Prey by Night

∎ ∎ ∎ ∎ ∎ ∎ ∎

Rain of Terror

Douglas Sanderson
WRITING AS MALCOLM DOUGLAS

INTRODUCTION BY GREGORY SHEPARD

STARK HOUSE

Stark House Press • Eureka California

PREY BY NIGHT / RAIN OF TERROR

Published by Stark House Press
1315 H Street
Eureka, CA 95501, USA
griffinskye3@sbcglobal.net
www.starkhousepress.com

ISBN: 978-1-951473-006

Book design by Mark Shepard, shepgraphics.com
Cover artist unknown
Proofreading by Bill Kelly

First Stark House Press Edition: June 2020

Douglas Sanderson: Pure Sweet Hell
BY GREGORY SHEPARD

Douglas Sanderson loved to travel. You could almost chart his travels in the books he wrote. Growing up in England, he initially moved to Canada, where his first five novels were set. Then off to Europe—Yugoslavia and Spain, in particular—where he set his next four novels. Then back to Canada for one more Montreal mystery plus a couple set in Southern California. Then back to Europe again, where most of his final books were set—with the exception of one in Cuba and another in Africa—and including four novels that were published only in France. There was even a solo trip across the United States in 1964, just for the hell of it. But really, it all started in Canada.

Sanderson had just published his first book, *Dark Passions Subdue*, with Dodd, Mead and Company. It got a few good notices. Sanderson himself called it "an analysis of Puritanism in Montreal's high society," and that is certainly one way of looking at it. It is also a frank look at a group of gay men who jockey for the attention of an effete artist. Banned in England, the book did not sell well. But interestingly enough, the fellow whom Sanderson used as a model for his main character made him a bet that he couldn't write a hardboiled thriller. As Sanderson paraphrased the challenge in a 1990 interview with Lucas Soler for *El Temps*: "Mickey Spillane has sold 32 million copies of his books. I'll bet you ten dollars you cannot write a thriller as he does."

The bet was on. Sanderson claimed that he had never read a tough guy thriller before, though in fact he had already published one mystery, *Exit in Green,* featuring a somewhat hapless main character, not at all in the Spillane mold. As the story goes, before writing this new thriller, Sanderson went out to a local drugstore and did a bit of quick research in the paperback stand. He met some members of the Canadian Mounted Police. They shared stories about local drug dealers. Douglas had his hook. The result was *Hot Freeze*, a story of drug smuggling in Quebec. His publisher didn't want him to use his real name because they were still trying to build a reputation around "Sanderson." For *Exit in Green* he had used a name that had a family history, albeit a tricky one—Martin Brett—which he again employed for *Hot Freeze*.

For the story behind the "Martin Brett" pseudonym, we must leave Canada and go back to England, where Ronald Douglas Sanderson was born on August 20th, 1920, in Beltinge, Kent, growing up in a large family with three brothers (one a half-brother) and two sisters. While he was still a child, his father abandoned them, leaving his mother to bring up the family. She and Douglas did not get along, two temperaments at opposite extremes. She was the hard-headed pragmatist, he the temperamental artist. And she had a family to feed. After Père Sanderson left, a Mr. Brett began visiting the household, and after each one of his visits, there would always be more to eat in the house. So, when it came time to pick out a pseudonym for his first thriller, Sanderson chose "Martin Brett" as a way of letting his mother know that he full well knew what was going on back in Kent.

Then in 1939 came World War II. Sanderson was only 20 when he joined the Merchant Navy and the RAF. But due to a perforated eardrum—caused, Sanderson claimed, by regular beatings from his father—he did not pass the medical tests to become a pilot. Instead, he started writing and performing, directing theatrical comedies for the troops. He even acted in a stage presentation of Patrick Hamilton's *Rope*, which Alfred Hitchcock later turned into a distinctive film.

Sanderson also wrote articles for the RAF magazine, then edited by René Brabazon Raymond, better known as thriller writer James Hadley Chase. It was Chase who first suggested that Sanderson start writing novels instead of plays.

In spite of this fortuitous suggestion, Sanderson joined a theatre company in London after the war. However, his mother still didn't approve of his artistic pursuits. And like many a brow-beaten son, Douglas moved as far away as possible, immigrating all the way to Montreal, Canada in 1947, where he eventually became a naturalized citizen. Here he did what he could to keep the wolf from the door—worked in a jeweler's shop, at a radio station, and in a Kellogg's factory. Somewhere along the line Douglas hooked up with the Canadian Broadcasting Corporation, and began to write radio comedies.

As Sanderson said in his interview with Lucas Soler, "For fourteen months I was writing a half hour comedy every week." It was then he made his first attempt at writing a novel. Feeling that his writing was too derivative, too strongly influenced by the authors he admired, he soon gave it up. But he tried again, and this time produced *Dark Passions Subdue*. The author biography on the dust jacket flap could have almost been written by Sanderson himself:

"His interests, now and always, have always been as wide as the world, and his travels have taken him over many areas.

"But what he has seen is unlikely to result in any pleasant travelogues. A keen and pitiless eye for dishonesty, a fierce distaste for self-deception—be it his own or anyone else's—and the very considerable dramatic-satiric gift that is revealed in this first novel, can be expected to provide us with provocative and disturbing books for years to come.

"Mr. Sanderson is a terrifying critic of the social scene. His Montreal frauds can be found in big cities everywhere. His hero's crisis is the crisis not of an individual, but of an era.

"This book is neither temperate nor kindly. It can not be flippantly read, or easily forgotten. The author's vast rage against the synthetic and cruel, emotional life, and the 'splendid isolation of the mind' that he finds everywhere, are conveyed with a sharp irony that will be felt long after the book is put away. His picture of utter vindictiveness, gathering force behind the façade of friendship, is shocking, terrifying, and disconcertedly recognizable."

The book definitely feels very personal to the author, as first novels so often do. It is at once verbosely overwritten, and a hothouse of restrained passions. There is no question but that he is railing against his restrained English upbringing. The flap copy goes on to explain the plot:

"Engaged by the sanctimonious hostility of his home life, Stephen lives in emotional and intellectual isolation until he meets Fabien—a wealthy, cultured and hedonistic young foreigner. Through Fabien he envisages a dazzling new way of life in which 'warm human contact would penetrate the intellect while embracing the heart,' and he sets out to intrench himself with his new friend by disposing of two great obstacles—his own inadequacy and a rival named Duncan. Stephen's campaign, increasingly feverish and tortured, abject and malevolent, provides a brilliant and haunting study of homosexuality in process of development."

The feverish quality to the writing lends passion to Sanderson's story of a young man awakening to his own talents and desires. Sanderson definitely evidenced a strong sympathy for some (though not all) of his gay characters. His son, John Douglas Sanderson, said that later in life he had many gay friends in Spain, "some of whom worshipped him as a father figure." Perhaps, in a more general sense, his true sympathies lay with the outsider in society, with a definite distaste for class consciousness and the thwarting of the artistic urge which can be traced back to his mother's rejection.

In fact, the thing that really hits the reader when encountering Sanderson's writing for the first time, is the anger and urgency which he uses to propel each story along. The Sanderson mysteries aren't always solved by cool intellectual minds interested in cracking a puzzle, but sometimes by sheer force of will; by frantic, haunted men with much to lose, and nothing less than their lives and freedom to gain. Sanderson's plots involve lots of running and chasing and falling and smashing and shooting. And after all that misery, it isn't even the solving of the mystery that really counts—though the payoff is always there—it's the getting out alive, which for most of Sanderson's main characters is the real challenge.

As Kevin Burton Smith observes in a recent introduction to David Montrose's *The Body on Mount Royal* (Ricochet Press, 2012), Sanderson's main characters are "desperate lone wolves [who] seemed to be always on the verge of losing it—politically, emotionally, even psychologically." This is a perfect description. As Smith says, Sanderson's books are "darker and messier" than the competition, propelled at a breakneck urgency.

Dark Passions Subdue was published in 1952, first by Dodd, Mead, then by Avon Books in a 1953 paperback edition. *Exit in Green*, Sanderson's first actual mystery was published in hardback only by Dodd, Mead in 1953 (and then expanded as *Murder Came Tumbling* when it was published as a hardback in England in 1959 by Hammond, Hammond & Company). The story concerns a fretful Boston playwright recovering from nervous exhaustion in a resort in the Laurentian Mountains who encounters murder when a vacationing British stage actress is found dead nearby. The tone of *Exit* is rather playful, almost teasing, and the action fairly restrained as Sanderson felt his way into this new medium.

Right after *Exit in Green* came *Hot Freeze* (also published by Dodd, Mead in hardback in 1954) the book which presumably won him his $10 bet, and introduced us to Montreal PI, Mike Garfin. In the words of Kevin Burton Smith from his introduction to the Stark House edition of *The Deadly Dames*, Garfin is a "former Royal Canadian Mounted Police officer of French-Canadian and Irish-Canadian ancestry who becomes a private investigator with an office in Montréal's *centre-ville* and an apartment in the Notre-Dame-des-Grâce district." Or, in the words of paperback publisher Popular Library from their back cover blurb: "Big

Mike Garfin, hired to tail a degenerate playboy, follows his quarry into a notorious sin-spot only to fall into a hornet's nest of kill-crazy underworld hoodlums. Here is a passionate suspense thriller written at machine-gun tempo!"

Quite a change for an author whose first book was a "brilliant and haunting study." But by now, Sanderson had found his footing and was off and running, and getting good reviews to boot. The *New York Times'* critic called *Hot Freeze* "entertaining... the tempo fast" and *The Saturday Review Syndicate* said "it's a rough winter in Montreal when Op. Mike Garfin takes on a case for a quality gal." Not ecstatic reviews, but much more positive than the drubbing Sanderson took on his first novel. He had found his niche.

Hot Freeze dealt with the drug trade and was quickly followed that same year by another Garfin thriller, *The Darker Traffic*, which was reprinted in paperback in 1955 by Popular Library as *Blondes Are My Trouble*, this time focusing on prostitution. For anyone who thought Montreal was a quiet, genteel city to the north of New York, *Hot Freeze* and *The Darker Traffic* set them straight. In *Traffic* "the story combines fancy floozies, sizzling smooching and gore... fast paced action with a surprise climax," according to the critic from *Tulsa World*.

The following paragraph from the back cover of *Blondes Are My Trouble* should give the reader a good example of Sanderson's brisk, declarative approach to thriller writing:

> "I slid the girl to the floor. She fell like dead meat, her dress up above her knees. At the same moment, Yellow-Head went after the pair of hoods. The blackjack whistled. One thug went down. The other guy swung around. The blackjack hit him right in the mouth. He was out cold. Yellow-Head grinned at me. 'We're in, pal.' I nodded. We were in, all right."

Mickey Spillane would be proud. Sanderson's career really began to take off. By this point, he had left Canada and was travelling around Europe, settling in Spain, where he met his soon-to-be-wife, Josefina Pastor. And this is where he bid adieu to Mike Garfin for awhile. As Sanderson pointed out in the Soler interview for *El Temps* in 1990, "I am a writer with no imagination who can only write about places and people I know. Mike Garfin, for instance, is based on a corporal of the Canadian Mounted Police I knew really well. When I started travelling...Mike Garfin made no sense anymore."

Sanderson's next book, *Prey by Night*, was set in Spain. It was also his first book written for the lucrative Gold Medal market. Gold Medal Books was the premier paperback publisher of the 1950s both in terms of sales and quality for the men's fiction market. Published in 1955, *Prey by Night* was also the first book to utilize yet another name change for Sanderson. Skipping over his contractual relationship with his original agent for a lucrative side deal, he was now Malcolm Douglas, named after his favorite brother, Malcolm Frank Sanderson. But Sanderson proved to be an uneasy traveler, often developing a love-hate relationship with each new locale he'd settle in. These telling passages from *Prey* say it all:

> "The road was like almost any other road in Spain—twisting like boiled macaroni, the only one in the district, and very bad. Spanish roadbuilders have a conviction that any distance tween two points should be made as long as possible...
>
> "There's nothing like that scenery anywhere else in the world. Range after towering range of peaks, sun-smitten Spanish rock, every shade from bright yellow to a purple almost black. Once in a while, thousands of feet below in the foothills, you catch a glimpse of man-made terracing, where people are trying to suck a living from the dry soil by growing olive trees. Tough people."

Prey by Night tells the story of a young smuggler named Bill Williams who is being forced out of business by a larger group called the Association. Over the course of a couple days, he has to find out who is out to get him, while keeping one step ahead of his partner Paco, who is murderously upset that Bill has fallen in love with his sister Maria. Like most of the Sanderson thrillers, this one never stops moving. Williams has his boat shot at, another boat exploded under him, and his car driven off the road; he's been roughly interrogated by the police, chased by a Spanish bull, and survived a knife fight. It's almost beside the point when he finally discovers who the bad guy is. By the end of the book, we're just relieved that he and Maria can finally sail off into the sunset, because they've just been through two days of hell. If *Prey by Night* is one of Sanderson's best thrillers, it is also a poignant love story, perhaps reflecting his own burgeoning love affair with Fina—the beautiful, dark-haired woman who in June of 1957 would become his wife—and with Spain itself.

The notices continued to come in. A writer for *The Naperville Sun* called *Prey by Night* "one of the most exciting...adventure yarns we've ever read," and that fellow from *The New York Times* was back with the opinion that this was one "tough action tale." Sanderson kept the folks at Gold Medal happy.

Rain of Terror came next, another Malcolm Douglas thriller published by Gold Medal in 1955, this one set in a small Italian mountain village south of Naples. The area is being deluged by rain and newspaper reporter Jake Abbott is sent up the flooded mountain with a photographer to write about the disaster. Jake is having an affair with his boss's wife and eventually they all end up in this small village where the water is knocking hell out of everything and everybody. Jake's boss is killed, an old World War II treasure is discovered, Jake is implicated and no one is who they seem.

This is one of Sanderson's most frantic novels yet. Weather always plays a major role in his books—a heatwave here, freezing snow there—but this book unleashes the full fury of Nature's forces as the characters dodge or are engulfed in rivers of water, mudslides, falling buildings and even a flooded automobile tunnel. In the following passage, Sanderson combines action with weather in a scene that leaves the reader winded:

> "The figure continued to advance, and Jake Abbott knew he was going to die. He wanted to dig himself in the earth. His scrabbling hand touched a large piece of stone. He snatched at it and straightened up and flung it with all this strength. Angelo gave a tiny scream of surprise. The gun clattered to the ground.
>
> "Jake ran. He cleared the arch and the heavens seemed to split. There was a brief roar, like the concert of a thousand caged animals. The rain was hammering down with renewed intensity. The gun barked again, strangely muffled. Jake couldn't get his breath... In the thundering of rain he couldn't tell whether he was still pursued or not."

Before the end of the day, Jake is being pursued not only by Angelo but the local police, while all hell continues to break loose from the skies. In 144 short pages—the page count of the original Gold Medal edition—Sanderson takes the reader on a trip to the Seventh Level and back again.

This brings us to the next Malcolm Douglas novel, *The Deadly Dames* (1956), and the return of his Montreal private eye. As he said, Sanderson liked to write about what he knew and while the family was still living in Canada he decided to write another Mike Garfin mystery set in his old stomping ground. Unfortunately, Garfin belonged to Dodd, Mead, or least to another agent, and for contractual reasons, Sanderson had to change his character's name to Bill Yates for Gold Medal. Same over-sized detective, same milieu, but a different name. And this time he gives his character a heatwave to deal with. And not just any heatwave—the mother of all heatwaves. Yates catches his image in a shop window: "six feet, brown hair, brown eyes slightly poached, and a hundred-ninety pounds, every one of them sweating."

Yates is first hired by a lush to tail his wife, whose mother-in-law then attempts to hire him away before she is hit by a bus. After that, things get messy. Yates is hired by the wife he was originally hired to follow. Then her sister gets in on the act, and pretty soon the bodies start to pile up. Eventually everyone is out to kill Yates. There is always a high body count in Sanderson's books, and the hero always seems to be the logical scapegoat. But in this case, Yates also has to do battle with rampaging mosquitoes. Stripped to his shorts in order to find out the identity of a body lying in a canoe on a nighttime lake, Yates encounters true torture:

"I kicked, not using my hands, gliding forward. My feet touched oozy bottom...In the stillness I heard the low whining of the insects. I almost swallowed my gorge.

"The boat started up with a roar. A bullet plucked the water beside me. I dived into the forest.

"...I put my forearms in front of me and pushed at the high undergrowth and the bracken whipped me. My bare feet twisted on the uneven ground. The boat roared closer. A bullet slapped into the woods. The mosquitoes came.

"They came in a cloud of millions. The needles pierced my skin and I went wild and the panic was worse than the pain because I couldn't get away from them...The whine of the insects rose to a scream."

Once again, Mother Nature wreaks havoc on our hero, and it's a toss-up whether he gets a worse deal from the mosquitoes or the guys who are chasing him.

After *The Deadly Dames*, Sanderson produced one more book from his European travels. This was *Final Run*, published in hardback by Secker & Warburg in London in 1956 under his real name, and reprinted in the U.S. in paperback by Popular Library as *Flee from Terror* by Martin Brett.

This time Sanderson gave us an Eastern European spy novel, utilizing his experiences travelling around Yugoslavia (around the same time he was in Spain gathering ideas for *Prey by Night* and *Rain of Terror*). In *Final Run*, an expatriate American named John Gregory is offered ten grand for a mission behind the Iron Curtain by an old spy named Blishen. The spy's wife offers her body to double-cross him. His best friend betrays him. The secret police want to beat the hell out of him. Written in an extremely abrupt, declarative style, this is Sanderson at his darkest and most cynical. This is also one of his most political novels as he lashes out at both the country and its leader, Tito:

"I once knew a man who liked Yugoslavia. He always talked of it with a defensive passion… He used to say that if religion was right and he was due for Hell, he expected to open his eyes after death in a replica of Ljubljana. There'd be no devils, no flames, no heat, no cold, nothing. Just a great grey drabness and over it all an electric sign spelling out the name of SATAN. In Ljubljana the sign says TITO."

He further makes his point by describing this street scene: "The workers were going home. I didn't hear a cheerful voice or a single sound of laughter. It was chilling. The only time an inhabitant shows animation is when he's drunk, which is often, and early." And just in case the reader doesn't get the point the author is trying to make about the drabness of the town, there is this: "I took my drink to a far table. I rolled back the cloth and watched the flies ascend. I sat down. The flies came back." By this point, Sanderson is beginning to sound more like Camus than Spillane. Or as the critic for *The Spectator* put it: "As pretty a talent for torture scenes as Ian Fleming. There is an echo of Hemingway *staccato* in the prose."

Like *Rain of Terror* and *Prey at Night,* in *The Final Run* most of the action takes place over a 24-hour period, mainly at night, with a plot that involves a mad dash from situation to situation, each one seemingly worse than the one before—and each one involving lots of pain and discomfort for the main character before the final twist of betrayal is revealed at the end.

His fourth book for Gold Medal produced the climax of his European chase thrillers, the aptly named *Pure Sweet Hell* in 1957. This one is set in Alicante, Spain, where Sanderson would eventually return to and live the rest of his life. The settings are all places he knew well. The set-up involves an FBI agent named Bishop who is trying to break a drug ring by finding out who is smuggling cocaine into the country. He is under cover as part of a merchant ship's crew. When they land, the rest of the night becomes one long chase (another 24-hour dash through hell) down alleys, into bars, over fences and into various hellholes as he tries to track down his lead. Bishop has stuffed a wad of bills into his shoes to purchase the drug, so his feet are in constant pain from the pressure, and it's hot and miserable. He eventually finds his man, right under his nose the entire time, but nearly kills himself doing so.

Alicante turns out to be the perfect setting for a Sanderson book, every bit as colorful as the streets of Montreal. As another example of writing what he knew, there is a revealing story about the whore whom Bishop meets in *Pure Sweet Hell*. No single women could be seen walking the streets after 10 p.m., but Sanderson met a prostitute one night who had just won the lottery, and spent the evening drinking with her.

Her character in the book provides the one poignant moment in the book, and *Pure Sweet Hell* is certainly one of the high points of his writing career.

Sanderson's own favorite novels, according to his son John, were *Prey by Night* and *Night of the Horns*. The latter title is another split by-line book, published in England under its original title and under the author's real name. In the U.S. it was published as *Murder Comes Calling* and was the last of the "Malcolm Douglas" thrillers from Gold Medal. In it, Sanderson tries something a little different by creating a protagonist who is both naïve, clueless and just a little exasperating in his holier-than-thou attitude. Lawyer Robert Race has a good practice helping people he knows to be innocent; and he is married to a beautiful woman that makes other men envious. But Race has taken on a shady client by the name of Kresnik who wants him to pick up a suitcase for him and hold it in his apartment until he sends someone to get it. Race would like to refuse but Kresnik threatens to reveal their relationship. That night, while Race is retrieving the suitcase, someone jumps him, and in one evening his entire life is turned upside down. He is slapped and rejected by an old flame, told off by those he thought respected him, threatened by Kresnik's henchmen, accused of murder and worst of all, finds that his beautiful wife has been decidedly less than faithful.

In its own frantic way, *Night of the Horns* has much in common with *Pure Sweet Hell* as Race races from one situation to another, uncovering facts along the way in one revelatory night of hell on earth (it is never named, but the city here feels like San Diego). He finds out that his protégée, the man he got off on a murder charge, was guilty all along. He finds out that his morally indignant father-in-law has some nasty secrets. He finds that love can come from the least likely of places. But mostly he finds out that he has been living a lie, that everything he believes is wrong. The book's pell-mell pacing doesn't detract from the sting in its tale, making this one of Sanderson's best, and quite possibly the apex of his writing career. It is also the only one of his novels to have been filmed, adapted for a 1964 episode of the British TV series, "The Detective."

After *Horns* comes a real mystery of a book. His next novel, *The Shreds*, was only published as *Sables-d'or-les-pains* in France as part of the Série Noire from Gallimard in 1958 under the Martin Brett pseudonym. Though the French title seems to be a play on words—referencing the coastal town of Sables-d'Or-les-Pins on the coast of Brittany—the story itself is set in the Middle East, one of two books he set there. According to Claude Mesplède in his article "Avez-vous lu Martin Brett?" (Have You Read Martin Brett?), *The Shreds* "depicts some

English and Americans who, under cover of archaeological excavations, try to seize the exploitation of oil wells. This denunciation of foreign imperialism in a country where the most insolent riches rub shoulders with the filthy misery is matched only by the pitiless description of the sovereign Selim V, ready to sell his country and its subjects to keep power and wealth."

Sanderson had four of his books published in French only, and as far as I know, none of them ever existed in English editions, nor have the original manuscripts ever been found. In fact, we only know the original English titles from the copyright page of the French editions. And it's particularly frustrating for his English-only fans because Sanderson was writing in the late 1950s at the top of his form. But as son John pointed out, Sanderson "sold mostly in France." Invited to a convention there some years later, Sanderson was surprised that so many people showed up with stacks of his books to be signed.

Following *The Shreds* came *Cry Wolfram*, published in England in 1959 under the Sanderson name by Secker & Warburg, and in the U.S. as *Mark It for Murder* by Avon Books. This is a much lighter book than its predecessors, as evidenced by this almost-playful opening:

> "The night outside was filled with sea-sounds and the smell of flowers. The Regatta Club was full of cigarette smoke and expensive perfumes with an underwaft of perspiration. There was a band playing French jazz, loud but good, and a big-chested girl at the microphone singing loud but no good. The dancing couples were crammed hard together and an aerial view of the floor would have looked like a snood of boiling porridge.
>
> It was two o'clock in the morning. I should not have been there."

Like *Pure Sweet Hell*, the action is set in a Spanish coastal town (referred to only as "the capital city of the province") where Johnny Molson, hired as nursemaid and bodyguard to an old, hardened millionaire named Craddock, finds himself in the middle of a financial swindle involving the supply of wolfram, or tungsten. There are also two women involved, as is so often the case, one to tempt and the other to taunt. As usual, Molson soon finds himself unjustly accused of murder, and before long is subjected to ill treatment at the hands of the local police:

> "My jacket was pulled up, my legs were clamped. I lay there like a stretched pelt. The rubber hose whistled through the air and hit me across the kidneys. The agony was incredible."

Though the pace is no less frenetic than his previous novels, *Cry Wolfram* is leavened by occasional touches of humor that were completely missing from the last few books—for example, a drunken gypsy wedding that comes out of nowhere and provides Molson a brief opportunity to recover from his beating. You can't help but think that *Cry Wolfram* could have been hatched as a Hollywood film plot, with its tireless hero and bittersweet ending.

It was during this time, in 1959 while still living with Fina and his young son, John, in Alicante, Spain, that Sanderson decided to move his family back to Canada, where they would live until 1963. While there, according to son John, Sanderson "wrote some articles that he read aloud in a local radio station about life in Spain, what the wedding in Alicante had been like, etc." Wherever he lived, he loved to talk to his friends about somewhere else.

And it was here in Montreal where Sanderson wrote his next novel, *Catch a Fallen Starlet*—published in paperback by Avon Books in 1960—set right in the middle of Hollywood.

As his son John observed in his introduction to the Stark House edition of *Pure Sweet Hell*, Sanderson loved the movies. James Cagney was a particular favorite. In *Fallen Starlet*, the main character, Al Dufferin, is a former script writer who had left Hollywood after a scandalous death in which he had been involved. Now he has returned to work on a new writing deal which naturally leads to murder. As John points out, Sanderson himself had had a bad film experience when veteran director Marion Gering came over to Spain to talk about turning *Prey by Night* into a movie. After many meetings and letters, Gering turned down the proposal. Dufferin reflects much of Sanderson's cynicism about the Hollywood machine, as well as the author's disdain for television, which he considered a threat to the cinema.

And once the Sanderson family moved back to Spain, while Franco was still in control before his death in 1975, Sanderson wouldn't allow a TV set in the house. As John mentioned in one of many emails, his dad was a very popular author in Europe, but none of the Sanderson novels were published in Spain. The reference to cocaine trafficking alone in *Pure Sweet Hell* would have landed him in jail because Franco denied the existence of any such illegal drug activity. Sanderson certainly didn't want Franco's propaganda invading his house, so instead of television, the Sanderson father and son would spend a lot of time at the local movie theatre. And interestingly enough, wife Fina eventually pursued an acting career herself in both theatre and TV under her maiden name of Josefina Pastor.

Sanderson's last great mystery thriller was *A Dum-Dum for the President*, which also happens to be Mike Garfin's final appearance. Though still set in the Montreal area, *Dum-Dum* feels very international in scope—no surprise after all of Sanderson's travels—since it involves

Garfin's discovery of a deposed South American president hiding out on Mount Royal from his political enemies. Very much a hardboiled thriller, Sanderson also interjects a strong dose of cynical politics into the story, as he did in *Final Run*. Until Stark House reprinted it in paperback in 2006, *A Dum-Dum for the President* had been a fairly rare Sanderson novel, only available in a British hardback edition published by Hammond, Hammond & Co. in 1961.

Two years later, in 1963, Sanderson left Canada for good and moved his family permanently back to Alicante, Spain. Gone were the U.S. paperback deals. The next three books, in fact, were only published in France by Gallimard. The *The Dead Connection* came out first as *La came á papa* (1961; loosely translated as "Drugs for Daddy" a cynical and violent anti-drug novel set in Canada), followed by *Shout for a Killer* as *Chabanais chez les pachas* (1963; "Clash at the Pasha's," his second Middle Eastern novel, involving an American black marketer adventuring in a country controlled by a corrupt dictatorship) and finally *Score for Two Dead* as *Le moîne connait la musique* (1964; "The Monk Knows the Score," set back in the author's home turf of Alicante). Like *The Shreds*, these three novels had no non-French editions and we only know their original English titles from the copyright pages of the Gallimard books.

After this, there were only four more Sanderson thrillers which came out in England in small hardback printings intended for the library trade from Robert Hale Ltd. *Lam to Slaughter* (1964) is the story of a young man being chased across Europe by some shadowy figures when he ditches the safety of his uncle's care for that of a dubious friend. *Black Reprieve* (1965) is a political thriller about a group of escaped prisoners in Africa, one of whom is a traitor. *No Charge for Framing* (1969) takes the action to Cuba for an unabashed spy novel featuring escaped cons, warring government agents, two American girls and a Cuban assassin.

By now, Sanderson was no longer writing in top form. There were moments, but the edge was off. The last novel, *A Dead Bullfighter* (1975) feels more cantankerous than thrilling, returning Sanderson to Spain for a tale of political corruption set against the world of bullfighting. The ability to tell a good tale is still there, but the immediacy of the prose is gone. A final novel, *A Dead Heat*, was announced in 1984, but never written. Son John admits that his dad had been drinking pretty heavily in his later years, only quitting in 1995, twenty years after his wife Fina had left him. In Sanderson's own words, from his interview with Soler, "I have some Irish blood so I have always drunk a lot."

Nor had Sanderson made a lot of money from his books. He was never really able to keep his family comfortable with his book income. Sanderson's younger brother, Frank, was a successful businessman, according to John, and transferred money to his brother which allowed him to live off the interest in his later years. He did start one more book, a story about drug trafficking from Colombia, but never got around to finishing it. As in many a case, alcohol eventually replaced the creative urge. And though he was never in any physical pain, his later years were spent with very little to do.

Fortunately we have so many great hardboiled thrillers that he did write during his lifetime: the Mike Garfin books and the Gold Medal novels, in particular. Sanderson seemed to write at a fever pitch. He put his characters through trial by torture. These are dark, sometimes dream-like stories about men who search in the night for a small bit of information that they think will set them free. Most of them find a bit of redemption at the end, and some even walk off into the sunset with the girl. But Sanderson always made them work for it, as hard on his characters as he was on the people around him. In fact, he could be quite the curmudgeon when he wanted to. As he confessed to Soler in his final interview, "I hate the English; I guess that is why I became Canadian."

Sanderson wrote from the gut. As Kevin Burton Smith says of his writing, "his twisted and often nightmarish tales of obsession stand up amazingly well, even half a century later, and still boast a passionate no-holds-barred immediacy that's hard to deny." Like fellow thriller writers Cornell Woolrich and David Goodis, Sanderson could bring nightmares to life with a crazy kind of logic. As a man, Sanderson loved the outdoors; he loved canoeing, sailing and skiing. As an artist, he loved classical music, art and decorating; the Mediterranean. As a writer, however, he travelled down some very dark paths, reveling in the twisted by-ways, the ill-lit corners of the night—and of the soul. Sanderson died in Alicante, Spain, in 2002 at the age of eighty-two—irascible, irritating, argumentative, colorful and opinionated—and one hell of a great thriller writer.

—Eureka, CA
(2013, expanded 2020)

Sources:

Douglas Sanderson interview with Lucas Soler in *El Temps*, Spain, 1990.

John Sanderson introduction to *Pure Sweet Hell / Catch a Fallen Starlet* (Stark House Press, 2004); plus various email exchanges.

Kevin Burton Smith introductions to *Pure Sweet Hell / Catch a Fallen Starlet* (Stark House Press, 2004) and *The Deadly Dames / A Dum-Dum for the President* (Stark House Press, 2006).

"Avez-vous lu Martin Brett?" by Claude Mesplède (online article)

Prey by Night

Douglas Sanderson

WRITING AS MALCOLM DOUGLAS

For my friend
Elena Mirgová

Part I
The Evening Before

Chapter One

It was on this particular evening, just around sundown, that my little private world began to collapse. I got the first creaking sign in North Africa.

The blades of the fan were twirling noiselessly in the middle of the ceiling. I was waiting for Silva to say something else, but he remained silent, maybe because he couldn't add anything further without tipping his hand completely. I left him to stew at it, started to think of María. She was the best thought I'd ever had.

Two streets away, on the tower of the mosque, the muezzin began his evening cry. Long and drawn out, like a wolf's call. Summoning the Mohammedan faithful to prayer. He could have saved his breath. Most of the faithful wouldn't be paying much attention. Put an international port in the hands of representatives from eight different nations, all of them on the grab, and the Arab soon learns to follow the shining example. He doesn't stop for evening prayer anymore, because some other joe with a little less faith may be using the extra time to snatch whatever graft is going. In Tangier there's a great deal of graft.

I waited. Silva moved. He rolled the cigar around his oily face, put his elbows on the desk, and adjusted his fat stomach. He said, "Well, Mr. Williams?"

I walked to the window and looked out, taking my time. Two small birds were making love on the outside ledge. Down in the narrow street the usual mob of Arabs waved their hands and talked at the tops of their voices. An old 1932 Renault was trying to get through, the driver continually honking the horn, leaning from the side window, screaming at anyone who would listen. Somebody screamed back. A dirty answer. A hoot of collective laughter went up from the tables at the café opposite.

Griswold lowered the newspaper to see what was going on. Among all those swarthy hawk faces he looked very American. He looked also very nervous and very shifty, and I didn't like him one bit or trust him one inch. But there wasn't another man in the city who would work with me and I'd had to take what I could get. I watched him put the paper to one side and start toying with his coffee cup.

Silva stirred little white fat-man hands through the papers on his desk. He cleared his throat. I turned around. He said, "Did you reach your decision, Mr. Williams?"

"No," I said. "I don't need to make one."

"Oh." The cigar went to the other corner of his mouth and he picked up two of the papers: "Let me see," he said. "Cosmetics, nylon stockings, dress materials. Hmmm. Radio tubes, watches, cameras, gold-plated watch straps—"

"I know," I said. "I'm a good customer."

"And I am equally good broker. The goods were delivered to your boat an hour ago. Everything." He flashed gold teeth at me. "Except penicillin, streptomycin, antibiotics, sulfonamides, or any medicines whatever."

"That's right, I didn't order any."

"Quite," he said. He laid down the papers with a sigh. "Time again for the decision, Mr. Williams. Face the issue squarely."

"I have. I've stopped dealing in drugs."

The smile started to fade. He leaned back and folded his hands across his gut and blinked at me. The long ash splashed from his cigar onto his flowered white vest. He said, "But you haven't stopped, Mr. Williams. In your position nobody could. Where else is the big money?"

He laid a finger along the side of his big nose and rubbed thoughtfully. He said, "I'll be honest. I have enormous difficulty obtaining sufficient drugs to meet the needs of my customers. But with you, Mr. Williams, I will offer preferential treatment. Anything you ask."

"Keep them."

"Why?"

"I told you."

"But the true explanation, Mr. Williams."

"All right," I said, "since you ask. In the last shipment from you every drug I got had been fixed. Half medicine, half muck. There was a kid died of your penicillin. I've never needed money that bad."

"I see," he said. He put down the cigar, stared at me, and began sucking his teeth. "So who now is supplying your drugs? Your good drugs?"

"The Association."

"Mr. Williams," he said calmly, "that is a big fat lie."

"As you like."

He reached for the big silver cigar lighter on his desk and flicked at it until he got a flame. He said, "No, Mr. Privateer Williams. No and no. You work alone. The Association would not supply you, I think, even with a card of pins. The Association does not like the competition of private enterprisers. The Association, in fact, would probably remove you if they knew of you."

"And you, Mr. Silva," I said. "Never forget that."

He resumed sucking his teeth, slowly and lingeringly. I pulled the money from my pocket and slapped it on his desk, and I said, "Payment for the shipment. Operations are being stepped up, so I'll be back in three days. You have my next order. The decision is yours." I started for the door.

"One moment!" He gripped the arms of his chair and strained upright. "Very well, Mr. Williams, you force me to be firm. Here it is. Either I supply everything, including drugs, or I supply nothing at all."

"Fine," I said. "I'll go elsewhere."

"No," he said. "No, I think not. True that I am also outside the Association, but I am more powerful than you. I have influential friends. Continue to deal with me and you continue to have my protection."

"Thank you," I said. "No drugs."

He spread his hands, shrugged his shoulders, and smiled. "Then one thing, Mr. Williams," he said, "one little thing. I know to where you are smuggling your cargoes. Your boat is not capable of long distances and you seldom order cigarettes, so we eliminate Marseilles and Genoa." He blew out a huge cloud of smoke. "Leaving only Spain. A terribly dangerous coast, I believe. Anything might happen."

I said, "Fatty, don't threaten me."

"Nothing of the sort." He went on smiling. "But the Association is watching for people like you, Mr. Williams. And there are many Arabs in the city who remember how once you ran guns to Israel. You have enemies. Don't, I implore you, add me to their number."

He minced around the desk on tiny bee's feet, patent-leather shoes glittering. He laid a soft white hand on my shoulder. "Let us be friends and associates again, Mr. Williams. I have received a new shipment of sulfonamides. You shall have as many as you want. They are not, I assure you, adulterated."

"I've heard it before," I said. "You can stuff your sulfonamides."

He lifted the hand, studied his fingernails, and heaved a big sigh. "Then I am afraid," he said slowly, "that you will never do another dollar's worth of business in this port."

"With you, no."

"With anybody. I beg you not to rely on other operators outside the Association, because I shall see you never get to them."

"Nuts," I said.

He slowly raised his head. "One last appeal to reason, Mr. Williams." I walked to the door. "Those same nuts."

He flopped back in his chair, picked up the cigar lighter. "So good evening to you, Mr. Williams, and regrettably we must now consider ourselves enemies. A mistake. You are in danger. You are going to be very, very sorry for what you have done."

"Maybe," I said. I went outside and closed the door and descended the stairs.

Griswold folded the newspaper, uncrossed his legs, and didn't get up. He said, "I drank five cups of this stinking coffee. We might as well make it a round half dozen."

"On your feet," I said. "We're going."

He stayed there. He smiled. "Bill, I didn't get a drink, not all day. What say just one? A small cognac, maybe."

"Nothing," I said. "Tilt a bottle and you're out before you start."

I watched the smile harden. He shifted his seat, building himself up. He said, "Bill, you're getting tough. I don't like being pushed around."

"You don't have a choice," I said, "so make up your mind right now. If you think you're not going to like it, you can go back to selling dirty pictures to the tourists."

He held it a second longer. Then he relaxed. He grinned and stuck the newspaper in his pocket. "That was yesterday," he said. "O.K., Billy, whatever you say. Let's go." He stood up.

I gave him the quick study. I didn't like what I saw. Drink-puffed face and mounds of flesh around his eyes, and he hadn't shaved for days. His clothes were dirty and ragged. His hair needed cutting. He smelled as if it was months since he had taken a bath. He was a pimp and a bum and he looked it exactly, but he was all I could get at the time.

There was one consolation. He'd be safe from the complicating desires of the Marquesa. She liked them young and chipper and juicy, and Griswold would never be that again, if he'd ever been it before.

We moved away. His eyes flicked. He said, "There's been a fat man watching us from the window across the road. Who's he?"

"Just a guy," I said.

"Association?"

I didn't answer.

We turned the corner and we were in the meat market, glamorous North Africa, land of spices and adventure and mystery. It was the same as always: screeching voices, purple and black meat in open stalls, swarms of fat black flies, and a stink that would kill dragons. A kid about ten years old started pulling my sleeves. He inquired if I wanted his nice sister.

"The fat guy supply your stuff?" Griswold asked. "Christ, the Association would put out his light in a flick if they knew."

I said, "You know the ears in this town. Shut your mouth."

The kid was still tugging at my arm. He changed the line about his sister and suggested I might prefer him instead. I clouted him hard across the ear and he dropped back with a squawk. It's the only way to convince them. It's the only way to convince almost anybody.

Griswold said, "So I'm your man now, Bill. Wise me to the setup."

"Spain," I said.

"I guessed it. What part?"

"You'll find out."

"Yeah, but how—"

"Shut up," I said.

The tropic darkness was closing fast. I was thinking of who I'd go to now that Silva was out of the running. I wasn't especially worried. There was still a reasonable selection of semi-honest small-timers. We got through the meat market, went down past the mosque, and on toward the port. Griswold smiled amiably and started making conversation again.

He said, "I hear the Association gets a sweat when anyone even mentions Spain. If they get put out of business it'll be the Spanish runners done it." He patted my back. "But I'm with you, Bill, I'm right with you. Them bastards been grabbing all the gravy too long. We'll clean up on them, eh?"

"Maybe."

"Anyone ever find out who the top boys of the Association really are?"

"No," I said.

He paused. "Bill, you working for yourself, or is there a boss?"

I said, "Look, Griswold. We'll have it straight from the start. At the moment I don't think much of you. You're a boozer and a bum and you need a bath. But you claim you can handle a boat and drive a car, and you have a reputation for keeping your mouth shut. O.K., keep it shut. That includes questions."

He grinned. He said, "There you go getting tough again."

"It's the sort of business we're in, tough. Prove right and you'll make money. Till then, pipe down."

"Bill," he said, "you're straight from the shoulder. I like that. Man knows where he stands."

"Yeah," I said, and I was thinking that maybe I'd get used to the guy. At the moment he was giving me the creeps.

I nodded to the man at the gate and we went along the dockside. The fleet was there, same as every night, the smuggling fleet, looking good, perhaps the sleekest, fastest collection of small boats in the world. Dutch, British, American, Italian, French, and pretty well every flag you can think of, most of them false. Manned by the toughest crowd ever gathered in one place, the *contrabandistas*, the players in the nightly charade, all of them legally waiting for the last light to disappear, all waiting so they could go streaking off to their illegal destinations.

I went down the steps and jumped aboard. Paco was up forward, sitting on the deck, back to the gunwale, legs spread in front of him, trousers rolled up, feet bare. He was tilting a goatskin of wine, streaming the liquid straight down into his throat. His eyes skated over Griswold and came back to me. Without expression.

"Everything here?" I asked.

He reached a hand and I pulled him upright. He said lazily, "The man with the big consignment asked many questions about drugs and medicines. The man with the drugs and medicines asked nothing at all. Me, I say nothing to neither. Have a drink, Beel."

Griswold was beside me, grinning. He said, "Nice boat. Looks fast."

"It'll do," I said, and Paco waited with a mild blank look on his face. I said, "Paco, this is Griswold. He'll be working with us."

They studied one another. Paco said, "*Mucho gusto,*" and gave a little bow, and then he offered Griswold the wineskin.

I got between them. I said, "Show him the layout. I don't want anything busted this time, so make sure everything is properly stowed. How's the weather outside?"

"There is a strong wind." The kid relinquished the wineskin to me. He'd gone back to his blank look.

"How far we go?" Griswold asked.

Paco took his arm, gave him a flash of the teeth. "Now I show you the wheelhouse, Señor Griswold," he said, and drew him aft.

The light switched on. There was barely room for the two of them in the wheelhouse. I looked around and the dusk lay thick across the harbor, but the mackerel sky beyond still held a last touch of orange and mauve. Five more minutes. I took a swig of the strong Spanish wine and laid the almost full skin on the deck. I leaned against the gunwale, wishing there had been someone other than Griswold. Something warned me it wasn't going to work out after all.

The footsteps came softly along the harbor wall. I looked up and in the dusk I couldn't see the man's face. He descended the steps and hesitated. Then he jumped lightly onto the deck. I put a hand in my pocket and got a grip on the gun butt. I said, "Get off my boat, mister."

He kept coming, hands hanging loose at his sides. He got close and he was about forty, a well-groomed man, dark-eyed, smiling, wide awake in every inch of him. He spoke in Spanish. He said, "A social visit, señor."

"I don't speak your lingo, mister. Get off the boat."

He switched to English. "I was impolite. Forgive me. I wish to pay a friendly call."

I said, "Tonight I'm not entertaining. Beat it."

"Do you desire to see my credentials?"

"So you're a cop," I said. "What do you want?"

"Thank you. One question only. To where are you shipping?"

"Israel," I said.

"Ah," he said, "Israel. Israel as usual. Señor, in Madrid we tell a funny story, all about a simple country boy seeing the city sights for the first time. In the evening he goes through the Plaza Mayor and a pretty colored girl stops him. 'Would you like to go home with me?' she asks, and the country boy gapes at her. He says, 'What—all the way to Africa?'"

He waited for me to laugh. I didn't. He said, "Señor, when I see the size of your boat I feel like the country boy. What—all the way to Israel?"

"I'm legal," I said. "You can see the manifest and the consignment papers."

"*Naturalmente.* The Association takes care of everyone. In all this harbor is not so much as one illegal cigarette—while it is in the harbor. Every item has a bona fide destination, papers to prove it, just like you."

He nodded toward the dimming sky. "But when you get outside, señor, somehow the destination always is changed. Where again did you say you were going?"

"Israel. I have the papers."

"I think you lie, my friend. You are going to Spain." He looked over my shoulder to the wheelhouse. "The Spanish boy who never comes ashore is proof enough."

"He's legal, too," I said.

"No doubt." The cop sucked in his breath and stopped smiling. He said, "In Cádiz last week three people died of adulterated sulfonamide drugs. The southwest of my country is flooded with goods on which no duty has been paid. You come here twice a week. I have watched you. You—"

I said, "Show me those credentials."

He smiled thinly. He said in a whisper, "Señor, I spit on your mother." Then he waited.

He'd given me the biggest Spanish insult. He was waiting for me to hit him so he could raise a shout and have me clapped in jail for striking a representative of one of the eight nations. There's only one law in the whole port: You don't hit a cop. Usually you buy him. But with this one it didn't look possible.

I said in Spanish, "Señor, I am an orphan. *Pobre de mí,* I never had a mother." I picked up the wineskin and held it out. "Here, take a drink."

He knocked the skin from my hand and it went flying over the deck. He said, "I speak with the boy," and tried to push past me.

I held him. I said, "In that case, I want to see credentials and a warrant."

He slapped me hard across the face. He said, "You *hijo de puta*, you son of a whore!"

I kept my fists unclenched. I took it slowly. "Go on, beat it, flatfoot. Chase a pickpocket. You're wearing out your welcome." We froze, staring at each other. Then I heard the footsteps behind me as the other two came out of the wheelhouse. I said, "Stay where you are. Our friend is just leaving. Prepare to sail."

In the full darkness the cop didn't move. There were more sounds and Paco pushed the starter and the engine coughed. The boat started a soft shaking purr. I walked past the motionless figure, up to the bow. I said, "I'm casting off now. Come if you want, but I don't guarantee your arrival."

He moved then. He shoved me aside and made a jump and got back on the steps. He wheeled around and looked at me wide-eyed through the darkness, speaking quickly, softly. "Señor, my name is Blasco. I wish to make you a promise, a strong promise. I make it on the grave of my father. I, Blasco, am going to smash the Association. Tonight, next week, next month, but one time for certain. You will be caught. You will be sent to prison and they will say that Blasco did it. And if you are killed, the biggest wreath will bear my name. You should not have tried to operate in Spain."

I unbent the rope and snaked it in. The boat began to back, churning the water. I said, "Señor Blasco, it was rare to have met you. You're a very funny man, *muy chistoso*. And now wish me Godspeed to Israel."

"*Hasta luego*, Señor Oovilliams," he said politely. "We meet again."

We backed right out and the boat swung around and we cut clean across the harbor with all our lights on. Few Spaniards can say a *W*, but he had the name right. I wondered from where. From Silva. Moving like greased lightning, I coiled the rope and went aft and Paco was at the wheel with Griswold looking over his shoulder. We picked our way through the other craft and opened up, and then we shot through the harbor mouth.

The wind hit us. It wasn't good. Only a few stars in the blackening sky, and the sea rising up in long gray running stretches. I looked back to the string of lights of the harbor. Nothing else anywhere around us. I stuck in my head and nodded to Paco. "O.K.," I said.

He reached a hand for the switch. All our lights went out. Griswold said nothing. I left them there and went below to the tiny cabin and deadlighted the porthole. Then I got out the manifest. I tried to figure out how much profit the Marquesa was going to make this time. She was the only association I'd ever had.

Chapter Two

I got back on deck and we were nearing the home coast. The night had worsened, the sea whipping into tall frothy crests, the wind increased to a roar, full of stinging spray. I hung onto the gunwale and dodged down behind the wheelhouse. Paco was already crouched there, trying to smoke a cigarette, cupping the burning end in his hand.

I sat close to him. I took the butt, had a couple of drags, and filled my lungs with smoke. Then I looked up at the handful of stars.

Something was wrong. I turned around and peered past the bow and knew what it was. We were off course, a long way. I pointed upward. I shouted, "Why?" The wind snatched the word from my mouth.

But the kid understood. He pulled me closer. He took the jacket from around his shoulders and draped it right over our heads. His mouth came next to my ear. "Beel," he said, "this Griswold, there is a smell comes from him. He is no good, I am certain. Why you bring this man?"

"The Marquesa's idea."

"But why not another Spaniard, Beel? Why not El Mudo?"

"The same reason you're not allowed ashore. You live too close. Twenty miles across the water isn't far enough. That was a Spanish cop came aboard tonight. One more Spaniard in the crew and we'd be traced."

"You mean like the friends of this Griswold will trace us?"

It was a thought. I'd had it since I hired the guy. I used the same arguments on Paco that I'd used on myself. I said, "He has no friends. He's nobody. When I found him he was steering tourists to brothels, selling dirty postcards on the side."

Paco sniffed. "What sort of man would do that? Like I say, no good."

The kid was jealous. I understood. I said, "Take it easy. Even if he had friends, they'd never find us in this sea."

The boat bucketed. I had to hang on to him. The bow began pounding as it hit the oncoming waves. He said, "In this sea all the world could follow us, one hundred meters away, and we should not hear. That is why, with permission, I stay off course until we pass the Point. Five minutes. The wind will drop then. We shall hear any pursuers."

"A good plan, *chico*," I said, but I was on guard because of that "with permission." We were not usually on those terms. When he began speaking again I'd guessed what was coming.

He took a deep suck on the cigarette and started slowly, hesitantly. "Beel. There is something I must say. About María. It is for me to tell you that I have heard a bad story. I do not like the necessity to repeat it to you."

"Then don't," I said. "María is your sister, a good girl. I know the sort of stories that get around among Spanish servants. I think probably that someone has lied to you."

He paused. "That is all?"

"All."

"Good." He put an arm around my neck and laughed. His voice warmed. "Then we forget, and I have said nothing. Tomorrow night we will go to Santa Faz and get drunk. It is the fiesta of the Christ. Everybody gets drunk."

"Good idea."

"No," he said. "Your voice. You are uncomfortable and it is my fault. You do not wish to get drunk with me."

It wasn't that. I had to tell the kid sometime. I said, "Look, Paco, an important thing. The Marquesa is putting a second boat on the run. Probably next week."

I felt all his muscles bunch up. I knew what was in his head. He hadn't a hope. Apart from his being only seventeen, the Marquesa had a hard and fast rule—no Spaniards for shore dealings. And the skipper of the new boat would have to handle all the ordering. Paco was ruled out.

"*Claro*," he said bitterly. "A new boat with this Griswold in command. It is clear to me." He gave a dry laugh. "But perhaps she will not like him when she sees that he will be no good in bed. There is no joy anywhere in him for a woman. He is withered with drink."

"Maybe," I said. "Which reminds me, don't allow him near a drink for a week or so."

"No?" he asked. "*Chico*, you should tell me these things. Your Griswold has my skin of wine."

I flung the jacket from my face and groped around the wheelhouse with the wind tearing at my hair and the spray cutting me. Griswold was standing in the wheelhouse. He was steering one-handed and he had all the lights on. The other hand was holding the goatskin over his tilted face. A continuous stream of wine was shooting down his throat.

I crushed through the door and pushed him in the side of the face and he fell over. I knocked off the lights and for a couple of seconds I couldn't see anything. The wheel started spinning. I grabbed for it and a spoke hit me hard on the wrist.

I was trampling Griswold's legs. He grunted. He hit my shin with his fist and squeezed against the bulkhead and eased himself slowly upward, standing so close that his chest heaved against my arm. He snapped, "What the hell's got into you, tough guy?"

"You're out, Griswold," I said. "I told you no drink."

"Jesus Christ, you think I'm an alky or something? I could take a gallon of that stuff without feeling it."

"Sure," I said, "with the coast half a mile to starboard and all the lights on. Why didn't you send up flares, you bastard, so the coast guards could really get us? You're fired."

He went quiet. I heard him swallow and his throat was dry. "Jesus, what a fool trick!" he said. "Yeah, I'm sorry, Bill. I didn't even think. Hell, I'm sorry." He hesitated. He sounded empty. He said, "Two more days, Bill. I'll be used to it. What say?"

I said nothing. The Marquesa had got greedy and insisted on a new man, and now she had one. And he was useless. I didn't want him. I was going to get rid of him. Either I turned round and took him back to North Africa, or I pulled inshore and beached him in Spain. One thing for certain, I wasn't taking him with me to land the stuff. You don't put a man wise to your layout and then fire him so he can go back and spread the news to all who'll listen. Maybe in other places, but not in the western Mediterranean.

I stood there trying to decide. The sea lifted and the wind whistled. Paco stuck in his head. He knew Griswold was in trouble and he sounded happy. He said, "We are passing the Point, *amigo*. Now we have speed."

It was as if he'd recited a charm. The wind fell to nothing and the water went flat as a mirror. He said, "You are sticking to my original course, Beel?"

"Yes."

"It is wise," he said, and he laughed and shut the door. I heard him get back behind the wheelhouse.

I opened up the engine. We skimmed over the sudden smoothness like a greyhound out of the slips. In the clearing air to starboard the mountains were a darker darkness against the night sky. I knew the area and it wasn't a good one. Shark-toothed shoals for two hundred yards out to sea, six inches below the surface. I'd have to put Griswold ashore ten miles farther on.

He cleared his throat softly. He got the edge of a whine into his voice. "So it's O.K., eh, Bill?"

"No," I said. "You're through, mate. I'm beaching you in a few minutes. Find your own way back across the Straits, or you can stay low a couple of days and I'll take you back myself. Now get out on deck."

He made no motion. He said, "One more break, Bill. I know I'll be all right. Hell, I don't want to go back to what I was doing yesterday. You wouldn't wish that on me, would you?"

"Without a second thought. Go tell the kid to give you a thousand pesetas. Any fisherman will take you back for half that. Now get out of here."

"O.K., if you've made up your mind."

He started to move. I squeezed onto the wheel to let him pass, and I seemed to be hanging there. There was a terrific pounding on the roof. Paco howled at the top of his voice. Three times. "Pursuers! Pursuers! Pursuers!"

I heaved at Griswold. I shot a glance aft. Through the tiny window, in the uniform darkness of sea and sky, was a tiny white crest. A boat coming after us. Fast. Too fast. Less than a mile behind.

I swung the wheel, headed seaward. They were coast guards or hijackers, and I'd soon know. Cops have a beam. Hijackers use bullets. The preparation for both is the same. I snapped, "You're hired again, Griswold. On deck. Paco'll give you a rifle. Prepare to stand these guys off."

"Yeah," he said, "yeah," and his voice was different. Eager. He was alive with something. He scrambled through the door and slammed it hard and I heard his footsteps clump on the deck. Then something more happened. The engine stopped dead. Just coughed once and cut right out.

I punched the starter. The spray had a dying hiss. We were losing way. I punched again. The dynamotor hummed full strength, but the engine didn't even catch. The water lapped. The whine of the other craft was getting louder. There was a shuffling out on deck and then a frantic kicking. Then Paco started shouting again.

I'd been sweetly crossed. It came in a big framed picture. I didn't want to do it. I turned on the lights and ducked low and a bullet whistled in from the beam and went right through the cabin and shattered both windows. Then another. That proved they weren't cops. And Paco had been right about Griswold. I should have known when he put on those lights.

I fumbled along the fuel pipe and twisted on the main feed tap that Griswold had turned off as he went through the door. I knocked off the lights, straightened again. Another bullet hummed through. They had the range. The fury was choking me and I could hardly breathe. I reached for the starter, to get away, to deal with Griswold. Then there was a big splash. Paco yelled my name. He was over the side.

A beautiful fix. I hurtled through the door and a bullet smacked the woodwork and I didn't know from which direction Griswold would attack. Then I saw them. They were both in the water. Paco was hanging onto a stave, trying to claw Griswold with his free hand. Griswold had him by the throat.

The other boat was about five hundred yards off, making a sweep across our bow. The shots boomed back from the distant mountains and the bullets were humming through the air like mosquitoes. There must have been two or three of them firing. I jumped forward and thrust my belly against the gunwale and leaned over. The heel of my hand hit Griswold's forehead, my fingers crushed into his eye sockets. He let go. I hit him one punch, made soft by water. Then I grabbed Paco's hair and pushed the kid under and bounced him up again like a cork.

He got a smacking grip on the gunwale. He was gasping. He swung over and fell on deck and his hands were scrambling, and then he'd picked up a fallen rifle. He squirmed to his feet. He fell across the gunwale just as Griswold was reaching for the stave. The rifle jerked and the butt smashed into the side of Griswold's head, and he sank below the surface without a sound.

I left the kid hanging over the side. I wriggled back through the wheelhouse door and the bullets were making it sound like a beehive. I pushed the starter. I was praying. The engine didn't catch and I felt sick.

Somebody on the other boat opened up with a machine gun. The bullets drummed into the woodwork and all the glass shattered again. I kept my hand flat on the starter and profanity was flooding from my mouth. The dynamotor whirred like an electric sewing machine.

Then the engine fired. The wheel spun and the boat started to whirl like a dervish. There was a crack out on deck and Paco was pumping away with the rifle. A high scream came over the water.

I couldn't crouch any longer. I had to be sure we weren't running for the shoals. I stood up and something plucked my cheek and I gunned the engine and swung round and headed for the Point. I looked back. Griswold's pals were pouring on speed. They weren't going to make it. My arguments with the Marquesa were being justified. Better many trips in a fast boat than one trip in a big junk that hijackers can pick up at will. I left the guys standing.

We shot past the Point and hit rough water again. There wasn't a chance of their finding us in this, with no Griswold to signal with the lights. I set course and headed for base, not bothering anymore to lay a false scent. But neat, that. Maybe I could persuade the Marquesa to give Paco a bonus. It was due to him. It was due to me. But I'd need to be careful what I told her.

I pushed open the door and held it with one hand. The wind blew fresh and the waves made a sound like music. I put back my head and hollered for Paco. I heard him putting the rifle away. He came in beside me and shut the door and lit one of his stinking Spanish cigarettes. He was exhilarated.

"That Griswold! That unmentionable! He snatches my rifle and throws it overboard and we fight. Teeth and knees." He took a breath. "That dirty unmentionable profanity of a son of a whore."

"He was all of it."

"That unprintable improper profaning profanity of his father's profaner."

"Also," I said.

We stood and rocked with laughter at each other.

"A thing," I said. "We don't mention this to the Marquesa."

"Naturally not. This is you and me, huh, Beel?"

"Sure it is. You and me. You hurt, kid?"

"Nah!"

He held the cigarette to my mouth, grinning in the dark, teeth glinting white. "You heard when I got one of them?" He imitated the scream. "There was a man with pain, my friend. Who were they, Beel?"

"Association. Or hijackers, maybe. Either way, Griswold was a plant. They were waiting somewhere. He was tipping them off with the lights as we passed the Point."

"Bastards," Paco said. "Trying to find our base. On that strip of coast they will find nothing but how to lose the bottom of their foolish boat." He roared with laughter again. Damage is a Spaniard's idea of humor.

He said, "So I eat no more fish till that Griswold is dead and digested six months. Not even Fridays do I eat fish." He paused, reached out a hand, touched my arm. "Beel, you stayed to pick me up. I wish to say that if ever you need—"

"Vete a joder," I said.

He said, "My friend, it takes two to do that. The bottom one always gets the worst of it." The traditional Spanish reply. He got the kick out of it they always do. We both laughed, because it is also a form of politeness.

He was so happy he was gurgling. He said, "There is no Griswold any more. Possibly I shall captain the new boat."

I knew he wouldn't. But he stood there grinning in the dark and he was a good kid and María's brother, and I couldn't dishearten him. I said, "I'll speak to the Marquesa."

He stopped grinning. He said, "That one."

"Yes, she," I said. "Here, take the wheel. I feel safer when you're steering."

I squeezed against the bulkhead while he moved into position. All the joy had gone out of him. His shoulders were slumped. He said, "You are a good friend, Beelito. Possibly you can arrange that I talk with her."

"Sure."

"Yes," he said, "but one thing. I will not go to bed with her. Never will I go to bed with that old American bitch." He shrugged, dropped his cigarette, crushed it underfoot. "Therefore I will never be a captain, will I? Not like you, Beel."

"No," I said, and I stood in the darkness and had to swallow it. I had no choice. He was speaking the truth.

Chapter Three

I cut the engine. We glided through the break in the reef, straight into the coolness of the cave, and instantly the dark lantern came on. My nerves must have been worse than I fancied. I shouted, "Kill it, you fool!" Immediately I was slightly ashamed of myself.

El Mudo scrambled out from the corner of the ledge with the lantern at shoulder level. I saw why he was breaking rules. There was another boat moored inside, a beautiful boat, a long fast sleek boat with lines as lovely as a woman's. The Marquesa had followed advice again. If the engine was like the exterior, then the western Mediterranean belonged to me. Or maybe to the Marquesa.

I tossed El Mudo our forward rope and he made us fast, our bow just kissing the new boat's stern. I jumped ashore and slapped his huge back and said, "*Hola*, Mudo," and I wanted to stop and gloat over the new craft, but the rule about lights at night was mine, and I don't break my own rules. So I said, "*Vámonos*, no hanging around," and he doused the lantern. We went back along the ledge and out through the mouth of the cave, with Paco behind us, whistling.

The cliff was Spanish rock. There's nothing harder in the world. You could march an army up and down it without leaving a single track. And that was important. No tracks. We got to the top and the wind had died and stars were coming out in a clearing sky. It was one of those soft Spanish nights when the sea and dry earth mix up their smells and stick in your nostrils.

We went down into the hollow and pulled aside the dead brush, and I got behind the wheel of the big Volkswagen. It looked like a miniature bus. El Mudo squeezed against me to make room for Paco and I passed round the cigarettes and we sat a few seconds, listening to the chirping and scratching of the night insects. I was thinking of Griswold. I was telling myself that the world was a better place without him. I felt unsettled about him, but not very much.

El Mudo nudged me, nodding, pointing out to sea. The moon was lifting from the horizon like a great blood orange, spreading a crimson wash far up into the night sky. It's a custom in that part of the world to watch four or five minutes till the moon is clear of the sea and begins to change color. I hadn't the time. "Beautiful," I said in Spanish, and the big man nodded happily and patted my arm. I let in the clutch.

We bounced over ruts and rocks and got to the track. The surface was no better, but now we could go in a straight line. I stayed at a steady thirty. The night air stirred through the windows and the cigarettes smelled strong. It was good. In a world like that, along with men like that, it is enough just to be alive and have five senses and arms and legs. Paco was singing softly to himself, one of those off-beat Andalusian songs that irritate till you get used to them. El Mudo was snapping his fingers in rhythm with the song.

I rounded the bend by the cluster of palms and pulled up, motor idling. The small wooden house was through the olive trees, a hundred yards off, a light shining from the window. María was there. I tried to imagine what she was doing, what she looked like. I couldn't picture her face at all, only the shape of her mouth. I got the familiar scooped feeling, the vibrations like hunger all the way from my knees to my chest. I hadn't seen her now for almost twenty-four hours.

Paco got out and slammed the door and came round the other side. Looking in the window, he said, "Usual time in the morning, *amigo?*"

"Sure."

"And in the evening we go to the Santa Faz fiesta and get drunk like everybody."

"Will be good," I said.

He threw away the cigarette. The glowing end made an arc through the air. He said, "Again, Beel, for what you did tonight *muchas gracias.*"

"Bury it, kid," I said, and grinned at him. I should have driven off, but the feeling was still in me. I had to send her some sort of message. I said, "My regards to María." He didn't answer. I think he nodded. I couldn't see properly. I said, "*Hasta mañana, chico,*" and meshed the gears and started off again for the big house. El Mudo still snapped his fingers. Maybe the tune was running through his head. I felt sorry he couldn't sing it, but he'd been born without any vocal chords. He was completely voiceless.

I coasted past the house, around by the lower orchard, and all the windows were open and all the lights on. Piano music was coming from the big room off the patio—Page playing a Chopin nocturne, playing it badly. I looked at my watch and there wasn't a great deal of time. I drove straight on and pulled up in front of my own shack. I told El Mudo to get rid of the Volkswagen.

He had the look on his face. He gazed at me with his great brown eyes and tried to communicate. I knew what he wanted. I could sympathize with him. Our targets were a long way apart, but maybe, basically, our feelings were about the same.

But I shook my head at him. I went inside.

Some of the blood had run down my face and dripped on my jacket. When I took a wash I saw that the bullet had nicked the center of my cheek. Not much, but when I used the towel the blood ran again in a thin trickle for a couple of minutes.

I put on a clean shirt and clean pants. I felt fresher that way, and it wasn't because I wanted to impress anybody. She'd start thinking that as soon as she saw me. She thought it no matter what I did, thought maybe I'd changed my mind about her. She couldn't understand that, outside of business, she hadn't influenced my decisions since that first fortnight.

I knocked off the light and went outside and El Mudo was still there. He fell in beside me. It was useless trying to dissuade him, so we went through the orchard together. The moon was higher now, changing color, hanging like a big gold doubloon. Over at the pickers' tents somebody was playing a guitar and a man was singing *"Adiós, chata mía"* in a high rough tenor. We passed one of the last uncollected mounds of picked fruit. The smell of it curled into my nostrils.

The lights of the house shone through the trees. El Mudo started dragging his feet. We were nearly to the edge of the orchard and he stopped altogether, plucked at my sleeve. I turned around. He stood and gazed at me, imploring, the moon throwing a pattern of branches across his face.

I said, "You will be waiting here?"

He nodded.

A dangerous game, and maybe I should have given him a lecture or something, but where was the use? The poor guy couldn't answer me anyway. And it was none of my business. I said, "All right, I'll tell him."

He nodded again, eagerly. A smile began to spread slowly over all his face. He made little movements with his throat as if he were trying to talk to me. I turned away and went through the trees at an angle, to approach the house from the back.

Page was still at the piano. Brahms now. But he was getting drowned out because the guitarist over with the pickers had switched to a fandango. A whole bunch of them were clapping in rhythm. After every few bars they called, *"Olé, olé!"*

I stepped onto the lawn. The Marquesa was proud of her lawns. Even in the very dry season she had them sprayed daily by one of the *criados*. The moon was appearing over the roof of the house, shining down on the big stone fountain in the middle of the garden, drawing glitters from the tinkling water. The wild music was still coming from over at the pickers' tents, and this girl on the lawn had her arms above her head and she was dancing to the guitar music.

There was moonlight in her hair. I realized suddenly how long it had been since last I had seen a woman who was blonde. I went slowly across the lawn, watching her, not wanting her to stop dancing, and then she turned her head. She saw me. She lowered her arms and without pausing in her motion she came running to meet me.

I thought she was smiling. She got close and it was just that her lips were drawn back.

She said, "You!" and snapped her fingers. She stared at me. She said, "I'm bored. I'm horribly bored. I want to go where that music is. I want to meet a real man, the one who was singing just now. Take me there!"

She was drunk. Absolutely hepped. She eyed me from head to foot and she said, "Black hair, isn't it? I can't tell in this light. Anyway, you're big. That's something." She took a step forward. She said, "No response. Might I inquire from which chill northern clime you hail? Perhaps you're a fellow American. That would be ghastly."

She reached up and put her arms round my neck. She tried to bite my mouth. Her hands slid up my arms and she was trembling and her lips were pressing all over my face. I felt her teeth graze my cheek. She giggled. She said, "You're bleeding. It tastes like salt."

I pushed her to arm's length and looked at her face. She was doll-like, groomed, expensive, about twenty-six. I hadn't seen a woman like her in years. She tried to close with me again. She said, "I don't want the music any more. Let's go among the orange trees and you can sing me romantic songs. You do sing, don't you? You look like a singer." She laughed. She said, "Are you understanding a word I say? What do they call you? We can do anything once we've been introduced. I'm Lavinia. An old-fashioned name for an old-fashioned girl."

"You're cute," I said. I let her go. I didn't want her. There was another like her in the house, twice the age but the same type exactly. I said, "Been nice knowing you. So long."

She stood in the way. "I'm drunk."

"I thought it possible."

She said, "Then you're a lousy sonofabitch not to take advantage of me. You'll never get the chance when I'm sober."

"Maybe I'll survive," I said, and put her to one side and went on toward the house. The guitar music rang through the orchard. I looked over my shoulder and she had started dancing again.

Through the back door and the kitchen, and the fat cook gave me the leer I always got from the servants. She didn't speak. I was beneath her. At one time it had bothered me, but not anymore. I nodded to her and continued up the back stairs and along the landing to the Marquesa's bedroom. I walked straight in. The place reeked with a gritty perfume.

I guess it wasn't her fault, but I hated her. She was sitting in front of the dressing table, the everlasting glass of Pernod in her hand, getting her hair fixed by one of the maids, a kid of thirteen or fourteen. She muttered something and jerked her head, and the girl lowered her eyes and went out of the room without a sound. The Marquesa sipped her drink, looking at my reflection in the mirror, waiting till the door clicked shut. Her negligee was open at the top. The fat flesh of her shoulders had a sort of white glow.

"Learn to knock!" she snapped.

"I had a rough trip," I said. "Save the great-lady act for someone else."

She swung around, hand out, the negligee opening over her big thighs. "What's the consignment? Give it to me."

She snatched the manifest and held it to the light, her lips moving as she read the list. The frown settled. Her mouth got smaller. She looked up again with eyes like chips of flint.

"Drugs from the new man. Twice the price. What's the matter with

Silva?"

"He still can't get any. I'm not sorry. That little boy who died a while back—"

She snorted. She said, "He had thirteen brothers and sisters. Quit the slop. If Silva's holding out for a higher price, pay anything in reason. Just so it's lower than this."

"No more handling adulterated stuff."

"You will if I tell you."

I said nothing.

Her eyes went slowly over me. Her expression changed. She said, "You've cut yourself shaving. Wipe it," and she threw me a cloth from the dressing table and sat watching while I dabbed at my face. She said, "Billy-boy, you look sort of sweet tonight. On whose account would that be?"

"Whose do you think?"

"Mine?"

"Maybe."

"I'd like to think that."

"I thought you would."

She smiled. "Yes, sweet. Very sweet. You know, Billy, I'm fond of you."

"Enough to give Pagey-boy the heave-ho?"

"Depends how you ask me. Go on, ask."

I said, "This was a bullet, not a razor. We had trouble. There's new glasswork needed on the boat and maybe some other damage."

She straightened up, stopped being a tart. "Who, hijackers?"

"Don't know. What does it matter? This is nothing new."

"So long as it wasn't the Association," she said.

"If it was, they're still searching the coast fifteen miles from here. One of the rifles went overboard."

She finished her drink and pulled a nearly full bottle from the drawer. She said, "The overhead in this game is getting too goddamned high for my liking. How'd the new man behave?"

"He wasn't there."

"What do you mean?"

"He'd changed his mind. Gone off on a job in Israel."

"Oh, for God's sake!" she snapped. "Why the hell couldn't you—"

"You're not missing a thing. He was a completely squeezed orange."

She poured another drink. Her mouth tightened again. She said, "Quit the smart-bastard wisecracks, Billy. And don't kid yourself I miss you. You weren't such a steaming hunk of meat."

"O.K.," I said, "we've got that out of our systems. Back to business. That's a nice-looking new boat down there. I'll try her tomorrow evening. What's fixed for delivery in the morning?"

"The medium Citroën."

"For who?"

She was drinking again. She frowned to herself. She said, "So what do we do now about a man for the new boat?"

"The kid who crews with me. Paco."

"No Spaniards. That's final."

"Talk to him," I said. "Maybe he'll persuade you. He's seventeen, good-looking, curly hair, full of juice. Good for a lot of years yet."

She turned back to the mirror. She said, "Go away, Williams, you bore me. If I could find someone to replace you, you'd be out on your ear before you got your breath." She picked up a comb, dug at her hair. "Send the maid back. Leave by the rear entrance. I had company arrive ten minutes back."

"I know," I said. "I met the blonde doll in the garden."

The Marquesa stood up quickly. The comb bounced on the glass top of the dressing table and fell to the floor. "Doll? A girl? Nobody told me anything about a girl. The servant said it was just Don Luis. Where was Page?"

"Inside playing the piano like a good boy," I said. "Calm down. Page knows where his bread's buttered."

She tried to recover her poise. She said, "Oh, well, if you spoke to this girl, you'd better go downstairs and meet Don Luis. They'll think it funny if you don't put in another appearance."

She bent down and picked up the comb, pulled the negligee tight around her. "The girl," she said. "Is she pretty?"

I didn't answer. The outline of her thickening shape was nauseating me. I went out the door and along the landing and down the front stairs. The little maid was waiting. She was new. But the nearly blank look she gave me was enough to show that she'd already been told by the other servants about the first fortnight I'd spent in this house.

Maybe even the orange pickers knew about it. So what? I walked across the patio, toward the music, and wondered how I could feel so old when I wasn't yet thirty.

Page looked up from the piano. He grinned, ran his fingers through an arpeggio, and went back to murdering a Mozart fantasia. The gray-haired man stood up from his seat in the corner, gave a preliminary bow, and waited in grave Spanish fashion for the introductions.

He wore an Andalusian suit: short black jacket, skintight gray pants. He was very slim and he looked like a young man until you saw his face. He could have been anything up to a hundred years old. His skin was tobacco yellow. There wasn't a square inch of it that didn't contain a hundred fine wrinkles. He had an eagle-beak nose, expressionless eyes, and a chin held so high that it looked painful.

"Good evening," I said.

Page didn't stop playing. He sounded tired and bored. "Don Luis Navarro, meet Mr. Williams." He stroked several notes in the upper register, then hit a deep chord in the bass. "Mr. Williams is yet another of the Marquesa's nephews. Which, I suppose, makes him my cousin, in a way."

Navarro gave another bow. I took his outstretched hand. It was like holding a small bag of dry bones; no return pressure. We murmured the usual Spanish nothings about what an overwhelming joy it gave us to meet each other, and I went to the sideboard and poured myself a drink. I watched him sit down again. He did it without bending his back.

He spoke in English. His voice had as little expression as his eyes. "This is an unceremonious intrusion," he said. "I trust your aunt will forgive me for being so unsociable a neighbor. It is now almost a year since I called upon her."

"Really?" I said.

Silence.

He moistened his lips. "You gentlemen have been staying long?"

"No."

"Ah. Are you liking Spain?"

"It's a fine country."

He nodded. "The guests at my *ganadería* have the same agreeable opinion. To a Spaniard it is gratifying."

"It must be."

He smiled. All the wrinkles creased and his face turned to parchment. "My guests supply a reason for the intrusion," he said. "The young lady is American. I thought possibly that the Marquesa would like to meet a fellow countrywoman again. There is a small fiesta tomorrow evening in the local village of Santa Paz—the procession of the village Christ. I am hoping the Marquesa—and, of course, you gentlemen—will honor my *ganadería* with your presence at dinner."

"Thank you," I said.

Page said in his bored voice, "I could give a better answer if I knew what the hell a *ganadería* was. You run some sort of saloon?"

A faint flush crept under the nicotine skin. The old man stood up and looked toward the piano. "I beg your pardon. There is no word in English. At my establishment I raise bulls, fighting bulls." His chin tilted even higher. "The Navarro bulls."

"Never heard of them," Page said.

"Mr. Williams—"

"Afraid not," I said.

"Of course. You are not long in Spain. Perhaps you have yet to see a *corrida.*"

"A bullfight? No, I've seen maybe a dozen."

He said, "The greatest art in the world, is it not?"

"Not to me."

More silence.

He moistened his lips again. He said, "Yes, I hear many foreigners are upset about the horses. But these days, with the heavy padding, the horses are seldom hurt."

"I know. It wouldn't have bothered me, anyway."

He said, "Then what is your objection to the bulls, Mr. Williams?"

"You're asking seriously?"

"Of course, señor."

"Then I'll tell you. Bullfights are dull. They're unbelievably dull. An animal is let into the arena, a bunch of overdressed men pick and gouge at it until it's played out, then another man gets in and waves a rag until the creature doesn't know whether it's coming or going. After a while, a long while, the man kills the bull with a sword, usually not very quickly. The band plays the same corny tunes, the animals all look alike, and the men invariably go through the same limited motions. It bores me. It bores me so much I most always get up and walk out. If that's an art, so is American burlesque."

Under the tight pants he sucked himself right in, made himself two inches taller. He said, "Señor, you are a stupid ignorant fool."

I shrugged. I went to the sideboard and poured another drink. I crossed to the piano. I said to Page, "Your friend's waiting. The customary place. If you go out there you're as dumb as he is, only in a different way."

"Mind your business," he replied softly. "Give the nice señor a drink."

I turned to Navarro. He was standing motionless, nostrils pinched, chin up. We stared at each other and he made a small movement with one of his thin hands.

"Mr. Williams, I have abused the Marquesa's hospitality. I most humbly beg your pardon."

"Forget it. Have a drink."

"No, thank you."

"Well, I will," Page said. He rose from the piano and mixed himself a big Martini on the rocks. He was very small when he stood up, like a doll version of Joe College, blue eyes and cropped curly hair. He was twenty-two and he didn't look it. If he'd really been my cousin, I'd maybe have wrecked his setup and sent him packing back to the States. For his own good.

He gulped the drink and got himself another, nervous because he had cause to be, trying to pretend that he wasn't in a hurry. He sipped and smiled and overplayed it. He waited too long. The Marquesa made an entrance.

"My dear Don Luis," she said musically, and swept across the room with both hands outstretched. She had on an evening gown of black lace. She'd tightened her figure and she looked not younger than she was, but peculiarly majestic, handsome, the way she was when first she picked me from a gutter in North Africa, when I looked at her, undeceived, and told myself I could go through with anything.

She held Navarro's hands and stood a little way from him with a bright smile, her eyes flicking round the room for signs of the girl I'd mentioned. "An unexpected pleasure, dear Don Luis," she said in Spanish. "How well you look, and how natural that you should! I have read in the periodicals of the magnificent performance given last week by your bulls in Sevilla. My husband would have been proud of his friend."

In his eyes the pride swelled fantastically. He kissed her right hand. "Too kind, dear Marquesa."

She switched to English. "You are staying to dinner," she said in a playfully commanding way.

"Ah, unfortunately I have another guest at the *ganadería*. I came only to ask if—"

Page said, "I got a mission among the Spaniards. I'm going to teach the bastards to eat their dinner before eleven o'clock at night."

He started fixing himself a third drink. He never could take it, and he was getting high. The Marquesa smiled at him. She said gently, "Why don't you play us something, Page?"

"Because I don't want to," he answered, imitating her tone of voice. "The mood is not with me."

She gave a deep throaty laugh. It sounded almost natural. "You must realize, Don Luis, that America has changed since I was a girl. They no longer raise the young with quite the same severity. Page, do play us something."

"No," he said. "The hell with it."

All at once we had a thick, uncomfortable atmosphere. The old man smiled awkwardly and looked at his shoes. The Marquesa gazed across the room completely unruffled, except for her eyes. I knew what would come afterward and I didn't want to be there. I wanted to be far away with María.

I made a motion to leave. Out on the patio there was a sharp patter of high heels, and then the blonde came in through the French windows.

She was more beautiful than I had thought. She stood languidly on the threshold, hands hanging at her sides, her hair sleek and wet. She was not drunk any more.

She said, "Sumptuous night. I had an unnerving experience and stuck my head in the fountain. It sobered me."

Nobody answered her. She advanced slowly into the room. She said, "Well, now, you must be the Marquesa. I am plain Lavinia. I feel I should curtsy. I'm not going to. And I simply cannot go around calling you Marquesa. You too must have been plain somebody before you left the United States."

They studied each other. Don Luis made a move, but the Marquesa beat him to it. She said, "I was christened Ethel, my dear."

The girl laughed. "I knew it all the time. Ethel Knapp. Debutante of 1926. Married the pick of the season's visiting titles. Then your dad lost his money in 1929 and you were isolated in this hole. That was tough on you, I'm sure." She wasn't helping the atmosphere any. She clearly didn't care.

"Strange, Ethel," she said. "I heard you were an only child. Here you turn up with all sorts of nephews. Where did they come from?" She waved a hand, walked toward the piano. "Don't bother with introductions, I've met them already. This one's as cute as could be."

She reached out and patted Page on the back of the neck. She said, "Be an angel child, darling, play me something. You have the loveliest touch."

He gave the Marquesa a hint of a malicious smile and without a word sat down and began to play.

The girl smiled at him. "Oh, goody. I just love those lousy little Brahms waltzes." She turned the smile around the room. "Ethel, you have a talented nephew."

"Thank you." The Marquesa sat down and clapped her hands twice in the Spanish signal. A servant came in, passed around a tray of drinks. Navarro's face was a mask of composed politeness. He was looking everywhere but at the blonde.

She swayed a little in time to the music, sipping her drink, one hand lightly on Page's shoulder. She said, "Been visiting Auntie long, darling?" and it was as if the rest of us weren't even there.

He got right into the vein, played it back at her. I didn't know what he'd suffered with the Marquesa since he became my successor, but I could imagine. He went after his revenge, melting smiles and a dreamy expression, intimate music, just him and the blonde. "Been here a month," he said. "North Africa before that."

"Lion shooting?"

"Trying to run a magazine. *Avant garde*, as they say, modern stuff. I put out exactly one issue and my old man cut off the dough. He's waiting now for me to crawl back home on my hands and knees."

"You won't, though."

"No."

"Good," she said. "The older generation makes me puke. Show them any sign of a creative spirit and they go crazy till they destroy you."

She got right behind him, both hands on his shoulders, leaning until her chin almost touched his curly hair. "I adore artistic people," she said. "When you come over tomorrow I'll lend you some annotated Kafka. Do you like Kafka?"

"Not much."

"Then you'll love my marginal notes. Weren't you delighted when they took out that miserable Mr. K. and cut his throat? He was a bourgeois. All his trouble came from being too damned respectable. I loathe and despise respectable people." She rumpled Page's hair. "Don't let it happen to you, darling. Don't let the swine pin you down to convention."

"I won't."

Don Luis took a step forward. "Lavinia, perhaps we should go. Rex will worry."

"Not while you're with me, he won't," she said. "And you haven't yet told Ethel about tomorrow. We're going to have a perfectly lovely time tomorrow, Ethel."

"Are we? I'm so glad." The Marquesa stood up suddenly and the drink splashed over her bare wrist. She clucked her tongue. Her eyes were bright. She said, "Now what have I done? Page, dear, do fetch me a handkerchief right away."

He stopped playing. Lavinia straightened up with a hand still on his shoulder. She said, "Send the other nephew, dear. He can't talk, let alone play the piano."

"Page, dear," the Marquesa said, "fetch me a handkerchief."

He got up, gave me a half grin. The orange trees were outside, and he'd been awaiting his opportunity. "Of course, dear," he said, and went lightly across the room and out to the patio. I listened to his retreating footsteps, wondering if he'd get caught. I wondered how he had got away with it for so long.

Don Luis had a nice sense of timing. He pulled a snowy white handkerchief from his pocket and gently mopped the Marquesa's wrist.

The girl narrowed her eyes, looked at me from under her lashes. "And what can you do?" she asked. "Anything?"

"Yes," I said. "I can go home and get something to eat."

Navarro put away his handkerchief. The Marquesa purred a little. She said, "Bill has a cottage on the other side of the orchard. He doesn't live here."

"I guessed that," the girl said. "The place would be sort of crowded up with two nephews, wouldn't it? All right, Bill, I'll walk across with you. You can show me the orange trees."

"I'm sorry," I said. "I have some business to do."

The smile on the Marquesa's face almost made me change my mind

and take the girl with me. Not quite. Because María would be waiting.
I said, "Well, good night, everyone."

"Until tomorrow," Navarro said. "Perhaps when you have seen my
bulls you will form another opinion of bull fighting."

"Perhaps," I said. *"Buenas noches."*

"Buenas noches and *adiós,* you punk," the girl said. I left it at that.

I looked down the road to the cottage and the light was on in the
kitchen. It meant María was having trouble getting away. I lit a cigarette and sat on the edge of the fountain and gazed at the moon and
smoked. The night air was full of tree scents, orange smells, the smell
of rocks, the smell of Spain.

Maybe that had been a part of falling in love with her. Maybe I
wouldn't love her so much if I took her away. Maybe she wouldn't love
me so much.

It's a fool's game to regret what is passed. But I wished now that I were
legal, had a passport. More than anything in the world, I wanted to
marry her. But in Spain that means a church, a sheaf of papers, a
checkup by the civil authorities. I was an illegal entrant. I couldn't stand
a checkup by anybody. I felt as if I'd enticed her to my bed by false prom-
ises.

Perhaps one day she'd change her mind, come away with me. Somewhere I could marry her without difficulty. There didn't seem much
hope. She was stuck with the Spanish idea of family, the female's duty
to the male. She'd made the promise to her mother. She wouldn't leave
Paco until there was another woman to look after him, till he got married himself. It looked like a distant prospect. Paco was seventeen. In
Spain they don't tie up that early. So now we lied to the kid, continually, because he too was stuck with something, that fierce Spanish thing
about the protection of women and the honor of the family name. I did-
n't feel good about it.

And I could guess María's thoughts. I could do nothing about them.
In Spain there are only good girls and bad girls, and nothing in between.
She was thinking that she was a bad girl. Take a girl like her to your
bed and she always has that thought at the back of her mind no matter what you tell her, no matter what she tells herself. That, and the fear
of having a baby. I sat there on the edge of the fountain and tried to figure a way out of the mess.

The big car came sliding up the drive and halted, and a man got out
dressed in sports clothes, a knotted scarf at his neck. He was of medium
height and about my own age. He stood on the drive, looked uncertainly
about him, then saw me and came heading across the lawn. I stood up.

He was smiling. He said in halting Spanish, *"Perdone,* but is this the house of the—er—Marquesa—" He stopped in front of me and the grin became broader. He said, "Oh, hello, old chap. I thought you were a Spaniard. Awfully sorry and all that." He hesitated. "I say, you do speak English, don't you?"

"My native tongue."

"What a relief!" He sighed humorously. "British, you know. We can never pick up a foreign language, and I'm the worst of them. This is the house of the Marquesa del Varco del something-or-other-else, isn't it?"

"Sure."

"Good show." He thrust out a hand. "Name's Hatherton, Rex Hatherton. How do you do?"

"Williams," I said.

"Oh, I once knew a fellow called Bill Williams."

"They call me that."

"Do they? Yes, I suppose it's sort of automatic, isn't it?" He went on laughing. "Sorry, but I'm not a very brilliant conversationalist. Matter of fact, I'm looking for my wife. Haven't happened to see her, have you?"

"If she's a blonde named Lavinia, she's inside."

Maybe I conveyed something. The smile faded. "You've met her," he said, and he had that slightly flat tone in his voice with which the British always try to disguise that fact that you've registered something on them. He said, "Shall we join her? Perhaps they'll give us a drink. My wife enjoying herself?"

I said, "How does anyone tell?"

He smiled again, but it wasn't the same. He said, "You sound a little humpy, old man. Come and have that drink. It'll make all the difference in the world."

"Some other time."

"Oh, well," he said. "Sorry I interrupted your meditations." He nodded and began to move away. "Cheerio. Hope we run into each other again."

"We will," I said, "at the fiesta tomorrow. I'm invited to dinner."

He turned back. The moonlight made his face like marble. "That's nice," he said, and his voice was flatter than ever. I was looking at a jealous husband.

I said, "Yes, it was kind of Don Luis to invite me. I hear he raises bulls."

"Yes," the Englishman said. "Good night." He turned on his heel and went toward the house.

I crossed the lawn and entered the orchard. The climbing moon had turned silver, and the dry earth was patterned with sharp shadows from the trees. I was back to thinking of María.

I had to face it, I was in love with her, hopelessly. We belonged to each other, and I'd never belonged to anyone in my life before. She was the only reason I'd gone on working for the Marquesa after that first fortnight. María. And if I went away now it would be like stopping my life.

I heard a rustling over to the right. Page said something softly in his very bad Spanish. They didn't see me. I kept walking. They were standing against a tree, faint in the moonlight, their arms tight around each other.

It wasn't to my taste, but all the same I felt sorry for them. Page was not the first guy to take it up in order to forget the embraces of an old woman. It's a popular pastime in North Africa, so maybe he'd had previous experience. I was still sorry for him. I was especially sorry for the poor big guy who couldn't talk. There was going to be hell to pay if the Marquesa ever found out about them.

María wasn't there. I poured myself a drink, undressed, went into the second room, and lay down on the trestle bed in my underwear to wait for her. Moonlight was coming through the open window, going through the adjoining arch into the other room, glinting on the latch she would lift. I lay watching it. I couldn't keep still.

Over at the pickers' tents it sounded as if the wine were going round. They'd broken out with two more guitars. There was a flurry of music and then a woman with a typical Spanish voice—deep and throaty, artificially hardened—began a slow song about how it was better to be dead than in love, because your heart aches until it bleeds and after a while you die anyway, and then your relatives come and put little white flowers on your grave.

I lay and listened to her. The smell of oranges drifted from the mounds among the trees. By noon they'd be all collected. The pickers would vanish until another year. Which means that most of tonight would be spent in drinking and singing and warming up for tomorrow night's fiesta at Santa Faz.

I listened to the woman. I wanted María so fiercely I got to feeling sick. A colossal ache and something like a fever.

And with all that I didn't hear her coming. I'd been walking around. I was standing in the middle of the floor. Then suddenly she was there for me, breathing heavily from running, her back to the door as she slid the bolt. She whispered, "Beel," and ran toward me. The nearness of her flooded me and I was kissing her and running my hands over her, and it was so fierce by then that I couldn't wait. I picked her up in my arms and carried her through the arch. We sank to the bed.

She whispered something. It wasn't words. The woman outside was still singing and María's arms were tight around me and she was pulling at my undershirt and her hands were smoothing at the flesh of my back. I wasn't conscious of anything except the feel of her and the smell of her and the scorching warmth of her body. And faintly the singing. Her shoes dropped noisily to the floor.

After that there was nothing in the world. There wasn't even a world.

I sat on the side of the bed and looked down at her. The moonlight was shining on her face and she seemed a child instead of nineteen years old. Her black hair was spread on the pillow. Her eyes glowed in the dimness.

I said, "Stay with me till morning."

"Is not possible, my Beel."

"Say 'Bill.'"

"Beel."

"Williams."

"Oovilliams."

"Now say, 'I will stay with you till morning, Bill Williams.'"

She took my hand and held it to her breast, shaking her head. "Beel, I must go home now. Paco suspects."

"No," I said, and held her where she was. "He does not. I talked with him. Everything is good."

"No, Beel. No. Tonight he spoke of you at the meal. He spoke of you and the Marquesa. He said that—"

I put a hand across her mouth. "Everyone says that. It is not true."

"Never?"

I made no answer.

She said softly, "I am glad you do not lie to me, Beel. The servants from the house have told me. They say it is still so, but they are wrong. Tonight I knew it and always I know it."

I said, "I am with her now for business only. She has her other boy."

"She still wants you."

"I think not."

"She does. I watched from the trees on Sunday when you were both in the garden. I saw how she looked at you. Beel, you will never do it, will you?"

I leaned over and kissed her, lifted her so she lay across my lap. Her arms twined around my neck and I lowered my face to her throat. The fires were starting again. I smoothed my hands over her body. I whispered, "Once more, María, before you go," and I pulled her tight against me. The flesh was hardening. I said, "I love you, María. We have to go away. We have to be married. Come with me."

The world blew up. Something smashed against the outer door. The bolt winced in its socket. There was another blow and fists began to pound. I scrambled to my feet. María was gripping my arm, terror-stricken, whispering, "Paco, Paco, Paco," over and over.

I got in front of her. I shouted, "Who is it?" There was no answer except the hammering.

She moved behind me. Then she was standing on the bed and climbing through the window. The humiliation of it was like a drink of filthy water. I reached to pull her back, but she was gone already, stumbling over the rough earth toward the orchard. I went through to the other room and jerked the door open. Paco ran past me and straight into the bedroom.

I walked slowly after him. I snapped, *"Qué pasa?"*

His jacket was open. His hand was on a knife at his belt. He stared at me through the gloom, and the moonlight was shining across the rumpled bed and right on the shoe that María had left on the floor.

"Where is María?" he demanded.

"How should I know?" I made a casual movement and sat on the bed and slid the shoe out of sight with my bare foot.

"She lied to me," he said in a dead voice. "Never has it happened before. She told me she was going to bed. I looked in her room and she was gone."

"For a walk, maybe. It's a fine night."

The sound of guitars came through the open window. The pickers were singing and clapping. Paco said, "Is not customary to answer a door when you are naked."

"I sleep this way. I wasn't expecting visitors."

His gaze went over me, slowly, scrutinizing. "You were having dreams, perhaps?"

"Yes," I said. "I often do. Now please go. I am tired."

He turned and walked away. He got to the open door and paused with his hand on the latch. He said, "I will kill the man who makes a whore of my sister. Any man."

"Good night," I said.

"Hasta mañana."

"Yes," I said. "See you in the morning."

He went out and closed the door behind him.

There's a Spanish proverb that says, "Always the father or the brother breaks in." I had laughed when first I heard it. That seemed a long time ago. I lay on the bed; watching the moonlight creep over the wall. After a while I pulled the sheet over me and listened to the singing. It went on for hours.

Part II
The Day and the Following Night

Chapter Four

I awoke just before seven, the sun on my face. The wild canaries were singing from the surrounding trees. El Mudo was cooking my breakfast in the other room. He seemed to like doing it. The pan sizzled.

A thin mist lay low around the boles of the trees. The pickers were already in the orchards, gathering the last of the oranges. Some of them still sang. Put a group of Spaniards together and some of them are always singing.

I washed, had breakfast, and Mudo came back with the medium Citroën. The morning air outside was like wine. I got behind the wheel, drove down the track, and stopped near Paco's house. I whistled through my fingers. The kid came running over the field, squeezed in beside us. But without his usual morning grin, just staring ahead through the windshield, face set, dark circles under his eyes.

I wanted to ask what was the matter, what happened when he got home last night. But El Mudo could hear, even if he couldn't speak. You don't question a Spaniard about his sister in front of another Spaniard.

We went to the cliff and down the face, the salt smell very strong, freshening the inside of my head. The mist was thicker on the sea. In that part of the world you can pretty well count on it. It simplifies matters. All you need do is run the boat in at night, with no lights, then unload at leisure in the morning when offshore craft have a visibility of only a few yards.

We got the stuff ashore, up the cliff, into the back of the small truck. We covered it finally with a tarpaulin. It took about an hour and a half and we really needed three more men, any men, but it was no use speaking to the Marquesa because she'd start off again about the Spanish wagging tongue. Some of her employees had been with her all their lives. She still didn't trust them. She had that racial-superiority complex that some Americans get when they live abroad. She wanted me to recruit other Anglo-Saxons from North Africa. It was almost funny. Superior types like Griswold.

I looked again at the new boat and she was lovely. I checked the other craft. There wasn't much damage outside of bullet scars and shattered glass. I told El Mudo to spend the day doing what he could in the way of repairs, and his face lit up. He was one of the mechanical Spaniards. You find a lot of them, able almost to make an engine out of a pile of scrap. He worked like a dog for the Marquesa. She paid him the equivalent of four dollars a week. In the rural areas of Spain that's considered a good wage. All the same, she was a stingy bitch.

I checked the drums of gas at the back of the cave and we wouldn't need new supplies for another week. We went back outside and the mist was lifting. The sun started shining strongly. It was going to be a hot, dry day. We drove back along the track and all the oranges were gathered and most of the pickers were sitting around making breakfast. Slices of sausage and hunks of dry bread. The wine circulated. One man who was a gypsy had his hands above his head, fingers snapping, dancing. His pals were gathered in a circle, clapping their hands, singing *"Qué bonita es mi niña,"* what a pretty thing is my girl. You get used to the songs after a while. You get to like them.

Paco had said not a word. I was worried about him. We reached the big house and I got out and the other two drove off to get the oranges piled on top of the tarpaulin. I entered the kitchen, had a cup of bitter coffee from the stove, and ate one of the new loaves the cook was taking from the oven. She watched me with customary disdain. For some reason it bothered me this morning, maybe because of Paco's attitude. I felt lonely. I wanted the cook to be friendly.

"Going to the fiesta at Santa Faz tonight?" I asked.

"Everyone is."

"Pretty far from here, hah?"

The contempt flickered in her eyes. She shrugged, face unchanged, and turned away. There was no point in pressing it. But I was sorry. I went looking for the Marquesa.

She was alone, sitting at a desk in the room that once had been her husband's library. She wasn't dressed yet, or made up, and her face looked greasy. She was nibbling a hot roll, negligee open, a glass of Pernod at her elbow.

"Everything ready?"

"Yes," I said. "A big load this time. I need more men."

"Get them."

"Like that, eh?" I took a roll from her plate, spread it with butter, and started eating. I said casually, "What about letting Pagey-boy in on the game?"

She grinned, just as casually. "And what the hell use would Pagey-boy be?"

"He could carry."

"Him? He can barely carry his own name." She sipped her drink. "No, dear, he's staying out. Right out. These past few weeks he's told me everything he and his family ever did or thought. I'd hate him to have the same opportunity with my affairs."

"Suppose I tell him."

"You won't," she said.

"Then how about some of these faithful old retainers you've had kicking around for years?"

"Nothing doing. I don't trust them. All Spaniards talk too much. They're not faithful to me so much as to my husband's memory. Anyway, it would be too much. They're accustomed to thinking of me as the Marquesa."

"The Marquesa," I said. "How nice. On your account I've fought hijackers, dodged cops, and broken pretty near every law of the high seas. Now you're going to start talking snob values,"

"Needn't get irritable, Billy. You're making plenty." She stood up. "You could make more if you liked. I've been thinking."

"Again?"

"Yes," she said. "About drugs."

"We're already making the maximum profit."

"Not that sort of drugs. Narcotics."

I said, "You're a lovely person. The answer's no."

"Why not? They're used as medicine, too."

"Oh, sure. Medicine. Especially through illegal channels. All the little junkies up a dark alley, doctoring themselves with a safety pin."

"There's a lot of money in it."

"For God's sake," I said, "no."

"We'll talk it over later."

"No, we won't."

She said, "Well, we'll see. Run along now, Billy. Have a nice trip."

I didn't move.

"What are you waiting for?"

I said, "The stuff you drink is beginning to fog your brain. Where am I supposed to be going this morning?"

She looked momentarily confused. It gave me a rotten pleasure to see her like that. She walked to the bookcase, removed four big books, and turned the dial of the flimsy-looking safe concealed in the wall.

All her money was inside. And my money. And all her papers, accounts, markets, names and addresses of her Spanish outlets. I'd never seen them. Nobody had. The Association would have paid a lot of money for just one look. She pulled out the big black daybook and ran her finger down the list. She said, "The Citroën. I told you last night."

"Sure you did. The Citroën can be either Ruiz or Ferrer. Which?"

She had to look at the book again. She didn't like doing it. "Ferrer," she snapped, "and there'll be hell kicked up when he learns the price of the drugs. See he pays cash. American bills."

She replaced the book in the safe, swung the dial. When she turned round again she was smiling. "I don't know, Billy, there's always an air of tension between us these days. Why? Why don't we make it up and be friends again? We could celebrate. Let's get really decked out tonight for this dinner at Don Luis'."

"And Page?"

"He's not going."

"No?"

"No," she said calmly. "Think I'm having him frisk around with that bitch of a girl?"

"Page or nobody."

She leaned back against the desk. "Jealous, Billy?"

"*Adiós*," I said. "I'm off to make you some money."

I crossed the room and went outside and turned around to close the door. She was staring after me. Her face looked old and pouchy. She said, "You sonofabitch, just what do you think you are?"

I shrugged. I didn't answer. I shut the door and went along the passage, and I didn't know what I was. I'd quit thinking of any definition for me after the first time I got in bed with her.

The Citroën was in the small barn. El Mudo and Paco hadn't finished piling on the camouflage of oranges. I went over to my own place to get a gun.

Through the orchard the pickers were sitting in the sun, work finished, some of them drunk already. They looked happy. There was a lot of singing and some of them waved a hand and said, "*Hola*," as I walked past. A beautiful gypsy girl looked a lot like María, so I smiled at her. A man stood up abruptly, dislike in his eyes. He was either her cousin, her brother, her boy friend, or maybe her husband. I had to smile at him too to make everything all right. In Spain you smile at the man exactly as you've smiled at the woman or you have a fight on your hands.

I walked to my shack, still thinking of María, wondering how she was. I pushed open the door and something moved. Don Luis Navarro stood up from an old wooden chair, looking fantastically out of place. He had on another Andalusian suit. He bowed. It was like bending a stiletto. He said, "Good morning, Señor Williams."

"Good morning," I said, and then I said, "This is your house," as you always do in Spain. "May I offer you something, Don Luis? Coffee? A little wine?"

"Thank you, no."

He didn't sit down again. We stood and looked at each other. I said, "Excuse me," and went into the bedroom and got the gun and tucked it behind the waistband of ray pants, inside my shirt. When I got back he was standing in the same position, looking uncomfortable.

"I hope you were not waiting long," I said.

"No." He shook his head. He hesitated. "Señor Williams, forgive me for coming at this early hour uninvited to your house. I have not disturbed the Marquesa. I wish to see only you."

I waited.

He flushed faintly, moistened his lips. He said, "My conduct last night was inexcusable. I insulted the hospitality of your aunt and I insulted you. You will be thinking now that all Spaniards are abominable. The fault is mine. The amendment must be mine."

In another language you say drop it, think nothing of it, forget it, something like that. In Spanish, talking to the hidalgo type, you make circles. I said, "Señor, the matter was of small importance."

"You are courteous, señor. Your very kindness puts me deeper in your debt." He hesitated again. "At my *ganadería* this afternoon is the shooting of the clay pigeons. At five o'clock will come Hernando Zerpa, the *torero*, to demonstrate his skill against my brave bulls. In the evening will be the fiesta and the dinner and the dancing. All my friends will be there from many miles. But my closest friends will arrive at two o'clock this afternoon. I shall be honored, señor, if you are among them."

He held out a thin dry hand. I shook it. I said, "Thank you."

He gave a peculiarly tremulous smile. "I will esteem it an even greater pleasure, Mr. Williams, if you can return with me now. I have many fine horses. This morning we shall ride. I can explain to you about the Navarro bulls, and we can lunch with my *ganaderos*. They are very good men. Very enthusiastic for the bulls."

There was something weird about the old man. But he was going out of his way to make amends. I was trying to figure a refusal when the truck pulled up outside.

I said in Spanish, "Don Luis, I have gratitude at your kind offer. This is an unfortunate day. I must work."

Instantly he was contrite. "How stupid of me. You help the Marquesa. And I am delaying you. Forgive me."

He walked with me to the door, into the sunlight. Paco saw who it was and got out of the truck and stood waiting respectfully. The oranges were piled high in the back, a fine job, not a trace of the tarpaulin underneath.

I said, "Don Luis, I will endeavor to arrive in time for the demonstration of the bulls. I owe it to you, and to my ignorance. And tonight, with your permission, I will drink all your wine and eat your table bare." I offered a hand. "*Hasta luego*, señor."

He started to answer. Another car came bucketing up the track and stopped beside us with a squeal of brakes. Lavinia Hatherton was behind the wheel, blonde hair all wind-blown.

"Hello," she drawled. "What a marvelous day! Have you seen all those

wonderful people lolling around under the trees? They simply fantas-
ticate me."

"Good morning," I said.

She ignored me. "Luis, what is the idea, running out and leaving your
guests to fend for themselves? I looked everywhere for you."

Navarro smiled, moved toward her. "I thought you were still asleep,
my dear."

"Rex, yes. Me, I have too much vitality. Tell you what. I'll race you back
to the *ganadería*."

"Excuse me, please," I said in Spanish. "I have to go now."

Paco took his cue and climbed into the cab of the truck. She looked at
me then. She said coldly, "Do we have the pleasure later in the day?"

"Don Luis has kindly invited me."

"I can hardly wait," she said.

I got behind the wheel, started the engine. I said, "Mrs. Hatherton,
your manners need a little fixing." I eased the accelerator and we
pulled away. Paco said nothing. I glanced back. Navarro was getting into
the car beside her, their heads close together.

We rounded the bend and by the cluster of palms Paco tapped my arm.
I drew up and he leaned across me and sounded the horn. María came
running from the house. She had a package of food and a small goatskin
of wine. She was barefooted. I lit a cigarette and sat back. Paco was
watching very closely.

I said, "*Buenos días*, María," and smiled at her. She did not smile back.
I saw the bruises on her face, the big one under her left eye. I said, "You
have hurt yourself. What happened?"

She lifted a hand to her face. Her eyes flicked to Paco. She was frightened. She said, "It was nothing. I stumbled."

I leaned out, took the wineskin and the package, managed to brush
her hand. "No matter," I said. "Tonight you forget it. Tonight we all go
to Santa Faz and enjoy ourselves."

"Yes," she said, and her eyes glowed. "There is dancing in the streets.
They have the most beautiful Christ in all of the province."

Paco reached for the wineskin, put it under the seat. He said, "I have
changed my mind. I am not going."

"I am," I said.

"We are not going," he corrected himself. "Not me and not María. Come,
Beel, we leave. It is late."

I started the engine. María had a helpless look on her face. "The food
is if you get hungry," she said. "There is fried squid and two loaves of
bread."

"Thank you," I said.

Paco said, "*Vámonos*, Beel."

I let in the clutch and headed for the mountains. I looked back and María was standing in the middle of the track, staring after us.

Chapter Five

The road was like almost any other road in Spain—twisting like boiled macaroni, the only one in the district, and very bad. Spanish road-builders have a conviction that any distance between two points should be made as long as possible.

We were climbing through baked-looking scenery, beautiful, somehow bruised, turning bends so sharp that sometimes it seemed we must topple two thousand feet down to the plateau. Then we went higher and the valley disappeared.

There's nothing like that scenery anywhere else in the world. Range after towering range of peaks, sun-smitten Spanish rock, every shade from bright yellow to a purple almost black. Once in a while, thousands of feet below in the foothills, you catch a glimpse of man-made terrac-ing, where a people are trying to suck a living from the dry soil by grow-ing olive trees. Tough people. They've never seen an automobile or a lo-comotive.

There was once a man who said the Spanish mountains had to be ei-ther heaven or hell, but he wasn't sure which. The people in the villages could tell him.

In an hour my ears began to pop gently because of the height. I glanced at Paco. He was slumped in the corner, a withdrawn expression on his face, still not speaking. He hadn't opened his mouth since we started.

I didn't like this high barrier between us. Maybe, since he stood be-tween me and all I wanted, I should have resented him. But once you fall in love and discover that you can't get through life alone, then you find yourself getting mixed up with all sorts of affections beside the main one. I liked Paco. More than liked him. He was María's brother, a good kid. He was proud and he was brave. In his shoes, with his idea of fam-ily honor, I probably would have been acting the same as he.

I said, "Paco, what's picking you?"

"Not your affair," he growled.

"As you say."

We drove a long way in silence. He stirred. He said, "Beel, I must do something regrettable."

"Go ahead."

"I must ask again if you spoke the truth about María."

I said, "Yes."

He wet his lips. "You will look in my face and say it?"

I said, "Sure. Then we go off the road and over the edge."

I laughed. I hated my own guts. But I'd promised María.

"You do not speak a lie, Beel?"

"Of course not."

"Then," he said quietly, "she has a lover among the orange pickers. One of those filthy *churumbeles* of gypsies. She was with him last night. I am young but I have many women. I know how they look when they have been making love. I will beat her again. I will beat her till she tells me who he is. Then I kill them both."

I said, "Keep your hands off her."

"Why? Why are you concerned?"

I cut the engine and we slid to a stop. The silence of the mountains lapped all around us. The heat haze shimmered from the rocks, and from somewhere far off a bird started singing. I reached under the seat for the wineskin, took a drink. I said, "Paco."

He was crouched forward, face tense. I said, "Look, *amigo*."

He snapped his fingers furiously. "*Escucha*, Beel! Listen!"

The silence rolled. The bird sang again. Then it came: the sound of a car, climbing at high speed, the noise echoing faintly from wall to wall of the mountains.

I couldn't tell how far away it was. There were rock barriers between us. But one thing was certain: It was bound to pass us. There was no other road.

"Onto the back," I said. He scrambled out, the gun already in his hand. Through the rear window I saw him burrowing among the oranges. I started up again, my own gun on the seat beside me.

I went slow round the bends, fast on the stretches, so as not to be caught in the open. Ten minutes passed. I got scared that we'd meet Ferrer before the other car caught up. I'd have to stop then. The two of us would be sitting targets. I was pretty sure that if there was violence, Ferrer would be useless. I was wondering what to do when Paco rapped on the window.

We turned a hairpin bend. I steered with one hand and held the gun in my lap with the other. I drove thirty yards farther on from the corner to give them enough clearance, then I pulled up sharp. It was suddenly a very hot day. The sweat ran off me. I looked back and Paco was full length among the oranges. I waited.

There was a roar. A whistling. The car came screeching around the corner at about forty. It was a big, long-bodied black Italian car, with enough room in the back to hold a party. Maybe they were doing that. I couldn't see. All the sun blinds were pulled down, side and back. There were three men in the front seat. They barreled past and disappeared around the next bend. I knocked on the rear window.

Paco was off the back and up the road like a hare, hugging the mountain face all the way. He reached the bend, flattened himself against the rock wall, and peered round the corner. His hand came up. He waved me on.

I drove forward. He climbed into the cab again. I shut off the engine and we sat listening. The sound of the car ahead got fainter, died away. I let out a long breath.

Paco opened the package, handed me half a loaf and three slices of cold squid, and we sat munching. "Foreigners," he said. "A Spaniard would have shouted at you for parking there."

"They looked Spanish."

"There was a glass partition in the front and a blind was drawn. I saw only the men in front." He took a drink of wine, wiped his mouth on the back of his hand. "They drove fast, as if they knew the road. Maybe Spaniards. I wonder."

We drank some more wine, finished the food. The silence washed round us. Stationary in the sun, the cab was getting hot as an oven. I turned the ignition switch, made to press the starter. Paco put a hand on my arm.

"You were going to tell me something."

"Huh?" I said.

"When the car came, you had started to speak."

"I do not remember," I said. He stared at me, "Yes, I do," I said. "Yes, I remember. About the new boat. We test it this afternoon when we return. Afterward I talk to the Marquesa of you."

"Nothing more?" His face was stony.

"Nothing."

He spat from the side window. "Then we go," he said, and reached over and pressed the starter for me.

The engine pulled well. The performance always improves in the thinned air of the mountains. We were nearing the topmost peak.

We rounded a corner. The road became more level. The sun was cut off for a moment's coolness while we went between tall pine trees, a group of them growing thickly on the immediate edge of the precipice. I looked at my watch and accelerated. Almost there, and late. We turned several more bends, leaving the trees behind, and in a long flat stretch was waiting an identical Citroën, motionless, empty, facing the way we were coming.

Ferrer had heard us. He stood in the roadway, flagging with his hand. I pulled around his empty truck, stopped right behind it, and he hurried over while I was getting out, face drawn, mouth twitching at the corners. Ferrer was in the wrong business. He hadn't the nerves for it.

We shook hands.

"You're late," he said impatiently.

I pulled the manifest from my pocket. "A black car pass here?"

"About ten minutes ago. What do you carry? I want more of those gold-plated watch straps."

"You have them. Plus radio tubes, a few cameras, nylon stockings—"

"No," he said. "No nylon stockings. I am overstocked. The prices are too high for my market."

"Everything or nothing." He opened his mouth to complain. I said, "There are drugs again."

His face changed. "Those I can use. How many?"

"Enough. And all unadulterated. Leave them that way and you won't kill any more people in Cádiz."

"Cádiz?" He reached for the manifest. "What do I know of Cádiz? I have no contacts there."

"You must have. It's your area. We're the only people operating on this part of the coast. I heard last night that three Cádiz persons had died."

He shook his head. "No." He was studying the manifest. Suddenly he snapped, "*Hombre!* You are crazy? You expect me to buy drugs for these prices?"

"Good ones."

"So I do not care. I do not pay this amount. Blood of God, you wish to bankrupt me?"

"I am indifferent. The total for the delivery is thirteen thousand dollars. Yes or no?"

"No! And again no!"

"*Bueno!*" I started to climb back into the truck.

He grabbed my arm. "*Amigo.* Look. I do not carry so much money with me."

"*Qué lástima.*" I knocked his hand away.

"Nine thousand I have, yes. Suppose I pay the rest in pesetas?"

"Suppose not. Thirteen thousand dollars. American or Canadian."

He stood in the sun and sweated. A long quiet stream of Spanish oaths came from his mouth. Then he reached into his pocket. Paco got down from the cab and started changing over the number plates from one truck to the other.

Ferrer counted the money into my hand. I rolled it into a bundle and tucked it away in my hip pocket. There was no receipt. Not for contraband.

A Spaniard, like an Oriental, is chary of losing face. Ferrer suddenly smiled and shook my hand warmly as if he'd just received a bargain. "My turn again two weeks from tomorrow," he said gaily. "Until then, *chico mío*. And please, no nylon stockings."

"Many thanks," I said, and Paco had finished switching the number plates. I got into the empty Citroën, the same model as the one I'd driven up, with the same number plates now. I waved a hand and called, "*Adiós*," started away. The engine definitely was not the same. It groaned. Ferrer was one of the unmechanical Spaniards, and he'd given the vehicle a beating.

I looked back. He was disappearing round the bend. The camouflage of oranges shone bright in the sun.

Paco tilted a stream of wine into his mouth and offered me the skin. "Have a drink. It is hot."

"Hotter when we stop," I said. "We get back and test the boat."

He nodded. He bent to slide the wineskin under the seat. He straightened up with a jerk. "What was it?"

"What?"

"A noise."

"This engine," I said. "El Mudo has a job with it."

I turned a corner into a long straight stretch. Paco was sitting hunched, his eyes closed. "Slower," he said. "I hear it again."

I dropped to fifteen. Paco put his head out of the side window. The engine started to cough.

"Imagination," I said. He didn't hear me. I listened carefully to the engine and it wasn't doing her any good to go slow. We were approaching a bend. I got a slight turn on the wheel and for no reason at all I looked back. Paco started to yell. He didn't need to. I had seen it. I stamped on the accelerator and the Citroën leaped forward.

The big black car was screaming up behind us. A man leaned from the side window, a gun in his hand.

I took the bend. There was another, fifty yards ahead. We screeched around it, our tires on the edge of the ravine. Paco had his gun out. I fumbled for mine, trying to think of where we could stop and fight it out, because we'd never outstrip them. The engine was racketing. It wouldn't last at this speed. I knocked Paco's arm, shouted, "The first corner past the pine trees. Jump quickly. Get them as they go by."

He nodded. "Those were guns I heard," he yelled. "Maybe they got Ferrer."

I didn't care about that. I had Ferrer's money and he was good for nothing else. I had other things to think of. The boat last night, now this. The Association had latched onto us. Maybe they hadn't got Ferrer, maybe he'd turned us in. There was no one else that knew about the appointment.

I snatched another look through the rear window, but I could see nothing. We were raising a dust storm. I took a bend and there was one more before the trees and one more after that and then we had to make a stand. I looked at Paco. He grinned, waved his gun. I swung around the next corner and the trees were on either side. The men were waiting. It was too late.

I couldn't have braked anyway. There wasn't time. I pushed my whole weight on the accelerator.

They had a thick rope stretched taut across the road between two trees. I had a glimpse of a man on either side of the road. Then we hit. The windshield buckled. I sat in a cascade of glass. The men ran from the sides. Paco's gun clattered to the floor. He started to scream. Everything was suspended, slow motion, engine roaring, Paco sobbing, the men firing. I saw them. One with a small mustache. The other wearing a hat.

The rope snapped.

It lashed sideways. It wrapped itself all around the face of the man with the hat. He clawed at himself. He howled. The Citroën was already beyond him. I screeched around the next bend. The black car was right behind us.

I was still holding the gun. I smashed the small rear window and snapped a shot. It was no use. I couldn't get aim. Paco was trying to straighten from his corner, holding his shoulder, moaning, blood running through his fingers.

The dust poured through the broken windshield and caked us. I looked at my hand on the wheel and there was a big piece of glass embedded in it. I swung around another bend. The road narrowed. The engine was grinding.

Paco leaned over, tried to pick his gun from the floor. Blood ran all down his arm and dripped off his fingers. We turned another corner. He fell over. His head dropped into my lap. I pulled him up by the hair and there was blood on his face. His brown skin had turned the color of the inside of an orange peel.

Behind us they were firing. A bullet spanged off the cab roof. Then they seemed to open up with a volley. The bullets hit the mountain face on my right. Little plumes of dust spurted out, joined the channel of it that peppered through the windshield. I turned the last bend, and I knew we were finished. The road stretched straight ahead for more than a mile. The mountain crowded one side. The other side was a drop.

I drove with one hand, turned around, tried to get another shot through the window. Paco toppled against me in a heap. I didn't know what was happening. My gun scraped the back of his head. I got an arm around him, tried to pull him upright, but he was a dead weight. Then there was more gunfire, and a screech, and the back tire was gone. The wheel went wild. It wrenched right out of my grip.

I saw all the different colors of the rock, then the mountain was gone. My feet were jammed against the floor board and I was tilted at a crazy angle. My head was almost through the windshield. I was gazing down at nothing.

We hung there. The truck teetered like a seesaw. I kicked at the door and twisted the handle and I was yelling at the top of my voice, as if that would help. The other car pulled up. The men were getting out. I was still shouting, still with my arm around Paco. Then the door flew open. I pitched out and the kid came with me. Somehow in mid-air I got both arms round him.

A man, maybe two men were firing guns. Paco hit the edge of the road and I fell on top of him. All the breath gushed from his mouth. A bullet smacked the earth beside our heads. The men were running toward us.

I hugged him hard against my chest. I dug a knee between his legs and heaved. We slid two inches. My mouth was full of dust. I rammed my knee again, pushed with all my strength. We slid a long way this time. We fell over the edge.

The world was stones and dust and sliding shale, a pain in my shoulder, and going to hell in a handcart. I clung to Paco like a last hope. We slipped and rolled and all the breath was being knocked out of me and he was not making a sound. We were gathering speed. The bullets plucked feathers of earth all around us. I tried to brake myself with my feet and I got all tangled up with Paco's legs. My arms were still round him. The skin was coming off the backs of my hands.

I saw the second ledge. I tried to heft him in a different position, to brake, but there was no way. The rock hit my ankles. I put a hand behind his head and rammed his face into my shoulder. We slid, started to roll, seemed to hesitate right on the brink. Then we were falling through the thin, thin air.

I shut my eyes. We hit a tree or a shrub or something and bounced and did a complete somersault. We were falling a long way farther. I couldn't hang on any longer. I dug my nails into Paco's shirt and the pain went through my fingers, up my arms. Then I clutched nothing.

I opened my eyes. A long way off, high above my head, the burning Citroën truck somersaulted after us like a tiny meteor. I knew it was going to hit me. I didn't care anymore. I wanted a drink, wanted to go to sleep, wanted to talk to María.

A big pain went all through me. I closed my eyes again. I hit something else and I could no longer breathe. From a long way off I heard someone moaning. Myself. I started to fade out and the last thing I realized was that I'd probably lost the thirteen thousand dollars.

Chapter Six

I was on my back, stretched at an angle, staring at the sky, vividly blue. I shut my eyes tight and lay there. I had a panicky feeling I was about to fall again.

A lot of time passed. I moved my limbs separately, an inch at a time, ran the palms of my hands along the earth at either side of me. The angle didn't seem steep after all. I sat up slowly. I couldn't yet trust myself to stand.

Fifty yards behind me the mountain sloped sharply to an overhanging ledge. I knew there was another mountain beyond because the sun was behind it. I could see the shadow of the peak, flung across the valley below. I couldn't tell how far we were from the road.

A little way back was a stunted tree. Most of the branches were snapped where they had broken my fall. The wood showed white, like bones. I got a hand on either side of me, pushed back until I could get an arm around the gnarled trunk. I eased myself upright.

Everything whirled for a couple of minutes. When finally it straightened I took stock. Abrasions, minor cuts one leg of my pants missing. Shirt all gone except for the row of buttons at the front and the collar. The watch was not on my wrist. Neither was the thirteen thousand dollars in my pocket. My nose had bled, caked my upper lip.

I lifted my hand to pick off the dried blood. I saw Paco then.

He was farther down the slope. A boulder had stopped him. He was curled around it like a landed fish. I started toward him. I turned my head and there were mountains all around as far as I could see, one ring behind the other. Below was the valley, a thousand feet, maybe more. I'd soon know. There wasn't a hope of going back up.

I knelt beside Paco, rolled him over. His mouth was open. There was so much dirt on his face that he looked like someone in a minstrel show. The blood from the bullet wound was spread all over his chest. He was as limp as wet washing.

I got an arm under his shoulder, put my ear to his mouth. I couldn't tell whether he was breathing or not. I put a hand inside his torn shirt and his heart seemed to be beating, so I patted his face a couple of times, shook him a little. I said, "Paco! Paco!" I brushed back the hair from his face. "Paco!"

His eyes opened. He stared at me. His lips moved a few times before the words came out. He said, "They will get us."

"No," I said. "No way down for them. We're safe, *chico*."

He lay there, eyes glazing. He wasn't blinking. After a while he said,

"Beel, what about María?"

"I don't know," I said. "What about her?"

He made no answer. He was trying to wet his lips. The heat shimmered from the rocks and there was no water. There wouldn't be any till we got down to the valley, maybe not even then.

My throat was suddenly parched. I said, "Can you move, son?"

The grime creased on his face. He tried to grin. The word for "son" is *hijo*, but it resembles another word that Spanish men sometimes call each other, especially up in Murcia. Farther south you make jokes about it. Paco said, "You trying to make a fight, Beel?"

"Later," I said. "I'll knock from you the father's milk. Now stand up. Can you?"

"Certainly." He gave a weak nod, started slowly to move. I got behind him and took him by the elbow and chin and eased him to his feet.

He stood alone a moment. A faint moan came from his mouth. He began to slump forward. I thought he was going to pitch down the slope. I got beside him, tried to straighten him up. I clamped an arm around his chest.

His head jerked. He grinned at me and showed all his teeth. His eyes rolled up and he fell against me and suddenly a great howl of pain came tearing from his throat. I let him go. He fell to the ground. I dropped beside him and the cry was still echoing all around the mountains. He was unconscious.

I couldn't bring him round. I went over him with my hands, and his arms and legs were all right. I touched his chest and felt the broken ribs, and I didn't know what to do. I sat and looked at him. His face was set in the grin, eyes half open, the irises rolled up into his head. The bullet wound under his left armpit had started to bleed again.

I wanted to put him across my shoulder. I got the idea that the broken ribs would go through his lungs. I put an arm behind his knees, another at his back, and staggered upright. The valley was a long way below. It looked cool.

I went down the slope holding Paco in front of me like a wet baby. All the loose surface was sliding under my feet. I went twenty yards and fell over. I slid twenty yards more.

I made a second attempt. I kept stumbling. The valley got farther away. The mountainside was hotter than the hobs of hell. I fell over again. My tongue was swelling. I lay there and looked at Paco.

After a while I sat up. I tore a piece from his shirt and plugged the wound. I moved him gently, took the shirt right off. I put it on myself, for protection. It was a lot too small.

I got him on his side, held him in position with one hand on his shoulder, and stretched full length beside him. I got him under his other shoulder and tried not to think of his ribs as I pulled him on top of me. I kicked at his legs until his feet were clamped between my ankles, put a hand at his backside, the other on the nape of his neck, and pressed him hard against me. I wriggled. We didn't move. I did it again and we started to slide.

I attempted to keep up my head, look over his shoulder, dig in my heels if we seemed to be heading for another drop. Soon it didn't matter. We were traveling too fast. I couldn't have stopped if I'd wanted to. The shirt was ripping from my back, and the stones tore me, and I didn't much care if we went over a drop or not. I only wanted a drink of water.

I went into a sort of semiconsciousness. I wasn't thinking of anything, yet I was thinking of everything. It was funny. Half my thoughts seemed to be in Paco's head. Stones and dust and half-felt pain, and the strangest part was when finally we did reach the flat ground. I couldn't believe it. I said so, and it was as if he had said it to me. So I answered myself. Then I lay there and went off to sleep.

I walked. I kept walking. The valley was going on forever and I was fantastically irritated. I swore continuously, all the oaths I knew. The earth was rutted. Every time I put a foot down, my knees started to buckle. I was carrying Paco and my arms seemed dead to the shoulders and mortified into position. But that was not what irritated me.

I looked at the sinking sun. The fact that I did not know the exact time infuriated me. I was muttering, "Two o'clock, three o'clock, eight o'clock, nine o'clock," then saying it in Spanish and swearing some more. Then I told Paco that we were bound to hit a village where someone would tell us the time. I imagined the faces of several different persons, but they all went away without speaking. I imagined other things.

I returned to Ohio. I went up to the river and caught some catfish. The water was so cool I jumped right in. My clothes were still wet when I got home.

The old man was drunk again. He beat the guts out of me. I didn't like that so well. I imagined myself a little older and a lot bigger, and then I beat the guts out of him. It was very enjoyable.

It didn't last. The old man knew about Mr. Phillips' store. He discovered the stuff in the cupboard in my room. He'd been waiting for an opportunity like that, though he didn't have the nerve to face me himself. Next thing I knew, I way lying on my bed reading a book and he was there with two cops. I had to fight the three of them. They counted that against me. It was on my records when I arrived at reform school. They used to beat me every so often on the strength of it, to prove that authority was tougher than I.

I laughed at that. When I shipped to sea, the same authority told me

I was finished if ever I jumped ship. So I jumped ship. With no passport, nothing. And not a thing happened. Five years. Up and down and a lot of money and all of it spent. North Africa, Israel, North Africa again, Spain. Frenchmen, Arabs, Jews, Germans, derelicts from all over the world. Derelict me. A bunch of foxes, loose in the world's poultry yard. A marquesa whose father had bought her a title when he had money. A big canopied bed with silk sheets. A fat body. I was one sweet, swell person.

I thought of the kid dead from penicillin and I had to sit down and take a rest. I held Paco across my knees. If I let him out of my arms, I'd never be able to lift him again.

After a while I stood up and went on.

My tongue stuck out. I slid into a dry watercourse, up another ridge and down again. Paco was grown onto my arms. I had been born carrying him. The sun disappeared behind a range and the light was turning yellow. The opposite mountains were every color from lemon to burgundy. They were beautiful.

I turned an elbow of rock. It seemed like the greatest of my imaginings. The running water was a hundred yards away, a river no more than six feet across, a stream. I went toward it slowly, waiting for it to disappear. I got to the rocky bank and it was still there. I walked right in.

The water came to my shins. I sank to my knees and the coolness reached my back. I lay down on the river bed and took Paco with me. He gave a feeble kick. I got him to the surface again and swallowed about a gallon of water, then I floated him as best I could and splashed water over his face and chest.

I stretched him on the bank. I cupped my hands and trickled water into his mouth. His eyes opened. Panic glittered. He said, "The guns."

"Lost," I said. "Don't worry. No one is coming."

He didn't seem to hear. He looked stupefied. He started to move and I helped him to a sitting position, and all at once he burst into tears. He went on crying. He said, "This Griswold. I killed him. I could have pulled him aboard. I thought he would take the new boat."

"Forget it."

"God is punishing me," he said. The tears coursed down his face. Hysteria crept into his voice. "I killed him because I want the boat. I am a better sailor than anyone. I want the boat! I want the boat! I want the boat!"

I hit him across the face. His eyes widened. He lowered his head and shuddered. He said quietly to his knees, "You son of a whore, you are giving the length to my sister." Then he made a sudden lunge and I hit him again. He went face down on the earth and stayed there.

I put my face back in the stream to take another long drink. I didn't feel bad now. I got more water in my hands, ran it over the back of his neck, and I said, "Come on, *chico*, we have to be going." I rolled him over and put my arms under his knees. He shoved me aside.

"I walk," he said. He started to rise and fell down again. I made no move. A Spaniard says he'll do something and you let him do it. Without interference. He made another effort and was on his feet.

I listened to the almost inaudible sounds in his throat. He lifted his head and stared at the sky. He gazed all around him. He said conversationally, "The sea over there," and without looking at me he scrambled away across the broken earth, stumbling as he went.

I hurried to keep up with him. He wasn't going to last long.

It was worse than not knowing the time. My head filled up with blood. I was thinking of Silva, of the danger he had threatened.

Paco was back in my arms, delirious, talking to himself, chattering about Griswold and the boat, the boat and the Marquesa, the Marquesa and me, and then me and María. Occasionally he took time out to insist to somebody that I was the finest, bravest, most loyal man he'd ever met, the best friend he had. Then he'd return to María again and begin cursing me. He had to protect her, he said. He was the only male relative. He started a long line about the honor of the family name. Finally he said something about his dead parents. Then he went completely limp, as if there were no bones in him. I continued to think of Silva, his oily face, his big cigar.

The last fingers of light were withdrawing from the sky. I heard the sea. A long time afterward there was a cluster of palm trees. I was staggering off the track, trying to get across the field.

The curtains were not drawn. The light shone strong from the window. I could see her in the room, waiting, sitting at a table.

I tried to call out. My mouth was too dry. I had a feeling then that I couldn't go another inch. I dragged my feet. All at once I was leaning against the door, wondering why she didn't open it. I got my elbow on the latch, pushed hard, and fell into the room.

She said nothing. I heard the door shut. Then she was pulling me upright and I felt an odd pleasure because she was strong. I said, "Yes." I smiled at her. I got Paco under the shoulders and said, "Watch his ribs."

She took his feet, straining. We carried him into the other room, put him on the bed. I said, "Get a doctor."

She moved swiftly to the window, drew the blinds. She came back and fell to her knees and cupped Paco's face in her hands. "He is dead," she said.

"No," I said. "There was trouble. He got shot. I think some ribs are broken. Get a doctor."

She looked up at me, stunned. I reached down and raised her to her feet. She said, "No doctor," and shook her head.

"The bullet is in him."

"No. The doctor will report a bullet. Paco will be sent to prison."

I put my arms around her. "María *mi vida*, María—"

"No." She held me away, a hypnotized expression in her eyes. "A man must be asked if he wishes to go to prison. When he awakens—" She sat down on the edge of the bed and looked at her brother. She was getting the look that most Spanish women have in the face of dire trouble; patient, resigned. "No doctor," she said again, and the tears started running down her face. "No doctor."

I yanked her up. I shook her. "All right, there will be no bullet. Get some hot water." I dragged her to the kitchen and thrust a bowl in her hands. I started looking through the knife box for something I could use.

She came to her senses. Her eyes cleared. She said, "You are hurt too, Beel."

"No," I snapped, and I wasn't. I was still looking for a tool, wondering if I could adapt a big fork, bend one of the tines. I saw the basket she'd been making. I picked up the long-handled hook that is used for pulling the reeds through the framework. I dropped it in the water.

The bullet didn't worry me. It was buried in the soft flesh under his left armpit. But I suspected he had concussion. I'd carried him a long way and the important thing was for the doctor to see what had happened to his ribs.

No telephones in that part of the world. I'd have sought a doctor myself, except that European medicos have a mania for reporting anything untoward. My presence would be on the report. No passport. It was enough to involve everyone who had even spoken to me.

I boiled the hook, went back into the bedroom. She was on her knees again beside the bed, wiping Paco's face with a wet cloth, kissing him. She looked lovely and sweet, and though there was nothing I wanted less at the moment, I got a swelling feeling. I said, "Out of the way, María. I remove the bullet, then you fetch the doctor?"

She was pale as a ghost.

"Sit on his legs."

She said, "Will it hurt him, Beel?"

I went to her and kissed her. I held her a moment. I said, "María, do me a favor. Go to my house. There's a gun in the cupboard beside my bed. Bring it. Bring me a complete set of clothes. I'm not handsome like this."

She tried to smile. She looked like Paco when she did it. She nodded a couple of times and turned around and ran out of the door.

I returned to the bed. I picked up the hook, sat on Paco's chest, and dug the curled end into the wound. The poor little guy started to whine. I couldn't help that. I dug deeper. He went limp again. I probed around and the blood was running, but it was easier than I'd thought. I finally got it out. I put it on the table beside the bed. Paco was a Spaniard. He'd want to keep the bullet for the rest of his life, to tell his grandchildren.

There was cognac on a shelf in the kitchen. I took a stiff drink and poured a lot of it into Paco's wound. Then I took off what remained of his clothes and propped him against a pillow to stop the bleeding. I went to the kitchen and put two pails of water on the stove. I returned to the bed, sat on the edge, and then I stretched out alongside the kid to relax myself.

It was too good. I relaxed too far. Five seconds later I was fast asleep.

I awoke refreshed. I felt I'd slept all night, but it could not have been more than fifteen or twenty minutes. María was just coming back into the room, the clothing over her arm. I got off the bed, went to the kitchen, and got the pails of water. I stood them in the center of the bedroom floor.

I took off clothes, shoes, and socks. I was naked. The tiled floor was so cool to my feet I wanted to lie down on it. I started to wash. I needed it. The first bucket changed to mud. María said nothing. She kept her back to me, turned to the bed, studying Paco, touching his face with her fingertips.

I said, "A towel, María." She left the room and came back with two in her hands. I took them. I meant nothing, but I touched her. Then we stood looking at each other for a long time. I held out my arms and she came forward and the roughness of her dress was against my chest.

We simply stood together. I loved her more than my life and all the world and everything else. Her hands were low on my back and I held her so tightly I was lifting her. I kissed her. I laid my cheek on her hair. We stood close like one person and whispered beautiful foolish things to each other.

Paco moaned and I let her go. She wheeled around. I took a step backward. We both looked at him. His eyes were open and he was stark crazy. He said, "You filthy bastard," and he tried to get off the bed.

She flung herself forward, fell to her knees, tried to speak. His hand lashed across her mouth and knocked her sideways. She sobbed, "No, Paco."

A stream of names poured from his mouth. He looked at me with insanity all over his face. He said, "You! I am going to kill you. I am going to kill you now."

He put a hand on either side of him and tried to swing his feet to the floor. He couldn't manage it. His chin jerked up, teeth gritted. The wound was flooding his chest with blood. He gave a long low moan and fell back on the bed. He whimpered once more and was unconscious.

María seized one of the towels, mopped the wound, whispering to him, although he couldn't hear. I put on my clothes, tied my shoes, stood around until the bleeding stopped, waiting to do something.

There was nothing I could do. She did not turn to me. I said to her, "Get the doctor now."

She stood up, holding the towel. There was blood on both her hands. The misery in her face was an anguish. She said, "Go, Beel."

"I'll wait while you get the doctor."

She shook her head.

I said, "I'll go through the window when I hear you coming with him. Make a lot of noise. If he asks about the wound, say you know nothing."

"Go, Beel," she said. "Please."

I looked into her eyes. I said, "You know that I love you."

"Yes," she said, and began to cry.

I reached out a hand and touched her hair. "Good-by," I said, and went out into the night and stumbled across the field to the track.

Shame tastes ashen. The blood was filling my head worse than ever.

The pickers were all gone. There was no sign of life anywhere. I drove the Volkswagen up the driveway of the big house and the place was deserted. There were no lights even from the servants' end.

The darkness was thick. I got out and crossed the patio. The French windows were open, so there had to be someone home. In Spain they don't leave unlocked houses without a guard.

I felt my way through the sitting room, out to the hall. I shouted, "Anyone here?" and the big Moroccan clock began to strike. I counted the chimes and they almost made me laugh aloud. It was only eight o'clock.

I shouted in Spanish, "Anyone in the house?"

The staircase light flicked on. There was movement above me. Page appeared round the corner and descended the stairs. His feet were bare. He was wearing nothing but the silk dressing gown he'd received from the Marquesa as an initiation present.

"Lo and behold, look who's here," he said, and he grinned. "I fear, chummy, that trouble awaits you. You didn't show. The cow got mad. It was sharpening its horns when it left."

"Where is she?"

"At this Santa Faz fiesta, along with everyone, servants and all. There was an exhibition of bullfighting this afternoon at Don Luis' farm. A car came to pick us up a three-thirty and the dear lady waited until four. Imagine her feelings when she had to leave without an escort. She, my friend, as we both can testify, is a lady who cannot get along without an escort."

His tone changed. He squinted at me. "You don't look good, Bill. Anything up?"

"Nothing."

He passed a languid hand across his brow. "Not so well myself. That's the reason I went to bed instead of to the festivities. Not that the darling Marquesa really wanted me to go."

"I can imagine," I said. "El Mudo around?"

"Why, no." Page straightened up and walked toward the sitting room. "I've an idea he went with the others. It doesn't sound like very much, do you think? Only a very small fiesta. Fancy a drink, Bill?"

"No. I have to make a trip."

"Really? Not going to the fiesta?"

"I need a companion."

"For the fiesta?"

"For the trip."

"Well," he said, "I don't think anyone's around. What will you do? Wait?"

"I can't," I said. "How about you? Want a ride?"

"Me?"

"You."

He laughed. He said, "Me in a boat. That's funny. I get seasick even when I go in wading."

I said, "What makes you think it's a boat?"

"Isn't it?"

"Why not a car?"

"I don't know."

I said, "You'd better tell me, Page."

He said, "Oh, horse manure."

I reached out and took him by the lapels of his dressing gown. I might be wrong about Silva. About other things. There were maybe complications I didn't guess at. But I couldn't think. It had been a hard day. I said, "Tell me."

"Horse manure," he said.

I hit him.

He let out a yell. I hit him again. I played an open-handed tattoo across his face. He tried to struggle away. He wasn't strong enough. He shouted, "Well, Godsakes, I'm not a fool. I see things, don't I?"

"No," I said. I stopped hitting him. I said, "We beach the boats six miles from here. You see nothing. Neither does anyone else. How'd you find out?"

"Horse manure," he said again.

I said, "I'm going to knock your guts out."

He stood there and suddenly he quivered like a kid who should have been with his mother. He said, "All right, Bill, you'll discover it anyway. El Mudo told me. I know about the smuggling."

"Liar," I said. "El Mudo can't talk, he can't write."

"Honest," he protested. "I asked where he went all those evenings in the Volkswagen. He told me with signs. Hell, I'm not stupid, I knew what he meant."

I half believed him. But somebody had tipped off the men in the black car, got Paco hurt, made María turn away from me. Somebody had to pay.

"What else?" I asked.

"Nothing."

I hit him and kept on hitting him. I beat him. He struggled with me and yelled, and it was a continuous rising roar. I looked over his shoulder and El Mudo came leaping down the stairs, four at a time. He rushed at me, looking like the giant he was. It seemed to be a night for naked men. The guy hadn't a stitch on him. He slammed me.

I skittered across the hall and hit the floor. That was it. I was big, but he was a lot bigger. He could have broken every bone in my body. I reached for the gun. It wasn't worth it. I picked myself up and stood looking at them.

El Mudo had his arm around Page's shoulder. He tried to back. He couldn't make it. The color crept slowly from his bare chest and all over his face. He removed the arm, moved away a little, and gazed fixedly at his bare feet.

Page said in his bad Spanish, "It was you that told me about the smuggling, wasn't it?"

The big man nodded like a shamefaced child, hanging his head.

I said, "*Bien*, Mudo. Finished. I must tell the Marquesa."

He looked up miserably. Page said, "No, Bill. She'll send him away."

"So?" I started for the door.

"Why not take him with you now?" Page said. "I won't let him tell me about it afterward."

"Impossible."

There was a silence. I got to the door. Page shouted, "Then wait till I start opening my mouth about you and that girl. I know all about it. I know quite a few details. Wait till the Marquesa—"

I didn't hear any more. I shut the door behind me, got in the Volkswagen, and drove for the cliff.

Someone was moving behind the drawn curtain as I passed her house. I couldn't tell which of them it was. I didn't stop. I wondered if she'd got the doctor yet.

In the cave I was full again of senseless anger. I nursed the new boat out to the clear water, opened her up. She went like a swallow. For no reason, that made me even more angry.

Chapter Seven

The trip took little more than half an hour. I throttled down and nosed through the oily water, the harbor lights all around me, the engine of the new boat purring like a cat. Business with her would be good. If we were still in business. It was one of the things I meant to find out.

I moored on the far side of the harbor, away from the usual place. Blasco, the Spanish cop, wouldn't recognize the craft, but he'd know me at a glance. He was the type. And this was one time I didn't want him on my heels. I hugged the shadows until I got outside.

Through the stairwayed streets of the port residential quarter and on through the red-light district. The place was packed with the customary smelly crowd. I tucked my two hands tight in my pockets, so no one could lift the gun. I thought of the lost thirteen thousand dollars. The Marquesa would have a hard time believing that, might even decide to deduct it from my share of the money she kept in her safe. It was another aspect of my visit. If Silva was responsible, I wanted thirteen thousand dollars damages. And I wanted his hide.

Past the bazaars. A beggar came whining beside me, pulled at my arm. I told him in Arabic to get the hell away, and he dropped back, shouting abuse. On the other side of the narrow street a cop glanced at us idly.

He glanced again. It wasn't much of a second look. I told myself it was merely my nerves, he was already gazing up the street again. I took no chances. I turned down an alley, doubled on my tracks, and worked to the business section through a succession of back streets.

In any other city in the world the business quarter would have been deserted at that time of evening. Here, business was in full swing. I looked back to see if the cop had followed. There was just a swirl of noisy, sweaty Arabs, walking slowly, holding each other by the hand. I sat down at the café where Griswold had waited. I waved away the waiter and studied the office building across the way.

Lights all over the façade. None in Silva's office. But I knew he worked evenings, wouldn't be away long. I decided to go up and wait for him, give myself the element of surprise.

I sat five minutes more, to be certain of the cop. Then I told myself it had been nerves for sure and got up and crossed the road and walked quickly through the entrance.

Voices came from behind doors on the ground floor. I went up the stairs to the floor above, walked on the balls of my feet, and stole along the corridor wondering suddenly what I'd do if Silva's office was locked. It was quieter up here. Breaking and entering would sound like a clap of thunder. I reached the door with "J. A. Silva, Broker," painted on it, and slowly turned the handle.

It squeaked. The door swung open. I slid into the pitch-blackness and turned the key on the inside of the lock and tried to get my bearings. I couldn't see a thing, only the dim outline of the curtained window.

I crossed the office, lifted the corner of the blind, peered down into the street. Two birds slept side by side on the narrow ledge, maybe the same two that had made love the previous evening. The Arabs jabbered in throngs. But there was no sign of a cop. I dropped the curtain. Darkness again.

I didn't want to turn on the light. I fumbled forward, hands outstretched, until I touched the desk. I skimmed my fingers over the top. Some papers fell to the floor. I felt the cool shape of the cigar lighter, gripped it with the de-presser under my thumb, and pushed.

The sparks leaped. The wick did not catch. But I had seen. I didn't want to try after that. I had to, I pushed once more and the orange flame sprang up, and I looked at Silva.

His hands were folded across his belly. He had no features.

The front of his head was a shapeless mess because someone had shot him in the face with a soft-nosed bullet. I held the flame nearer. A cloud of black blowflies rose from him with a dull buzz. He had been dead for more than a few hours, and had already begun to rot. He smelled.

I looked at him, listened to my own breathing, and the phone started ringing. I snapped out the light.

I wiped the lighter carefully on the inside of my jacket. I placed it back on the desk. I withdrew my hand into my sleeve, picked up the ringing phone, and said, "Hello?"

"Meestah Seelvah, pleess." A man's voice with the local singsong intonation.

"Speaking," I said.

It was the night shift, a male operator. He said, "Long deestance call from Spain, Meestah Seelvah."

"Who's calling?"

"I check, sah."

The phone went dead except for a high oscillating note. I waited, staring through the dark at what had been Silva. The flies were still buzzing. The receiver clicked. I heard the faint background noises, a lot of people talking in another room, then somebody laughing. The operator said, "You're through, Meestah Seelvah."

In that other room the person went on laughing. Loud above everyone else. It was the Marquesa.

I said, "Who's speaking?" She still laughed. She was drunk.

"Who's calling?" I said. Whoever was at the other end drew in a deep breath. I heard it distinctly. Then the phone went dead.

I put down the receiver, stood in the darkness. The flies were fighting, droning at one another. The voices came up from the street, chattering wildly. I stood there with my mind a complete blank. I couldn't sort anything out. Then I heard the other sound. A pair of feet was shuffling softly along the corridor, coming toward the door of the office.

I pulled out the gun and stood against the wall, away from the window. I waited. The handle squeaked. There was a faint creaking of wood and the handle squeaked once more. I held my breath.

There was a shuffling of feet. A body hurtled against the door. I changed my mind. I dropped the gun in my pocket and jumped for the window. Only the law could afford to make that much noise. There was another crash, a splintering of wood. I yanked at the window sash. He must have heard me. He started shouting and I recognized the voice. It was Blasco.

I was already outside the window, hanging from the narrow ledge, telling myself to let go. Someone saw me, shouted from the café opposite. A huge roar went up. They cheered as I fell.

The impact nearly drove my thighbones to my shoulders. I wrenched myself upright and saw the grinning faces. All the people at the café were on their feet, applauding. Blasco shouted from the window, something about a reward. I hurtled through the crowd, started to run. He was still shouting. Maybe they didn't understand him. Maybe they didn't care. They drowned him out.

They hooted. They jeered. Only rich bastards could afford offices. Rich bastards deserved to be robbed. They hoped I was getting away with millions. Curses on all rich men. Allah loved only the poor. Blasco stopped shouting. I didn't look back. I heard footsteps pounding behind me. I ran down a long dark alley.

A bullet sang off the wall beside my ear. The blaze of light lit up the whole place. I looked over my shoulder. The silhouette of a man was coming after me. He opened up again, spraying from side to side. I tried to weave. The alley seemed endless. I wrenched the gun from my pocket.

But I didn't fire. It was the law. They had me tabbed. Shoot a cop and they reach anywhere in the eight nations and get you. I kept running.

I saw the end of the alley coming and grabbed the corner and swung myself around it and stopped dead. The feet pounded toward me. I reversed the gun in my hand, waiting. The man had stopped firing. His feet slithered on the cobbled ground. He was about to burst into the street.

I swung my arm and the gun butt caught him square in the middle of the forehead. He gave one cry and slumped against the alley wall. He started to fall. I was already running again, fighting down an insane desire to scream. The light had fallen briefly on the man's face. I knew who he was. No cop. Not the law. He was Griswold. And Griswold was supposed to be dead on the floor of the Mediterranean Sea.

A cross somewhere. A crisscross. I couldn't think of anything now. I yelled at a crowd of Arabs in front of me, waved the gun, and they parted like the Red Sea. I looked back. They had closed in again, shouting at the tops of their voices. A lot of people ran out from the bazaars, Arab faces, a mass, front, back, and side. I couldn't see if anyone was following. A group of small boys started after me, howling pursuit. But Arab children are too undernourished to run far. I tore on. The crowd thinned. I swung into the quietness of the tortuous back streets and my lungs were being burned away.

After an eternal distance I leaned against a dirty wall and sobbed.

I approached the harbor entrance and held my breath, so that the man at the gate would not see how much I was panting. He wasn't even there. I slipped inside and started racing round the rim of the water, and all the lights were on. I pulled up short. A hundred yards ahead the man who should have been at the gate was talking to two harbor cops. Farther on were two more. They had in their hands what looked like flashlights.

Maybe they were looking for me. Maybe not. I couldn't take a chance. I leaped from the harbor wall onto an unlighted boat. I ran to the end and slipped into the oily water. I wished I had more breath left. I kept choking, swallowing mouthfuls of muck.

The harbor is a semicircle. I swam across the diameter on a breast stroke, to avoid splashing. Halfway to the boat I looked back. A cluster of men had gathered at the spot where I jumped from the wall. I rolled over and watched them. They were examining every boat, pencils of light stabbing the dimness. They were seeking the craft that Blasco would recognize as mine.

I had the new boat. They might examine it closely simply because it was new. I had to be there before they were. It was fifty-fifty. I rolled over again and did a crawl. I kicked off my shoes.

When I was ten yards from the boat they saw me. They were still on the other side of the harbor. A shout went up. They started running. I made a final gasping effort, dragged myself aboard. I cast off the mooring, ran for the wheelhouse, wondered when they'd start shooting.

I pushed the starter. The engine caught. I heard Blasco shouting in Spanish for me to stop. All the others started shouting. They had about forty yards to go. I backed out and swung the wheel and cut a U. Then I was streaking for the harbor mouth. I was safe. There wasn't a thing they could do to stop me.

Three miles out I'd be beyond North African jurisdiction. Nothing to fear until I came into the territory of the coast guards at the other end. And tonight I was carrying nothing. They'd have nothing to go on even if they did hold me up.

I shot through the harbor mouth and automatically turned off the lights. The rim of the moon was showing above the horizon. Bad timing if I was carrying a load. Tonight it was unimportant. Tonight it was about the only thing that was unimportant.

I've never believed in coincidences. The hijackers last night, the black car, Silva dead, Blasco arriving, Griswold waiting. Griswold especially. It stank of frame-up, reeked of the Association. They wanted to crush Spanish competition. They'd succeeded neatly as far as I was concerned. Put my nose inside the city again and I'd be in jail on a murder charge. The cops would be able to find at least a thousand motives for it.

I opened the engine right out. For the first time in a long time I thought of going back home to the States.

The sea was like glass. The moon was leaping above the horizon. I looked astern and the harbor lights fell from sight. There was another light I had not noticed before. A launch. It was fast. It was following me.

I crammed on all speed. They were police for sure. Whoever had framed me would never edge in the game at this stage, with the cops right at my heels. But I couldn't figure it. This was a violation of rules. Nobody ever got followed from the city. The reason was simple. None of the eight nations had authority to reach onto the high seas.

And then I thought of Blasco. A Spanish cop. He had authority in North Africa. He'd have the same authority once we got within three miles of the Spanish coast. I got the binoculars, looked back through the clearing moonlight. The boat was a police job for sure, a fast one. I could neither outrace them nor elude them.

The swiftly ascending moon turned slowly from gold to white. The sea lit up like a festival. For all the hope I had of dodging, I might as well have been driving down the Grand Canal in Venice.

I knew then that I was finished. But if I was caught, the Marquesa was finished too. Once the police laid hands on me, they'd trace my connection to her. She'd join me in jail. Busted. No chance to reorganize with other men. And I had not the least desire to be caught. So I rehearsed the logic of my argument until it was fixed solid in my head. I knew I'd need it, later this evening. There'd have to be a lot of rock-hard logic before I convinced her that what I was about to do was the only way out.

The Marquesa was going to lose her new craft. I didn't know where she purchased either boats or cars. That was one of the details she kept strictly to herself, like the list of names and addresses. But I was pretty certain she'd have covered the purchases, as she did everything else. And if something should misfire, if they traced the boat to her, she could always claim it had been stolen.

It was a chance to be taken. I had to take the chance whether I wanted it or not. But not until I reached the other coast. I was tired. I wanted to make the swim as short as possible.

I punished the engine until it screamed. It didn't matter anymore. I kept it screaming. The other craft stayed right with me. The moon climbed and the spray flew, and the Point loomed ahead. I was in Spanish waters. The boat behind knew it too. They wasted no time.

They had some sort of small cannon mounted on their bow. They opened up. The shot splashed well to starboard and the report reverberated from the onshore cliffs. Maybe just a warning. I could expect one more. Then they'd take aim.

I curved around the Point and worked fast while they were still out of sight. I picked up a rope, lashed it to the wheel, and swung inshore. The cliffs loomed high. On top, and over the fields, the house was less than two miles away.

The moon made the water like a flat mirror. I could see the underwater shadow of the shoals. I got inshore as far as I dared and headed for the rocks. Then I turned her sharply around, put her nose to sea, and lashed the wheel in position by bending the rope to a cleat in the bulkhead.

I got out of the cabin, ran to the stern. I murmured a good-by to the boat because she was a pretty thing and deserved a better fate. I jumped overboard.

The water closed over me. I swam deep. The rocks scraped my knees. I stayed down until my lungs were bursting, then I rolled upward and put my face above the surface. The moon shone strong in my eyes. The roar of boats sounded so near I wondered if I'd set the wheel in the wrong direction. I went under again, hearing a low boom as the police opened up with the cannon. I touched bottom.

Five minutes later I dragged myself up on the beach and ran for the shadow of the cliff. Under the brilliant moon the distant craft looked like scudding water beetles. The police were firing round after round, throwing up high white splashes from the still water. There was no longer any question of warning. Both craft were heading directly out to sea.

They fired a last shot. A sudden red flash lit up the entire area. The sound of explosion rolled slowly toward me. I stood and watched while the Marquesa's new boat blazed like the Fourth of July; red and yellow flames licking into the night sky.

The police boat throttled down, waiting for a second explosion. It came with a roar. There was a huge cloud of black smoke, and then the flames disappeared. The Marquesa's new boat went down like a stone. Briefly, I wanted to weep.

I didn't wait for any more. I went slowly along the face of the cliff and sought a handhold. In a little while I began to climb.

Chapter Eight

Stopped at the little house, but they were both gone to the hospital. I wondered how long she'd be allowed to stay. I had to see her, talk to her, make a last attempt at persuading her. This was the end for me. Tomorrow morning I'd be far away. But first I had also to see the Marquesa. I wanted the money that was due to me.

I went back to my own shack, set the alarm clock, and slept for half an hour—a trick I picked up years before. I got up, took time out to shave, and then put on an inconspicuous dark-blue suit, a white shirt, and a maroon tie.

I returned again to Paco's house, to see if María was back yet. The lights were on, the door open as before, nothing disturbed. The place was still empty. I crossed the field, got back in the Volkswagen, and drove up to the big house.

Page was playing Liszt, better than usual, very melancholy. I crossed the patio and entered the big room. He was bent over the keyboard, as if he played to himself. On the other side of the room El Mudo was deep in an armchair, his face buried in his hands.

I said, "Hello."

The music stopped. Page stood up. He was fully dressed, sparkling white shirt front, tails. "Hello," he said. "Going somewhere?"

He looked at me nervously. El Mudo rose slowly from the chair, stood waiting. Page said, "Bill, I'm sorry."

"For what?"

"I'm sorry."

"Forget it," I said. "It's not important now."

He was silent a moment. "You mean you won't tell?"

"I couldn't be bothered," I said.

He reached for a glass on top of the piano. He took a sip. He said, "Bill, I just got back from Navarro's place. I went there looking for the Marquesa: I was going to tell her about you and the girl before you got in your story about me." He paused. "That wasn't very nice, was it?"

I didn't answer.

"No, it wasn't," he said. "I'm glad now I didn't find her. She was out somewhere in the village with a bunch of the other guests, watching the beginning of the procession, I didn't search for her because I was pretty sick with myself by then. I came straight back."

I said, "Make any phone calls while you were there?"

He looked at me in surprise, possibly faking. "Why, no."

"Do they have a phone?"

"I don't know. Why do you ask?"

I said, "Seen any sign of Paco and his sister?"

He shook his head. He smiled, turning to include El Mudo. The big man smiled back. But he still couldn't bring himself to look in my direction. Page said hesitantly, "Bill, I'm glad I'm in your confidence. I won't mention her, of course, ever. That was a lousy thing I shouted at you before."

I wanted to catch him off balance. "Sure about that phone call?"

"Sure I'm sure." He was bewildered.

I said, "All right. How do I get to Navarro's place?"

He came nearer, smiled broadly, reached out and patted my arm. "Good old Bill. We could embrace if we were Spaniards. I feel like it." He patted some more. He said, "Bill, I want you to do me a favor. Let El Mudo drive you to the *ganadería*. He's suffering about you. He's a gentle sort of guy and he's sorry he hit you."

Page switched to laborious Spanish. "It will please you to drive Bill to Don Luis', eh, Mudo, no?"

Mudo looked at me shyly.

I had nothing to lose. I said, "How about it, *chico?*"

He smiled. He nodded. He started immediately for the patio.

At the French windows he hesitated. He turned around. Maybe they did it unconsciously, but they looked at each other very softly. It was their business.

"I will be waiting here, *amigo*," Page said. El Mudo smiled once more and went out.

I said, "If the Marquesa returns, tell her to wait. It's important."

"Did you have a good trip, Bill?"

"Lovely."

He looked into my eyes. He said, "Thanks again, Bill. You're a good guy."

"Yes," I said. "Someday you can make a pass at me."

He flushed. He said, "You didn't have to say that."

"I did," I said. "At least once. But don't let it worry you."

He said, "You're still a good guy."

I nodded to him and went out. I'd got to the other side of the patio and he called from the French windows. He said, "Hey, Bill. Who would I have been phoning?"

"I don't know," I said.

I continued on across the lawn to the driveway and climbed into the big Volkswagen, and El Mudo started the engine.

"Got a gun?"

He nodded.

"Give it to me."

He reached inside his shirt and handed me the weapon. I stuck it slantwise in the waist of my pants, just above the hip. "All right," I said. "We go. Fast."

He looked at me with friendship and gratitude in his eyes. Smiling with all his white teeth, he let in the clutch.

The wounded-looking Spanish countryside was drenched in moonlight. The breeze fluttered through the windows. Spain was in my nostrils. My heart was sick at the thought of leaving it.

But I had no choice. Blasco was nobody's fool. He was out to smash the Association. He seemed to think I was a member. Even if he believed me dead, he'd still be seeking my associates. And now he had a location to work on, the stretch of coast I'd led him to. He needed to make only one inquiry about *americanos*.

In that part of Spain Americans are rare. Everyone gossips and news travels fast. If I didn't shift rapidly, Blasco would have me pin-pointed, extradited to North Africa on a murder charge. I had to get out. And I had to take María with me.

Even if it meant taking Paco. But I knew that was impossible. Africa was finished for me. There was only Europe. With María I could head for the nearest American embassy, marry her, and get us both repatriated to the United States. As the wife of an American citizen, she'd be granted immediate entry. But Paco needed a passport, a visa, means of identification. I might smuggle him out of Spain, but he'd get sent right back again. Communists have put the European police on their toes. Illegal entry is no longer the easy jaunt it once was. And if Paco went back, María would go with him. Duty. I doubted she'd marry me until she was completely certain of his security.

I had to find a way out.

We bumped toward the village. The place was strung with colored lights, flags, banners, the rest of the panoply that Spaniards use for a fiesta. They're never halfhearted about anything. El Mudo reduced speed and I could hear the band playing as we entered the main street. We drove a couple of hundred yards more, reached the big village square, and could get no farther. I stood up and opened the roof panel. I looked out.

You have to see those things to believe them. To anybody not a

Spaniard they seem beautiful and barbaric and crazy. The whole population was turned out. They stood packed and silent in the square, holding flaming torches, clutching rosaries. They were praying as they stood. They were all looking in one direction. Because Christ was coming up the street. Their Christ.

They were carrying him on their shoulders. They had been taking him to look at his village. They were waiting now in the square, waiting to welcome him back to his home in the church. They looked at him with pride and love, and with an almost delirious happiness.

It happens every year. Christ's day. They and their fathers and their fathers' fathers worked and saved for years to buy their Christ. He is beautiful. He is more beautiful than the Christ in the next village or any village anywhere. And they are Spaniards. They know pain. They know that the world was saved through pain. So the huge image is always a crucifix, the figure an intensity of the agony of the salvation.

But pain is a normal part of life. And Christ is a part of life. Why mourn? Rejoice in your heart and your joy no man shall take from you. Behind the religion is gaiety. Behind the wildest enjoyment is a deep piety. They are jubilant about their salvation, jubilant with the Man who saved them.

So every year, on an elected day, they take this Man and show him the people, the houses, the streets, the whole village for which he did so much. His village. The band plays slow marching music, and some of the people walk behind the band, barefooted, carrying lighted candles, the men and women in two separate lines; and last of all, lifted high on the shoulders of twenty sweating men, comes the agonized figure, triumphant Christ.

I crossed myself. The band played and the torches guttered. The great figure swayed into the main square. The men halted at the foot of the church steps and waited. The music ceased.

A priest emerged from the church, leading by the hand a little girl dressed all in white, a small pair of white wings attached to the back of her dress. He lifted her up and placed her on a parapet to one side of the church door. She faced the Christ.

She spoke. She was not nervous. Her voice was clear and loud. She spoke with respect and friendship, and she was speaking for the entire village. She gazed up into the agonized face and thanked Christ for what he had done for them all, and she said she was happy that he was here, and she hoped he was happy too. She asked him to bless everyone in the world, but especially the people here gathered because they were his particular people in his particular village.

She thanked him because life was good. She thanked him because he was good. She smiled up at him as she finished, and then her voice rose and she shouted, "*Viva Cristo Rey!*" And the air was split as the whole population echoed, "*Viva! Viva!* Long live Christ the King!"

The twenty sweating men began to move slowly up the steps. The people were waving and shouting and cheering, and the music burst out again, gay and cheerful and fantastically loud. I looked over the heads and clearly saw the face of one of the men who carried the statue. Then the statue was inside the church. All the fireworks started going off in a terrific cannonade.

I was already out of the car, trying to fight my way through. I didn't have a chance. The people were packed together in the square, laughing, shouting, some of them already drinking wine. I got into the press. I couldn't move. They were waiting.

Then they broke. The great open door of the church was suddenly framed in a flaming outline of Roman candles. Everyone was trying to run through, trying to get into church before the fireworks burned out, to ensure good luck throughout the coming year. They surged all around me. I was swept forward up the steps.

The church was a Spanish church. It had no seats. I got through the door and the Christ was up by the altar. Between us was a packed mass of people. A woman raised her voice in song, and suddenly the whole crowd of them were singing at the tops of their voices, one of those vivid, joyous, massive Spanish hymns so old that no one has ever seen the music.

I eased over to the stoup, stood up on its base. Some of the men were lifting their children to glimpse the altar. The place was banked with flowers. Through the upraised arms I could still see the man who had helped carry the image. I had seen his face before. He had a small mustache. He was one of the men who had appeared from the pine trees during the morning ambush.

He said something to the man standing next to him, smiled. He looked all around, and his head jerked back again, and he had seen me. His eyes flew wide with fear. He knew I had seen him.

He moved. He melted quietly into the shadows at the side of the altar. A door opened and closed. Then he was gone.

I fought my way back to the main entrance. In the square the fiesta was on. The fireworks were blazing and banging, and the band was playing a wild tune, and a lot of people had started dancing. I ran right around the church. I entered the back door, opened the other door beside the altar, looked out onto the massed faces of all the singing people. But the man was gone. I went back outside. He could have vanished into a thousand places.

I cut across the square and a pretty girl seized me. I danced a few steps with her and told her I had to go and I'd see her later. I got back in the car. El Mudo was still behind the wheel, looking eagerly from the side window, eyes glowing, watching the dancers, smiling.

I said, "Stay if you want, *chico*."

He looked momentarily surprised. He shook his head.

"*Bien!*" I said. "*Vámonos!* We get out of here. Quickly."

We edged through the dancers, across the square, reached the other side. Some people waved to us. El Mudo waved back. I was wondering about the Association. They must be already well established here to be employing local men. Only a local man would be permitted to carry the statue.

The *ganadería* was roughly four miles beyond the village. We turned off the main track onto another road lined with palms; then we emerged into the open on completely flat ground. The buildings were in front of us, the long rambling hacienda to one side, all the roofs gleaming silver under the moon. Even when we were still a long way off I could hear the music. Lights were shining from every window.

El Mudo throttled down. There was fencing all around us, good fencing, a rarity in Spain. We were nearly to the hacienda, passing some outbuildings, and I saw what looked like a miniature football stadium, an arena surrounded by rising rows of bleachers. Three animals were in the ring, standing quite still. The man who was looking at them heard us coming and turned around and lifted a hand.

"Williams!" he shouted.

El Mudo put on the brakes. I said, "Wait here," and got out of the Volkswagen. In the still air the noise from the house was suddenly very loud, a lot of people laughing, talking, back of it all the clacking of castanets, the sound of guitars.

The man came forward to meet me. One of the bulls, startled by the movement, charged at the fence and then veered off. The three of them ran to the other side of the arena and stopped abruptly, flanks heaving, snorting.

The man held out his hand. "Hello, old chap."

I said, "Evening, Mr. Hatherton."

"Gracious! Couldn't you manage to call me Rex?"

"Sure."

He smiled and nodded. Over at the house a group of voices began singing "*Aires de Huelva*," very fast. I realized they must be in the open air, in a patio maybe, an inner courtyard.

"Quite a party," I said.

"Glad you enjoy it. It's a little noisy for British tastes. Spaniards *are* very noisy, aren't they?"

"Sometimes."

On the other side of the arena one of the bulls moved. The three animals wandered slowly back to their original positions.

Rex Hatherton looked over at the Volkswagen. "Beautiful night," he said, and there was a fever in his eyes. "Have you been down watching the procession?"

"Yes. A little while."

"Was it good?"

"Yes."

"I envy you," he said. "I'm absolutely incapable of getting enjoyment from that sort of thing. In England, you know, they teach us to distrust anything too colorful, especially when it's performed by foreigners: I get embarrassed."

"I'm Catholic," I said. "That helps."

"It would." He nodded. He said, "I didn't notice you leaving with the other guests. Not that I blame you. It all rather smacked of an organized trip to see the quaint peasants, didn't you think? I don't much care for that sort of thing myself, patronizing people, I mean, do you? Did you go down alone?"

"I didn't go down at all," I said. "I'm just arriving here. I saw the tail end of the procession on my way over."

"Oh." His face cleared a little. "Well, that's very wise of you, arriving just in time for dinner. It saves you an awful lot of previous agony."

He took me lightly by the arm, started moving away, still talking. He didn't approach the house directly, on a diagonal. He chose the road instead, the long way. He was saying, "Dinner, of course, will be fantastically drawn out, lots of toasts and everything. A little dreary after the second hour."

He stopped. He nodded to El Mudo, still sitting behind the wheel. He said, "Admirable job, these big Volkswagens. How many people do they seat?"

"Up to twenty if you squeeze hard."

"Really?" He swung open the door and looked in the back. "I see you've knocked out all the back seats. A friend of mine once did that, and then installed a bunk and a sort of stove. Toured all over Europe, living in it. Had a wonderful time." He slammed the door, smiled faintly. "Love to take a run in her sometime. Maybe after I've settled down. We've only been here three days."

"Any time," I said.

He put a hand on my arm again, started walking toward the house. "So you just came over through the village," he said. He laughed. "I say, Bill, don't think me dotty. I assure you it doesn't happen as often as you'll think. But actually I'm looking for my wife again. Didn't happen to see her down there, did you?"

"No," I said. "It was pretty crowded."

"I suppose it was."

I said, "Did the Marquesa go down?"

"Your aunt? I don't think so, not with the main party. I'm not sure."

"Maybe she and your wife went together."

"Oh, I doubt that very much."

He smiled again. He didn't want to say any more. But he couldn't stop talking. He hadn't been able to stop since first he spoke to me. He was a man with an obsession, one of those people who get love and hate all mixed up. He was so jealous about his wife it was a sickness. You find guys like him making fools of themselves all over the globe.

He said, "I thought perhaps she'd gone with Don Luis, but of course his type of Spaniard never leaves the house when he has guests. A fine man, Don Luis."

I said, "Have you known him long?"

He looked at me in surprise. "Oh, yes. Did he never mention us to you? It's a couple of years now since we met. I have a place at Vence, on the French Riviera. Navarro was staying nearby." He blinked at me. "He never told you? Honestly?"

"I don't know him well enough."

He said, "I thought you were close friends."

"No," I said.

We reached the archway of the main patio. Hatherton stopped. I looked through to the courtyard and the party was in full swing. Pretty. Lanterns strung all over, a small fountain in the center floodlit in changing colors. Luxury. In a corner the professional entertainers were playing their guitars. A girl with a lot of skirts was dancing a fast *fandangillo*, heels rapping like machine-gun fire, castanet held high above her head, rattling a counterpoint.

One of the guitarists stood up and began to sing, high and wild, his face transformed. He didn't give a damn for the guests. Or they for him. He was interested only in the song he was living. To them he was simply a background color, a noise behind their own noise, a pepper on the meat of being alive. I was reminded of the bullfights, when the shouting thousands suddenly realize the band has stopped playing. They howl, "*Música! Música! Música!*" over and over.

The din was fantastic. Full of joy. I knew the guests had not yet had dinner, because they were still rousing their appetites in the Spanish manner. Two long tables with servants behind them were spread with *aperitivos*: shellfish, prawns, pickles, meats, potatoes with garlic, small octopuses, sausages, anchovies, smoked fish, stuffed olives, a dozen other things. The guests were eroding slowly through them. Mention dinner to any Spaniard and he immediately starts eating his *aperitivos*, and keeps right on eating them even though the meal may not be served for another five hours. Then he sits down and eats an eleven-course dinner, washed down with wine.

The sight of the food made me realize I'd eaten nothing since morning. I said, "Let's go in, Rex."

"No, I don't think perhaps I will," he said. "Don't speak much Spanish, you know, and these people will insist on talking to me. I'll—uh—I'll see you later."

Abruptly he turned on his heel and strode back toward the small bull ring. I wondered where finally he'd find his wife. I didn't much care.

In the patio I looked among the crowd for the Marquesa. She was nowhere. I worked through to one of the tables and got myself a big plate of food, a glass of white wine. It was good. It tasted like the local vintage. I had some more. The conversations around me were being conducted in a roar, lots of laughter, the men patting each other, putting their arms round each other's necks. But never touching the women. Never even standing too near to them.

I waited for the Marquesa, listened to a big jovial middle-aged man with an enormous belly wrapped in a cummerbund. He was drunk. He talked about bulls. He was a little like a bull himself. The circle around him kept laughing.

He said, "No, señores, I do not abuse the hospitality of Don Luis Navarro. He and I both raise the animals and are therefore immune from the normal rules of courtesy. It is permitted absolutely for me to say that our good friend deceived us this afternoon. Four bulls he showed—"

"Fine bulls," somebody said. "*Más bravos que nada.* No braver bulls in the world."

"Ah-ha, yes," the fat man said conspiratorially. "But they are the only fine bulls he has. Four! Now if you come to my place—"

He was drowned out in a roar of laughter.

"No, no, no!" he shouted. "It is true! I have a *ganadero* working for me whose wife has a cousin with a husband who is a *ganadero* working for Don Luis. We have our spies. It is legitimate. And I say to you that the Navarro strain is finished."

They jeered at him.

According to Spanish rules, he was drunker than he should have been. He got red in the face, a little too vehement. "I tell the truth. Four bulls! And how many must he raise to find four that are brave enough to show the public? Forty! There is a number for you. Forty! And the other thirty-six fit only for the slaughterhouse."

He took a deep swig of wine. "Listen! One fighting bull costs Don Luis more money than any twenty of mine cost me. The Montero strain is great, the best in Spain. The Navarro strain is finished."

He had gone too far. They laughed again, but uncomfortably now. They began edging away from him. I put down my plate and glass, skirted the fountain, and went up the three steps to the house. I was getting nervous. I wanted to find the Marquesa before any cops found me. She had sounded drunk when I heard her over the phone. Maybe she was somewhere upstairs, lying down.

There were as many guests inside the house as out, and there was just as much noise. I didn't know anyone present. I walked into rooms, nodded to people, and walked out again. I tried several doors. One of them opened into an empty room. There was a telephone there. I entered, closing the door behind me.

I crossed to the phone and stood listening. The last vestige of doubt was removed. The noises from the other side of the door penetrated very distinctly, men talking, women laughing. Silva had been called from this house.

And so the hell with it. That was solely the Marquesa's worry. All I wanted now was my money and a fast getaway. And María. I went out among the people again, threaded my way through to a big hall. There were a lot of servants flitting around with trays. I couldn't catch the attention of any one of them. I went alone up the wide staircase to the next floor, meeting no one. I turned into a broad passageway, a succession of arches. Suddenly everything was very quiet. My footfalls made no sound on the thick carpet.

I opened the doors of three bedrooms. She was in none of them. I turned into a second, dimmer passage, walked a few yards, and quietly opened another door. She wasn't there either. But two other people were.

Don Luis was on the bed, his back to me. He was not wearing his Andalusian suit. In his arms was Lavinia Hatherton, her chin on his shoulder. I saw the recognition in her eyes.

I swiftly shut the door and went back downstairs.

I hung around for another half hour, taking more food and wine. The Marquesa didn't show. Through big windows I could see the servants in the house laying the long tables for the midnight dinner, glittering silver and glass and dazzling napery.

I couldn't wait any longer. I nodded to the fat man, who was still denigrating Don Luis' bulls, nobody listening, and I went through the archway and back along the track, trying to keep in shadow lest Rex Hatherton should see me. Jealous husbands have an extra sense, more delicate than radar. If he spoke to me for even two minutes he'd deduce something about his wife. And I was interested in nobody's business but my own.

The Volkswagen showed soft blue in the white moonlight. There was nobody behind the wheel. I opened the door to see if El Mudo were stretched out sleeping in the back, in the shadows. He wasn't there. But Lavinia was.

I left the door open. "Good evening," I said.

She didn't answer for what seemed a long time. Then she moved forward. The moon glinted on her blonde hair. She said harshly, "Well, go on, say something."

"For instance?"

"Something witty. Tell me it doesn't take me long to get dressed."

"Come to that, it doesn't," I said. "Now get out, please, Mrs. Hatherton. I have to go to the village."

She said, "I'm going, too."

"Not with me, you're not," I said. "It's nearly dinnertime and your husband'll be looking for you. In fact, he's looking for you now."

"As always," she said.

I said, "Yes."

She started to cry.

She looked pretty when she cried. She cried skillfully. I stood it for three minutes, a long time. I said, "Look, Lavinia, beat it, will you? Get out of my hair. Stay out."

She didn't move.

There was nothing I could do short of throwing her out. And her husband was somewhere around, and I'd wasted enough time anyway. I climbed behind the wheel, shut the door, started the engine. I made a turn and drove fast for the village.

She sniffled a few times more. I said, "Where's the man who was waiting for me?"

"I sent him away."

"Why?" I asked. "What's the attraction?"

She made no answer.

"What did you tell your husband was the attraction?"

"I only said you were good-looking."

"Yes," I said, "I'm as cute as could be. So tonight he comes searching for you in the back of this car. He'll do it again. There's going to be hell to pay if he finds you. And you'll pay it, not me."

"I don't care," she said. "At least it'll be a little variety. He's good for nothing but losing his temper."

"I don't want to hear about it."

She shrugged. "I suppose not. You know most of it already. You can guess the rest."

There were no signs of tears any more. We drove away and I said nothing. The silence seemed to annoy her. She leaned against the back of the seat, talked to the side of my face. She said, "What exactly did Luis tell you about me?"

"Nothing."

"I don't believe you. You're a liar. There isn't a man in the world that doesn't yatter over his past triumphs."

"Is that what you were?"

"No!" she snapped. "Just his mistress. Just for his money. And then I found he didn't have any. Oh, my God, what a bore he was! His eternal talk of bulls!"

She had a handbag with her. She reached into it, lit a cigarette, and blew out a jet of smoke. "On the French Riviera he talked about bulls, even."

"You mean yet."

"So I'm being vulgar. The hell with it. You want me to start acting the Vassar deb after what you saw?"

"Whichever way you like," I said. "But it's nice you've made up with him again."

She gave a short laugh. "We never quarreled. Even at Vence, when I first met Rex and began going with him, Luis didn't complain. And when finally I left him for good on Rex's account, he merely bowed and said how happy he'd been with me and thank you."

I remained silent. I wasn't interested.

She paused reflectively, blowing out more smoke. "So I persuaded Rex to marry me. Imagine that! I thought it was going to be exciting after living with Luis. I've been looking for a man to Rochesterize me, like Jane Eyre, ever since I was a child. I knew Rex lived a tough life. I thought he was the one." She laughed again, raspingly. "Ye gods! Do you know about Englishmen?"

"Lavinia," I said, "shut up. You're boring me."

"Not all Englishmen, of course, just the upper classes. There's a system to it. When they're about seven years old they get sent to monastic little schools where the teachers spend years plucking out any sign of a spiritual whisker. Then the bald little bastards are sent to a university for the major operation. The resultant creature is like something that just crawled out of a Foreign Office wastebasket. The only things that can bring Rex to life are jealousy and money."

I said, "Take your choice. Shut up or get out and walk."

"Oh, sure, you like Rex," she said. "Why not? The whole breed is reared to get along with their own sex, jolly good chaps all of them, rugged rulers of the outposts of empire. It's tougher for a woman."

She threw her cigarette out of the window. "He was bad, I knew that. So I thought he'd be exciting with me. He isn't. Just money and jealousy."

I said, "You're beginning to repeat yourself."

She paused. She said, "You don't like me, do you?"

"You're all right."

"But I interest you."

"No," I said.

She laughed. "That isn't possible, dearie. I know about myself. I know my effect on men. What's holding you back?" She drew nearer. "Another woman?"

I said, "We'll soon be in the village."

"Not the Marquesa," she said mockingly. "Would you really deny yourself for your auntie?"

"Lay off," I said.

She leaned over the back of the seat and reached a hand for me. I gave her a shove and she went sprawling in the back of the car. For a long time she remained silent, not moving. The moonlight glowed. The Volkswagen bumped over the rutted road. We were almost to the outskirts of the village. I could hear the band.

She said in an amused voice, "Well, you insolent sonofabitch. That's the first time in my life I ever had a deliberate brush-off."

She came forward again, leaned over the back of the seat. She was smiling. "All forgiven, Bill. It did me good. Why are we going to the village?"

"To look for the Marquesa."

"Auntie again," she said. "Little auntie-wauntie. Bill, I know you stay there because you're onto a good racket, but don't you think sometimes you're wasting yourself?"

"What good racket?"

"Let's not get sordid," she said, and laughed and lit another cigarette. We drove into the village.

I stopped the Volkswagen at the square. Once again I had to. Through the open door of the church I could see a few women praying in the yellow interior, black mantillas on their heads. Otherwise the religious aspect of the fiesta was finished. On the church steps the village band was playing. In the square almost the entire population was joined in a series of huge concentric circles, revolving slowly, dipping, swaying, very graceful. There was a blare from the band and the circles broke into couples, whirling through intricate steps. They were dancing a *jota*. It looked like a lot of fun.

I slowly scrutinized the square. No cops. No Marquesa. The village lads were loose. Those same village lads you find everywhere. Fifteen or sixteen years old, growing up, and drunk for the first time. This bunch was over by a flare-lit kiosk where an old woman sold doughnuts, fried potatoes, and fried shrimps to sustain the wineskins being handed out from the *taberna* behind her. A bunch of young girls surrounded the boys, clapping and giggling. One of the kids was trying to walk on his hands. Too drunk. He fell on his face. Everyone laughed some more.

Lavinia Hatherton threw away her second cigarette. She said, "This dance doesn't look half bad. Care to shake a shoe, lover?"

"No time," I said.

She said, "Look! O.K., you repulse me, fine, but let's hang on to the normal amenities, shall we? I want to dance. I'm asking you."

I was still searching the square. "Sorry," I said.

"There's a lot of awful good-looking boys out there."

"They'll be glad of the opportunity," I said. "Spaniards love blondes. Jump out. You're bound to run into a party from the *ganadería* sooner or later."

She said, "You sonofabitch."

"I know," I said.

"Where are you going?"

I didn't answer. María came out of the church.

She dropped the mantilla from her head to her shoulders, looked about her. She saw the Volkswagen, hurried down the steps, and came running around the great outer circle of the dancers. I scrambled out to meet her. I heard Lavinia ask what I was doing. I didn't answer. My whole heart was filling up just at the sight of the girl. I called, "María!"

She didn't run into my arms. I knew she wanted to, but a Spanish girl never permits herself to show public affection to a man. She halted in front of me, wide-eyed, her face pale, horribly frightened about something. She whispered, "Beel. It is Paco. You must not see him."

Then Lavinia Hatherton was beside me. She put a hand through my arm. She laughed. "Well, well. Lavinia the seeress. Her crystal ball tells all. How are you on crystal balls, Bill?"

She eyed María slowly, contemptuously, from head to foot. "Pretty little thing, Bill. Where does she work—in the Marquesa's scullery?"

María didn't move. I disentangled my arm. I said, "If she could understand English I'd beat in your face."

"I can see it," she said. "The crystal ball never lies. Tell her I offer a better job. She can be my maid. Is she pretty hot stuff in bed, Bill? She looks it."

"Beat it," I said. "I've got private business."

"Couldn't be more private, could it? Spurned again."

Lavinia Hatherton suddenly broke into perfect Spanish. She smiled at María. "Do you mind if the Señor Williams drives me back to the *ganadería?*"

María looked dazed. Shook her head. "No, señorita."

"No for certain, señorita," I said in English.

"Then how do I get back?"

"You walk," I said.

Her eyes went reptilian with venom. Her voice was like honey. "But Bill, dear, I thought you wanted to see the Marquesa. She's at the *ganadería*, you know. I was talking to her just before we left."

"Why didn't you tell me?"

"Why didn't you ask me?" She laughed again. She said, "Well, then, let's all pile in," and she got in and slid quickly past the wheel to the far side, so that María would have to be in the middle. She was up to a game. I didn't know what. There was nothing I could do about it. I had to see the Marquesa.

And at least I had María now. I put her on the seat between us and got in and started the engine. It was necessary to back to a side street. The dancers were still filling the square with the figure of the *jota*. Somewhere behind us, on the far side of the crowd, another car commenced a continuous hooting of its horn.

"We didn't stay long," Lavinia Hatherton said, "did we?"

I didn't answer. María was sitting very close to me. I could feel her trembling. Lavinia Hatherton would feel it too. I wanted to ask a thousand questions. I kept my mouth shut. We bumped over the rutted road and in the white moonlight the countryside looked suddenly stark.

The blonde put an arm around María's shoulders. "Would you like a cigarette, *chica?*"

"*No, gracias*, señorita."

"Then let us converse, shall we? What is it like to sleep with the Señor Williams?"

"Keep your trap shut," I said, "or I'll slap it shut."

"I'm not talking with you. This is a woman-to-woman conversation. We like to discuss such things, don't we, *chica?*"

"Ignore her, María. She has a bad mouth."

The kid had stopped trembling. She went as still as stone.

Lavinia Hatherton said, "Young lady, there is no use attempting to stand on your dignity with me. Once you start sleeping with a man there is no dignity left. I speak as an authority." She was having a wonderful time. She said, "You must be very good at it, my dear. He turned down even me on your account. Do you have any special tricks you would care to pass on?"

María said in a low voice, "Señor, please, I wish to get out."

"She wishes it also. Stay where you are." I stood on the accelerator.

"She called you señor," Lavinia Hatherton said. "I like that. It touches me. Does she always call you señor, Bill? I mean, even when?"

I said in English, "You filthy, dirty, foul-minded tramp."

"Well, if you insist, it's a pretty accurate description." She laughed lazily, switched back to Spanish. "My dear, you must be more careful if you wish to keep your little secret. Rule one is not to look at him as you did back there in the square. Rule two is not to have him return the look. Any observing woman of experience will guess immediately." She removed her arm from María's shoulder, reached into the handbag, got a cigarette. She said, "Imagine my thinking it was the Marquesa. She will be amused when I tell her. Although annoyed too, I should imagine. She will probably discharge you, both of you. The Marquesa is also a woman of experience, isn't she, Bill?" She leaned very close to María. "Has not the señor told you of his own experiences with the Marquesa?"

"Señor," María said, "please let me out."

"I heard every little detail. Don Luis has given me a personal maid. She gossips. I learned all about the Marquesa and her big *americano* the very first night I was here. Now I must bring the maid up to date and tell her of the big *americano* and his— What did you say your name was, dear?"

I said, "All right, you cow. I turned you down twice. You've had your revenge. Now quit."

She leaned back. Up ahead were the lights of the *ganadería*. The music came faintly through the open windows. She laughed. Then she said softly to María, "My dear, I understand certain things about your religion. How on earth do you manage about it?"

María began to cry.

I said, "O.K., Mrs. Hatherton, the method is yours. I tell one man at this party that I found you in bed with Navarro and the rest will know within ten minutes."

"What's that to Lavinia?" she said, but not nearly so lightly as she intended. "Rex will be insane for a week, but hardly surprised. After all, I was Luis' mistress when I first met him. As for the rest, I don't give a damn. I expect to be in this odious hole for no more than another week. I shall certainly never return." She reached across María and patted my knee. "Threaten me some more, Bill. It means I'm getting somewhere. I'll teach you to brush me off, you unlettered bastard."

We flashed past the outbuildings. Rex Hatherton was over by the arena, smoking a cigarette, waiting. I stood on the brakes. He looked up. I jumped out and went around the other side and opened the door. I said, "Get out!"

She descended slowly. She looked up in pretended surprise and saw her husband coming and waved a hand. She called gaily, "Rex, where have you been? I looked all over for you."

He almost ran toward us, his eyes glittering in his tense face. He snatched her by the wrist and jerked her angrily, for no purpose at all. Her voice changed. She was frightened of him, almost in terror. She said, "No scenes, Rex, please. I was in the village. Mr. Williams was kind enough to give me a lift back. We were suitably chaperoned, see for yourself."

In the patio the music stopped. The voices surged louder. I heard the Marquesa laughing. "Excuse me," I said, and turned away from them. I looked in the Volkswagen. María sat like a graven image. I said, "María, wait for me."

She made no reply.

I said softly, "María, please do. Because I love you. With all my heart and soul and life I love you."

I felt a hand on my shoulder. Hatherton said, "A moment, Williams. I have something I wish to talk to you about."

"Later," I said, and shrugged him off. I made my way swiftly toward the patio.

She'd been making an impression. She hadn't liked my dragging her away. I closed the door behind me and the voices from outside still sounded loud.

"What's so urgent?" the Marquesa demanded.

She was drunk, slurring her words. The aniseed smell of Pernod reeked all around her. She weaved across the room, flopped into a chair. "Dinner's just beginning. What do you want?"

"All right," I said. "I'll make it brief. Someone's onto us. Maybe not you, but certainly me."

"What are you talking about?" she asked irritably.

"We had hijackers again today. Up in the mountains. An ambush. Paco was hurt and I think they got Ferrer. The truck's somewhere among the peaks, a burned-out wreck."

"The Citroën?"

"The Citroën," I said. "It may be discovered. Take any necessary steps to cover yourself."

She was pushing herself to her feet, her face gone paste white. She said, "What are you telling me, you goddamned boob? Do you realize what that Citroën cost me? What the hell were you doing to let it happen?"

"Better sit down again," I said. "That's not all. Not by a long shot. Ferrer paid me the thirteen thousand dollars. I lost it."

She remained completely motionless for fully half a minute. Not a muscle moved. She said, "That's the racket, is it, you bastard?" and then she flew at me, clawing for my face.

We had a short tussle before I grabbed her fat wrists and forced her down into the chair. She lay there gasping. She wasn't nearly so drunk now.

I said, "Brace yourself, honey, because here comes one other item.

You've also lost the new boat. Gone. Bang. The bottom of the ocean. I was going to explain it to you in detail. I don't think I'll bother."

She sat there looking a thousand years old. Her voice was a croak. "Say your piece, Billy-boy."

"All right," I said. "The police blew it out of the water a couple of hours back. Spanish police. They know me. I'm getting out of here tonight. I want whatever money is coming to me."

She stared at me for a long time. She said, "You've loused it up for me, you sonofabitch."

"Skip the compliments," I said. "I'll give it to you straight. I've an idea they're only on to me. Not you. I've never mentioned your name or where I was operating from. The police will be searching this strip of coast for me. If I hang around they'll get directly to you. So I vanish. They'll get to you anyway, through gossip, so cook up a story for them. Say I told you I was writing a book. Say, if you like, that I was your lover. You're a nice respectable marquesa, an old title. That counts for something in this country. I doubt they'll even think of connecting you with contraband. After a while they'll get tired and go away."

She was still staring. She said, "You realize how much that boat cost me?"

"I'm no longer interested," I said. "This is for your benefit, not mine. Clear your boozy brain and listen."

"You've loused up everything," she said. Then she called me the filthiest name she could lay her tongue to.

I ignored it. I said, "I don't know whether the hijackers are Association or not. I had an idea Silva sicked them on me, but I must have been wrong. I went to see him tonight. He'd been knocked off. Nastily. And someone had arranged a tight little frame. It nearly fitted."

She started to say something. I said, "Let me finish. Listen. Silva got a phone call tonight from this house. I heard you in the background. I don't figure it. Maybe a chance acquaintance just wanted him to dash across for the party or something. I don't know. Anyway, Silva was dead by then. Whoever called was pretty obviously not aware of it. Make of it what you can. And when you're looking for my successor, stay away from a man named Griswold. An American. Griswold. He's a rat."

She stood up.

I said, "That's about all. I have to be on my way now. Come back to the house and give me the money due me."

"What?" she said, and suddenly she laughed. She said, "Are you crazy?"

"What now?" I said, but I knew.

She said, "You lose me thirteen thousand dollars, a truck, and a brand new boat, all in one day, and then you expect me to give you money." She laughed again, contemptuously. "You poor silly bastard."

"There's no giving to it," I said. "I earned that dough." Her mouth snapped shut. She looked mean as a snake. "You don't get a nickel."

"Right," I said. "I inform on you. An anonymous letter. All the details."

"What details? What do you know except Silva? And he's dead." She laughed with real enjoyment. "Sonny-boy, I couldn't be better covered if I had ninety-seven umbrellas. Details! Write all the anonymous letters you want. Take it up as a hobby. But you'd better not do it from this district, because if you're still here in the morning I'm going to set the police on you. I'll figure a reason."

She walked past me and got to the door. She paused. She said thoughtfully, "Know something? After the way you treated me, this is really rather pleasant. I don't think I so much mind the cost after all."

She went out. The voices from outside flowed into the room. I stood there and sweated.

Through the crowd and out to the Volkswagen and El Mudo was in the front seat, sitting next to María. I got behind the wheel, started the engine. I said, "I'll take you home, María."

She shook her head. "I must find Paco."

"What do you mean? Where is he?"

She glanced at El Mudo, shook her head again, lapsed into silence. She looked pretty near dead. I said, "I'll take you home."

Back in the patio I heard the Marquesa laughing. Right then I almost admired her. I revved the motor and the noise startled the three bulls so that they ran from one side of the arena to the other. As we passed through the village, the people were still dancing.

Chapter Nine

El Mudo waited in the car, cigarette glowing through the dark as I closed the door of the house. I faced María.

She had been silent all the way home. She said nothing now. She stood looking at me and the love filled me up, and I put my arms around her, and then she started to cry again, long-drawn sobs that made her shudder from head to toe.

I laid my face against her hair; whispered to her. I said, "No, María mía. No! The woman was bad, una sinvergüenza who knows nothing of love. It is not as she made it seem between us. She speaks of animals. Do not let her turn that which we have into a dirty thing."

I held her tightly. Kissed her. Tried to comfort her. I couldn't live away from her. I had to persuade her. I held her from me and felt the hopelessness before I started to speak.

I said, "María, tonight I must leave this place. I want you to come with me, to Portugal. The American man in the embassy there can marry us, and I will take you to a new home. Please."

She stopped crying, put out a hand, and touched my face. She seemed all at once almost calm.

I said, "I have to leave because the police want me. I am going to the Marquesa's house for some money and then I will return and we'll take the boat and go to Portugal. Tomorrow you will be my wife."

She looked at me a long time. Then she shook her head. "Beel, there is Paco."

I started to protest.

"No, Beel. Before my mother died I made to her a big promise. Paco has no one else. And he is sick."

"The hospital will make him better."

The tears started filling her eyes again.

"What's the matter?"

"He is not in the hospital. I must go now and look for him once more."

"Wait. What happened?"

She went slowly across the room and sat in a chair. She looked suddenly exhausted, grief-stricken, and it crushed my heart to see her.

"I went to the big house of the Marquesa," she said, "to find someone who would bring the doctor for me. But all the windows were dark. Nobody was there. I knew I must go myself, but first I came back to see that Paco had not too much pain. The door was open when I returned. He was gone. I have been seeking him. I cannot find him anywhere."

"Stay here," I said. "I'll get him."

"No!" It came from her mouth like a cry of terror. She flung out of the chair, gripping my arm.

"Why not?"

"No. You must go away or the police will take you."

"I can afford another hour."

"No."

There was something else wrong. I said, "Tell me more, María."

"It is nothing."

"Tell me."

She held it another half minute. Her shoulders drooped. "Paco has a gun. He has taken also the big knife that once was my father's. He is looking for you, Beel. He will try to do a terrible thing with the knife."

"How do you mean?"

Her voice became almost inaudible. "I have heard how two brothers in a village near Cádiz did this same thing to a man who loved their sister. Paco told me. He said it was justice. Now everybody makes fun of the man and it would be better if he were dead. And if Paco sees you—"

"Hush," I said. "He will neither kill me nor do that to me. I shall talk with him, say that his suspicions are wrong. We have been good friends, Paco and I. He will believe me."

She shook her head wearily. "He will not. He saw us. A girl does not stand with an unclothed man unless there has been love between them. He knows for certain. Soon everyone will know."

"Don't worry about the American bitch. She was only talking. And Paco won't advertise it."

She smiled faintly. "Advertise, no. Soon there will be no necessity."

"*No comprendo*."

She said, "Beel, I tell you this because you are going away. In another year more happy, perhaps the knowledge will bring you back."

"What?"

"In a few months I have a baby." She gave the faint smile again. "It is good to have a baby."

I didn't take her in my arms, kiss her, do any of the things I'd heard about. For a little while I felt too good even to move. Then I said, "Yes. Damn right it's good to have a baby. Possibly the best thing in the world. Now I find Paco. Tell him how we must marry immediately. Guns and knives are not important. The baby is important. He will be a boy."

She said, "You do not understand the temper of Spanish men."

"No, but I understand the temper of American men. It is enough. Look, *chica mía*. Paco is grown up, almost a man. He must look after himself. I know you promised your mother, but we will manage that also. Established in America, I can send for Paco, look after him there. But this one thing for certain: I leave no baby of mine to be called a bastard. And especially not in Spain, where he would be stamped for life through having only the single name of his mother, instead of the names of both parents. So I go now and look for your brother. I tell him everything, even if I must sit on his head to do it. You stay here. Don't move. Promise me that."

"I am frightened," she said.

"Don't be. In my life there have been many things worse than a delirious young man with a gun and a knife. And have no fear for me. We are going to have more children, you and I, and no silly boy with a knife can prevent it."

I began laughing. I felt good. I held her tight against me. I said, "Nobody will get hurt, not me or Paco, I promise you. *Y la policía?* I can run faster than all the policemen in Spain, even if they wore roller skates. Promise you will stay here and wait."

She nodded uncertainly. "Beel—"

"No more." I hugged her, rocked her to and fro as if we were dancing, kissed her. I held her face between my hands and looked at her and she was beautiful. "Sit here," I said. "Think of all the names we might call the baby. And do not fret because you cannot say Williams. It is a false name I use only because it is common. Now tell me that you love me."

"I love you."

"Enough." I kissed her once more. "A small farewell, my little one," I said, and I grinned at her because I couldn't help it, and went outside, still grinning, and over the field to the car, where El Mudo was still waiting for me.

But first I had to get the money.

We pulled up on the driveway, outside the house. I cut the engine. There were no lights showing and I guessed Page had gone to bed. I turned to El Mudo.

"*Amigo*," I said, "I intend to do something bad. I am going to commit a crime. I may need you to help me."

Without hesitation he nodded eagerly, grinned. He put an arm round my shoulder and pulled me against him, the way Spanish men do when they want to be friendly. In a little while he'd be patting the back of my neck. They do that too.

I said, "Yes, but think carefully. It is not smuggling. It is against the Marquesa. Right now I am going in there to rob her safe."

He went on nodding, grinning.

"If she discovers you were connected, your life will not be worth living. And I go away tonight, for always. You will be left to face it alone. Think again. Deeply."

He didn't. He simply put his big hand on the back of my neck, squeezed a little, and began to pat. I said, "*Bien!* Thanks, Mudo. Get some tools from the box, something strong with a levering edge. Maybe we can discover the combination to the safe. If not, it must be forced." I slapped him on one of his huge biceps. "You."

He scrambled happily from the car. I didn't feel so good about using him like that, but he was pretty shrewd, despite not having a voice, and there was no reason for anyone ever to know the part he played. I just hoped he could play it successfully. I had a wife and child to think of. And basically I was doing nothing dishonorable. I intended taking only the money I had earned—earned the hard way, the hardest way.

I stood on the driveway, fingers crossed, and prayed the safe would be as flimsy as it looked. El Mudo made chinking noises in the toolbox, his face lit up with excitement and delight, eyes glowing like moons.

We went together across the patio, into the big room. There was no reason why lights shouldn't be on. I tripped the switch. The chandeliers blazed out. Several sheets of music had fallen down from the piano. The big guy paused to pick them up, arrange them neatly, lay them on the piano stool.

We got into the big hall. El Mudo's eyes flicked to the staircase, then he looked at me and lowered his head and blushed slightly. I said, "It is better for him to be in bed. You can decide afterward whether to tell him." I took the guy's arm and led him along the corridor to the library. So far as I knew, he'd never before been in that part of the house.

I paused in front of the door. "You are sure about this?"

He nodded.

"Why?"

He hesitated, shrugged humorously. His hand came up and patted me fondly on the back of the neck.

"Then thanks, *chico*. Someday the same for you." And as I opened the door I was thinking how strange it was that none of the Spaniards liked the Marquesa, when as a rule they're loyal, even devoted, to their employers. Something like that I was thinking. I was feeling for the light switch, fumbling along the wall. The room that had once been a library was flooded with light.

I can still hear it. The tools fell from El Mudo's hand. He stood perfectly still. Then from his big voiceless throat came a long and awful cry of anguish. It was the first sound he'd made in his life.

He staggered past me in absolute silence, sank to his knees beside the desk. His hands reached out slowly. They were shaking. It was as if he were afraid the final touch would destroy him. His body heaved with sobs and the tears flooded from his eyes and fell onto Page's face. But they didn't revive him.

Page was as dead as a doornail.

They'd used a professional cracksman. The safe was neatly and correctly picked, not a thing inside, everything gone, money, books of addresses, every last paper. The Marquesa had lost the ninety-seven umbrellas of which she boasted. She was no longer protected. And I wouldn't get my money. But somehow it no longer mattered.

For no reason, I closed the safe and put the books back in position.

I searched. Everything was tidy and clean, nothing to indicate who the visitors had been, not a footprint outside the window. Then I had to get out because I couldn't bear to watch El Mudo anymore. I touched his shoulder. He paid no heed. He sat on the floor, Page's body in his arms, the dead, burned face pressed against his chest. He rocked to and fro, like a mother with a child, tears streaming down his face, his body racked by dry, silent sobs. I just couldn't take it. I picked up the fallen tools and went out and shut the door on him.

In the big room I poured myself a stiff drink of cognac and sat on a chair near the piano, trying to figure things out. I got nowhere. I was numb, shocked, filled with a stupefying sense of unreality. My very life seemed unreal and unbelievable.

In the first flash I had thought that maybe Paco was responsible, that he'd killed Page instead of me. But it didn't stack up. Paco had no interest in safes. Paco would not have tortured Page by holding lighted matches to his face. This had been someone trying to extract information, probably something that Page couldn't tell because he knew only what El Mudo had been able to communicate in sign language. And he was not tied up. That indicated a group of three or more. At least two men were needed to hold him down while the flames were applied to his face.

I thought about that. I got to feeling sick. There were no lethal marks on him, except the burns. Maybe they hadn't meant to kill him. He looked as if he'd died from shock, brought on by pain. But I didn't suppose the questioners had minded the death. Or much else. You have to be beyond a lot of things before you stick a lighted match into a man's eye.

I dwelt on it too long. Then I told myself angrily that it was none of my business. I was out of the game. The police were after me. The smart thing to do was hit out for Portugal right away. Right away. I said it twice. Aloud. I didn't move.

I got another drink and tried to think back to the beginning. Griswold. Everything had been going smoothly except for Silva selling me bad drugs and the Marquesa wanting to expand. So I'd purchased drugs from another source and got myself a new man. Griswold. I'd heard of him before. Neither good nor bad. Even had a slight contact with him a few years back, when I was running guns to Israel and he was contact man for the munitions firm. Everyone said he drank. They said also that he could keep his mouth shut. A risk. I took it.

So where did he fit? Clearly a plant, but whose? Not Silva's, because I'd completed negotiations with Griswold before any trouble arose with Silva. Then he was a finger man for the Association. It fitted. He'd also spotted Silva, had him knocked off, tried to frame me for the murder. It meant the Association had decided finally to eliminate Spanish competition, invade this section of the coast, and make it their exclusive territory.

I took that one again. If Ferrer spoke the truth, then the Association had invaded already. Three people dead of fixed drugs in Cádiz. Ferrer claimed he didn't work Cádiz. Somebody did. The Association.

Cádiz. Nearer than that. Near enough to employ a man who lived in Santa Faz. Because no man not a villager would be allowed the honor of carrying the Christ.

I hit a brick wall. I thought of the ambush. How had they discovered the appointment with Ferrer when only the Marquesa and I knew of it? There was one way to get an answer. Return to Santa Faz. Find the man with the small mustache. Beat the truth out of him.

Fine. While I sought him, the police would be seeking traces of me, getting nearer all the time. Meanwhile Paco was wandering around. Maybe ill. I liked the kid. I'd promised to find him. All this other stuff was none of my business.

Except ... I had a beautiful thought. Except that the Marquesa might think I had robbed her safe, which I had certainly intended to do, and killed Page when he tried to stop me. She'd fancy herself still covered. She wouldn't have the least compunction about sending the police after me on a second murder charge.

Out of Spain I was probably safe from Blasco. He wouldn't care once he'd driven me from the country, so long as I didn't recross his path. But the Marquesa was another kettle of fish. Lavinia Hatherton scorned wouldn't be a patch on the Marquesa scorned. She was robbed of money, vital papers, and a last remaining boy friend. I could imagine her sending the police of five continents after me, poking them, prodding, nagging, using her title on them until they got me.

I had a sudden empty feeling that I wasn't going to be safe anywhere. I crossed to the piano, struck a couple of chords, and they sounded bad. I always wanted to play the piano. I never made it.

I finished the second drink, poured a third, a small one, and mentally I was a moth, its wings torn off, limping, hobbling, not knowing where to go. I sank back in the chair, paralyzed with weariness, not wanting to move. I wanted María to be there, to put my arms around her, draw comfort from her. I wanted to be five thousand miles away with her, for the baby to be a boy, for the three of us to be safe and happy.

But I had to do something. What? To search for Paco seemed simplest—at least an immediate thing. I tossed down the third drink, shuddered, and stood up. Then I didn't move anymore. I felt deathly ill. I got the feeling that comes when you're trying desperately not to vomit, when all your pores start yawning and you sweat hot and cold.

Blasco, the Spanish cop, was standing at the open French windows, smiling. On either side of him was a uniformed policeman, holding a gun, covering me. For some reason I thought of the unborn baby, of the life he'd lead after all this was through. I said croakingly, "Good evening."

Blasco stepped into the room, his smile growing broader. "*Buenas tardes*, Señor Oovilliams," he said. "How good to see you alive again. Did you enjoy your swim?"

Chapter Ten

I looked at him frozenly. The events of the past thirty hours flashed through my mind. I tried to reckon the extent of his knowledge. My brain wouldn't work. I twisted my face into a smile, my voice all wrong. "This is not my house," I said, "but come in. Can I offer you a drink?"

"You can, but I shall refuse it. I am very much on duty."

I looked at the other two. "Gentlemen?"

They gazed back stonily.

"You move around too freely," Blasco said. "Once ashore, I was able to trace you easily." He advanced on me, the others flanking him. The chair seat pressed against my calves and suddenly I was claustrophobically hemmed in. I sat down abruptly, my limbs feeling disarticulated. I wanted to reach for a cigarette. I couldn't trust my fingers.

"Well," I said, and continued smiling at them. One cop was thin and fair, an Asturian. He seemed all right. The second was a thick, squat man with a round pudding head and a brutish face. I was afraid of him. They stood like statues. Blasco settled himself, feet apart.

"Who else is at home?"

Across the hall, along the passage, was the dead body of Page. "Nobody," I said.

"There is a light on the other side of the house."

"Yes," I said, "in the library. I was looking for a book. I must have forgotten to switch it off."

Blasco looked all around him, his gaze hesitating at the tools I'd put on the table. "I do not see a book."

"No, I couldn't find anything light enough. I've been at Don Luis Navarro's *ganadería* since this afternoon and I'm about exhausted. Spanish fiestas are great fun but—"

He interrupted, smiling thinly. "Do you have Spanish blood in your veins, Señor Oovilliams?"

"I'm not sure. Americans seldom are."

"You lie like a Spaniard, like a Spanish gypsy. I would admire to hear you expand yourself, embroider the story. Unfortunately we have no time."

"I don't understand."

"It is not important, señor. Now, on your feet. We will tread a soft way to the library and seek that book for you."

"No," I said.

"I am asking politely."

"Yes, but this isn't my house. I can't give you leave to go roaming over it."

He leaned forward. He hit me across the face with an open hand, with all his strength. My ears rang. He said gently, "Stand up." The two policemen moved to either side of me. "Stand up," he repeated.

It wasn't so bad then. I stopped shaking. The blow had restored my sense of immediacy, cleared my head. I knew I had to keep my temper. I put my hands on the armrests, leaned back in the chair, looked expressionlessly at the three of them. I didn't move.

"I am about to do it again," he said.

I nodded. "Go ahead. I'll sue for double the amount. Our governments are pretty friendly at the moment, but maybe we can make an international incident of it if you try hard."

He regarded me blandly, a full half minute. He took two backward steps, nodded to the cops. They were highly trained. They swooped. They dragged me to my feet, bent me over, and twisted both arms up my back. I tried to push at them. There was no hope. They rushed me resisting through the door and into the darkened hall. I began to yell.

The dark chunky cop hit me in the neck with the butt of his gun. I went right on yelling. I started to kick. We stood together in the darkness and struggled. I thought my arms were being torn out.

A flood of light burst into the passage ahead of us. The library door opened. I stopped squirming and waited for El Mudo to come out, because he hadn't had time to get away. Nobody appeared. And then I realized that Blasco wasn't with us, that he must have run ahead as soon as I began shouting. I didn't shake anymore. I went empty, with nothing inside me, no longer resisting. The cops ran me up the passage, flung me through the door, and I staggered across the room and fell to the floor beside the desk.

Page should have been lying there. He wasn't. The French windows were open. In the neat, tidy, traceless room was nobody but Blasco.

I picked myself up slowly. I stood and prodded with my fingers at the joints of my shoulders. I felt my neck where the man had hit me. I said, "Items two and three. Now find me this nice light book and get the hell out of here. Tomorrow I visit the nearest American consul. I don't know what your rank is, Blasco, but you'll be without it by tomorrow night."

He no longer smiled. His face was wooden. "In that case," he said, "I set myself no limits. As well to be hung for a sheep as a dog."

"Leave out the colloquialisms. Your English isn't good enough."

"Possibly," he said. "But I want no comments from people of your breed."

"You'll get none. Find your own way out. Good night."

I turned around. The two cops were waiting. The dark guy punched me in the chest and I fell over the foot of the other one. I skittered across the room. I was off balance. I reached with my hands but somehow I missed. My head hit the corner of the desk. I went out.

I came to sitting in a chair. Blasco was standing over me, gazing down unblinkingly. "You were unconscious for three minutes," he said. "How do you feel?"

I made no immediate answer. I was thinking of El Mudo, wondering where he had taken Page, hoping he was far away. I said, "Item four. It'll make interesting headlines. Spanish police third-degree American citizen."

"Item five," Blasco said. "American citizen will now show Spanish police his passport. Complete, I hope for his sake, with visa."

"I don't have it with me."

"Where is it?"

"In my place at the other side of the orchard. I don't live in this house."

"You did once." His lip curled faintly, probably unconsciously. He'd heard the story. I felt the flush creeping over my face. I couldn't prevent it.

I said, "Yes. Yes, I did."

Almost imperceptibly he softened. He was silent a while. He pulled some cigarettes from his pocket, offered me one, and the fair-headed policeman struck a match and held it out. I inhaled deeply. I said, "Thanks."

It was the sort of strong cigarette that Paco smoked, dry black tobacco and very strong. The smoke went down the wrong way and I had a fit of coughing. They stood and watched me, not moving. There was a peculiar deadened atmosphere in the room that made me seem to be coughing in a cave. I kept it up as long as I could. I was trying to perfect a story.

Blasco said quietly, "Tell me about yourself, Mr. Oovilliams."

"Why?"

"Because," he said, "this time I have both credentials and a warrant. I am doing my duty. Tell me about yourself."

"All right." I shrugged. "I'm twenty-six years old, an American citizen born in Ohio. I have been working in North Africa."

"Illegal work."

"Not exactly. It's neither one thing nor the other. Outside the spirit of the law, maybe, but well within the letter."

"Your employers use that same sophistry," he said. "The Association."

"Wrong," I said.

His face began to harden again. The other two cops might as well have been wearing masks. "Continue," Blasco said.

I said, "Right. I'll tell you why I'm here. I like Spain, especially this part. I've visited here pretty often. One day I met the lady who owns this house and she—"

"You can leave that out."

"Yes," I said. "Well, anyway, she offered eventually to let me stay at the little place beyond the orchard. For as long as I liked. Since then I've lounged around and occasionally helped with the oranges."

"Occasionally gone across to North Africa."

"If you like."

"For what?"

"Some of that legal-illegal work. I'm being honest with you. I've needed to earn money."

"By running contraband into Spain."

"Into Israel," I said.

He punched me so hard in the side of the head that I thought my neck had snapped. The cigarette went flying. My chin dropped. The other cops took two automatic steps forward. "Into Spain," Blasco repeated softly. "Spain."

"No."

He hit me again in exactly the same spot. I made a lunge at him. The boys were ready for it. They slammed me down hard and twisted my arms behind the chair, and the squat dark cop grabbed my hair. He jerked my head back, straining my neck. I was looking up into his face and he was still without expression, except for the dull gleam in his eyes. I had been right to be afraid of him.

"Let him relax," Blasco said in Spanish. The pressure was released. The man retained his hold on my hair. I was thinking of María, Paco, El Mudo, especially María. I had to keep a grip on myself, get out of this somehow.

Blasco said, "Now I will tell the truth about you. It is well known. In the past few years you have been connected with nearly every illicit activity along the entire length of the southern Mediterranean. There is almost nothing you have not done. You have a reputation for courage, plus an astuteness that has kept you always within the fringe of the law. In short, you are precisely the type of man to be selected by the Association as a pathfinder, when they decided to extend their activities to the south of Spain."

"Interesting and flattering," I said. "But not true."

The cop started to yank my hair. Blasco snapped his fingers. The grip was released altogether. But I wasn't silly enough to try to move again.

"Nevertheless," Blasco resumed, "how very stupid of the Association. In North Africa, in that unpleasant sink of a city where I work, they are perfectly legal and safe. Simply an import-export firm with transferable and untouchable licenses, under cover of which they have since the war exported goods with unassailable legality to every obscure spot on the map. Some of the places have been so obscure that the goods never arrived. They were never intended to arrive. My harassed colleagues of the French and Italian police could tell you the true destination of the consignments." He looked down at me. "You find this interesting?"

"It's more or less common knowledge," I said.

"I did not expect it to be news." He smiled bleakly. "But now consider the mistake of your employers, their foolishness. The French and Italian coasts are wide-open territory of great length. To police them properly is an impossibility. Until now the Association has done exactly as it pleased, with only a few minor irritations."

He lit a cigarette. This time he didn't offer me one. He said, "The Spanish coastline is also fairly long. But the Association has established already a network over the north of Spain by smuggling across the French-Spanish frontier—a simpler process than landing cargoes by sea. So we are left with only southern Spain, just across the water."

"Too near for comfort," I said.

He nodded. "Traceable. Which is why the Association delayed for so long. They knew that, unlike their French and Italian coastal activities, landing goods on the Spanish coast would give us a chance to smash them from this side. But finally they were overcome by greed. As always, it blinded them, and you, to several salient facts. They thought fast boats would be safest. But fast boats of necessity are small boats, capable of traveling only small distances. We knew at once that you were shipping to Spain. A small distance. And there was the question of the moon. Few people care to smuggle under the threat of a full moon, but you were able to take off only a little before moonrise. Again it indicated a short distance. Spain."

He was no longer asking, he was telling me. He waited for a comment. I made none. He walked to the desk, stubbed his cigarette in an ash tray, and turned back to me.

"You have been very clever. You established yourself on this deserted coast by taking advantage of an aging woman. I will say no more of that. Apart from that regrettable weakness, I understand the lady is highly respected, a woman of title." He turned to the fair-haired policeman. "It is true?"

"Yes, sir."

"But you missed on the little things," Blasco said. "You have brought in an accomplice, another young American who is taking the same advantage. Perhaps you have instructed him. The subject is unpleasant. However, both of you have made a bad slip. So far as I can ascertain, there is no record of your visa at any police station in the vicinity. You are illegal entrants."

He drew a long slow breath. "This was not minded so long as you were thought merely to be guests of the Marquesa. But tonight I traced you here. I have given to local police a report of your previous activities. They look at you now in a different light."

"You mean they are going to deport me?"

"Cease to be foolish!" He stared coldly. I knew then that I was in for a bad time.

I said, "Señor Blasco, let me tell you straight. I do not work for the Association."

"Then for whom?"

I wanted to tell him. I couldn't. Any confession whatever of smuggling into Spain would land me in jail, no matter who my employer was. "Not the Association," I said.

"You are repetitive."

"I'm sorry." I was. But I had to protect myself and María. And there was something about Blasco that indicated that he was not so much the master of the situation as he pretended.

He said, "Would you care to give an explanation of what happened tonight?"

"Tonight?" I said. "I don't know. I was at Don Luis Navarro's *ganadería* from five o'clock on. I just got back."

His expression did not alter. He said levelly, "At about nine this evening, in my office, I received a phone call that you had just landed and were in the office of a man named Silva."

"Your office here in Spain?"

"My office in North Africa. The caller did not identify himself. He told me that you had murdered this Silva."

"Who's he?"

"Silva?" Blasco asked patiently. "A man who had the same business interests as the Association but was not a part of it."

"And he's dead?"

"Very dead. I was given his address and advised to go there immediately, to catch you red-handed. But I didn't catch you, did I? For reasons entirely your own, you fled seaward, instead of staying in the city. Why, Mr. Oovilliams? I would have encountered greater difficulty arresting you there. The Association could have hidden and protected you."

"I'm not clear," I said. "Are you taking me in for murder?"

He waited a long time, then shook his head. He smiled at me with great friendliness. "That is why I desire an explanation. In this climate the time of death can be established fairly exactly by the state of decomposition. Silva was killed around ten o'clock this morning—let us say between nine and eleven. You were not in the city at that time. You could not have entered the city at any time during daylight today. Seven policemen and myself were watching the harbor for any sign of you."

"Thanks for that."

"Inadvertent," he said. "Accidental. But you see, don't you, that you didn't have to run away when I entered Silva's office?"

I nearly fell in. I bit my tongue. I said, "I don't know who Silva is. I've been at Navarro's *ganadería* since five o'clock. Do you think I go out in a boat dressed up like this?"

The friendliness faded. He studied me. I saw him looking at the scratches on the backs of my hands. "Three people dead in Cádiz," he said. "Tonight I learn from these gentlemen that a boy died thirty miles from here. I am going to smash the Association. You will help me."

"I don't work for the Association."

"Your sentence might be reduced."

"I don't work for them."

"For whom, then?"

"For nobody."

He suddenly snapped his fingers. My arms were clamped and then my head was jerked back. My throat was taut. The dark cop had a grin on his brutish face. He said, "Señor?"

"A little," Blasco said.

The man's hand was apelike. He reached a stumpy thumb and forefinger and delicately took my Adam's apple. Then he squeezed. Hard.

I gagged. I struggled. I thought my head was going to burst. He let go of me.

"Señor Oovilliams," Blasco said. "Only a little information about the Association. For example, what are the contacts here in Spain?"

"I know nothing."

He nodded. "A little more this time."

My head was yanked back and the fingers closed, and then the pressure increased. The pain went up through my temples, thrusting at my ear drums, and then it exploded all over my skull. I fainted.

I pushed away the glass of water. Blasco said, "Castillo does not know his own strength."

"I'd like the chance to show him mine." I put a hand to my neck. My head felt fragmented. I had difficulty swallowing. I looked at the cop and he gazed back without emotion. I said, "You son of a whore."

Blasco struck me casually across the face. He said, "No, not to a policeman. You have forced these methods on us. I am prepared to go even farther to get my information. To any length."

I thought of Page and had a crazy idea. I said, "Even to sticking lighted matches in my eye?"

"You have listened to too many stories of the Spanish Inquisition." He shrugged. "But perhaps lighted matches. My nation does have a strong streak of cruelty. And nothing can be too bad for those who make a business of poisoning sick people with polluted drugs."

"I agree with you," I said. "Nothing."

"What?" He looked at me strangely. He laughed. "Oovilliams, you are peculiar. You sound almost as if you mean it."

"I do," I said. I was thinking of Paco, the Citroën, the boat, the money, all the things that had been done to me. "There's nothing I'd like better than for you to smash the Association," I said.

He took two swift steps and swung hard. He hit me again. The cops bore down on my arms and his open hand beat back and forth across my face. He continued till he was breathless. He said, "You mock me, Mr. Oovilliams."

He slapped me once more. My head rang. "You mock me."

He walked away and banged the palm of his hand on the top of the desk. He stood a while, shoulders bent. When he turned around again he was calm. "Oovilliams," he said, "tell me something. Anything. Talk to me. Ask me questions."

I put my head in my hands. My skull was splitting. I raised my face and said, "Blasco, what are the penalties in Spain for smuggling?"

"They are heavy for all concerned." He looked me straight in the eye. "I give you no false hopes. But will not the Association also be hard on you? Your foolhardy seaward escape tonight cost them a boat."

He continued talking. I didn't listen. If I could have thought only of myself, I'd have gone to jail without a qualm, dragging the Marquesa with me. But there were Paco and El Mudo, both implicated. Most of all there was María and the baby. I couldn't do it. I still had to figure a way out.

"I'm sorry," I said. "I know nothing."

There was a long oppressive silence. Blasco sat on the desk, lit a cigarette, and in the stillness the waxed Spanish match sputtered unnaturally loudly. The cops remained motionless. I sat and listened to the sounds in my aching head. It seemed that hours were passing.

"A last chance," Blasco said dispassionately.

"Look," I said, and I stopped. A car was coming up the driveway. We froze into position and waited.

There were feet on the gravel and a murmur of voices. Somebody said in Spanish, "Stay here." The cops slid across the room, guns in their hands, and stood on either side of the French windows. Blasco backed to the wall, took a flat black automatic from his pocket, and leveled it at me. The footsteps approached and I stared at the French windows, and then Don Luis Navarro appeared on the threshold.

He hesitated diffidently. He stepped into the room. He turned his head, saw the fair-haired policeman, gave a start, smiled, and said, "Good evening, García."

"Good evening, sir." The cop returned the smile, put the gun in his pocket, and bowed.

The throat squeezer already had his gun slipped from sight. He stepped forward. He said, "It is a great pleasure to see you, Don Luis." His voice was like oil.

Navarro ignored him. He was looking at Blasco, eyebrows fractionally raised. The fair-haired policeman bowed again, smiled a lot more, and turned from one to the other. "Don Luis Navarro, this is Señor Blasco, head of the division in Cádiz. Señor Blasco is in this vicinity on business."

They shook hands, telling each other how they were overwhelmed and enchanted. I stood up. I said, "Good evening, Don Luis."

He turned to me then. Slowly he held out his hands, palms upward, in mock supplication. "My good friend," he said, "here I am once again to solicit your pardon. I was not on hand to receive you for dinner. It was right that you left in disgust."

Everyone looked at me. The cops had their hands in their pockets in case I should make a run for it. I said in Spanish, "On the contrary, señor. It was rude of me to leave without explanation. But there is a reason. At your *ganadería* this afternoon I witnessed for the first time the true splendor of the perfect fighting bull. A great and uplifting experience. I am afraid that afterward it caused me to drink too much wine. I left to avoid making a spectacle of myself."

He gazed at me fully ten seconds, not moving a muscle. Then his eyelids flickered and his face withered into a smile. He said warmly, "You make me happy. My bulls were good."

"They were magnificent," I said. "I celebrated them. I became very drunk in the company of a fat man named Montero. Later I discovered that we were drinking for totally different reasons."

Navarro slapped himself lightly on the thigh. He burst into a deep chuckle that slowly grew to a full-sized laugh. "Poor Montero, I fear he is jealous," he gurgled. "He knows his strain will never be as great as mine. Poor Montero."

I laughed too. I said, "He was still complaining just before dinner when I left. Red in the face and very bitter and very drunk. Carrying it too far, I think. I left for fear of doing the same thing in the opposite direction. I would have argued with him."

We were laughing together. "Very kind, my good friend, very kind. I was most upset when the servants told me you had left, just as the tables were being set."

"I was not hungry," I said. "I was emotionally exhausted from the bulls." I put a hand on his shoulder and made the gambit. "But now I am rested."

"Excellent!" He reached up and patted the back of my neck. Coming from him, the ordinary Spanish gesture surprised me. He said, "That is why I am here. To take you back. My car is waiting for us outside on the driveway."

"Then we go," I said, and waited. The policemen didn't move.

Don Luis smiled from one to the other, bowed to Blasco. "Enchanted to have made your acquaintance, señor."

"I as much."

The two cops still had their hands in their pockets. I looked slantwise at Blasco. "Good-by," I said.

"Good-by, Señor Oovilliams. We will take up in the morning the matter of your visa."

"Visa? Nothing else?"

"To be truthful," he said, "I have nothing else. I am very sorry about that."

"I, too," I said, "if you can believe it."

"I cannot."

"It is difficult," I said. "*Adiós.*" And for nerves, or for no reason, I held out my hand.

He ignored it. "Good-by." He turned away.

I walked toward the French windows, my arm linked with Don Luis'. The dark-haired policeman watched us go, slowly turning his round pudding head.

Blasco had been working a bluff. Nothing to go on. For the first time I could think clearly. I took it in detail. First and foremost, I was absolved of Silva's murder. What else did Blasco have that he hadn't had last night, when he'd been helpless to stop me? No evidence to substantiate my smuggling. No proof I was in the boat he'd helped to sink. No proof that I'd even been in Silva's office. Nothing. Only my lack of visa. It was not sufficient reason for pulling me in.

I thought of that again. And I was wrong. The visa supplied ample reason if he wanted to make it so. He could have taken me to a secluded police station, indulged in more questioning. So why not? Because he was an honest policeman? Maybe, but it wasn't enough. Then what?

The thought dropped over me like a big dank cobweb. He'd let me go in the way a cat releases a mouse. I tried to figure his reasoning, his scheme. I could think of only one obvious aspect: that he'd need to keep a tail on me.

I had to get rid of it. Now. Try to find Paco, avoid El Mudo, not talk to anyone lest I implicate others. I tried concentrate on what Don Luis was saying.

His car was on the driveway. There were two men beside it, waiting respectfully, their hands held in front of them. I looked over my shoulder and Blasco had stepped outside the window. He was watching us. Navarro was saying, "And the car will be at your disposal any time you wish to drive back. I shall tell the man to wait only for you."

I tightened my grip on his arm and steered him toward the Volkswagen. "But you will have many guests who will wish to go home," I said. "I would not ask so much when I have conveyance of my own."

"It is nothing, nothing at all," he protested. He made a small movement as if to pull away. I held him tight.

"I insist," I said, and looked back again. Blasco was still there.

I opened the door of the big Volkswagen. I said, "I wish to show you how Americans drive." I almost pushed him in under the wheel to the far side. He began to protest. I drowned him out. I started the engine. I said loudly, "Very interesting. The policemen were looking for a man who did a murder in Cádiz." Don Luis leaned from his side window and called something.

All at once there was an air of craziness about everything. The two men ran from Navarro's car and shouted something either to him or to me. One of them tried to open my door. Blasco left his post at the window and began walking swiftly toward us. I roared the engine very loud. I leaned from the side window and pushed away the man who was trying to open the door. I shouted, "Look out, I'm going to turn!" I worked the clutch and the car leaped forward a few yards. I swung the wheel and backed, swung again and hit Navarro's car a grating sideswipe. We went barreling down the drive.

I wanted the second vehicle. The cops must have left it on the road, since I hadn't heard them coming. I turned the corner of the drive and the car was a hundred yards away, standing to the side. I swung onto the adjoining field. The Volkswagen rattled and jumped. I turned diagonally and stood on the accelerator and prayed.

We hit sideways. I heard the metal crumpling. The small police car turned right over and then we were back on the road again, weaving drunkenly. I felt I could breathe.

"Señor!" Navarro gasped. "Señor, what are you doing?"

The chance had paid off. A good big car will always get the better of a good little car. I wasn't sure about the one back on the driveway. I wanted to leave them some conveyance and maybe I'd hit it too hard. I said, "I'm sorry about this, Navarro."

He was leaning hard against me, gasping with every jolt. The night air whistled through the windows. He said, "Señor, it is the wine. Please, I will drive."

"No," I said.

"You have damaged this fine big car."

"Yes," I said. "It is not important."

He fell silent. The moon was sinking. I turned the headlights up full, scanning the rocky radius of the beams for Paco, but the countryside was deserted. I said, "To where does this track eventually lead?"

He was gripping my arm with both hands, to keep himself from bouncing. The words came jerkily. "If you do not turn off at my establishment, then you continue right around the southern coast of Spain. It is a bad road, little more than a mule track. Farther on the surface deteriorates even more."

Somehow he was still contriving to be formal. I thought of the way I'd seen him with Lavinia Hatherton, wondered what his reaction would be if I brought up the subject. I could see how she might have been attracted by his unshatterable exterior. A polite man always has an edge with a naturally ill-mannered woman.

"I don't mind about the surface," I said. "You mean if I keep going, I'll get eventually right around to Cartagena?"

"Yes." He released my arm. His two bony hands gripped the seat. "Señor, you are thinking of leaving us?"

"Yes."

"I trust not for a long time yet."

"Now," I said. "I'm going immediately."

We were halfway to the village. We hit a large rock. Navarro bounced almost to the roof and clutched me again. He was wheezing. "I am distressed to hear it, señor. I wanted that we should get to know each other better."

"Yes," I said. "Sorry about that. And sorry I can't take you back to your *ganadería*."

"You wish me to accompany you all the way to Cartagena? I do not understand. I am afraid that—"

I said, "Enchanted to have made your acquaintance, Don Luis. Forgive me for the last time, but you're part of the delaying tactics." I pulled up the car with a jerk. "Get out."

"I don't—"

I thrust across him, pushed open the door. "Get out!"

"But Señor Williams—"

I shoved him hard. He fell out and sprawled in the dust. "Good-by," I said.

I slammed the door and drove hell for leather for the village.

Chapter Eleven

Twenty minutes had gone by. The moon was sunk behind the village houses. The Volkswagen was parked in an inky-shadowed village street, invisible until you walked into it. I waited with my back flat against the side wall of a house, my head edging the corner so I could peer across the square.

The fiesta was still on. The village band, in the center of the square now, puffed valiantly at a *paso doble*. The crowd had thinned, mainly because most of the children had been put to bed. But there were still a great many people.

The atmosphere was drunken, highly excited. The couples stepped frenetically in time to the music. Over by the kiosk the village boys, inexhaustibly energetic, were wrestling and jumping and horsing around, their yipping cries echoing up toward the waning moonlight.

There was a girl. She was perhaps the local bad lot. She was twisting and weaving in a solitary dance, castanets high above her head, a group of men surrounding her, their expressions growing slowly more wolfish as they said, "*Olé, olé,*" to encourage her. In the church was darkness. Through the open door I could see only the red glimmer above the altar.

I waited, wondering if my thin scheme would succeed. I had picked up Don Luis solely to plant an idea. I wanted the police to spend the night chasing me three or four hundred useless miles in the direction of Cartagena. But maybe they wouldn't see Don Luis in the darkness, and would pass him by. And in my eagerness to lay a false clue, maybe I'd hit the first car too hard. I stood back in the darkness and hoped.

The band switched to a Mexican tune. You seldom hear them in Spain. But all the men were a little drunk now and they took it up with gusto, yi-yipping enthusiastically at every eight-bar interval. The solitary girl stopped dancing because of the erratic rhythm. It was strange to her. She just rattled her castanets. The circle of men moved in on her, all laughing. The boys at the kiosk had turned to new delights. They'd got a blanket from somewhere and were tossing a yowling friend high in the air. From the corner of my eye I saw indistinctly a very drunken man, head bent, run staggering from somewhere and into the church. Two things happened at once.

Paco appeared. He was walking slowly, weaving, head flung back like an epileptic's, feet going down toes first as if his legs had lost their use, only one more tottering man among many. He looked dazedly about him. He started in the direction of the church. I jumped into the square to get him and Navarro's car came chugging from the main street. I ran back again.

The light from the flares gleamed over the crinkled metal where I'd hit it with the Volkswagen. The two servants stood on the far running board, to balance the vehicle from the smash or because they weren't allowed to sit inside with their superiors. Blasco sat at the wheel, the fair-haired policeman beside him. Navarro was in the back with the other cop. They were all talking.

They drove straight on in the direction of the *ganadería*, in the direction of Cartagena. I heard the fading throb of the engine above all the noise. I waited. I counted sixty. Paco was falling up the steps of the church. I ran frantically around the edge of the square.

The boy from the blanket landed at my feet. He straightened up. He grabbed me. I fell. I stumbled backward and the blanket tightened and I was flung high into the air. The band played. The dancers yipped. The boys made screaming rocket noises every time they tossed me.

I shouted, "Let me down!" They laughed. I went higher. Among all the screams I heard a different scream from the church. Nobody noticed. The music continued. I was flung so high I could see the roofs of the houses.

"Let me down!" They gave a final great heave, caught me, lowered me. I lay on the ground, surrounded by their grinning, toothy, drunken young faces.

"*Qué cosa*," said one of them. A dozen hands reached out and dragged me to my feet. I shook them off. I ran for the steps of the church, stumbling. I hurtled inside and I could see nothing. I stood motionless.

I said, "Paco." The walls whispered *pacopacopaco*. There was no reply. I walked halfway down the aisle and stood still again. "Paco," I said. "Paco, it's me, Bill. Where are you, Paco?"

There was a long silence. I took a soft step forward and the shuffling of my foot sibilated around the vaultings of the roof. The music outside, all the dancing, shouting people, belonged to a different world. "Paco," I said.

He sobbed. He was up by the altar rail. I ran toward him.

He was sprawled with his back on the shallow step, his feet wide apart. In the glimmering red light I saw him. The knife had been driven deep into his chest. His two hands were gripping the hilt, trying to pull it out again.

I fell beside him. I said, "Leave it alone." He groaned. The knife clattered softly on the carpet. My tongue was cleaving to the roof of my mouth. The music outside was still playing.

"I did not kill him," he whispered.

I got an arm behind his neck, raised him gently. I didn't know what to do. I said fatuously, "What have you done?"

"I did not kill him," he repeated. "I was looking for you, Beel, to kill you, Beel. He was drunk when I saw him. He ran away and I followed. In the church he was waiting for me."

I looked around. There was no sound. I lowered Paco to the step and stood up and struck a match, held it until it burned my fingers. There was no one. I dropped beside him again. The altar light was shining on his face.

"Griswold," I said.

He nodded weakly. "Beel, I think really I could not have killed you. But I believed already I was responsible for Griswold. It makes a man insane."

"Don't talk," I said. "I'll get a doctor."

His hand gripped my wrist with unexpected strength. "No, I wish to go home. The doctor is in the opposite direction, a long way."

"Then a hospital," I said.

He shook his head again. "It is no use, *amigo*. Take me home to María. I am going to die."

"No," I said. But I knew he was speaking the truth. "I don't have many friends. We'll go to a hospital. I can't afford to lose you."

"Hah," he grinned, "the way you talk. Is not a bad thing to die, Beel. I did not kill Griswold. I am happy. Take me home."

"I'll get—"

His hand on my wrist was a clamp. "There will be trouble for you. For everybody. I die anyway. Promise to take me home. Promise."

"I promise," I said.

He nodded to me. He smiled. Then he closed his eyes wearily.

I picked him up, holding him against my chest. Through the main door of the church were the band and the dancers and somebody else being tossed in the air by the screaming boys. I went out through the door by the altar, along the passage, into the open air. The noises from over in the square burst with fantastic loudness into the blackness of the almost deserted back street.

Two men were passing. They dragged a third between them. His arms were over their shoulders. "Good night," one of them said happily.

"Good night," I said.

They passed. The second sober one looked back. He laughed. He said, "In every man's life comes a time when he has to take home his drunken little brother."

"Yes," I said. "Good night."

I went past the *carbón* shop, hurrying. I turned into the pitchy street and ran for the Volkswagen. I was thinking of nothing anymore. My brain had stopped. I opened the door and put Paco in the back and pulled aside some ropes in order to rest him on a pile of sacking, taking off my jacket to cradle his head. The gun was still tucked behind my waistband. The cops had missed it. I slid it under the seat. I said, "Paco."

He moaned softly. His eyes opened.

"A hospital."

"You promised," he said. "Why make the trouble? Think of María."

"I do," I said. "All the time. I love her."

I put a hand to his chest. He was soaked with blood. I stroked his forehead. I was thinking of how he'd be shaken by the trip home.

He reached out feebly and pulled at my shirt. His eyes seemed twice their ordinary size. He said, "You think maybe a priest, Beel? A priest says nothing unless you give permission."

"Anything at all, Paco."

"But we go home as you promised. María will prefer it."

"I'll get him," I said. "You'll be all right?"

"*Sí.*"

I shut the door and ran. Round the corner, past the *carbonería*, along the deserted street and into the square. No one was dancing. The band had switched to a song: "The Four Mule Drivers." The people surrounded them thickly, double-clapping their hands, singing the words at the tops of their voices. "Of the four mule drivers, Mother, the one with the gray mule has stolen my heart." They sounded happier than I'd ever be again.

I grabbed a man on the fringe of the crowd. I swung him round. He thrust his wineskin into my hands and grinned, still singing. "Oh, why do you look for light for the house, when from his soft face are shining live coals?"

The man nodded at me. He tapped the wineskin. "Drink, *amigo*," he said drunkenly. "Tomorrow we work for another year."

I said, "Where does the priest live?"

He pointed at a small house next to the church. "Drink my health," he said.

I pushed the wineskin back at him and ran weaving between the straggling edges of the crowd. The band switched to another song with no break but a change of tempo. The clapping stopped. I hammered on the door. It opened immediately.

"*Vete!*" the woman snapped without looking at me. "Go!" She tried to close the door again. I stuck in a foot and pushed with my shoulder.

"I wish to see the priest," I said.

She snorted with derision. She was a tiny old woman of about eighty. She looked tired. "Another one," she said. "Every fiesta it happens. They drink too much wine and they get drunk and they want to talk to Father Juan about the state of their miserable souls. Well, he's gone to bed!"

"Please let me see him," I said.

She looked at me then, little black eyes flickering over my face. "Oh," she said grudgingly and opened the door wide enough for me to get in, closing it immediately. "I bring him," she said, and disappeared.

The room was small. It looked like a study. The oil lamp gave enough light to see the walls, lined with devotional books. Out in the square the crowd sang mutedly of how the shepherds were leaving for Estremadura, how the mountains were sad and shadowy and the girls were weeping because the shepherds were going.

The priest came in. He was a tall, thin man, perhaps sixty, very brown-faced from the sun. He wore a nightshirt covered by a dressing gown, and on his feet were black slippers decorated with gold thread. He hesitated, looked at me keenly, then came over and put a hand on my shoulder. He said, "Why do you cry, son?"

I hadn't known about it. I wiped a hand over my face. I said, "Can you come with me?"

"Yes." He took the material of his dressing gown between thumb and forefinger. He shook it. "It will take only a moment."

"A boy is dying," I said. "There is a long way to travel, but I have a car outside. I will wait while you dress."

"It is unnecessary. I have a car. Tell me where to go."

I feared that. Paco might die on the way home. María would never forgive me if I had no priest. I said, "Come with me."

He shook his head. "In a few hours I have a Mass. I must be certain of returning. I will drive myself."

"Then follow me," I said. "I shall wait on the other side of the square. A big blue car like a small autobus."

He looked at me curiously. "I saw you this evening. You are a foreigner. Are you a Catholic?"

"Yes," I said. "Please hurry."

He studied me an instant more. He nodded and disappeared through a doorway. I let myself back into the square.

The band had stopped playing. The bandsmen were drinking wine from skins. The sadness of the last song seemed to have dampened a little the high spirit of the gathering. People were dispersing to their homes. I moved with them. I started across the square.

I was halfway across when someone tapped my shoulder. My heart jumped. The police, I thought. Griswold. I wheeled around. It was Rex Hatherton. He said, "What-ho, Bill? Enjoying the shindig?"

I stared at him.

"Breaking up now, I think," he said. "By Jove, can these people sing! Did you see the dancing?"

I said, "Excuse me, I'm in a hurry." I turned from him. He fell in beside me and walked fast, almost trotting. I said, "I don't want you along, Hatherton."

"Are you angry with me about something?"

I said, "I haven't seen your wife and I don't want to see you. Go away."

"Now look here," he said. "I want to talk to you. It's quite important. Can't we go to that tavern over there?"

Without pausing I shoved him sideways. He fell over his own legs and sat down. I ran around the corner, past the *carbón* shop, down the dark street to the Volkswagen. I got behind the wheel and looked over the seat. "You all right, Paco?"

There was no answer.

"You all right?"

He moved slightly. I saw the whites of his eyes. "Hello," he said.

I said, "Paquito, listen. We go now. I have the priest. He will follow us home in his car. Tell me if it hurts you and I will drive slowly."

He moved again. "I no longer bleed," he said. "I am good. I do not hurt one bit."

"Let me take you to a hospital."

"Beel, I wish to see María."

"Yes," I said. "All right. We'll go to the square and wait for the priest. He won't be long. Try to lie still, Paquito. Do not speak."

"I told you," he said. "I am good."

"Good," I said, and started the engine and backed up the narrow street.

I parked on the far side of the square. I was almost hoping now that the police would appear, to take matters out of my hands, force Paco to go to a hospital. The band had resumed with its second wind. A lot of people were gone, but there were still more than a hundred present, all split into circles for small *jotas*. There were not enough women. About twenty men were dancing with each other as partners, horsing it up, some of them pivoting on the other man's arm to swing both legs high in the air, then falling on their backs and lying on the ground and curling with laughter. I sat watching the door of the priest's house. Paco made no sound.

"Williams," a voice said.

Rex Hatherton came along the side of the Volkswagen and reached for the door handle. I thrust myself through the window and pushed him hard. He staggered back two steps. He stood there, staring at me.

I said, "The car isn't yours. Keep your nose out of it."

A man and his wife walked by, going home. The man had a sleeping child over his shoulder. Rex Hatherton said, "Oh, I see. That's what it was offended you. You're perfectly right, of course. I had no justification whatever."

I said, "Beat it, go away! Your wife isn't here."

He didn't move. "I know," he said. "She's back at the *ganadería*. It's you I've been looking for. There's something I want to talk about, something important."

"Not to me."

"Yes," he said. "It's two thousand pounds important. That's about six thousand dollars." He turned his head. "The tavern's still open. Let's go and have a drink."

I looked at him closely for the first time. I'd had an idea that he was a weak man, somehow ineffectual, an impression helped by his light-sounding accent. He turned back and I saw that I'd been badly mistaken. His eyes belied the voice. His face was like stone. He was tough without a trace of fake.

"Well?" he said.

"You drunk?"

He smiled. "I repeat, six thousand dollars drunk, and that possibly only a down payment. You have information of value to me. Perhaps more than I think. We might end by working together." He paused. He said, "Let me sit inside with you. It's as good a place as any to talk. We can come to terms."

He reached again for the handle. A horn started honking. I shot a glance in the rear mirror and a battered old black car came streaking up behind us. The priest was at the wheel, pumping the horn button.

"What about it?"

"Some other time." I started the engine.

"There won't be another time. You'll regret it."

"I don't know what you're talking about."

"Yes, you do," he said. "You'll regret it bitterly. Don Luis isn't that much of a friend to you."

I didn't answer. I let in the clutch and rolled away. The priest was three yards behind us.

The road had never seemed so rough. The rest of the village lay silent. We passed the outskirts and I listened through the window to the dying sound of the band. The moon was almost gone. The rocks rattled under our wheels. I turned my head to the side. "How is it, Paco?"

He was a long time answering. His voice came weakly. "Good, Beel. I am very good."

"Anything I can do?"

"I don't know," he said. "Yes. The song about the shepherd—you know it, Beel?"

"Yes."

He said nothing else.

"You all right, Paco?"

"Yes."

So I sang it to him. The headlights from the priest's car kept catching in the rear-view mirror and flashing into my eyes.

A light shone from the window. She was waiting. I lifted Paco from the Volkswagen and the priest saw what I was doing and came running forward. I started across the field. He said, "Is this the boy?"

"Yes."

"Why did you deceive me?"

"Go ahead and open the door," I said.

Paco was making no sound. A sickness was on me. I walked through the rectangle of yellow light and into the room just as María stood up and said, "Father Juan!" She saw me. The color drained from her face. She said nothing more.

I carried Paco through to the other room and put him on the bed. He lay weightless. The priest came in with the lamp, placed it on the table, and stood about a yard from me, staring at the side of my face. María had dropped to her knees beside the bed.

The priest's mouth was a thin line. "Are you responsible for this?"

I couldn't make my own answer. "Am I, María?" I said.

She turned her head, looked up into Father Juan's eyes. "He is Paco's friend," she said without hesitation. "He would do nothing to him."

The priest said, "Why do I get no answer from you?"

On the bed Paco made a faint movement with his hand. I got down beside him. "Paco!"

He spoke without opening his eyes, his voice coming faintly. "What a foolishness to cause so much trouble," he said, and gave a weak grin. "Father, I hear what you ask my friend Beel. He has done only what I tell him."

The priest pushed me aside. He sat on the edge of the bed. "Who harmed you, son?"

"There is an American named Griswold, a bad man. He put a knife in me." The kid drew a deep shuddering breath. "All the same, it is better this way, Father. I thought I had killed him before and it made me mad in my head."

The priest looked at me again and said, "Forgive me." He put a hand on my shoulder to indicate that I should stand up. He said gently, "Take María into the other room. I will tell you when to return."

Paco opened his eyes, turned his head, looked at his sister. He reached out and managed to touch her cheek. He said, "María, don't think of those bad things I told you because you are in love with Beel. He is a good man. I am happy you love him. There is nothing else important."

He closed his eyes again. "You are not angry with me, huh, María?"

She leaned over and kissed him.

"Please," the priest said.

I put my arm around her shoulders and took her into the other room.

"He is going to die," she said.

Through the closed door I could hear faintly the whispering of Paco, the low murmur of the priest. I said, "Yes." I held her in my arms.

She didn't cry. She said, "Beel, why? He is only a little boy. Why is he going to die?"

"I don't know," I said. I wanted to comfort her. "Circumstances," I said. "They begin and end somewhere, but no one can ever tell. Maybe this started when Paco was in his cradle. Maybe it was only yesterday. We get to know only the immediate things. I suppose the rest belong to God."

I was thinking of Griswold. He wasn't God's. He was mine.

She broke from my arms and sat in a chair. Her elbows rested on the table and her head was lowered. She remained like that and I tried to think of something to say. There wasn't anything.

She looked up. Her eyes were fixed on my face. Her expression was altered. "I cannot go away with you now, Beel," she said. She was Spanish. I knew what was in her mind.

"No," I said, "and I can't go. In a few weeks Paco would have been my brother. He's my brother now. Today brought him all the way back from the mountains. It will be for him and for me too."

"You know who the man is?"

"Griswold, an American. In a little while I'll go look for him. I won't get hurt."

"I know," she said.

"We will go away together afterward."

"Yes," she said.

I said, "Do you love me, María?"

She rose from the chair and came and put her hands about my face. She started to cry. I took her shoulders, shaking my head. I said, "No, not now. He doesn't want to see you like that. It is the wrong memory for him."

She raised both hands and wiped her eyes. She smiled at me. Love is a devastation and an agony. In the other room the voices ceased. I heard footsteps cross the floor. The priest opened the door. He said, "Come in now."

The kid had his head turned, waiting for us. His eyes were wide open. He grinned broadly, as if he were playing a joke on us. He tried to raise his hand. He didn't have the strength. He said, "Foolish ones, here."

She knelt down and put her head on the pillow beside him. They gazed long at each other and he was still smiling. I sat on the edge of the bed.

I took the kid's hand and held it tightly. The priest was standing over us.

"These two," Paco said. *"Qué tontos!* Their children will be all lunatics."

"The worst will be the first one," I said. "A boy named Francisco that we will call Paco for short. A bad handicap for any child, but I'll do it anyway."

He tried to turn his head. He couldn't. "The poor little one," he said. "But a good idea, huh, María? Beel will think of the fine times we had together. Isn't it a good idea, María?"

"Yes, my loved one," she said. "Yes, my little brother."

"A very good idea," he said. "You and Beel are my people."

She moved her head and kissed him on the lips. They smiled at one another.

The priest touched her shoulder. He said, "You must stand up now."

Chapter Twelve

María talked to the priest. I didn't know what they were saying. I was in the kitchen, drinking the last of the cognac, trying to stop myself from shaking. It took a long time.

I went back into the other room. Paco was dead. I took a last look at him. He lay on the bed with a crucifix held to his blood-matted chest. I said, "I'm going now," and the priest came over to me and we went through the door.

María was making a supplication. I could have repeated it with her, and that surprised me. I hadn't said a prayer for the dead since my mother died when I was seven. I walked across the field with Father Juan and tried to remember what my mother had looked like.

The priest said, "Well, son?"

It brought me to earth. I tried to think clearly and didn't do so well. I started for the Volkswagen and then I knew I had to stay away from it. Now above all times I didn't want the police to get me. Not yet. I said, "Can you give me a lift to the village?"

"Of course."

We drove a way in silence. The darkness formed a wall around the car. The priest could drive well, and his hands were thin and hard. I could see he was used to manual labor. I wondered what sort he did. I said, "Want a cigarette?"

"Thank you, I don't smoke."

I lit one for myself. In the flare of the match his face was grim. He started without preamble. He said, "What has been happening?"

"It's a long story. Too long to tell."

"I have time."

"I haven't."

"The boy said a great deal, but I can reveal nothing unless I hear it from you."

"You won't."

"But he mentioned the name Griswold while you were there. That at least I can tell the police."

"Stay away from them a while," I said. "Leave it till morning."

"It is nearly morning now."

He gave a sidelong glance at me. He stiffened. "No, son," he said. "You are not a Spaniard. There is no need to do anything. Revenge is an evil."

"And murder?"

"The fusion of two bad things does not result in good. Come with me to the police. It is a long drive, forty kilometers on the other side of the village. We can talk."

"I don't wish to talk. And I daren't see the police. I'm a *contrabandista*."

"I know. María told me."

"Is it such a bad thing to be?"

He didn't answer.

I said, "Stay away from the police for María's sake. I'm going to settle my business, then go back to the house and take her out of the country with me. I'm in love with her. I'm going to marry her. She's expecting my baby."

"You misbehaved with her, that fine girl? I have known her since she was a child. It was bad of you."

"All right," I said. "I'm ashamed. But don't preach me any sermons. Not now."

His car was very old. It rattled. We drove almost ten minutes before he spoke again. "When were you last at confession?"

"It's none of your business."

"Then what is my business?"

"I'm sorry," I said. "I apologize." I looked at his profile. I felt he was a good man. "I'll go soon," I said. "Maybe next week."

His face relaxed for the first time.

I said, "Can you promise me two things?"

"I don't know."

"If I get out of this, María will go with me. We shall have to leave Paco. I want you to look after him."

"Certainly. And the second?"

"The man I am looking for is drunk. I know now it was he that ran into the church ahead of Paco. He may be collapsed somewhere. Perhaps somebody has seen him. Stay away from the police for two hours. Give me time."

"Impossible. There is a duty to God and a citizen's duty. Both must be fulfilled."

"Paco told me you'd say nothing."

"Paco was dying. You misunderstood him."

"It's not much to ask."

"No," he said.

There was nothing more. I knew he was inflexible. We drove the rest of the way in silence.

On the outskirts of the village all the lanterns had been put out. We drove up the silent main street and into the square and a scattering of people still remained. The bandsmen were sitting on the church steps, drinking wine. The others, all men and mostly drunk, were gathered about them. A low buzz of conversation rose out of the quietness, sporadic bursts of laughter that echoed from the walls of the dark houses. I wondered what time it was.

Father Juan said, "You are sure you will not accompany me?"

"Quite."

He pulled up. I got out and walked around to the other side. "Thanks for the lift."

"It was nothing." He leaned from the side window. "What is your name, son?"

"They call me Williams. My real name is Robert Aliston."

"A very pronounceable name for a foreigner." He smiled faintly. "It is a long forty kilometers to the police station," he said. "A bad road. But I shall go as fast as I can."

"Good-by," I said.

He drove off.

I went up the steps past the men and searched the church. I did not have much hope that Griswold had stayed in the immediate vicinity, and he was not there. I came back outside and a drunken man, not a bandsman, had seized a trumpet. He was trying to play a tune. All the others were laughing.

I had to speak loudly to make myself heard. I said, "I am looking for a foreigner." No one paid any heed.

I selected the man who seemed least drunk. I put my arm round his shoulders to get his attention. He turned a smiling face to me, a set of very white teeth. "I am seeking a foreigner," I said, "a tall man like myself, but fatter. He has fair hair. He is probably drunk. Have you seen him?"

The smile got broader. The man widened his eyes. "*Probably* drunk!" he exploded. "Any man who is not drunk by this time is no man." He poked an accusing finger at my collarbone. "Friend, you are not drunk," he said, and thrust his wineskin at me. "Here, *chico*, tilt it." He turned back to laughing at his comrade.

The trumpet was emitting a series of squawking blasts. I sat down on the church steps and held up the goatskin and the wine jetted coolly into my throat. I was not tired anymore.

I laid the skin down and looked up at the sky. It was black. I compressed the aching grief in me and tried once again to think, going right back to the beginning, covering everything.

A time passed. And then the amateur at the trumpet began to play a recognizable tune. Everyone applauded. I rose to my feet and said good night and walked away.

The darkness was thick. Somehow it was permeable. Maybe my eyes were getting used to it. I could see a few yards in all directions, the rocks on the road ahead of me, the scrubby plants a few yards out in the fields on either side. I still looked for Griswold, but the hope of finding him had left me. A drunken man will stagger anywhere and sleep.

Up ahead the outbuildings of Navarro's place showed dimly. In the main building was one yellow light, shining from an upstairs window. The party was over. I wondered again what time it was. I wondered about a lot of things. Silva dead. Paco dead. Griswold responsible in both cases. Then Page. Which meant that Griswold had somehow discovered the base from which I operated. So he had gone himself, or sent other men, to burgle the Marquesa's house when he thought that all the occupants would be away at the fiesta.

But there was something that didn't fit. How had he known that everyone would be away? And once he had the papers, why did he hang around? I shifted to Rex Hatherton.

This was the thought that had struck me as I sat on the steps of the church. An insanely jealous husband had brought his wife to stay at the house of a man he knew had been her lover. It made no sense. "A tough life," she had said of him. "Money and jealousy." Maybe the former emotion had overcome the latter.

On his own admission, Rex Hatherton had been in the district only three days. The trouble started thirty-six hours ago. It fitted neatly. Until I gave it a second thought.

Six thousand dollars for information. A lot of money. Plus the possibility that we might end by working together. It sounded fine. But what information did he want? The Marquesa's safe had already been robbed when he made the offer. If he was implicated even remotely, he would have known by then that any information I could give him was already in his possession.

There was one point more. Spain is an insular country, full of insular people. A three-day acquaintance is not sufficient to secure the confidence of a Spaniard to the extent that he'll undertake dangerous work for you. The man at the ambush, the one with a mustache, had been a local man. Very clearly, somebody was working from this side.

Which brought the biggest problem of all. How had they known about the appointment with Ferrer?

I went softly toward the *ganadería*, avoiding the small rocks, the loose pebbles. I had to see Hatherton. I wanted to know what he expected to buy for six thousand dollars. It was a starting point, my only one. And I'd start anywhere if it led eventually to Griswold.

I thought of him. There was no anger anymore, only a consuming and implacable hatred. I was going to kill him. I owed it to María, and to myself, and most of all to Paco. I was the one that had to do it, not the police. It was I that had first brought Griswold into the picture.

I got off the road. There might still be someone about—the police, Blasco; conceivably he had stayed in the company of Don Luis. I sidetracked to the field and went at an angle. I wanted to approach the house from the left-hand side, staying in the shadows of the outbuildings. The solitary light shone down from the window. The darkness seemed to be getting thinner all the time.

I wondered if any guests had stayed the night, whether the Marquesa had stayed. Perhaps she was in bed, too drunk yet to have discovered about the safe. But she'd be puzzling about Page. He too should have been in her bed. She was like that when she got drunk.

I thought of El Mudo, trying to speculate where he had taken Page's body. I wondered if he was still weeping. Then I remembered the moment I had seen Paco die. I wanted to weep myself.

I slid along the wall of the outermost building and crossed an open space. I got to another building that smelled strongly of cattle. Up ahead the three bulls were still in the arena, snorting and scuffling, as if they fought each other. One of them kicked against the fence.

I got to the corner of the wall. There were two more buildings between me and the house, but they were widely spread. I looked around. The safest way to go was to skirt the arena. There was a narrow alley opposite me, running between the first row of bleachers and the arena. I dodged into it.

On the other side of the railed fence the bulls still butted each other. There was a *burladero* in front of me, one of those rectangular shields inside the ring, jutting out from the fence, with just enough room at each side to permit a man to slip into the alleyway. It's where the bullfighters dodge when something goes wrong, or they are unable to dominate the bull when he charges. I edged forward a little. I looked into the ring.

I could see nothing distinctly at first. Then the animals drew closer, their heads near the ground. They weren't butting each other, except in-advertently. Between them was a bundle. They were trampling on it, goring it, tossing it jerkily across the ring. One of them retreated a lit-tle and ran forward and flung up its head. The bundle soared through the air. It hit the fence. It fell soggily to the ground. I was so near I could have touched it. It was the Marquesa.

I reached out. The bulls were quicker. They wheeled together and ran flank to flank across the ring, scooping the Marquesa in front of them. I acted instinctively, without thought. I slipped through the narrow opening at the side of the *burladero* into the sandy arena and started across the ring. Then I came to my senses. But I was too late. One of the bulls turned from its companions. It charged. I ran for my life.

There was no time for the fence. I streaked for the *burladero* and hur-tled behind it into the alleyway. The bull's horns crashed into the other side. I stood motionless and listened to its snorting. It butted again, en-raged.

My heart pounded up in my throat. I heard hoofs on sand and the other two animals came over. They rubbed against each other. Suddenly, with terrific impact, they all seemed to smash into the fence at once. The wood shivered. There was a shuffling. One of them came to the side and tried to thrust its head into the slot between the *burladero* and the fence. Another tried to vault the fence, and would have made it if he'd had a longer head start. Fighting bulls are all huge. The darkness made this one seem the size of a locomotive.

It was idiotic to have jumped in. The Marquesa was beyond help. I had to get myself out again. I turned my back on the fence that the bulls were battering and put up my hands to climb up to the first row of bleachers. Something brushed my hand. A gun jammed against my fore-head and a voice said softly, "Get down again." I did as I was told.

The quietness was absolute. The bulls seemed to have stopped breath-ing. I waited an eternity. I said, "Can you help me out of here, please?"

"On the contrary," he said. "It is my intention to force you into the ring."

"But why?"

"There are many reasons," he said. "Let us say it is because you mocked my bulls. Go now and mock them to their faces."

"You have it wrong, Don Luis," I said. "This afternoon I thought they were magnificent."

"Liar," he said levelly. He hopped down into the alleyway and gestured with the gun. "Turn around." I turned around. He pushed the gun into my back. "You were not here this afternoon. You used the story simply as an excuse to get away from the policemen. You will not, however, get away from my bulls. Try. Go and rescue your mistress. It will make a fitting end for a sordid story."

"You put her in there." I said.

"Yes," he said, "I did. She had an unfortunate recovery of memory. Last evening I excused myself from her to make a phone call. Less than a minute later she opened a door and saw me putting down the receiver. A very short call."

"To North Africa."

"Yes. That is what the Marquesa said when she remembered. She mentioned Mr. Silva. She was very unpleasant and very drunk."

"Let me out of here," I said.

He ignored me. He said, "Very drunk. Some of my guests remarked upon it. They will make a good story from all this. The woman who got so drunk at the party that afterward she wandered into the bullring. Being Spaniards, they will laugh over it. But they will not laugh about you. The fact of a young man being killed while trying to rescue a woman will make a strong appeal to the romantic side of their natures."

He prodded me with the gun. He said, "Go now, Señor Williams. If you do not, I shall shoot you. I can do it with impunity. The police are scouring the countryside for you. They warned me. I shall plead self-defense. It will not be difficult." He laughed softly. "But naturally I prefer the bulls. Considering your views on bullfighting, it is the more poetic method."

I said, "Navarro, you're insane."

"You know I am not," he said. "This is merely a business move. I am ridding myself of a rival, as I did with the Marquesa. I thought you had been taken care of already today. My men assured me you were lying dead at the foot of a mountain. Then this evening one of them thought he was seeing a ghost. He reported to me. I came to fetch you, to deal with you, but unfortunately the police were there. Were they investigating the death of the other young American?"

"No," I said. I was so frightened of the bulls that my brain had thickened into utter confusion. He couldn't be the Association or he never would have dealt with Silva. Yet he had been responsible for the ambush.

Suddenly I got a glimmering of light. I said, "Did you know Silva is dead?"

It got a reaction. Momentarily the gun wavered. The voice remained smooth. "Did you kill him, Mr. Williams?"

"No," I said. "I left all that to your side. May I ask a question?"

"Well, yes," he said. "I am rather enjoying this situation. Do not think, though, that you can alter our ultimate conclusion. Should anyone arrive, I shall shoot you immediately."

The bulls moved. One of them brushed the barrier, then all three trod softly to the other side of the ring. I said, "Silva phoned you about me last night."

"It is now the night before last. Yes. Mr. Silva said you had just left. He described you and told me your name. I had never seen you, but I recognized you at once. The countryside has talked for a long time now about the old Marquesa and her imported lovers."

"You drove over to the house."

"At once," he said. "I was pleased at last to locate my competition. And remove it."

"I think I understand now," I said. "Silva knew that you and I were privateering the same district. He was supplying us both. But I wouldn't buy his drugs and you would. That was where the money lay for both of you. He knew that if I was got rid of, the whole territory would be yours. You'd continue buying all the drugs from him and he'd have his double market back again."

"Is that the reason? I don't know. But it was good of him to wish me to increase my income."

"Yes," I said, "you need the money. Bulls are an expensive hobby, especially when the strain is petering out."

"You think so?" The gun rammed viciously against my spine. "Go and see for yourself."

The bulls began scuffling again, butting each other, snorting. I thought of the Marquesa. I wanted to be sick. My tongue was thick with fright. I started talking, much too fast, foolishly. "You came over," I said, "and sized up the situation, and I arrived on schedule, corroborating all Silva had told you."

"You were a little later than I expected."

"I had trouble on the way over."

"Really? What sort of trouble?"

It was at that moment that I think I saw the whole set-up. I knew why the Hathertons had thought Navarro to be such a close friend of mine. I said, "So then you and I had a brush at the house. Maybe you did it intentionally, I don't know, it's not important. But you used it as an excuse to come back in the morning, to get the lay of the land. You saw me get in the truck. You checked the direction I took. There was only one road, so you could afford to give me a start. Then you sent your *chulos* after me."

"A pity the scheme failed," he said. "So neatly planned. I guessed it was a rendezvous and I instructed the men to go ahead first and check how many people were waiting. There was only one, a man named Ferrer. He is to be the first of my new customers."

"Yes," I said, "only one. You wanted a list of all the rest. So you sent over your men tonight when you thought the house was empty and I was dead. Page was there. He didn't know anything at all about the business. But they killed him."

A bull hurtled across the ring and crashed into the barrier. Navarro prodded me again with the gun. "They are waiting for you, Señor Williams," he said. "Go into the arena. You will find that bullfighting is not so dull as you claimed."

I said, "Do you know a man named Griswold?"

"I have never even heard of a man named Griswold. Get into the arena."

"You'd better listen to me," I said. "You're in trouble."

"I?" Navarro laughed again. His voice changed. "Go and bring back the body of that poor woman. It will be a noble deed."

I didn't move. I couldn't. I was petrified with fear of the bulls. I preferred the gun.

"Go," he said.

"No."

Everything was silent. I waited for the bullet.

He grunted. The gun went away from my back. I heard a snapping sound. Somebody started to scream, a split second of it. The voice was cut off. Then there was no sound, no movement.

I whirled around. I said, "No, Mudo, no!" I tried to pull him away.

His knees were clamped on Navarro's legs to keep him from struggling. The gun was on the ground and one of Navarro's arms dangled broken and useless. El Mudo had a huge hand over the old man's face, another at the back of his head. He was trying to crush his skull.

"No," I said. I tried to pull his wrists apart. "Mudo, it's not worth it. Leave him." He took no notice. His hands pressed remorselessly. I couldn't shift them. I grabbed his waist, trying to pull him away, but he was rooted to the ground like a tree. I hit him in the face. He heaved me away with his shoulder. I could see the muscles standing out on his bare forearms. The silence was awful.

"No," I said for the last time. I punched him hard in the middle of the back. He moved then, only three steps. Navarro started feebly to kick. I didn't see clearly what followed.

El Mudo made a turning movement with his hands. The old man's body swung up by the neck. It happened in one motion. El Mudo's back jerked and Navarro cleaved the air and went flying over the fence. He landed with a thud in the sand of the ring. El Mudo grabbed my arms and held me fast. I watched.

The bulls were on the far side. They didn't move. The dark heap that was Navarro stirred faintly and then, hideously grotesque, he picked himself to his feet, holding the one good arm rigidly in front of him, his hand clawing at the darkness. I don't think he could see. He took two drunken, staggering steps forward, stumbled, and dragged himself upright again. He tried to run.

A bull charged. Navarro's body was transfixed at the first thrust. He rode a few seconds on the single horn before he fell off. Then the three of them were on him, trampling, tossing him high. They snorted in the darkness. El Mudo released my arms. I turned away.

We stared at each other. El Mudo's eyes were huge. His arms hung loose and the palms of his hands were dark with blood. I said, "Yes, you got the right one. He was responsible for Page." I reached out and put my hand on the back of El Mudo's neck. "Thank you."

His mouth quivered.

I said, "*Chico*, what have you done with Page's body? Will it be found?"

He shook his head. The tears began rolling down his face.

"Be very careful, Mudo. How did you find me?"

He pointed back toward the village, still weeping. He made drinking motions and I guessed that the men on the church steps had told him the direction I took. It wouldn't mean anything to them. They were too drunk. I said, "Better to get away from here, Mudo. Everything is finished. Paco is dead. The Marquesa is dead. There will be no more smuggling. Stay out of sight for a week or two, get out of the district. Go now."

He stood still a moment, then reached out and embraced me, his cheek touching first one side of my face and then the other.

I said, "*Adiós*, Mudo."

He nodded.

"See you in the future at a better time, *chico*."

He drew a forearm across his eyes. He nodded once more. Then he turned and walked slowly away. The darkness swallowed him up.

I stooped down and picked up Navarro's fallen gun. The bulls were snorting but I did not look again into the arena. I went toward the house.

Chapter Thirteen

Lavinia Hatherton took up with Navarro for his money. She found he didn't have any. The fat man at the party, the other bull raiser, had claimed it was necessary to breed forty Navarro bulls to get four fighters. Bulls are a fantastically expensive hobby, anyway. Perhaps Don Luis had originally been rich and lost everything when the strain began to fail. He needed more money.

The animals bearing his name were his pride, probably his very life. To a Spanish hidalgo the two things are practically the same. He had to sustain the reputation of the bulls because it was synonymous with his own reputation. So he'd taken to contraband running, willing to go to any lengths. It explained the deaths in Cádiz, the local man at the ambush, Page, the murder of the Marquesa.

But it didn't explain Griswold. Or the hijackers. Or Silva's murder and the attempted frame. Neither did it explain Rex Hatherton's offer, six thousand dollars for information.

I saw my error. The pieces began falling into place. I had thought I was fighting only one faction. There were two.

On the upstairs floor of the house the light had been switched off. The whole place was in darkness. I eased along the wall of the final outbuilding and there was only one more open space between me and the house. My nerves were bad.

I started for the gate of the patio, going swiftly. From the corner of my eye I saw something move. I stopped and turned my head. There was nothing. I continued forward and then I had a sudden feeling that the patio gate would be closed, that it would squeak as I opened it. I reached out. My fears were groundless. I walked into the courtyard and it was all at once very dark. I could hear the tinkling of the fountain.

From the shadows of the arched veranda a voice hissed, "Luis!"

I backed to the wall and waited.

"Is that you, Luis?"

Lavinia Hatherton. I could see the whitish blob of her golden hair. I brushed along the wall to the veranda, walked toward her. She said, "Luis, I thought you were never coming." Then she saw who it was. She said, "Oh!"

"Hello," I said.

"Why are you prowling round here?"

I didn't answer.

"Not that I'm not pleased to see you. I'll take you against Luis any day. Have you come to make an attack on me?"

"On nobody. I have business with your husband. Take me to him."

She hesitated. "He's in bed." I held the gun firmly in my right-hand pocket. The lightness of her hair moved as she nodded her head. "All right," she whispered, "come on. But don't make a noise. No need to let the servants know everything."

She moved lightly, with no sound of footsteps. I followed her and I was raising a whisper of echo. We went through a doorway. She looked over her shoulder. She said, "Ssshhh!" It was like a children's game.

We crossed the central hallway, went up the big stairs I had ascended earlier when I was seeking the Marquesa, and it seemed a century ago. We traversed the landing. Lavinia Hatherton drew close to me. We turned into the second noiseless corridor, and I recognized it. Dim light bulbs were burning in sconces on the wall.

She halted in front of the second door, grasping the handle. She lifted her face to my ear. "My room," she whispered. "Wait here while I go wake up Rex." She opened the door and I stepped inside. The door closed behind me and the lights came on.

His gun jolted into the base of my spine. He'd been waiting in the darkness behind the door. He said, "Put up your hands," and reached into my pocket and took out Navarro's gun. I heard it drop softly somewhere. He told me to turn around.

She was in the room too, smiling a cat smile. She must have sneaked in behind me. She said, "An unexpected surprise. I got this one instead." She went over and sat on the edge of the bed.

"No need for guns, Rex," I said.

He smiled. "Of course not, old chappie, but just in case. Where is your boss?"

I didn't know what he knew or where I stood with him. But I wanted one thing only and maybe he'd give it to me. Griswold. I said, "I've come to make that deal with you."

He backed a few steps to get beside his wife. He said, "Hasn't Navarro returned yet?"

She shook her head, smiling. But her eyes flicked. She was frightened of him. She didn't like me in the room with him, Navarro's name being mentioned. She thought I might say something.

She said, "I think he took the Marquesa home. Maybe she passed out or took sick or something, and he's had to stay a while. Anyway, he knows where to meet me. You want me to go back outside and wait?"

"In a little while. We'll deal with this one first. It may necessitate a change of plan." He smiled at me again, waving the gun at a chair. I sat down. He said, "Now, old boy, what's all this about a deal?"

"I'll give all the information you want in return for the answer to one question."

"What's that?"

"Where's Griswold?"

He shot a quick glance at his wife, then looked back at me. He said, "Dear, oh, dear, so you know of the connection with Griswold. What else do you know?"

"That's where the deal comes in."

He sat on the arm of a chair and dangled the gun lazily between his knees. Lavinia Hatherton watched me from the bed with bright unblinking eyes. He said, "I have information about you and you appear to have some about me. Let's exchange. We can judge afterward whether the residue merits a deal."

"You first," I said.

He cocked an eyebrow. "That's a bit cheeky, Williams."

"Maybe so. Mark it down to nerves. I'm in a difficult position."

"You're in worse than that, old sport, much worse. However."

He reached into his pocket with his free hand and pulled out a loose cigarette. Lavinia leaped forward and lit it for him, then returned to her seat on the bed, still watching me.

He said, "Righty-ho!" and inhaled slowly several times, as if he were thinking. "Here's how it stands," he said.

"The south Spain trade has been bothering us for some months. A thorn in the side, you might say. You know the hazards of this coast, the dangers of the short distance between here and North Africa. Well, we held off. We thought direct shipping was an impossibility."

"It's not," I said.

"You proved that," he said. "We did have a market here, quite a large one. But the material had first to be shipped to France, smuggled over the frontier, then brought all those hundreds of miles down here by truck. An expensive business. It made the price of the goods far too high."

He pointed the end of his cigarette at me. "You, old man, had the intestinal fortitude to demonstrate the possibilities of direct shipping. Your running costs were lower. You could undercut our prices by a third. So our market disappeared; you took it over. We called a board meeting and decided that if you could do it, so could we."

"But you had to get rid of me first."

"Or amalgamate with you. The matter was not really important. Either way was agreeable. After all, we are businessmen, you know, we must think of the good of the company. Myself, I voted for amalgamation. I said you could teach us valuable lessons of method."

"How long did you lie in wait?"

"Oh, hardly any time at all. We suspected immediately that you were trading in Spain by the size of your boat. A few weeks later our market had gone. Then word got around that you were looking for another man. My wife recommended that we plant Griswold."

I looked at her. "Not him, too," I said. "Not Griswold."

"What the hell are you talking about?" she snapped.

Rex Hatherton stood up from the chair, his mouth gone taut. "Yes, Williams, what do you mean?"

"You picked a bad one," I said. "He muffed it from beginning to end. All he wanted to do was get at the booze."

Hatherton looked at me for a long time. He was losing some of his poise. He said, "Don't underestimate Griswold. He drinks, yes, but he's reliable. He's even courageous on occasion, if the pay is high enough. He acted exactly according to instructions. He was either to locate your base or, if you got suspicious, sabotage your craft and jump over the side. The theory was that our boat was supposed to blow you out of the water. You proved too good for us. By the time Griswold had been picked up you were gone."

"I want him," I said. "He killed a friend of mine tonight. He also murdered a man named Silva."

Rex Hatherton looked faintly amused. He twirled the gun around his finger, very expertly. "Now, that was an unexpected plum," he said, "the discovery of Silva. We removed him, naturally. If we remove all the private brokers, the runners will have to come to us for everything, no matter where they're shipping to. Of course, the really plummy part happened tonight. Griswold was down by the harbor and by absolute accident he saw you coming ashore. He guessed where you were going and instantly phoned the police."

"It didn't work," I said.

"No, I know. You seem to have a quite fabulously charmed life. I understand you caught Griswold a nasty knock on the forehead. He was very grieved when he came over here to make his report to me."

"Look, Hatherton," I said. "Lead me to Griswold. I'll tell you everything you want to know."

"Everything?"

"That's what I said."

"Well, now, that might be interesting." He twirled the gun again.

Lavinia Hatherton said nervously, "Stop playing about, Rex. It's too dangerous. The police are looking for him."

Hatherton nodded at me. "They are, you know. They arrived earlier on with your boss and told everyone to keep an eye peeled for you. It was rather droll, really, seeing Don Luis with the police. I wonder if he was nervous. He isn't aware yet that we know about him."

"My boss?"

"Yes," he said, "and perhaps we really should stop playing. You see, there is nothing you can tell me, Williams. I know it all. I came over three days ago to spy out the land from this side. It was rather sweetly coincidental that we came to stay with Don Luis only because he's an old friend of the family."

"I heard about it," I said. "An intimate friend."

Lavinia didn't move. Rex Hatherton slapped me not very hard across the face. But all his jaw muscles had gone tense.

"No," he said evenly. "That wasn't very gentlemanly. Navarro should not have told you. Williams, there will be no deal."

"As you say."

"I do say. There's no need. I learned everything last night." He glanced at his watch. "No, it is now the night before last. I quite thoughtlessly picked up a ringing phone in this house and the operator said someone was calling from North Africa. You, of course."

"Silva."

"You or Silva, it's a detail. But remember I was here to find rival contraband runners on this part of the coast. A phone call from North
Africa. I felt suspicious. Immediately afterward I was convinced. Don
Luis marched straight from the phone and suddenly announced he was
going for a short drive. It was most unlike him, especially since we were
in the middle of a conversation about bulls. I sent my wife along to keep
an eye."

"I guess she didn't mind," I said. "It's nice to ride with an old friend."

He said, "You're making it very difficult for yourself, Williams."

"Am I? You'd be astonished at the needless difficulties you're making
for yourself. So you thought he came over to see me. You knew I was running the stuff and you deduced that he and I were working together."

"Quite. And the following morning I knew for certain. He sneaked over
again to give you orders before anyone here was out of bed."

"That six thousand dollars tonight," I said. "It was for me to cross him
up."

He nodded. "Unfortunately, I have to withdraw the offer. The police are
seeking you. The Association has no use whatever for a marked man."

"May I inquire your intention?"

"I'm going to kill you," he said lightly. Lavinia Hatherton smiled. He
said, "You see, the police will get to you eventually, Williams. In these
past few minutes you've demonstrated that you know far too much
about me. You might decide to share the knowledge. I can't take the risk.
I must now deal directly with your boss."

I got to my feet. I said, "Mac, you couldn't be more balled up." He
planted his feet and aimed the gun at me. We stood in a long silence.

It was very easy to hear the car. It was coming up the road toward the
house. It was traveling in second gear.

Rex Hatherton backed from me. He spoke to his wife without turning
his head. He said, "I'll take care of this one. That'll be Navarro. Get him."

She stood up. She started for the door. I said, "Why not bring him back
for a roll on the bed, as I saw you doing earlier this evening?"

Hatherton moved with the speed of a snake. He wrenched her by the
arm and flung her clear across the room. She fell in a corner. It happened
too quickly for me to capitalize on it. He was covering me again.

"What is this?" he asked. He looked down at her.

"He's lying." She pushed back the hair from her forehead and got to
her feet. Her face was flaming. "He's lying, Rex," she said. "I don't know
what he's talking about."

"Perhaps he will explain."

I was willing to explain anything, at any length. I didn't know who was
in the car, but it wasn't Navarro. Anybody else represented hope. I said,
"Remember the first time I saw you over by the bull ring?"

"Don't believe him," she said. "He tried to make a pass at me. I would-n't have any of it. He's getting his own back." Only her lips moved. The rest of her face was petrified.

Rex Hatherton was holding the gun so tightly that his knuckles looked on the point of bursting through the back of his hand. He said, "Go on, Williams. I'm listening."

The car pulled up with a faint crunching of gravel. I heard no footsteps. Lavinia Hatherton made a slight move toward the door, looked at her husband's face, and stayed where she was. I concentrated on two things: It wasn't Navarro, and this was the only light burning in the house. Whoever it was might come here. I had to give him time. I made a big effort and managed a short laugh.

I said, "Luis is no gentleman, believe me. He told me all about him-self and your wife, with details. He liked to brag about it. I guess he had reason. You thought you'd snatched her from under his nose up there on the Riviera. You couldn't have been more wrong. Ask him to show you the letters she's been writing."

She gave a tiny shrieking gasp and started for me. He jerked his head. He said, "Stay where you are, Lavinia." His voice had no tone.

"But the lying bastard," she said incredulously. "The filthy rotten—"

"A tattletale," I said. "You write a good letter, Mrs. Hatherton." I turned back to him. "A little dirty, maybe, but very frank and descrip-tive. Do you know the only things you're good for?"

He remained perfectly motionless.

"Money and jealousy," I said. "Nothing else. Your wife has a nickname for you. She calls you Unsexy Rexy. She also puts forward a theory that you were emasculated at school. She gets very derisive about it. You should hear her tell Luis in those letters how she prefers the Spanish methods. It makes him very proud, naturally. He's a pretty old guy and Spaniards set a lot of store by that sort of thing."

I thought then that he was going to shoot me. I counted on the aspect that starts jealous husbands off in the first place, the fact that they like to torture themselves.

He said, "What were you going to tell me about tonight?"

"I guess you've had trouble with her right from the start," I said. "Funny. She's not a type that appeals to me."

"Rex, for God's sake! Don't listen to him!"

"Be quiet," he said. "Williams, I'm waiting."

"Well, it's not very pleasant. You were over by the arena. I came up-stairs to look for the Marquesa and opened this door by mistake. Luis and your wife were on the bed. That was it. It's pretty raw, I guess, when a man gets the horns planted on him in his own bedroom. I'm sorry to have to tell you this."

The stillness was broken only by the jerky sound of Lavinia Hatherton's breathing. He spoke. He said, "Lavinia, come here. Stand next to me. This side."

She moved slowly. She got to the left of him. The gun in his right hand stayed unwaveringly on me. She said, "What, Rex?"

His empty fist flashed up and hit her a terrific smack on the side of the jaw. She went to the floor like a log and stayed there. Rex Hatherton said, "And now you."

"There's still the deal. I have a lot of good stuff."

"No," he said.

"Why? Don't you have the authority? Are you just a little wheel in the Association?"

He looked at me in an almost friendly manner. He smiled. He said, "Williams, I *am* the Association. Good-by. I shall say I shot you when you attacked my wife."

"Wait," I said. The door opened. I dived for the floor.

My nose hit the carpet. I didn't see what happened. There were two shots close together and the clunk of a falling gun. I rolled over. Rex Hatherton sat slowly down beside me. He was gazing stupidly at his shattered wrist.

Blasco walked into the room, a gun in his hand. There were about eight cops at his heels and they all had guns. In back of them, peering over their heads to see what was going on, was the priest. Blasco looked pretty pleased with himself.

They all got to looking pleased with themselves. Two of them helped Lavinia Hatherton to her feet, politely called her "señora," and then stayed never farther than six inches from her, watching every move. They didn't treat him nearly so gently. He got slammed into a chair, where he continued to study his wrist, and then one of them asked him a question.

He smiled upward. He said, "I'm most awfully sorry, but I really don't speak Spanish."

The priest came over to me. "Is this the man you were seeking?"

"No."

"Did you find him?"

"No."

"I'm glad," he said. He looked across the room to Blasco. They held it a moment. Then without another word Father Juan went out the door.

Blasco said to Hatherton, "But I speak English, señor. Not very well, I fear, but sufficiently to understand that you were going to kill this boy when he discovered you were the Association."

Hatherton said, "I haven't the vaguest idea what you're talking about, old man."

Blasco said, "No, señor, I am aged only forty-three."

The squat dark-haired cop was standing close to me, staring at my face. He blinked his expressionless little black eyes a couple of times and smiled faintly. I didn't like it. I said, "Blasco."

He turned, speaking to me for the first time since he had come in. "Ah, yes," he said. "You." He walked across to the door, opened it, and made a beckoning motion. "This way, please, Señor Oovilliams."

The dark cop made a move to follow. He was waved back. Blasco said in Spanish, "I shall return in a few moments." He closed the door behind us.

We went along the passage and down the stairs with no word being said. We got outside and the fresh air smelled good, the odor of dry rocks dampening under mist. Blasco fumbled in his pocket. I thought he was after a gun. He pulled out a pack of cigarettes, offered me one, struck a match, and leaned against the wall.

I waited.

He said conversationally, "Did you ever kill a man?"

"No."

"Never in your life?"

"Never."

He sucked at his cigarette. "You are a strange one," he said. "Very. I did not believe it when you said you wished to smash the Association."

I remained silent.

"You damaged a police car," he said.

"I'm sorry about that. I didn't know where I was at."

"To be candid," he said, "I still don't. Can you help me?"

"I'll try. To begin with, I am not of the Association."

"Clearly. I heard as much."

"There have been two factions working this section of coast, unknown to each other. The Marquesa and Don Luis Navarro."

"Oh," he said slowly, widening his eyes, making his lips very rounded.

"I worked for the Marquesa. Don Luis found out about us and took steps to get rid of the competition. He did pretty well. He claims his men killed the other American who was staying with the Marquesa—I don't know about that. There's a whole gang of local men working for him. One of them helped carry the statue in the procession tonight, front right-hand side as they went into the church. A medium-sized man, small mustache, about thirty-five."

"I am sure he will prove informative."

"I hope so. His boss overreached himself. Tonight he murdered the Marquesa."

"What?"

"And got killed himself in the process."

"How?"

"They're over in the arena. The bulls did it."

I waited for comment. None came. I drew on my cigarette and covertly studied his face in the glow. His expression betrayed nothing.

"Meantime," I said, "the Association was trying to break in. Hatherton, the man inside, is the head of it. There is an American named Griswold working for him. He was the one that phoned you last night when they tried to frame me in North Africa. I think probably he killed Silva. He tried to kill me. He killed a friend of mine named Paco Sierra. He's still at large."

"I heard of that," Blasco said mildly, and I guessed Father Juan had said as much as he could. Blasco said, "Were you responsible for the three people in Cádiz?"

"That was Navarro. But the little boy around here, maybe that was me. I'm not sure."

He remained leaning against the wall. I listened to the fountain. Almost imperceptibly the sky was lightening. The day was coming.

He said, "Now this person Hatherton. We have his identity, so he will be unable again to operate in North Africa. Reasons could be found for his deportation. Fairly satisfactory, but not completely so. With what can I charge him in Spain?"

He paused. He flicked his fingers and the cigarette curved through the air and hissed into the fountain. "Attempted murder," he said reflectively. "Threats. That will require you to appear as a witness. Or I can hold him until the Griswold man is found and then charge him with complicity in the killing of— Who is it?"

"Paco Sierra."

"To be sure, Paco Sierra. I hear you liked him well. That is sad. Mr. Hatherton and I will have long talks, I think."

"Ask him about his organization for smuggling into Spain across the French frontier."

"So! Oh, yes!" Blasco straightened from the wall and gently rubbed his hands. "Now, therein lies possible promotion. I shall question him closely about it. He appears to me a man who will not remain silent for long, not like you. There is a little police station down the coast that will—"

He stopped. He added thoughtfully, "I feel very sorry for the lady who is his wife. I think he ill-treats her. What a pretty woman, and how charming! We do not see many blonde ladies like her in Spain."

"No," I said.

"I fear we shall have to keep her in the vicinity, though not necessarily in a cell. I shall question her also. Less harshly."

He slapped my arm. "Oovilliams, you have friends in this district, one very good friend especially. For whom did you say you worked?"

"The Marquesa."

"Ah, yes, the oranges. A very healthful occupation. But is not the season finished?" He lit another cigarette and looked at me in the flame. He threw the match at the fountain. He missed. He said, "You have been a great help, Señor Oovilliams. I shall be coming over later to question you about your visa."

"What?" I said.

"Your passport, you fool," he said. "In about an hour. I cannot possibly make it more than two hours. Good night."

He shrugged, waved the cigarette, walked across the patio, and entered the house. I ran for the gate.

A solitary car stood on the road. Its headlights were on. A man was waiting, one foot on the running board. He straightened up. "Williams."

"I'm in a hurry, Father."

"I know," he said. "I can give you a lift to the village."

I nearly kissed him. I said, "Thanks."

The rolling early-morning mist lay knee-high over the countryside like a layer of absorbent cotton. The false dawn was glimmering in the sky with an unchanging pearly light that left the earth still in darkness. I reached for a cigarette. I didn't have any. The priest's old car rattled in all its joints.

We were nearing the outskirts of the village. Suddenly he pulled up, the engine still running.

"Something wrong?" I said.

He opened the door, got out on the road, and stood looking in on me. "Nothing at all. I walk from here. Always in the morning I take exercise before Mass. It is my time for contemplation."

He slammed the door and leaned in the window. I didn't know whether or not to get out. I made a move. He said, "No, take the car. María will be waiting for you. Leave it outside of her house. The Señor Blasco will drive me over later this morning to pick it up. A good man, Blasco."

I slid behind the wheel. I said, "There are many about if you care to look for them."

"I like to hear you say that." He nodded. "Are you going to marry María in church?"

"As soon as possible."

He withdrew his head. His hands were still on the door. He said matter-of-factly, "Paco Sierra will have a decent Christian burial. He was a good boy. Get a passport and come back to visit his grave sometimes, Señor Williams. And forgive me that I do not remember your correct name."

He reached inside and tapped me sharply on the shoulder. "Lead a good life, son. It is more comfortable and more practical. I fail to comprehend why everyone does not understand that." He tapped me even harder. "Do you understand?"

"Yes," I said. "Thanks for everything."

"For what do you mean?"

"Well, for the loan of the car."

He stood back. "It is nothing." He slapped the palm of his hand against the door. "*Adiós, mi hijo.* You do not deserve it."

"I know," I said. "*Adiós, Padre.*" I waved a hand. When I looked back the mist was too thick for me to see him. I went on toward the village.

At the main street I slowed down. This was not the time to gain a minute and lose an hour. There might be drunks about. There were.

In the village square the mist was dispersed by the houses. Only a few stray fingers, like feathers, hovered motionless a few feet above the ground. A solemnly drunken man, apart from his comrades, was trying gravely to gather the mist in his hands. He had a musical accompaniment. The amateur trumpeter was still standing on the steps of the church, blowing his lungs out to the tune of "*Cielito Lindo.*"

The last of the revelers sat around his feet in desolately unmoving postures, contemplating maybe the bitterness of normal life when fiestas are done. In the center of the square a solitary bandsman was flat on his back, clutching to his chest his bassoon. I drove on. To myself I wished them all a good night and a good year. I reached the farther fringe of the village and speeded up. The windshield was bedewed. I turned on the wipers. The countryside lay hushed, as if the wavering mist deadened all sound.

I was thinking of María, of what I must tell her. That the police were bound to get Griswold in the end. But it was a lie. Blasco would do his utmost, I knew, but if Griswold had skipped back to North Africa, the task was going to be infinitely more difficult. News travels fast. By tomorrow the whole Mediterranean coast, both sides, would know of Hatherton's arrest. And Griswold had proved himself no fool. If he knew his boss was finished, he'd immediately put himself beyond the reach of extradition.

And I couldn't stay here now. Not just for my safety's sake, but because all at once I was beginning to feel different. I'd have to explain it to María. I didn't want to start our life with a lie. She must make the decision. She had that right. I hoped she would realize that it was not because I was being a coward.

The breeze hummed at the windows. I was a mile beyond the village. I turned up the headlights and they stabbed ahead into the wreathing white vapors. A man was walking in the middle of the road, waist-deep in mist. I sounded the horn.

He swayed off to the side and disappeared beyond my vision. I was already past him. I stopped the car with a screaming jolt of brakes and leaped to the road. I shouted:

"Griswold!"

He turned slowly. He was about fifteen yards away. "Yeah?"

"Here! It's important." I started toward him. He remained motionless.

I didn't know whether he was still drunk or not, or had a gun, or had recognized me. I didn't care. It was better this way. Suddenly I felt fiercely good. I was going to kill him after all.

He took three steps forward to meet me. His head was held back to give him better vision. "Who is it?" he asked, and he wasn't drunk. It pleased me. I didn't answer. "Who is it?" he asked again. Then he sprang. He knew who it was.

His right arm splashed upward. I knew he had a knife without seeing it. I jumped to the side and tried to close with him. He was too quick for me. He did a complete turn and we stood apart, shoulders hunched, staring at each other, waiting for the next move. He kept the knife a foot in front of him, gripping the handle for an upward thrust.

He grinned. "What's a matter, Williams, looking for trouble?" He guessed I was not armed.

Up ahead the mist did a slow dance in the beams of the headlights. I moved slowly to the side, looking for an opening. Griswold made a small pivot. He knew all the tricks. My foot brushed a rock.

"Me, I been asleep," he said. "You, you're just going to sleep." He took a slow step forward. I retreated. My heel hit another rock. I was temporarily off balance. I flung myself upright and Griswold halted his plunge. He knew his advantage. He had only to wait for an attack. He was holding a knife. If he waited long enough I'd run myself onto it.

I said, "The kid you stuck tonight is dead."

"Too bad." He was still grinning.

"If you'd been anything but a broken-down rummy you'd have had sense enough to get away, instead of crawling out here to sleep."

"Ah, shut up!" he said. "You're such a tough guy, come on and be tough."

"I'm leaving you for the police. The kid had time enough to talk."

"Did he? You won't."

I took the chance. Three fast backsteps out of range and he ran for me. I was on my knees, groping. The rock lay right under my hand. He didn't see it coming. I flung hard. He hit it with his chin. He toppled. I dug in my toes and lunged and my head hit him square in the belly. I was sprawling half on top of him, grabbing for his right wrist.

He tried to knee me. I was too low on him. The knee hit my chest. I reached out, grabbed his hair, dragged myself upward, and butted his face. We rolled across the road, writhing. I was still holding his wrist. The rocks were cutting into my ribs.

He bit my face. I released his hair and banged his forehead and his head hit the ground. I swiveled around on him. I sank my teeth into his wrist. He let go of the knife and I had it at his throat.

He lay without moving a muscle. I kept the point at his larynx, just breaking the skin, I moved slowly, gently off his body till I was kneeling beside him. I said, "Griswold, I am going to kill you."

His face went bloated. His puffy eyes started to bulge. The least motion and he knew the knife would be in his neck. He said in a whisper, "Bub, don't be crazy."

"I'm going to carve you up," I said. And then the ridiculous words started splintering in my mouth. "You're a murderer," I said. "A double-crosser."

The mist eddied around and over us. I was suddenly very cold.

There was a rock wedged under his back. He was afraid to shift. In the black-gray light his face seemed to have become jelly. He said, "You wouldn't do that to me, Williams, would you? You couldn't kill me in cold blood, eh?"

I looked at him. I didn't move for a whole minute. Then I knew he was right. I couldn't kill him. I got up swiftly. I flung the knife very far away into the darkness. I said, "All right, Griswold, on your feet. This is it."

I guess I didn't give him a fair chance. He was barely off his knees. I hit square in the face. I reached down and swung him up by the hair and held him away from me. I smashed him.

After a while his features began to disappear under my fists. When I was tired and my knuckles were all raw I dragged his unconscious body toward the priest's car.

Chapter Fourteen

Cape St. Vincent lay to starboard. Spain was behind us. The sun lifted slowly and the sea was a dazzling expanse of blue, dotted with white flecks. The early-morning breeze blew through the door, very salty. Life was a pretty good thing.

I looked aft. The four big drums of gasoline were secure. There would be a lot left over. I could sell it. I checked northward on the map to Sezimbra and I was trying to think of a Portuguese I'd heard of in North Africa, a man who ran a small shipyard and bought hot boats. He was known to all contraband runners who'd crossed up their employers. They'd skip with the loot and sell him the boat.

I thought about it. Then I no longer tried to remember his name. I figured it would be a bad start to a different life. I'd rather abandon the boat. There'd be enough from the gasoline to take me and María into Lisbon. After that I could come to some arrangement with the Embassy.

She was supposed to be down in the small cabin, sleeping. She came up on deck and walked toward the wheelhouse. Her face still held a lot of sadness.

She came inside and stood with me. There was lots of room because she was so small. I put an arm around her, steered with one hand. We ran into a patch of sea that was dancing more than all the rest.

"Not long," I said. "Two hours or so. I know where we'll land."

I thought of how she had risen from the bedside, come with me unquestioningly when I asked her. A last backward look at Paco and then the drive in the Volkswagen to the cliff. My arm tightened. I felt her body still tense with strain.

I said, "Paco will be taken care of by Father Juan. You can trust him."

"Yes," she said. Her voice was almost inaudible. She did not relax.

"There is nothing more to fear," I said. "I spoke to the policeman. Sometime soon, when we are married, we can return. We shall have passports." I put my mouth to her hair. "I love you, María."

She drew away then, stood a little apart, lifting her eyes to my face. She said, "Beel, I did a bad thing to you. I sent you after that man. You would not have come back unless you—"

I put a hand to her lips. "No," I said, "I didn't." And I was glad it had worked out this way.

She looked at me fixedly, perplexity in her eyes. She was making a decision. She said, "Good, Beel. It does not matter that he escaped. Someday the police will get him. Father Juan knows his name. Father Juan will see to it that he is punished."

It had been a bad night. But the morning was beautiful. I laughed. I said, "*Chica mía*, you have no idea how soon Father Juan will see to it."

"I do not understand."

"The old black car," I said, "the one that stood by the Volkswagen when we came from your house. It was the priest's car. A passenger is lying on the floor at the back and his name is Griswold. He has a note pinned to him that says so. There is a gag in his mouth and he is tied with ropes, very uncomfortably."

I looked up at the sun. "I think Father Juan should be there by now."

It was then that she relaxed completely. I saw the cloud lift from her face. She couldn't possibly be happy now, but she was going to be in the future. I'd see to it for the rest of my life.

She stepped outside. She was conscious for the first time of the sea and the sun. They were having an effect upon her. She lifted her head and inhaled the salt breeze deeply. She looked lovely.

I said, "Come back in here, María."

She was even smiling a little. I bent down and kissed her. I said, "Say Aliston."

"Aliston."

"Mrs. Robert Aliston."

The sunlit water sprinkled over the bow. We were cutting north, making good speed.

"Mrs. Robert Aliston," she said. She said it very well.

THE END

Rain of Terror

■ ■ ■ ■ ■ ■ ■

Douglas Sanderson
WRITING AS MALCOLM DOUGLAS

For my good friend
Claudio Ianora
who was there with me...

Chapter One

Mr. Turrido had thirty-seven canaries, all contained in a single large cage. He was feeding them.

It was past midnight, and most of the birds were already asleep on the perches, heads tucked under their wings and feathers fluffed. To Mr. Turrido they looked like little balls of puffed yellow cotton. He smiled softly.

He reached into the cage and whispered, "Lili." A small bird, almost white in color, hopped daintily on to his out-thrust finger and allowed herself to be drawn from the cage. Mr. Turrido lifted the hand near his face and whispered cheepingly, strong white teeth glistening in a smile under his stiff, neatly trimmed black mustache. The bird put her head on one side. He told her he loved her. She twittered at him.

He flicked his hand. She rose to the ceiling of the high room and fluttered among the plaster cupids and the convoluted plaster grapes. Then she returned with a swoop, sprang nimbly into the cage, and settled on her perch. Mr. Turrido, still smiling, crossed the luxurious crimson carpet to the sideboard, poured himself a drink of the very best brandy, moved to the window and gazed down with pleasure on the soft lights and pastel dimness of the Roman night.

No cloud of discontent marred his mellow mood. The customer was more than an hour late, but that was no cause for worry. Many Americans liked to be a little drunk before they conducted any business. It was part of their innocent charm. And who would complain? One simply adjudged the degree of their intoxication and adjusted the price accordingly. The maneuver was almost an art in itself.

Mr. Turrido put down his drink, gently lifted the smoldering cigar from a tray, careful not to break the long gray ash: this was one of the indications of a really cultivated gentleman. Mr. Turrido picked up little hints like that purely through observation. He was on the watch for them. He smiled again, drew up to his full stocky height of five feet three inches and turned with slow pride to survey the room. His corset creaked; he did not notice.

Such a fine room! Through a cloud of rich blue smoke he remarked the other signs of cultivation—fine tapestries, fine carved furniture, fine small and discreetly lit pictures, all pretending to be original. Briefly, from the depth of his soul, a wordless voice cried out for more and bigger pictures with fiercer lighting. Mr. Turrido stilled it to dumbness. Two years of admission into high Roman society had taught him that there are certain things to which a gentleman of taste must never succumb.

He lowered his gaze. A ravishing scent filled his nostrils from the two large spots of perfume under the tabs of his shirt collar. Mr. Turrido drew a long, contented draft of his cigar. He was pleased with himself. He had cause to be.

As a farm laborer many years ago in Sicily, the scent that drenched his armpits had been of the cheapest variety. His whole life at that time had worn a bargain-basement tag. Work fourteen hours a day, and drink on Saturdays. Little gained, nothing saved, no foreseeable future. The only thing he possessed of value was a pretty girl friend he couldn't afford to marry.

He hadn't liked the existence one bit, knowing as he did that he was made for better things. He used to get angry, especially when he drank. Then he'd take it out on someone in a good brutal fight. He always won; he was incredibly strong. But it never decreased his resentment by one iota. He got so that he was angry all the time.

Then one day everything changed, simply because his employer had guests at the farm. Mr. Turrido came in from the fields at eight in the evening and passed an open window. On a brown walnut dressing table he saw a bottle of expensive perfume. He slipped in and stole it.

There was a week of fearful waiting after that. He didn't dare use the perfume. He used to sniff it secretly at night. It smelled luxurious. Then abruptly he realized that nothing was going to be said about it. He was struck by the delightful easiness of the happening. He promptly went out and stole something else.

There was really nothing to it. After six months of increasing boldness and undetected petty thievery came the big opportunity. His employer had a large sum of money in the house. It stayed there for precisely one day. The following night Mr. Turrido was on a boat bound for the mainland of Italy. The money was in his pocket and the pretty girl friend was on his arm, smiling up at him, sharing his triumph. It made him happy just to look at her. He loved her very much at that moment.

But somehow he never did get to marry her. The money disappeared after a few riotous weeks in Naples. Somebody had to earn more. The girl was elected. With surprisingly little persuasion she entered the oldest profession in the world. Mr. Turrido entered the second oldest profession; he became a pimp. The work was not uncongenial and one met a great many interesting people, some of them with good ideas. Once again Mr. Turrido was impressed by the ease with which life could be lived.

Success prompted expansion. He recruited more girls, many more. After five years of intense opposition, and a fierce running battle that necessitated four murders, Mr. Turrido was the owner of the five most luxurious private brothels in the entire city of Naples.

Orgies and singular exhibitions were the specialty. Trade boomed. The pretty girl friend had long ago been lost in the shuffle.

But at bottom Mr. Turrido was never fully in favor of the business. Although his mind told him that they never were, there was still a lurking suspicion deep in his Sicilian heart that women should be sacred and inviolable. It was almost a relief when war came and he was able to turn his talent, muscles and money to the more manly affairs of the black market. Those were the exciting days. Other murders were involved, of course, but inconsequential ones. Mr. Turrido's mind was turning to other things. He was meeting a different variety of people—some of them even had titles.

Once the desire was born, it grew swiftly. For the first time in his life Mr. Turrido had a consuming ambition other than power and money. He decided that he wanted to be a gentleman. He set to work on it, and he succeeded beyond his wildest dreams.

The war ended, time passed, and the money solidified. For three years now he had conducted no business whatever except one elegant little racket fully in keeping with his station in society. Life was rewarding him for past labors. In the previous twelve months, representing himself vaguely as the owner of large sulphur mines in Sicily, he had begun to be accepted into the very highest of high society. He received at least two desirable invitations to dinner each week. People bowed to him on fashionable thoroughfares on the rare occasions that he walked.

It was true he sometimes felt a need for exercise, was short of breath, was at the moment wearing a corset to take in a minute amount of unsightly fat. But Mr. Turrido knew that at the age of forty-seven he retained all his old vitality and strength. He needed only a week of conditioning, a fortnight at most, to put him back into the pink.

Over in the big cage a canary cheeped sleepily. Mr. Turrido flexed the biceps of his right arm, tested them with his left hand, and sank contentedly into a chair. His smoking jacket rustled silkily. His patent leather shoes pointed fastidiously to the front. The drink was where he had left it on the table by the window. He felt too relaxed to get up again. He lolled back his head. He roared, "Angelo!"

The door opened instantly. The curly-headed pale-faced boy hovered on the threshold and gazed at Mr. Turrido with a worshipful look that was satisfying in the extreme.

"Are the servants gone?"

The eighteen-year-old boy nodded. He preferred to speak little, because Mr. Turrido made fun of his Sicilian accent. He wished very much that he was rich and powerful and cultured like Mr. Turrido.

"No sign of our American and his customer?"

Angelo shook his head. "They're late," he ventured.

"Clearly," Mr. Turrido said paternally, waving a hand. "Refill my glass. Bring a fresh cigar."

He watched fondly as his orders were obeyed, liking the lad almost as well as the canaries. Angelo would be even more useful if one ever decided to get back into business. He'd do anything he was bid; one could tell that by the adoration in his eyes. Mr. Turrido recalled Angelo's tears of gratitude the previous week when he had been presented with a .45 automatic. Too big for the lad, of course, but that didn't prevent his wearing it all the time in the inside pocket of his jacket.

Mr. Turrido sipped his drink, puffed his fresh cigar, smiled upwards and played God for a minute. "You like being here with me, Angelo?"

The eyes lit briefly, taking some of the cruelty out of the little white rat face. Angelo nodded eagerly. But there was nervousness in his answering smile. In his heart he still did not believe his luck. He had always a small fear that he might be sent away again. He looked anxiously at the cigar to see if it was burning properly. He longed with all his being to do something really important for this wonderful man.

Mr. Turrido said purringly, "It could have been very different. I might have sent for the police when I caught you stealing from my house."

He saw the fright on the boy's face and reached out and slapped him reassuringly on the buttock. "No," he laughed, "don't fret, *giovanotto*. There's a long life in front of us. You are going to be of great use to me in the future. You too will be rich." The boy reminded him of himself at that age, thinner, naturally, but the same Sicilian accent. And what if Mr. Turrido had been caught during his first theft? He opened his mouth to soothe further.

Downstairs a bell rang. Mr. Turrido's expression changed. He looked rapidly around at the pictures on the wall, snapped his fingers and nodded. Angelo cast him a final idolizing look and went down to open the door.

The footsteps came up the stairs. There were only two sets. When Angelo re-entered the room, Mr. Turrido was prepared through long instinct for some sort of emergency. But he smiled warmly at the other man who came in. He said with great grace, "Good evening, Mr. Abbott."

The tall American nodded tersely. A surly uncertainty revealed that he was half drunk. He sat down without being asked and gazed directly at the Sicilian with glazing eyes. He was trying to be brave about something. Mr. Turrido's sense of emergency increased.

"A drink for Mr. Abbott," he commanded genially. Angelo leaped to obey. The American took the glass without speaking. Mr. Turrido leaned forward on the top of his corset and offered a cigar.

Jake Abbott's voice was thick with alcohol. "Never smoke them," he said. "Do you have a cigarette? I'm right out."

"And I have only cigars in the house." Mr. Turrido smiled. "Angelo! The bars will still be open. Go buy the gentleman a packet of *Nazionales*."

They were a cheap brand; he felt delightfully superior at ordering them. It was really a neat little insult, a sign of contempt. He waited till the front door closed, then inclined his head and smiled benignly. "And how progresses your job at the Press Association?"

The American shrugged and looked up. It was a casual glance, but suddenly their eyes locked. They stared at one another. Mr. Turrido said, barely moving his lips, "Does the work still bring you into contact with all the more interesting Americans who visit Rome?"

Jake Abbott straightened. He said, "Sure. And the richest. Come out in the open, Turrido. Ask why I didn't bring Mr. Summerhill tonight."

"I was wondering," Turrido murmured. "I have gone to special pains for Mr. Summerhill. You say he knows something of painting. We cannot therefore sell him anything too obvious." He pointed a finger to one of the paintings on the wall. "He will buy that beautiful imitation of a Benedetto Bembo."

The American remained silent.

Mr. Turrido said, "Once again we will say that I am an impoverished nobleman. He will be happy to obtain the Bembo from me for twenty-two thousand dollars."

Abbott said, "I'm not bringing him."

Mr. Turrido continued unperturbed. "As second choice he can have the Matteo di Giovanni. Truly one of the best imitations I've ever seen. It will appeal to him and make him happy. Americans always expect a Madonna and Child from Italy. Who are we to disappoint them?"

He smiled. He said, "I shall cry a little as he pays me the twenty thousand. The picture has been in my family for generations. There will be a fee of an extra thousand dollars for smuggling it out of the country."

"He's not coming. Not tonight nor any other time."

Mr. Turrido shifted his weight. "Now, these other Americans you have in mind. You say they know nothing of art. I am having some Giottos prepared. He suits all tastes. And there will be two or three Canalettos. Those nice clean colors always seem to appeal to your fellow countrymen."

The corner of Abbott's mouth twitched. He said, "Get it in your head, Turrido. Summerhill won't be here, nor any of the others. I came tonight to tell you I'm through with the racket."

The Sicilian drew deeply on his cigar. He was being defied. A trembling started within him, the same feeling that in the old days had always preceded a fight. He let it flow unchecked. He said, "You want a higher percentage? But I take the risks, Abbott. You merely meet the people and bring them here."

"I want nothing," the American said violently. "Just to quit. As of now I've done it." He started to rise.

"Wait!" Mr. Turrido stood up so quickly that the ash dropped from his cigar. It infuriated him. The trembling increased. He said, "You have certain commitments. I have invested considerable money in future stock."

"Find yourself another contact man."

Mr. Turrido's voice grew louder. "One thing more. I've advanced money to you. You owe me precisely two thousand one hundred dollars."

"I'll pay you back."

"From your wages? How?"

"That's my worry."

"And mine. I don't like to worry. You will return the money in twenty-four hours."

The American said in English, "Nuts!" He began to get up. Mr. Turrido felt the angered strength surge through his muscles. He did not resist it. This was just like old times. He drew back his hand and hit the American hard across the face.

Abbott sat down again, a red mark spreading across his cheek. "That was interesting," he said. "What's the next move?"

"Whatever I say." Mr. Turrido felt suddenly twenty years younger. "For one thing we'll have no more disobedience," he snapped, reverting unconsciously to his Sicilian accent. "You bring Summerhill tomorrow, and the rest whenever I tell you. Your commission remains at three per cent. I want no more trouble."

"Or?" The American no longer seemed so drunk.

"Or your life won't be worth living. You'll lose your job. I'll spread the word about this married woman that you—"

The American scrambled up and made a clumsy lunge. The Sicilian's big fist swung hard. Abbott fell to the floor and lay there for a few seconds. Mr. Turrido towered over him, feeling immensely powerful.

He said contemptuously, "Perhaps I should beat you to show who's master." He said nothing else. The American seemed to spring clean from the floor. Mr. Turrido had no time to dodge. His nose crunched. He hurtled backwards across the room and smacked against a wall.

He couldn't believe it. The blood was running over his chin. He was terribly short of breath. He gasped, "You son of a bitch," and made a rush. With great ease the American hit him again. Mr. Turrido staggered. He hit the big cage of canaries. There was a fluttering of wings and a frantic chorus of cheeping. Mr. Turrido screamed, "Angelo!"

The canaries were whirring from the broken cage and beating in small yellow clouds to the ceiling. Mr. Turrido reached out and flung a box at his opponent; cigars scattered all over the floor. He snatched a small vase, smashed it against the edge of the table and ran again, swinging the jagged ends at the American's face.

Abbott stepped, to one side, grunted and hit. Mr. Turrido went flat on the floor, the remains of the vase shattered in his own bleeding hand. He looked up, suddenly very frightened; the sensation outraged him. He went berserk. He clutched Abbott's legs and pulled himself upright, not even feeling the blows that hammered into his face.

He bit. He pulled the American's hair and tried to kick him in the groin. The air was wheezing from his lungs; his corset was too tight, and he couldn't get his breath. In all the body of which he was so proud there was not an ounce of strength. He shrieked, "Angelo! Angelo! Angelo ..."

He relived the humiliation afterwards, many times. He knew exactly how it had happened. His jacket had been torn open. He'd been trying to bring up his knee, jerking his head in an attempt to butt the other man's face. The American had hit him in the stomach. Somehow his fingers had got tangled in the waistband of Mr. Turrido's trousers. Mr. Turrido had fallen backwards, but the fingers had held. There had been a rending of cloth, and Mr. Turrido had lain flat on his back and looked at the circling canaries—his shirt pulled up, his trousers down. The bright pink corset had been shamefully exposed for all to see....

Angelo ran into the room with a packet of cigarettes.

The boy came to a sudden halt. He gaped. In a frenzy of mortification Mr. Turrido shrieked, "Get him! Get him!" Angelo dropped the cigarettes and drove a hand at his inside pocket.

He was too slow. The American hit him in the side of the face and he went down, still reaching for the gun which glinted on the floor. He tried to raise himself. The American stamped hard on his wrist, and kicked. The gun skidded. It went clean through the door and clattered halfway down the stairs. Then the American ran and in a minute the street door slammed.

Mr. Turrido slowly picked himself up. He was trembling. He groped for his torn trousers. The boy sat on the floor and held his wrist, his pale face averted from the spectacle before him. The canaries flew, twittering, overhead. A few had settled on the frames of the pictures.

Mr. Turrido hissed breathlessly, "You son of a whore, you useless fool, why didn't you do something? Why do you think I gave you that gun?"

Angelo got to his feet, his head hanging. He still gripped his wrist. Mr. Turrido was vainly trying to recover a vestige of composure. He felt like screaming. He had been mocked, insulted, humiliated. He wanted his revenge. But he was too old, he knew now. In an excess of anger he struck the boy twice in the face.

It calmed his breathing a little, but the hatred was not lessened. He said, "There was an excuse for me. He hit me with the vase when I wasn't looking. But you! You!" It was too much. He hit the boy again.

Angelo gulped in a deep breath. He stood motionless, his eyes blazing. He whispered, "What shall I do?"

"What do you want to do?"

"I want to kill him," Angelo answered shakily.

Mr. Turrido nodded. "Good. Follow him, Angelo. He has moved again. Find where he lives. Wait your opportunity. He insulted us, didn't he? Don't come back until we have repaid him."

Angelo nodded once and ran from the room. He paused halfway down the stairs to pick up the gun, and then the street door closed quietly. Mr. Turrido remained rigid at the center of the room. His head ached, his nose was still bleeding, and his trousers were falling down. A sob of sheer anger rose from deep in his chest and he started to weep with fury. He couldn't stop.

The little white canary soared down from the ceiling and fluttered in front of his face. He raised his hand automatically. The bird settled on his palm and twittered softly. It was Lili, and Lili was laughing.

Mr. Turrido swore and clenched his fist. The bird died without a sound. The blood spurted out, ran down Mr. Turrido's wrist and dripped to the floor. He raised his arm, flinging the bloody mass of feathers across the room. Then he went outside into the passage for the phone.

A few seconds later he asked the operator for the number of the Universal Press Association. Back in the room the canaries cheeped feebly at each other as if they were scandalized at the dreadful thing that had happened.

Chapter Two

Jake Abbott turned into the dingy side street, saw his hotel, and stopped running. He looked over his shoulder. No one was following. It didn't quiet the panic in him. His heart beat hard in his throat. He needed a drink.

He told himself he'd been a fool. A few more days and maybe he'd be out of it, away to Paris, away from everything. He should have stalled along, not visited Turrido, pretended to play the game to the very end. But he'd got this crazy idea of having to do at least one thing on the level. After a few drinks it had seemed honorable to go to Turrido and say he was quitting.

Honesty, the best policy—fine way it turned out. He knew Turrido's type. The fat little swine would go to any length to get his own back. Jake Abbott walked into the shabby hotel lobby feeling empty.

The desk clerk was waiting with the key and a letter. He smiled as if he had a small, unpleasant secret. Jake tore open the envelope and read the note. His spirits plummeted. The job in Paris was not open for another month. He had no money; he'd have to continue working in Rome till then, He looked hopelessly at the clerk and said, "Anything else?"

The smile under the penciled mustache became a little more indecent. The man leaned across the desk with his secret. "The *signorina* is here again, Mr. Abbott," he whispered. "Waiting up in your room." Jake Abbott suddenly wanted to hit him.

He strode to the elevator, slammed the doors and put a ten-lire piece in the slot. The cage ascended jerkily. The nervous ache in his solar plexus was increasing. He went along the dusty corridor, hesitated a moment and pushed open the door. Grace was sitting on the sofa.

She rose to meet him, smiling. She said softly, "Darling, I've been waiting simply hours. I thought you were never coming." She held out her arms.

He walked past her. He went to the far corner of the room and poured himself a whisky. In the small mirror above the table his eyes looked puffy and oriental. He was drinking too much. He turned around with the glass in his hand and he said, "I told you not to come here again."

"I know. But you didn't mean it."

"Christ, yes I did!" he exploded. "Don't you women ever take a brushoff?"

"No. Not when we know the man is in love with us."

He stared at her, helpless with the truth of what she had said. It was more than love. He was obsessed with her. To see her standing there was enough to fill his heart, and not all the derisive words in the world could unpack it. He said, "Oh God, Grace, go away. We can't continue like this. Don't you see?"

She didn't answer. She went back and sat on the sofa. She said, "What are we going to do?"

"Nothing," he said. "There's nothing we can do. Let's face it. You've got a husband. He's been a friend to me, and I've repaid him by making love to his wife. Well, I'm tired of it. I want to go back to being a nice guy."

She said slowly, "Then I've really been kidding myself to think you loved me."

He took a step toward her, every instinct crying a protest. It was because he loved her so much that he was going away. A little less love and he might not feel this nagging urge to act decent. It was hard to explain even to himself. The affair had started with an almost casual intimacy after a party. Now the bounds had been overleapt. And because it was so profound and consuming he couldn't bear any longer that they continue seeing each other in out-of-the-way bars, in grubby little hotel rooms. Better to have nothing at all than that.

And she had a husband.

He said, "Grace, you owe Ralph something."

"Yes, I suppose so," she said quietly. She looked down at the folded hands in her lap. "I wish he were dead."

He finished the whisky, put the glass back on the sideboard. "Want a drink?"

"No."

He crossed to the sofa and stood awkwardly over her. He wanted to reach out, touch her, take her in his arms. He said, "Look here. Promise not to make a scene. I didn't want to tell you yet, but I've got to be honest. I am in love with you, yes. But we can't go on this way. There's no end in view. It's not enough anymore just to crawl into bed. I want all or nothing."

He paused. He said, "And you've got him, so I get nothing. Well, we'll bring it to a clean finish. A guy has offered me a job. I'm quitting the Press Association in two or three weeks and going to Paris. We won't see each other again. It'll be best."

She looked up at him and gave a jerky little laugh. Her face twisted. "Oh, of course it'll be best," she said. "It'll be lovely. And you don't want me to make a scene." A sob wrenched out of her. She buried her face in her hands and burst into tears.

He dropped to the sofa beside her and wrapped her tight against him. He said, "Don't make it difficult, Grace. How the hell do you think I feel?" He kissed the top of her hair, his hands smoothed her back.

"Jake, I'll go with you," she said. "I'll go anywhere with you." She turned her face to him, searching hungrily for his mouth. His hold tightened. The fire started in him. And then he knew he was lost, that he'd never get away from her. He was kissing her lips, her cheek, the hollow of her throat. His hands dragged hard over her shoulders, cupping roughly at the warm resiliency of her breasts.

The scorching warmth of her arms came tight around him, burning through the thinness of his shirt. They strained to each other. It was a flame that neither could quench. She was falling against him, making a little moaning noise. He pulled her across his lap and picked her up and carried her toward the bedroom.

On the other side of the door the phone began to ring insistently. He stopped.

"Leave it," she whispered.

"No," he said, "I can't."

"It'll just be some drunk at this time of the morning."

"I know," he said, and set her down. "They'll quit in a minute."

The phone continued ringing. He counted. Nine times. Ten. He looked at her again and shrugged and went into the bedroom, jerking the receiver from its cradle.

"Hello?"

"That you, Jake?"

"Yeah."

"Where were you? I been phoning all over."

"I went on a pub-crawl."

There was a pause at the other end. Ralph Ellison said, "Somebody else been trying to get you. A guy with a Sicilian accent. He wanted your address."

The nerves jumped all over Jake's stomach. "You give it to him?"

"No. Told him it was a rule never to hand out information about employees."

"That's good," Jake said.

There was another pause. Ralph Ellison cleared his throat. He said casually, "Didn't happen to see Grace around tonight, did you? I wondered if maybe you'd both wound up at the same party. She wasn't home when I left."

"When you left?" Jake said quickly. "Where the hell are you now? Not at the office, for God's sake, not at this time of night."

"Where else? Women and newspapermen—our work is never done."

"You mean me too?"

"I mean you especially, son. That's what the panic's about. We got a really dirty dilly. A village called Piscoli, up in the mountains way south of Naples. The place got flooded tonight. Thirty-two people were killed. I want you there. Harry Myers will go along for pictures."

"Right. I'll take the morning train."

"You'll take a train in two hours. It may be the last. The rain's still falling in buckets down there. You'd better pack a change of clothes."

"Two hours?"

"That's what I said. The train takes you as far as Asceno, population around a hundred thousand. There's a small branch line out to Piscoli. Or you may have to walk by that time. I'm calling Harry now."

"He may not be home."

"He will." Ralph Ellison laughed. "He's been married to that glorious babe for exactly three weeks. A man always stays home at that stage of the proceedings." He cleared his throat again. His tone changed. "You didn't tell me if you saw Grace."

"No. I haven't."

"No? I see. Any questions?"

"Money. I don't have any."

"Come over to the office and get some. I'll answer anything else when you get here. Okay?"

"Sure. See you." He hung up.

She had come into the room, was standing close behind him. He said in a miserable attempt at flippancy, "Your husband, dear. I'm going to quit newspaper work and write a modern little play about the situation. Cosy, isn't it?" He walked into the other room and poured himself a fresh drink from a new bottle of whisky. In the bedroom she started to cry again.

He couldn't take it. He shouted, "For the love of God, Grace, shut up!"

She appeared at the doorway, her face streaked with tears. "What did he want?"

"To know where you were. It's a game of tag. He gets warmer all the time."

"I'm certain he doesn't suspect anything," she said.

Jake tossed off the drink, walked to a cupboard and pulled out a small suitcase. He said, "After this he'll have no cause." He opened the case on the sofa and began throwing in a few clothes.

She advanced upon him, slowly at first then with a stumbling little run. Her eyes were large with tears and pain and bewilderment. She said, "You're not going to Paris now? Not leaving me like this?"

"No." He shook his head. A shirt dropped to the floor. She picked it up and smoothed it and placed it in the case. He said, "Don't come too near, Grace. I feel bad enough as it is." He bent over and swiftly kissed her cheek. They smiled at one another.

"How much are you packing?" She walked to the wardrobe.

"Only a change. I have to go to a place called Piscoli. It's raining down there. There's been a disaster. Thirty-two killed."

She took his trench coat from a hanger. She was trying to be impersonal. "Poor things. I did some committee work for that other business a little while back. The poor in this country have enough to endure without natural catastrophes."

"Yes," he said.

She was standing behind him. She said, "I'm going with you."

He wheeled on her. "Don't be so damned foolish."

"I can't help it."

"You're not going."

"I want to."

"Then you can go on wanting."

She looked into his eyes. She said coldly, "Dear God, what an ignorant swine you are."

He said, "When you're around, yes. Clear out. You're a bloody nuisance."

She slapped his face.

In the next moment they were in each other's arms, holding tight as if they were the only two people left in the world. They stood for a while in silence, not moving, feeling the warmth that flowed from one to the other. She looked up. She said, "I've bruised you."

"That happened earlier." He broke away. "Look, Grace, I can wait for you in Paris. See what Ralph says about a divorce."

"He won't, Jake."

"Maybe we can think of something else."

She said, "There has to be something else. Paris is such a long way away and I get sick when you're out of my sight for more than an hour." She came nearer. "Let me go with you to this village."

"It's out of the question. It might be dangerous."

"I don't care. And Ralph has to know some time."

"Yeah, but not this way. I'm tired of being underhanded. I'll tell him to his face when the time comes. Don't insist, or we'll quarrel again."

He finished packing, went over and got the bottle of whisky and put it in the top of the case. She said, "You drink too much, Jake."

"Shut up, Grace." He snapped the catches, picked up the case and looked around the room. "Let's go." They went out together to the elevator.

He didn't have a ten-lire piece for the slot. They had to wait while she fumbled in her handbag. They stood close together, both very quiet. In the confined space their breathing sounded abnormally loud. Her hand was trembling as she inserted the coin.

The cage descended. She turned to him. "When do you get back?"

"A few days. I'm not sure."

"Let me go with you." Her eyes brimmed with tears.

"No," he said. The elevator bumped the ground floor.

He pushed open the doors and went across to the desk. The clerk was waiting, a small smile, eyelids drooping intimately.

"Going out again so soon, *signore?*" His gaze flicked insolently to Grace.

"I'll be gone a few days. Forward any mail to the Universal Press Association."

The pencil mustache quirked. "I quite understand. And enjoy your holiday, sir."

"Thanks," said Jake, and turned back to Grace. They went slowly toward the door. Her shoulders were drooping. She said, "I can't help it, Jake, I feel rotten. I think I'm going to make a scene."

"I'll never forgive you."

A man bustled in from the street, carrying two suitcases. A taximan at the curb was getting slowly into his cab.

She said, "It isn't love, you know. It's a sickness."

"I know," he said. "Wait here."

He went swiftly through the entrance. The cab was pulling away. He leapt into the back and slammed the door and she had a glimpse of him through the window. He lifted a hand. He was gone.

She ran outside. A small figure collided with her and almost knocked her down. She saw briefly a thin, pale face. The boy flashed past without apology and hurried down the road in the direction taken by the cab. She stood helplessly in the middle of the sidewalk and wondered what to do.

At the end of the street Angelo paused for breath. Then he flagged another cab.

Chapter Three

Jake Abbott sat in the corner of a first-class compartment nursing his bottle of whisky and waiting for the train to start. He was getting drunk. Through the window he could see Harry Myers saying good-by to his new wife and the sight made him feel resentful and envious.

They were ill-matched in appearance. Harry with gray hair, tall and thin, looked older than forty-two as he bent down to whisper in the ear of his twenty-year-old Italian bride. But the love they had, the eager way their eyes sought each other's faces, made the physical disparity insignificant. They fitted. Jake caught himself watching them greedily as they kissed. He looked away, trying to ignore the sudden pang inside him.

Life was a mess anyway. He took a swig from the bottle and said, "Hello," to the only other person in the compartment, a small fat man with popping eyes. The man returned a stiff nod and looked away. The hell with him, Jake Abbott thought.

He realized how drunk he was becoming. He took another nip and settled deep in the corner, aware that the fat man's gaze had skated over him with disapproval. He closed his eyes. The train gave a preliminary jolt. Harry Myers shouted from the platform, "Jake, aren't you saying good-by to Lucia?"

"Sure." He flung out of the corner and leaned from the window his head spinning a little. The other two smiled up at him, the Italian girl's brown eyes soft with love as she clung to Harry's arm. Jake said, "*Addio*, Lucia, you beautiful *ragazza*. I'm getting rid of Harry this trip and coming back to snatch you for myself."

She looked at her husband to check whether it was all right. She saw he was smiling so she laughed. She said, "Goo'by, Jek. You tek care of heem, huh?"

"Him? He's indestructible."

There was a hiss of escaping steam. The train jolted again, and people began scrambling aboard. Harry kissed his wife and patted her on the backside. "Don't wait any longer, honey. Run along. Go straight back to bed. Do as I say, now." They exchanged a last kiss and she hurried off down the platform, a small figure in a fur coat, her chin buried deep in the collar. Jake sank back into the corner. The fat man tried not to look at him.

The third and second classes were packed in like sardines. The first class as usual was quiet. Harry Myers's footsteps sounded down the corridor from the end of the coach, then the door slid open and he entered the compartment and dropped into the opposite corner. His glance flicked over the luggage rack, checked his photographic equipment, skidded away from the fat man, and came to rest on Jake. He said cheerfully, "Boozing?"

"Some. Want a drink?"

"At this black hour of the morning? I'm a married man now. I'm respectable."

"So would I be, with Lucia. She looked good. Nice fur coat."

"I went into hock for it. She's worth every nickel. Want me to tell you how wonderful she is?"

"Not again."

They grinned. The train hissed, gave its final jolt, began pulling from the station. A thin chorus of farewells rose from knots of people huddled on the platform. Some of them cheered encouragingly as a thin youth with curly hair came streaking through the gates and swung up onto the last coach.

Jake put the cork in the bottle. He leaned back drunkenly. He shut his eyes and tried not to think of anything. The lights of the Roman suburbs shone through the window, flickering over his eyelids. There was a long sequence of darkness. He fell into a doze....

He sat up with a start. The door from the corridor slid open. He was trying to remember how Ralph had really looked back at the office. He blinked blearily at the figure about to enter.

It was a medium-sized man, maybe thirty, wearing a nicely cut Brooks Brothers style smoke-gray suit. He smiled confidently. His teeth were excellent. He said, "Sorry to bust in, but you're Americans, aren't you?" His voice was upstate New York.

Jake didn't answer. The fat man continued staring at nothing through the window. Harry Myers grinned and nodded. "Any way we can help?"

"If you have an American cigarette, I'm dying for one." The man came right in, still showing his fine teeth. He sat down next to Harry. "Nice night," he said as he took the cigarette. "Thanks. I hear the weather's not so good where I'm going."

He glanced around. Nobody was taking him up. He inhaled deeply.

"Name's Leverett," he said.

"Harry Myers. This is Jake Abbott." They shook hands all around. The fat man was pretending they weren't there. Leverett said, "I'm bound for a place called Piscoli. Supposed to be some sort of flood there. I represent the Italian-American Assistance Committee. They're sending me down to supervise immediate aid."

Jake said, "What, all by yourself?"

Leverett lost his smile. "Well, no, as a matter of fact. At the last moment they gave me a girl assistant." He rallied again. "Very blonde and very pretty. She'll console me, perhaps, if the going gets too wet. Have you heard about this flood?"

Harry nodded. "Pretty bad, they tell me."

"Very bad. I expect to find chaotic conditions. That's why it's best to be on the spot at once, to see what happens to the aid we give. You can't really trust these Italians. At the last disaster all the stuff we sent disappeared into the football stadium for three months. Then it reappeared in the stores. For sale. They're great boys for a swift dollar."

"Some of them are all right," Harry said. "I'm married to one."

"Oh, I like the women." Leverett's smile flashed broader than ever. "No offense meant. You boys going to Naples?"

"We're going to Piscoli," Jake said, "and I'm trying to get some sleep on the way down." He jerked his head at the Italian. "Harry, see what that fat little bastard says if you try to turn off the light."

Leverett looked from one to the other. "Piscoli? What for?"

"Press Association," Harry said.

"Really? That's very interesting. I once had newspaper ambitions myself. Have you been writing long?"

"No. I'm the photographer."

"Photography!" Leverett's eyelids flickered with interest. "I paint a little myself. That was my main reason for coming to Italy."

"You must tell us all about it," Jake said. "Some other time. Turn the damned light out, Harry."

The fat man turned from the window. He said in English, "Excuse me, gentlemen, but with your permission I wish to read later on." He resumed staring out into the night.

Harry Myers grinned. Jake took another drink and buried his face in the upholstery. Leverett said, "Personally I don't think I have much talent, but people keep telling me I paint like Calvani."

"Lucky if you can get those blues," Harry Myers said.

"Oh, you know something about it."

Jake was vaguely aware of them droning on. He started to doze again, counting the rhythmic clatterings of the wheels on the ties, determined not to think of Paris or Grace or anything. He sank deeper. A long time passed....

The train was jolting to a stop. He awoke, the dream still on him, head twisted back in an angle of terror. Someone was looking at him from down the corridor. It was Angelo. Jake Abbott closed his eyes then looked again and there was nothing. He'd imagined it. He stretched, tried to moisten his dry mouth and sat up.

Raindrops were pounding against the window. Leverett had gone. Harry was asleep. The other man was reading. Jake said, "Is this Naples?"

The Italian lowered his book. He replied pleasantly, "We passed Naples more than an hour ago. You have slept. We are almost to Asceno. I wonder why we stopped."

"Don't know." Jack kicked Harry's shoe. The photographer stirred, yawned, smacked his lips. "What?"

"Almost there."

"That so? Oh God, hark to that weather."

"I know."

The corridor door slid back. A train conductor poked in his head, looking worried. "Pardon," he said. "I think we go no farther. Passengers will now have to walk." He withdrew and went down the corridor.

"What was all that?" Harry said.

"Floods." The Italian stood up and took a small bag from the luggage rack. "It is possible that part of the mountain has washed down and blocked the tracks." He smiled at them and stepped delicately over their outstretched legs. "Good morning, gentlemen," he said, and vanished down the corridor.

"But don't we get the creamiest jobs," Harry moaned, gathering his gear. "Listen to that rain."

At his words the intensity seemed to increase. They walked into the corridor and it sounded like a tin tunnel being bombarded by a tornado of buckshot. Along at the end a handful of passengers were pulling coats tightly around them, being ushered out by the same guard, who was now saying something about a bridge. He waved a hand and added that taxis were waiting. They joined the crowd and descended the two steep steps and found themselves in the cold, leaden dimness of a rain-slashed morning. After the heat of sleeping Jake shivered violently. His shoes sank over the soles in mud.

The mountains rose all around them. Ahead of the train, through the thick curtain of rain, Jake discerned the bridge spanning a chasm. The noise of falling water was incredible. In a hundred places it cascaded down the mountains with a roar, bringing with it stones and mud and small uprooted trees. The raindrops beat fiercely, as if each had a venomous life of its own. Jake felt them penetrate. In two minutes he was soaked.

"Land of sunshine, song, and the tinkling mandolin," Harry said. "Our story. But how in hell do we get to it?"

Jake looked back along the train to where about thirty more passengers were descending. Mentally he made notes, picking the salient points for a possible story, the huddling people, the steep bank sloping from the railway line, the lights from a cluster of houses farther up the mountain shining dimly through the feeble daylight. He looked at his watch and was mildly shocked to see it said almost ten o'clock. He still felt drunk.

He had to get up front to see what had happened to the bridge. It might be further material for the story. He started to turn and he saw her descending from a carriage at the back of the train. For a blinding instant he felt more joy than he could possibly contain. Then fury filled him. He muttered something to Harry and ran toward her.

She saw him coming, and halted. She lifted her head and smiled, her eyes almost closed against the rain. She said, "Hello, Jake. I told you I had to come."

"You crazy bitch," he said. "You crazy bitch. What do you think this is?"

She flinched as though he had struck her. He said, "What excuse did you give Ralph?"

"I didn't," she answered dully. "He doesn't know I'm here. I expect the committee will tell him."

"What committee?"

Leverett emerged from the coach behind her, swinging himself lightly down the two steps. "Hello," he hailed brightly. "Hell of a weather. I see you've met my beautiful blonde co-worker. Her name's Mrs. Ellison."

"Is it?" Jake reached out and took her suitcase. "Let's get moving before we drown," he said, and turned on his heel and stalked back down the track. Harry Myers pivoted to meet them. His gray eyebrows shot high on his forehead. "Well lawsy-daisy and look who's here. Welcome to Atlantis, Grace."

She managed a smile. Leverett blinked suspiciously. "Do you all know each other?"

Nobody answered. "Been checking the bridge for you, Jake," Harry said. "All this water's eroding the foundations. They don't know how much it'll take anymore. We're to get down this bank and be driven into town by cab." He groaned. "My rheumatism, friends, is going to give me gyp after this."

Leverett said, "We can all go together."

Some of the passengers were already descending to the road, slipping and slithering down the high muddy incline to where a faintly seen line of taxis was waiting, the driving rain hammering their roofs. Harry Myers walked to the edge. "We're off," he said, and started down sideways, ramming the edges of his soles into the mud to retain balance, the photographic equipment banging heavily against his sides. Jake took Grace by the arm and dragged her forward, gripping her tighter as they went down the bank, feeling her tremble under his hand.

The anger was still in him. He said tautly, "You must have arranged this trip at pretty short notice."

Leverett was right behind them. "The committee needs a lot more workers like Mrs. Ellison." He had to speak loud to make himself heard above the rain. He said, "She volunteered as soon as she heard," and then he paused, a little breathless. "Where does Piscoli lie from here? Anybody know?"

"No." Grace stumbled. Jake pulled her closer, not knowing whether it was rain or tears that filled her eyes. His anger was subsiding. He said, "Hang on tight." They went down together to where Harry was waiting.

Some of the passengers were going to be stranded. There were not enough taxis. Leverett saw it sooner than anyone else. He broke away suddenly and streaked for the nearest of the remaining four, entering into violent conversation with the driver. Then he waved the others to him and opened the door and scrambled inside. They hurried through the rain and clambered gratefully after him.

"Everything fixed," he said. "I explained that we're newspapermen." He leaned on the back of the seat and addressed the driver in Italian. "How much are you charging us, man?"

"Two thousand lire."

"Robber!" Leverett laughed and lapsed into English. "Afraid he's got us by the short hairs, but I guess you boys have expense accounts, huh?" He switched back to Italian. "Can you drive us straight to the village of Piscoli?"

The driver shook his head. "As far as Asceno."

"Okay," Leverett cried gaily. "Lead on, Macduff. *Andiamo!*"

The driver meshed his gears. Jake rubbed his sleeve against the steamed inside of the window for a last look out. A few passengers were still descending the slope. He glanced upward.

Coming last, without an overcoat, drenched to the skin, was the thin little figure of Angelo. This time Jake recognized him for certain. A stab of fear shot through him; unconsciously he drew closer to Grace. She looked at him in surprise. Her fingers lightly brushed his wrist.

The cab leapt forward with a sudden burst of speed.

Chapter Four

Signor Attilio Drago, the mayor of Asceno, rested three chins on his cupped hands, brooded intermittently and waited for the phone to ring again. It had been ringing steadily since yesterday morning. He had answered it every time. He needed sleep. He pushed at his drooping eyelids with his forefingers and wished he were on holiday in Naples.

Capitano Ettore Luca, looking stonily at the mayor's bowed head, shifted his weight from one foot to the other and waited for a resumption of conversation. It didn't come. He cleared his throat and said coldly, "Then there is nothing?"

"No."

Mayor Drago kept his head lowered. He didn't like the policeman's heavy black mustache, he didn't like the policeman, and above all he didn't trust him. Nobody did. He was too silent. And that business during the war had never been cleared up. People still talked. The mayor would have been happy to get the man transferred elsewhere. But he was, after all, only a mayor.

He said, "The people from Piscoli?"

"All evacuated," Captain Luca said. "We found billets in various parts of the town. The mountain road is now completely blocked. The village is inaccessible. There will not be much left of it tonight, if this rain continues. The small aqueduct ..."

He was cut short by a wave of the hand. "Nothing will happen to the small aqueduct. As well to suggest the big one might collapse." Mr. Drago snorted in disgust. He not only distrusted the captain; he was now beginning to distrust God for sending so much rain. Unbelievable; it had never happened before. And it was bad publicity for the district; bad for the tourist trade if news got bruited around that Asceno, treasure house of art and culture, gem of the mountains, suffered from brutality of climate. It was bad for local trade, bad for the local mayor. Falling prosperity would demand new elections. The local Communists were sniffing for office.

Mr. Drago, who liked being mayor, felt bitter.

He gazed prayerfully at the ceiling. He said, "Perhaps the rain will stop soon." The phone rang. He snatched it up.

"Hello. Yes. What?" He gave a cry of anguish. "*Madonna mia*, not the bridge! Why wasn't I informed before? I want to be informed immediately of everything. Make certain the passengers are comfortable. Tell them the rain is due to cease at any moment. Welcome them to Asceno in the name of the mayor."

He hung up and looked accusingly at Captain Luca. "The railway bridge to Naples is no longer safe."

"I know. The foundations began crumbling at four this morning. I arranged taxis for the last lap of the journey."

"Why wasn't I told?"

"I thought you had enough to cope with."

It was unanswerable, and more infuriating for being so. Mr. Drago swelled slightly with temper. He wanted to swear many great oaths, but the dignity of his office prevented it. He contented himself with glaring balefully at the captain and trying to think of something cuttingly polite. The door opened. The mayor's expression immediately went soft.

The man who entered was chubby, thirty-three years old, had a pink cherub face, a pair of amazingly candid blue eyes, and a head of thinning hair. He was Giovanni, Mr. Drago's only son, the apple of his father's failing eye. He smiled at the mayor, a gentle honest smile, full of understanding and filial affection. He said, "Papa, there are some people out here. They want to see you. I think they're Americans."

The next moment four people were crowding into the office. They were indisputably Americans.

"Welcome to Asceno," the mayor said, standing up.

The gray-headed one quirked a grin. "A lovely little spot, and you must believe that we're very happy to be here. Unfortunately we leave immediately for a village called Piscoli."

Mr. Drago was caught completely off balance. He said, "Why?"

The handsome young man with the oddly frightened look in his eyes stepped forward and proffered a card. "Universal Press Association," he said. "We want a story on the flood."

Mr. Drago realized that the worst had happened—bad publicity, and on an awful scale. "Flood?" he asked, playing for time.

Captain Luca addressed himself to the gray-haired man. He said, "You cannot get to Piscoli. No one can. It has been evacuated. The road is completely washed out."

The mayor almost burst with fury.

"That's nice," said the gray-haired man. The handsome one said, "Where are the bodies of the dead?"

The captain looked at him in disgust. "Still in the village. We had no time to get them out."

"And the evacuees?"

"Scattered through the town. They're comfortable."

Jake looked at the policeman and got the feeling that for some reason he'd made an enemy. Leverett pushed to the front, smiling. "You mean anyone's comfortable in this town? In this weather?"

The gem of the mountains was losing its luster. The mayor shot a hat-ing glance at the captain, livid that he had mentioned the blocked roads. "But this is exceptional," he said quickly. "Never has it rained before like this. By tomorrow the sun will shine hot and strong again, and you will enjoy Asceno. There are fine hotels waiting to welcome you. You will write fine stories. Asceno is a treasure house of art."

"And we apparently are marooned in it," Harry Myers said.

The others were regarding the mayor with complete lack of interest. He was not holding them. He had to think of something special. Then he had an inspiration. It would also repay the captain for speaking out of turn. Without looking at the policeman he said, "Perhaps you gentlemen will investigate our great mystery. It also concerns art. During the war we had a German commandant living here on the mountain. He was an art fancier. He was also a great thief. He stole some of our finest objects for his collection."

From the corner of his eye he saw that Captain Luca was turning a dull red. The mayor continued blandly, "The commandant was later shot, by a policeman. Nobody has ever found the stolen articles, though everyone has a theory about them. Perhaps you will uncover something fresh."

The good-looking one grunted indifferently. "Where are these hotels? We'll stick around till the Piscoli road opens again."

"Stick around long enough with this rain," the gray-haired one said, "and there may be a disaster right here in Asceno."

"Never!" The mayor was suddenly very tired and irritable. He could no longer cope with these foreigners. He flashed his son an appealing look and Giovanni responded immediately. "Papa, I will take them to the Rialto Hotel."

Mayor Drago nodded gratefully. Then his heart sank. One of the Americans was shaking his head. "Not the lady and me," Leverett said. "We haven't started our business yet. I think you'll be happy when we do. We're here to give things away."

Grace said in English, "I could wait for you at the hotel."

Jake was already at the door. "Better stay here, Mrs. Ellison, to supervise the supervisor." He stepped outside with Harry and Giovanni and the door closed.

"Now?" the mayor asked wearily.

Leverett held out his hand. "We represent the Italian-American Aid Committee," he said with a huge smile.

Outside the rain was pelting down, pouring off roofs in great spouts and hissing through the gutters. The taxi sped toward the hotel, leaving a wake behind it. The people in the streets were scurrying from doorway to doorway, some with sodden sacks over their heads. Harry My-

ers said, "So what's the program, kid? Pictures and stories from the evacuees?"

"If you find them," Jake said. "Pictures first. I've written enough of this
stuff not to need interviews."

Harry laughed. "First I got to hunt up a local photographer and bor-
row his dark room."

Giovanni's honest blue eyes glinted helpfully. He said in English,
"There is a local newspaper. They will be happy to oblige another member of the same profession. I will take you there."

"You speak pretty good English."

"I have studied much." Giovanni smiled shyly and ran a hand over his
thinning hair. "Would you gentlemen like to visit a brothel?"

"What?"

"For girls."

"Hell, no, not at this time of the morning." Harry exploded with laughter.

Giovanni said mildly, "Then perhaps later. Americans always like to
visit brothels. I am friendly with the *padrona* of the best establishment
in town. She will make special prices for you."

"I'll bet," Jake said. He was feeling tired. His mouth tasted foul. He
said, "Just get us to the hotel so I can change my clothes."

"*Presto, signore.*"

They splashed up to the imposing entrance. Harry waited in the cab,
preparatory to seeking the local newspaper office. Jake and the mayor's
son padded into the hotel lobby and across to the desk, and the American saw the swift look that passed between Giovanni and the clerk. He
knew what it meant. There was going to be a special price here, too. He
was too fatigued to argue.

He handed his bag to an aging bellboy in a green baize apron and they
crossed to the elevator. As the doors closed he looked back and saw Giovanni holding out a hand for his commission. Maybe it'd be different in
Paris, but he doubted it. They went up.

The room was on the fifth floor, the replica of a hundred others he had
slept in across the country. He threw his unopened case in the cupboard,
lit a cigarette, put his typewriter on the small table and sat in front of
it, trying to think of a lead sentence for a story to fit the pictures Harry
had not yet taken. He couldn't concentrate. He was remembering how
Grace had looked when she'd held up her face against the rain.

He knew she'd come to this hotel, tap on the door and enter and kiss
him and be happy for the two minutes before they had a scene. He did-
n't want to see her now. He went and shook the door to make sure the
catch had caught. He hated himself for what he considered a sniveling
puritanism, but he was thinking of Ralph. Ralph had been a good guy.

The decent thing to do was call Rome and say Grace was here.

Jake picked up the phone, dropped it again and walked to the window. The rain was falling in sheets, laying an opaque brown veil over the city. The distant mountains were almost invisible through the tumbling water. The room was dim. He switched on a brass bedside lamp.

Farther down the street a car pulled up with a screech of brakes. A coatless man leaped from it and ran into an official-looking building. Jake Abbott stiffened. The fear he had tried to suppress came to his consciousness with a force that hurt his eyes. The man had looked like Angelo, who could be here for only one purpose.

He remained staring from the window, wondering if he should communicate with the police. No; the only evidence to offer was that he had himself been involved in a counterfeit painting racket. It meant jail. Mr. Turrido could easily wriggle out of it. The incident would only add to his luster. But for Jake, after jail, it meant blacklisting and no more jobs.

Another man scurried down the street, muffled to the ears in a coat, his face invisible. Maybe Angelo had purchased outer clothing from somewhere. There was no way of telling. Anybody could be Angelo until he got close up.

Jake crossed the room and sank to the bed in his wet clothes. The night's alcohol was telling on him. He wanted to sleep off his worry. He curled up and tried to think of nothing.

Some time later he heard a discreet knocking on the door. It was repeated several times. He ignored it. After a while the caller went away. He switched off the bedside lamp. The room was quite dark. The sound of falling rain beat soporifically on his ears....

At the other side of town Angelo was sipping a glass of strong wine, trying to drive the chill from his bones. His wrist was hurting badly where the American had stamped on it. All the other men in the place were talking of the disaster up at Piscoli and the continuing weather. He waited until the time seemed expedient, and then slipped in a question about the Americans in town and where they were staying.

Nobody knew. They looked at him curiously.

He felt bad. He had made an error, something that would displease Mr. Turrido. In the future he must keep quiet, bide his time, wait until he caught the American somewhere alone. He paid for the drink and left unobtrusively, the dampness biting his flesh.

The moment he was out the door all the other men remarked on his Sicilian accent. They wondered where he was from, what he was doing in town, why a boy in such a good suit didn't also wear a topcoat. Nobody could remember having seen him before.

Chapter Five

The rain outside was falling everlastingly. The key turned in the lock. Jake Abbott stirred awake, opened his eyes in the dark room and came to his feet with a cry. The figure was looming over his head. He struck out blindly. Somebody grabbed his wrist.

"Hell!" a voice said. "You crazy goon. You dreaming or something?" The light switched on. The bellboy was standing over by the door, still holding his passkey. The man gripping Jake's wrist was Ralph Ellison, Grace's husband, his big red face split in a grin, eyes glinting between the blond lashes.

"What the hell are you doing here?" Jake said. He trembled. He went across to the bellboy and angrily flipped his finger against the old man's shoulder. "This room's supposed to be private. Who gave you permission to let anyone in? Get the hell out!" He spun the bellboy into the corridor and slammed the door on him. "Fine damn hotel!" he snapped.

"I got him to open up because we couldn't wake you." Ellison looked surprised. "What's eating you, Jake? Guilty conscience or something?"

"Meaning what?" He realized at once he shouldn't have said it.

But Ralph Ellison continued smiling. "Meaning I'm the man who pays your salary, plus a ruinous expense account. And I come here at six in the evening and find you asleep."

"I see what you mean."

"What did you get today?"

"Nothing I can't write up in half an hour. Piscoli's isolated."

Ellison said happily, "Piscoli be damned. We've got the makings of a fat page-one catastrophe right here in Asceno, if the rain keeps up. People are leaving their houses on the mountains. The water's coming down those rocks like a river. How the hell long you been asleep?"

His grin got wider. He was always good-natured, but never this much. He said, "Fine newspaperman you are. Did you even know this town's been cut off from the outside? No trains? I had to come from Naples by hired car. It was a hell of a trip."

Jake sat down on the edge of the bed. "Why did you come? Keeping tabs on me?"

Ellison gave a curious smile and looked away. "That elegant young wife of mine," he said. "Florence Nightingale and Sister Kenny rolled into one. She left Rome for this committee of hers without telling me. I was worried."

"Yes," Jake said carefully, "I saw her on the train. There's a guy named Leverett with her."

"That fifi! Another bum trying to chisel a swift buck." Ralph turned back to Jake. He said with a sudden almost defiant spurt. "Anyway, if this story really breaks it'll need two of us. How about your hustling out and getting some local color? I hear the Communists are strong here. That's always a good angle for back home. And there's a yarn about missing art treasures stolen during the war. Might be something there."

"I heard about it." Jake stood up. "What about the evacuated suburbs?"

"Oh, I can take care of the main angles until the big thing comes, if it does." Ralph smiled sunnily. "Now don't say I've wounded your professional feelings. I'm not a rival."

"That's right," Jake said.

The smile vanished. The atmosphere went all at once peculiar. They stared at one another, held it too long, and both looked away at the same moment. Jake said, "Ralph." Someone tapped the door. Grace walked in.

They both turned to her in relief. Her eyelids flicked once. She said, "Ralph, Harry Myers stopped in; he says to tell you he'll be down at the local paper, developing today's shots."

"Okay."

She looked at Jake. She said in exactly the same tone: "Wasn't it a surprise, Ralph turning up like this? We've moved into a two-room suite just along the corridor."

"Have you?"

Ralph Ellison said quickly, "Good old Harry, always on the job. Now don't take that as another dirty crack at you."

"I didn't."

"You don't have to," Grace said. "He saves all of those for me. I'll tell you something, Mr. Abbott. My husband arrived here expecting to find me in a two-room suite with you. Or one room. The expression I believe is shacked up."

"Grace!" Ralph said.

She ignored him. She said, "He got a phone call this morning in Rome. Somebody with a Sicilian accent claimed that you and I, Jake, are having an affair. I've neither confirmed nor denied it. Do you have anything to say?"

Jake said, "It's crazy."

"That's what I thought," Ellison said eagerly. "Some screwball trying to make trouble. I hung up on him."

"Did you?"

They stood in a tight little group, none looking at the others. An extra hard flurry of rain tattooed suddenly. The two men glanced across to the window. Grace said, "Well, that very neatly settles everything, doesn't it?" She encompassed them both with a look of contempt, turned quickly and ran from the room, slamming the door hard.

There was a long silence. "I guess she's tired," Ralph murmured. "All night on the train and everything. I'll go talk to her." He hovered uncertainly at the door. "No offense meant, Jake. I wouldn't have said anything, but—"

"Forget it." Jake was pulling on a still-wet raincoat. He was thinking how he'd let her down. "I'll get on the job. Maybe I'll run into Harry."

"Yeah." Ellison eagerly accepted the change of subject. "He's probably hanging by his teeth from some bridge. There should be more like Harry. Wish I could increase his pay to help with that new wife of his." He slapped Jake on the back and opened the door. "Wish I could give you a raise too, Jake."

Jake didn't answer.

In the foyer a voice hailed him. He ignored it, striding to the entrance and out into the rain. Momentarily the intensity of the weather took his breath away. He lowered his head. The light from the dim street lamps splashed brokenly through his wettened eyelashes.

The soft pad of footsteps came behind him and he remembered Angelo with stabbing fear and started to turn. Leverett came up beside him, falling into step, managing still to look dapper. The teeth flashed. Leverett said, "Stout fellow, I've been trying to persuade myself to go out for the last half-hour. It's my duty to investigate. Where do we go?"

Jake wanted to say nowhere, but his back had turned cold. He felt an ache for the safety of company, even Leverett's. He said, "Looking for local color. Any suggestions?"

"The old part of the city," Leverett answered without hesitation. "I was there this afternoon. The houses looked due to fall down any moment. There may even be people killed. All right?"

"Sure."

They went swiftly through the drenched streets. Leverett was talking smoothly about the importance of his work, the necessity for supervising the citizens. The rain didn't seem to bother him. They passed through a dripping arch and entered the old quarter. The narrowing streets began to slope upward. Water was gushing over the entire paving in a two-inch flood that washed the uppers of their shoes. The street lamps grew sparser, dimmer, throwing up more sharply the lighted covered candles guttering under the religious pictures on almost every corner. Leverett was saying that all the Italians really needed was a trainload of spaghetti.

Angry voices raised suddenly in the next street. They turned the corner. Half a dozen men were having what looked like a free-for-all fight in front of a lighted doorway. Others were crowding to watch, but staying inside out of the rain, looking over shoulders. The figures broke apart then, and they saw it was no fight. One small man was being severely beaten up by the others.

They were slamming his face and body. Somebody cracked him from behind and knocked him down. He hit the street, fighting. The pouring water flowed around his shoulders. Methodically the other five men began to kick him in the body, stamping on him whenever he tried to rise. Leverett said amusedly, "Local color. How typical." Jake was already running.

He bulleted into the group and they drew back in surprise. Somebody shouted from the lighted doorway. The men stood uncertainly, shifting their weight, the violence still in their faces. The other man was lifting himself from the flooded street. It had all happened in two seconds.

One of the group struck at Jake, and the American feinted and jabbed and knocked the man flat against the wall. The small man leaped from the round. The others started to close in.

Leverett's precise voice said sharply, "All right, you men, that will be enough." He couldn't have been more effective had he fired a gun. He stood at a distance, hands in pockets, looking very straight and commanding. The men wavered for an instant and stopped.

"Communist bastards," hissed the small man beside Jake.

There was another threatening shout from the doorway. The men began to move again. Leverett said, "And that will be enough from you, little fellow. Break it up and we'll all get going."

A man in the doorway laughed suddenly. It hung for a moment, then they were all laughing. Leverett took the small man's arm and began to propel him gently down the street. Jake followed behind, feeling a sudden and unreasonable dislike for the other American. He drew abreast, walking on the other side of the small man. The small man was saying nothing. Leverett said cheerfully in English, "Abbott, you idiot, that was a Communist meeting. They were liable to have done you damage." He looked back over his shoulder and called, "Good night, gentlemen."

Jake was examining the small man—short, thick-set, curly hair, intense black eyes in a passionate face. A thin trickle of blood was running down his forehead. Jake said, "You hurt?"

"No." The answer was surly.

Leverett said in a shocked voice, "Aren't you going to thank the gentleman for rescuing you?"

The small man screwed up his dark eyes, examining Leverett as if trying to determine what he was. He turned to Jake. "I'll buy you a glass of wine," he said, and crossed the road to where a light shone dimly from behind a glass-paneled doorway. They followed him inside.

"Three wines," he grunted.

The man behind the small counter greeted him with a shout. "Three wines for Signor Luigi Moretti."

Jake leaned on the bar. "Got a toilet here?"

"What? The street, *signore*."

"Too wet."

"No one would ever notice." The bartender grinned and pointed to a rear door. "Through there, *signore*, and under the arch. It is very private."

"Thanks," Jake said. He went along the bar and outside. The rain struck at him. He stumbled over a pile of broken bricks.

He was at the center of a darkened alley, standing under a supporting arch. The rain fell on either side in two almost solid curtains, dispelling the feeble light that crept up the alley from the street lamp. He stood by the wall, shivering, the smell of fallen masonry in his nostrils.

He was thinking of Grace; he remembered her expression back at the hotel, the look she had given equally to both of them. He had to make amends. He had to go back and tell Ralph now.

The thoughts were crowding his head. The shadow of a man darkened the end of the alley and he looked up almost casually, feeling only a faint embarrassment at being caught in this position. He saw that the man was not wearing a coat or hat. The light gleamed darkly over the soaked head. He sensed the arm lifting and a shout started deep in his stomach, and then the gun spat, flaming very bright in the alley's darkness.

Chapter Six

He flung himself downward. The bullet sang viciously off the wall. The figure continued to advance, and Jake Abbott knew he was going to die.

He wanted to dig himself in the earth. His scrabbling hand touched a large piece of stone. He snatched at it and straightened up and flung it with all his strength. Angelo gave a tiny scream of surprise. The gun clattered to the ground.

Jake ran. He cleared the arch and the heavens seemed to split. There was a brief roar, like the concert of a thousand caged animals. The rain was hammering down with renewed intensity. The gun barked again, strangely muffled. Jake couldn't get his breath.

He flung himself around the corner of the alley, already sobbing. The rain beat into his eyes and blinded him. He ran uphill. Suddenly there was a rush of water and he was up to his ankles. He had to lift his knees ridiculously high to keep running. In the thundering of rain he couldn't tell whether he was still pursued or not.

He staggered, and his shoulder hit a wall. He groped frantically and

touched another corner and pulled himself around it, the water dragging at his feet. He was in another narrow alley, the close buildings
breaking the intensity of the rain. He could see a little. Ahead was a second corner. He ran for it and kept running, and then he was in a complete maze of alleys.

He ran until the breath scorched his lungs; his legs had become lead,
and he leaned against a wall at the end of a narrow street and waited
for his pursuer. The rain was so fierce as to be a parody of a tropical
cloudburst. The entire world was water, slashing from roofs, churning
through gutters, falling from the invisible sky like a sea. It ran down
his neck and under his collar. It beat straight through his clothing. He
waited, feeling he would never be dry again, flattened to the black wall.

At the far end of the almost lightless street the figure appeared. It was
tiny and staggering, bent over from the weight of something carried on
its back. Jake remained motionless. The figure tottered a little more,
then pitched forward in the flowing water of the street. A feminine
scream sounded briefly through the hammered night. Jake left the wall
and ran toward the dark heap.

He pulled her upright. She seemed to weigh nothing. Her bony hands
scrabbled. The sack that had been on her back was beginning to float,
dragging, down the street. He grabbed it, swinging it to his shoulder,
holding her up by the other hand. For a moment she scratched at him,
thinking he was trying to steal from her. Then he felt her relax.

She said in a cracked voice, "The Madonna bless you, fine young man,
helping an old woman on such a night." She lifted a rain-drenched face
to him. In the almost-darkness she seemed incredibly old and thin and
tiny. She said; "A handsome young man, too. Young." Her clawlike grip
tightened on his arm.

He had savored the relief of her not being Angelo. All at once he was
ashamed that he had run. He said, "I'll get you home; where do you live?"

Without answering she began to move, clutching at him with ex-
traordinary strength, moving with an agility almost unseemly in one
so old. She said, "Don't drop the sack, dearest," and went a little faster,
oblivious to the swirling water that plucked at her feet. Fresh from being pursued, Jake sensed suddenly that the old woman was herself in
fear of pursuit. He said, "What's the hurry?"

"We'll get wet," she answered, and giggled. She said nothing more.

They turned several corners, and finally she squelched up some stone
steps and into a street where comparatively little water flowed. There
was just a film of it across the paving. They stopped in front of a house
that was like a small grubby monument to poverty, and he released her
arm. She smiled up at him and said, "Bring it inside for me," and
pushed open the door.

They were in a single cluttered room. An oil lamp burned on a table where pieces of dry bread and slices of salami were scattered. Religious pictures crammed the walls. There were two beds. A middle-aged man was stretched out on one, snoring loudly in a drunken stupor. On the other was sitting the most beautiful girl Jake had ever seen. She looked at him quickly and lowered her eyes. He swung the sack to the table and tilted it.

The old woman jumped to prevent him, but she was too late. A clatter of silver knives and forks fell on the table, and the end of a rain-soaked bolt of silk protruded from the sack. The old woman pushed him to one side and snatched the sack from his grip.

The girl whispered, horrified, "Where did you get them?"

"None of your business," the old woman snapped. A frightened look appeared briefly on her face. Jake guessed she'd been on a looting trip, probably out to the suburbs. He looked into the girl's face and she lowered her eyes, flushing slightly. The old woman's gaze was flicking cunningly from one to the other.

She said, "Pretty isn't she, my granddaughter? Only sixteen." She swung the sack into a corner and pushed it behind a cupboard. The girl sat down again on the edge of the bed. The rain hammered against the door.

The old woman said, "I have little to offer, *signore*."

"That's all right. I have to be going."

She reached out quickly and touched him. Her hand was almost transparent. "Stay a little while," she said. "Talk to my pretty Fausta."

The man on the bed snored gutturally. Jake knew what was coming. He thought it might be offered as a bribe for his silence. The old woman raised up and began to whisper in his ear. "Sixteen. Never been touched. There's only her father, and he won't wake up. What do you say? Ten thousand lire."

He looked at the girl's lowered head. He couldn't judge by her stiffened attitude if she had heard. He shook his head.

"Never touched," the old woman persisted. "All yours. Pure. You men like that, eh? And only ten thousand lire. Less than fifteen of your American dollars."

The girl got to her feet. She was very small and very young. She said faintly, "I want to go for a walk."

"Stay where you are, girl," the old woman snapped, "until I've finished talking." She turned back to Jake, whispering again, little black eyes gleaming with avarice. He was overcome with revulsion. He shoved her aside, went out into the pelting rain, and shut the door behind him.

Faintly, almost immediately, he heard within the room the sound of a violent blow. The girl gave a cry. He walked away down the soaking street, hands deep in his pockets, thinking how pretty she had been. He reached the steps that led down again into the streets of running water. He halted, realizing he was lost. Then his hands whipped from his pockets. The footsteps were pattering swiftly down the street. He whirled.

The girl ran right past him to the steps, tripped, and fell—and her long brown hair was flung out into the water. He grabbed her under the arms and pulled her upright. The warmth of her body flowed into his hands through the thin dress. She wore no coat. He pulled off his almost useless trenchcoat and said, "Here. Put this on."

"Leave me alone." She shrank back.

"No need for both of us to be wet." He draped the coat over her shoulders and pulled it tight around her neck, feeling her shiver. He said, "Where are you going?"

"I don't know."

"Better get home again."

She shook her head. He didn't blame her. He said, "I'm lost. Do you know the Rialto Hotel?"

"Yes."

"Take me there."

He grasped her arm and they went together down the steps, into the gushing water. He heard her gasp. He looked at her and she seemed smaller than ever. He said, "This is bad, isn't it?" Then he picked her up in his arms and waded down the street carrying her in front of him, keeping her securely covered with the raincoat. She was very light. He was suddenly happy at being able to do something for somebody else.

He set her down when they reached the main part of town. The streets were clearer here, the lights better. The rain flogged the gleaming concrete, each drop bouncing high. The girl relaxed, saying nothing more. He could feel her increasing confidence. It gave him a growing sense of responsibility for her. He'd take her to Grace. Grace would know what to do.

Suddenly he wanted to see Grace more than anything in the world. After that he'd see Ralph.

They drew near the hotel. He'd been in Italy too long to take the girl in by the front entrance. Her reputation would be lost forever afterwards. Still holding her arm he walked around the block and found a rear entrance. He said, "Come," and drew her through the door. She followed without resisting. They went up the service stairway to the fifth floor. They met no one.

He didn't know the number of Grace's room. He went to his own door, opened it and beckoned the girl inside. "Wait," he said, then went back outside to look for an employee. He had to go clean down to the lobby.

The clerk told him that Mr. and Mrs. Ellison were in suite number 5B.

He returned in the elevator and knocked on the door. There was no answer. The elevator boy was watching from his cage. Jake shrugged at him and grinned and entered his own room. The girl was sitting nervously on the edge of the chair. The raincoat had dropped on the floor beside her.

The water had penetrated. Her clothes were plastered to her young body, delineating the firmness of her round breasts, the beautiful joining line of her thighs. The water dripped from her skirt to the floor. Her feet were soaked.

He said, "Would you like to dry your clothes?"

The panic jumped into her eyes. She turned away, shaking her head. He said, "Well, I'm going to change. I'm drenched. Turn your back, if you like."

He walked slowly to the cupboard, listened to the squelching of his shoes, and took out the suitcase. On top was a suit of pajamas. He held them out to her. He said, "I think you'd better. You're liable to catch pneumonia."

She hesitated a moment, looking directly into his eyes. Then she stood up, took the suit and whispered, *"Grazie."* He turned away, began stripping quickly. The hotel room was cold, the rain beating ceaselessly against the windowpane. He thought of Angelo somewhere out there in the darkness, and he shuddered. It was suddenly as though he were isolated in the room, imprisoned by the rain, completely alone in the world. He felt an aching need for human warmth.

He picked the towel from the suitcase and thought of the girl. He remembered the old woman had called her Fausta. He said, "Here, dry yourself with this, Fausta," and turned around, the towel extended. She was standing before him as naked as he.

For an instant they stood and gazed. He felt a scooping in his stomach. He trembled. He took two swift steps forward and wrapped the warmth of her tight against him, bearing her down to the bed, feeling the softness of her flesh yield voluptuously under his weight.

Her arms went tight around him. She was not resisting. His face was buried in her breasts. But the fierce animal heat was receding. He ran his hands softly over her in an attempt to sustain his desire. It was impossible. He knew he didn't want her. He wanted Grace.

The girl's arms went limp upon his back. She was whispering something. He raised his head to look at her. She was lying there with eyes closed, lips barely moving, repeating a name—Gino—over and over like a sad little dirge. The tears were escaping under her lashes, tracing raggedly over the curve of her cheeks.

He said softly, "It's all right, Fausta." He started to get up. Then he stiffened, not daring to move any more. He reached out a hand and pressed it over the girl's mouth. Somebody was knocking at the door.

From out in the corridor Grace's voice said urgently, "Jake. Are you there, Jake? Jake!"

Chapter Seven

He rose from the bed and all the mattress springs creaked. Despite the coldness of the room, he broke into a sweat. His hand was still on the girl's mouth. He looked down at her and her eyes were open. Their gazes met for an instant, giving almost palpable form to their mutual shame. Then he released her mouth. She turned her head aside. Color suffused her face, neck, even her breasts. The knocking was repeated. "Jake."

He told himself this was his opportunity, what he'd been waiting for. He had only to open the door, let her see him like this, and the whole affair would be over. No painful dragging out, no torturing farewells. A quick, clean cut of the knife. But he couldn't do it. The knife would cut out his own heart. He remained still.

"Jake," she said, and knocked for the last time. He heard the faint susurration of her shoes on the carpet as she went back down the corridor. He walked to the corner and picked up his dry clothes, beginning to dress. Over his shoulder he said, "I'm sorry, Fausta. It shouldn't have happened. It was my fault; you're much too pretty."

Behind him the bed creaked as she rose from it. He had on his shirt and trousers. He turned around, standing on one foot and pulling on a sock, trying to introduce a casual, almost comic note to dispel the vestiges of desire that lingered in the room. He looked sexlessly at the girl's naked form as if she were an infant, trying to reassure her with the neutrality of his gaze.

"No," he said, as she reached for her wet clothes. "The pajamas. It won't occur again. I'm taking you along the corridor to a friend of mine, a married woman." He turned away again and finished dressing.

There was no one in the corridor when they left the room. Within the loud beating of the rain the hotel seemed an empty shell, quiet as a tomb. Then the elevator started to ascend. He knocked on Grace's door, still holding Fausta by the arm. The girl was suddenly listless, almost entranced. He smiled encouragingly as they heard the footsteps inside the room. Grace flung open the door.

"Jake," she said, and saw the pajama-clad girl. A tight little smile flew to her face. She said, "How nice. Is this a casual friend or did you bring her from Rome?"

He bundled inside, shut the door, crossed the room to sink into a chair. A knot of words formed in his mouth. In dry clothes he could afford the luxury of being a little angry. But Grace forestalled any expression. "I'm sorry," she said, "I shouldn't have said that." She turned to where Fausta was still standing near the door. "Forgive me."

"She doesn't understand English." Outside in the corridor the elevator doors clanged. He said, "It's a long story. First off the grandmother tried to sell her to me. The attraction was virginity. I didn't buy. The kid still has it. Afterwards I found her wandering around in the rain. I brought her back here."

"She's wearing your pajamas," Grace said.

"I know. We were changing in the room when you knocked just now, both naked, backs to each other. That's why I let you continue knocking."

The words seemed evocative. Someone rapped on the door of Grace's room.

The girl turned as if in a dream. She opened the door, recovered herself and closed it again to a tiny crack, peering through. Jake heard the voice of the elevator operator. He was laughing. He said, "Tell the gentleman that Mr. Abbott along the way was trying to get him just now." Then he was gone. Along the corridor the doors clanged again. The girl turned and looked at them.

Grace said, "She's exceptionally pretty."

"Yes. And she's in love with someone named Gino." He wanted to tell the whole truth then. The words stuck in his throat. He said, "Can you look after her? She's had a tough evening."

"Of course." Grace put her arm around the girl's shoulders. She said in Italian, "To bed, dear, and get warm. Come along." Fausta smiled tremulously. The atmosphere lightened. Suddenly everyone was a friend.

They went into the other room. Jake watched as she helped the girl into the double bed. Grace came out and shut the door behind her and he said, "There's only one bed in there."

She had been smiling. It froze on her face. She said, "No. How could I, when I belong to you?"

He stood up, taking her by the arms, looking into her eyes. He said, "He knows."

"Yes." She nodded. "That phone call was only the clincher. I think he's suspected for weeks. Rome is a small town."

"That the reason he came here?"

She nodded again. "To confront me. We had a lovely little scene after you'd gone. But do you know what?" She laughed bitterly. "He's going to forgive me. Dear, placid Ralph is going to forgive me, whatever I do.

Which means he'll never give me a divorce."

"He said so?"

"Yes. Quietly and with great resignation. About five hundred times. I wanted to kill him."

Jake said, "I'll talk to him. I'm sorry about earlier. I should have done it then."

"It's no use. He'll forgive you too. He won't even fire you."

"All the same, where is he?"

She sank wearily into a chair. "That's why I tried to contact you. He wants you to go to some Capuchin monastery up the mountain. The water is beginning to pile up and he thinks you should both be on the job. Harry Myers is already there." She paused. "Jake, I hate him."

"Sure. But did you ever think he might be in love with you?"

She looked up for a long moment. She said slowly, "Yes, I did. I tried to think it for three years—long before I'd even heard of you. We've not discussed it before and we won't now. But Ralph is not in love with me. He never has been. He knew my father could get him this job in Rome, and he knows Dad can help him hold it."

"That's a lousy thing to say, Grace."

"Isn't it? Unfortunately it's true." She lowered her head miserably. He couldn't see her face. He touched her head and said, "Well, I'll cut to this monastery," then he crossed to the door. He opened it, but hesitated on the threshold. The light glinted on her bent head. An ache came inside of him. He said, "One thing, Grace, though. I love you. I love you more than I can tell."

"Do you?" She raised her eyes. She said, "Thank you. Thank you very very much." Then she began to weep. He went out and closed the door.

Down in the lobby the crowd was growing thicker, groups of small gesticulating men who exuded the clinging smell of damp clothing. Jake picked his way through to the desk and waited for the harassed clerk to give him attention. He said, "Can you get me a cab?"

The clerk stared in glassy surprise. He pushed back a well-greased lock of hair from his pale forehead and gave a short giggle. "No, *signore*, I cannot get you a cab. There are no cabs. There are also no vacant rooms, no beds, no nothing. There is only me, and I am going mad. There are no longer even telephones for me to cancel the guests who arrive tomorrow."

"They won't come in this weather."

"To Asceno," the clerk said, "they always come. It is the gem of the mountains. How else can I help you?"

"Which way to the Capuchin monastery?"

The clerk smiled with false brightness. "First you put on a diving suit.

Then you go right up the mountain via the road past the cathedral—always supposing the road still exists." Somebody else plucked his arm and he turned away with a groan. Jake pushed for the door.

Even in this protected part of town, the waters were now pouring over the streets. The rain fell in a solid curtain. Jake stepped back involuntarily, buttoning his coat tight to the chin, brushing against a man just emerging from the entrance. He turned to apologize. He said, "Good evening."

Mayor Drago wrung his hands and squinted up in agony to where the sky used to be. "It will be better tomorrow," he said, "but I shall not be here to see it. Everybody calls me. The hotel roof is leaking. The drains are flooded all over my city. I am dying of exhaustion. Now I have to go to a monastery and rescue a group of silly Capuchins."

"I'm trying to get there."

The mayor shot Jake a calculating look. It was good to be friends with the press, especially the influential American press. Really good publicity could make re-election a certainty. He lifted a pudgy hand and pointed. "My car at your service," he said. "We shall go together." He grasped the American's arm and ran across the sidewalk.

It was a small Italian car, little larger than a beetle. The rain beat on the roof with a cymbal roar. Jake slid behind the wheel. They were both soaked through. It seemed to be assumed that he would drive. He switched on the squeaking windshield wipers and let in the clutch. The car snarled over its partially stripped gears. The other man leaned forward, peering ahead with nervous intensity.

"Turn left," he said. "We must first pick up Captain Luca. He will be probably at his house."

A little scheme had entered the mayor's mind. The uses of bad publicity might be as effective as those of good publicity. A word dropped here and there might hasten the captain's departure to another city. Anyway, he could try. He reached across the American and pumped furiously at the horn button. He said, "Strange that a policeman should go home at such at time."

The American made no answer.

Mayor Drago punched the button again. "And did you investigate the great mystery of our missing art treasures?"

"Yes," lied Jake. There was no one in the rain-swept streets, and he was irritated that the little fat man should keep sounding the horn.

"Then you will know," the mayor said, still staring ahead, "why everyone in the city thinks him strange."

"Who?"

"Captain Luca, of course. It was he who shot the German commandant during the uprising. He was just a sergeant in those days."

"Interesting story," Jake said. It was, but he couldn't use it.

"Not," the mayor hastened to add, "that there was anything illegal in the killing. All of us had to fight desperately. I, too. And my son, my little Giovanni, he was a hero of the heroes. But the commandant died at night in his house, and no one knew of it till the following day." He paused, reaching out to wipe the inside of the windshield with his sleeve. "His collection of stolen art treasures was never found."

"Meaning Luca spent the night removing them."

"*Signore!*" The mayor spread his arms in mock horror, laughing. "There is a law against saying such things." He put his hands together again and rubbed the fingertips. "Nevertheless, everyone says them. Captain Luca is not popular."

"Has he never answered the accusations?"

"My friend, he says nothing. Nothing. That in itself is suspicious." The mayor shrugged. "Of course, he is originally from the north, and they are not like us. More secretive, you understand. But he should speak up. Those treasures were the cream of Asceno's heritage."

He started to enumerate them. Jake barely listened. He was concentrating on the driving. Every time they passed a downsweeping road the car had to ford the onrushing waters that spilled down from the mountains. The rain was continuing unmitigated, seeping through the cracks of the doors and windows, trickling onto Jake's lap. Visibility was almost zero. Suddenly the streetlamps went out.

The water immediately sounded louder, as if it were washing around the body of the car. The mayor said, "*Gesu Cristo!*" in a scared voice. Then he remembered the values of publicity, the need to establish his own qualifications for mayor. "Never fear," he said. "I know my city like my own hand. A little farther up is the wretched captain."

The house was the only one with a lighted window. Jake waited behind the wheel while the mayor waded through to the front door and began hammering. There was a brief flicker of light. He went inside. Jake sat and listened to the water and thought of Grace.

Without really considering, he had believed till now that the aching misery of the affair was all his. But back in the hotel he had glimpsed an intensity that surpassed his own. The responsibility to make her happy was suddenly greater than if she had been his wife.

He tried to make a concrete plan. Nothing would solidify. She had said Ralph would not fire him. But if they returned to Rome and lived openly together, Ralph would have to fire him. And after that? There were few openings for newspapermen in Europe. He had never pulled off any spectacular reporting, so there was nothing special to recommend him if there were any vacancies. If Ralph passed around the word that Jake's work was actually bad, the chances would be even less. So what followed? There'd be nothing to live on. He saw no way out of it. He couldn't even pay their fares back to the States.

The rain was literally smashing down. A hundred yards behind him a street lamp came on. He looked back away from the headlights and saw for the first time how deep was the water pouring down the hill. A spasm of uneasiness shot through him. The light slowly went out again. It was almost as if he heard the dying hiss. He looked at his watch in the dim light of the dashboard, and saw that the mayor had been gone at least fifteen minutes. In an irritation of impatience he jabbed the horn and kept it depressed.

The door opened. He had a brief glimpse of a woman holding a candle. The mayor splashed across to him and squeezed into the car. He said, "Straight on, or they'll be wondering what has become of me." The clutch ground again. They began crawling uphill, making the hissing splash of a small boat being launched. The mayor said, "I was a long time."

"Yeah."

"She offered me a glass of hot wine to keep out the cold. Fine woman. Pity she married Luca." The mayor became confidentially reflective. "Hasn't had much of a life, you know, what with everyone thinking as they do about her husband. She's aware of it, of course. And there's the little boy. I understand the other children shout after him at school. 'What's your father done with the objects, what's your father done with the objects?'" The chanting mayor sounded like a child himself. He paused, an edge of worry in his voice. "Aren't we going more slowly?"

"The water's getting deeper."

"Oh." Despite the sound of the rain, Jake heard the mayor swallow gulpingly. "Yes," the little man said, suddenly angry. "Damn Luca! We come out of our way to pick him up, and he's not even at home. There's a much safer way to the monastery round the other face of the mountain. This way—" His voice caught on another gulp.

"We'll be all right," Jake said.

Actually, he felt less confident. The darkness was almost impenetrable. The headlights crept forward a few yards, then blocked themselves against a solid wall of rain. The houses were thinning out. The sound of swishing water sounded louder than the rain that pounded the roof. He wanted to suggest that they go back, but his pride prevented him.

They turned left. Then there were no gutters any more. They were running level with the foot of a slope that reared to the right of them, its top disappearing in rain. In the shortened gleam of the headlights Jake could see the continuous films of mud and small stones sliding down the incline in small waves. From occasional rocky ledges the water spurted down with fire hose intensity. The ground flood was reaching to the axles of the car. The noise grew enormous.

"Hadn't we better turn back?" Jake shouted.

The mayor's eyes were glinting with fright in the dashboard's gleam. He shook his head and waved at the slope, his voice gone suddenly neuter. "The ledge is protecting us. This is the way you must have come this morning. The railway line is on top. The bridge is a little farther ahead. We can drive through a small traffic tunnel."

"Where's the monastery?"

"On the other side. There's another road. We won't have to come back this way."

"Good," Jake shouted, and trod on the accelerator. He had a growing fear that the car was going to stop and leave them marooned in the wet darkness. He pressed harder. There was no perceptible increase in speed. He looked again and saw the mud sliding easily down the mountainside. It gave him a choking feeling. The mayor was talking excitedly, cursing Captain Luca.

He saw the fierce lights high in the sky to the right of them and for a moment could not understand. Then the mayor was clutching his arm excitedly, pointing upward, relief making his voice go even higher. "Everything good now," he shouted. "Those are men working on the railway bridge. They have searchlights." His fingers dug into Jake's arm. He giggled. "We're safe. The tunnel is a little way ahead." The lights rushed toward them and seemed to hover overhead. They disappeared behind. The darkness fell again. The oozing slope closed in upon them. Jake peered ahead for the traffic tunnel. The mayor was chattering in self-fermented happiness about their safety. He bounced in his seat and pointed and shouted, "There! There!"

Jake saw the narrow mouth. He swung sharp right. After that it was too late.

It was a short, narrow, single-line tunnel. From halfway through he could see the other end. Then the water came. It came too quickly for thought. It filled the entire tunnel with a roar.

The headlights went out, and they were engulfed.

Chapter Eight

The mayor's flailing hands scratched across Jake's face, seized his throat and held hard.

Jake was choking. He wrenched at the door handle, heaved against the force of the water, struggled to get through the opening. It was too narrow. The door was wedged hard against the tunnel wall. He'd have to get out the other side, past the mayor.

The will to struggle deserted him. He wanted to lie down. It was as if he were in a lush meadow of soft green grass. The grip tightened on his throat. His senses returned with a spurt. He reached out with his hands and plucked at the little man's eyes. The mayor let go.

Everything was in slow motion. He thrust across his companion's body. His only feeling was irritation that the man was so fat, and the car so small. He reached the doorway, strained it halfway open. The water seized it and ripped it from his grasp. The doorframe scraped against his legs, and then he was outside the car. He planted his feet hard on the chassis and tensed his muscles against the fierce rush of the water. His only idea was to save himself.

Suddenly he acted differently. He had no intention of heroism. He had ceased to think. He got a hand-hold on the doorframe, reached inside the car and dragged out the still-struggling mayor. He felt the hands scrabble over him again, seeking a grip. He had a vague feeling that he should hit the man and knock him unconscious, but he hadn't the strength. Suddenly he wanted to go to sleep again.

He pulled the other man hard against him, and they struggled feebly. All at once the position changed. They were on the hood of the car, pressed against the windshield. It was very humorous; Jake wanted to share the joke. With great nonchalance he opened his mouth to tell about it. Water filled his lungs; his head rolled and he felt happy. He was drifting slowly away to Grace.

Another face pushed hard to the side of his own, the mouth against his ear. He heard the sucking of hungry lungs and knew there must be air now. But the dreaminess prevailed, the soft dim languor was pulling him down. There was no Grace anymore, and he didn't want to go there. He pulled up his head with a jerk and realized that a lot of the gasping was his own.

He was sucking at nothing, like a landed fish. The headlights were out. The darkness was pitch. He was still on the hood of the car, the mayor clinging desperately to him. The water had fallen. It swam over the hood of the car and lapped around his thighs, breaking into fierce currents on either side of the windshield. He took another deep breath and leaned over the mayor's back and vomited briefly. Then he thrust the little man away. He gasped, "We have to get out of here. There may be another."

The hands clutched him tighter. "I can't swim."

"Wade. The water's not deep."

"I can't."

"Then get on my back. Don't hold too tight."

He slid slowly from the hood and stood with his back to the radiator. The onrushing water washed round his chest. He could discern the tunnel mouth a few yards ahead, a lighter darkness. He shouted, "All right!

Andiamo!" Then the mayor was clamped to his back like the Old Man of the Sea. He struggled forward.

He managed it by a tacking process, letting the water buffet him first against one wall then the other, making a little progress with each tack. It seemed to take forever. The weight grew on his back till his spine was red-hot and he thought it was about to snap. He wanted to be sick again. Then all at once they emerged into the driving rain.

He clutched at a bank of mud. High to the right, the lights from the bridge shone spatteringly. He dug in his fingers and fell sideways, and he and the mayor were lying side by side panting deep in mud; it was nice to be there. He took several deep breaths. He said, "Mr. Mayor, which way to the Capuchins?"

For a moment there was no answer. The mayor sat up. He said, "You saved my life."

"Talk about it later."

"I shall talk about it always. You saved my life. You risked your own safety to pull me from the car, and you carried me from the tunnel. It was a brave deed. I was afraid. You fortunately were not."

"I was petrified."

"Then your deed was even braver. I shall see that you receive a medal."

"Better submit me to the Capuchins. My boss is waiting up there."

"Anything that you say." The mayor struggled to his feet, slipping in the mud. "We climb," he said, and started resolutely.

The rapid progress did not last; the going was too tough. They kept descending into gullies filled with rushing water, skirting them, having to clutch at rocks that scraped their hands. The mayor was in no condition for physical exertion. He began groaning again, cursing the unceasing rain. They climbed toward the lights of the bridge.

They were among tall black rocks. The lights disappeared. They scrambled across what seemed to be a small river, and from far above came a loud roar. They rounded a rock-face. By a freak of levels the lights were now below them. Jake saw other lights a little farther above. He said, "The monastery?"

"No. It's higher." The mayor was clinging to his arm. "I don't know what those are. They seem to be above the other road that leads back to town." He snorted. "If it hadn't been for that damned Captain Luca! Anyway, my car was insured."

The lights cast a faint glow. They could see each other dimly. The mayor looked up at Jake, started to smile reassuringly—and his face froze in horror. He tore madly at the American's arm, screamed, "Run! Run! It's coming again!" Jake swiveled his head. A great sheet of water had spread right across the mountain and was sweeping silently down at them in a turbulence of broken whiteness.

He acted faster than ever before in his life. He sprang for the point of a rock and dragged himself up, then he had his arm around a stunted tree and was pulling the mayor to safety by his collar. The little man dangled a moment, scraping against the stone. The water hissed whitely beneath his feet, traveling at incredible speed. The mayor was shouting.

Jake went suddenly calm. He had never thought of himself as being strong. All at once he felt like a superman. It was wonderful. He made a great effort and heaved the mayor up beside him and sat down on the rock, amazingly pleased with himself. He looked down at the water and laughed. He said, "Flash flood. Not more than six inches deep."

The mayor took a deep shuddering breath. "Again you saved—"

"There'll be more," Jake said. "We'd better get out of here." He got up briskly and hauled the mayor to his feet. "We'll head for those other lights."

"Yes," said the mayor. "You are a brave man and a modest man. I will not speak of what you did." He paused judiciously. "This is very bad rain."

It was, but somehow it was less ominous. Jake Abbott was soaked. His feet kept sinking in mud. He felt cheerful. He wanted nothing more than to face Ralph Ellison. He climbed eagerly toward the lights, hearing only half the words as the mayor made panting conversation.

"The monastery is up there to the right. Below it, more to the left, is the big house where the German commandant lived. We searched it from top to bottom, of course, but never found anything. Then there was a suggestion that we pull down the entire house, but as I pointed out the place is a jewel, one of the many that Asceno has to offer the interested visitor. Criminal to destroy it."

"Yes," Jake said. "Interesting." Through the drenching downpour, groups of figures moved around the arc lights. The noise of a power unit sounded above the drumming of the rain. He saw two brief white flashes. Harry Myers was taking pictures. Jake yelled, "Hello!"

The answer came immediately. The man was using a megaphone. "*Chi è?*"

"The mayor of Asceno," roared the mayor, and straightened up. "Accompanied by the man who twice saved his life."

"Then come and save some more," the man shouted back laconically. "We need all we can."

The night suddenly went black and miserable again. Ten yards from the lights Jake was up to his ankles in running water, and everyone else was. A little beyond, men were working frantically at a small cluster of collapsed houses, swinging picks that made futile splashes as they hit the water. The camera blazed briefly again. He saw Harry Myers, half crouched, his overcoat pulled right over his head like a hood in an attempt to protect his camera from the rain. Jake felt a surge of affection. He and Harry had been together on a lot of jobs.

Jake said, "Hi! This the worst yet?"

"Damn right! Should have brought an underwater camera, or a small boy with an umbrella." Harry looked up grinning. "But Jesus! What pictures! Look over there!"

Jake turned his head. The picks were swinging. The hands tore at fallen masonry. Some of the men were monks, working furiously, the skirts of their habits hoisted up to their girdles to give them easier movement in the ankle-deep water. In the strange light of the arc lamps the scene had the appearance of an etching.

"Been glued here ever since I arrived," Harry said. "Daren't move. There's still people under there. We've had about five flash floods. The damn things attack foundations. The monastery went first, then the big joint over there, then these houses." He misquoted grimly, "And that is why we loiter here on the cold hill's side."

"I'll get me a pick," Jake said.

"Better see Ralph first. He's hunted all over for you. He's somewhere around."

"Okay." Jake walked back toward the lamps, scanning the people. Leverett was at the other side of the orbit, looking incongruous with a pick on his shoulder. Ellison was nowhere. Jake walked to the far edge of the light, till looking. The rain fell hard; the water swished around his legs and his feet were frozen.

He didn't hear anyone come up behind him. The hand clamped his arm and swung him round and he was looking into the face of the man who'd been fighting outside the communist meeting. The guy looked very ill and very young. His eyes were sunk in his head. His mouth was a thin line. He said in a choked voice, "You're Mr. Ellison."

"No."

The man had one hand thrust deep in his pocket. His entire face twitched. He said, "You're a liar. The old woman described you. I went to the hotel, but they wouldn't let me in."

The hand came out of his pocket. He was holding a knife. His voice quivered and the words were almost incoherent. "The bellboy told me Fausta was undressed in Mr. Ellison's room. They all laughed at me. I tried to get in, and they hit me and threw me in the gutter. It's because she's poor and I'm poor."

"You mean you're crazy," Jake said. "What the hell are you talking about?"

"You know." The Italian started to cry. He said, "I'm going to kill you."

"That's stupid," Jake said. "Wait."

It was all too quick and silly. They were staring at each other, unmoving except for the Italian's slowly raising arm. The American opened his mouth to say something. It was going to be too late. The Italian boy gave a great sob. A voice called, "Jake Abbott, you old son of a gun. Where've you been?"

He remained staring into the other man's eyes. He didn't turn his head. He shouted, "What do you want?"

"Where did you hide yourself, Abbott?" He knew it was Leverett. He could hear the splashing approach through the water. He managed to smile at the Italian. He said, "My name's Jake Abbott. I remember yours, it's Luigi Moretti. Do people call you Gino for short?"

The Italian backed three steps, swiveled suddenly and fled into the darkness. Jake turned to face Leverett. He said, "I'm glad to see you." He meant it, then.

"Wasn't that our friend of the wine shop? What happened to you?"

"I met a girl."

"In that rain?"

They waded back to the base of the lights, the center of activity. Leverett still had the pick on his shoulder. He said gravely, "Plenty of committee work here, I think, when this is over."

"I wouldn't doubt," Jake said. He could see the mayor talking excitedly to four men. He had an embarrassed feeling they were being told the story of the rescue. He said, "See Ellison?"

"Why no, I've been too busy. Wish my assistant had stayed, but she disappeared."

"Who?" Jake said.

Harry Myers was sloshing toward them, camera at the ready. "Hold it," he said. "A picture of you two for reader-association back in the States. Gallant Americans Aid Rescue. The subway commuters'll fancy it's them for a moment. Give them a kick."

"No." Leverett turned abruptly aside. "Hell, we haven't done a thing. Get a picture of the monks over there."

"I've got a thousand."

"From this distance? Is that a good camera?"

"Good? Finest little bastard of a latitudinous wide-angled telescopic box camera you ever saw in your life. And it also takes pictures. Get set, men. The hero's smile."

"Quit Harry!" Leverett snapped. "There's work to do." He waved a hand, made a rueful mouth and went splashing off toward the fallen houses. Harry Myers stared after him in amazement.

"I was kidding him anyway," he said. "So what do you know? He turns out to be modest. Maybe I've been doing him an injustice."

"He's a pain," Jake said. "Seen Ralph?"

"That's what I came over to tell you." Harry nodded at the ruin of the big house, standing alone a little way up the mountain. "Guy tells me he went up there some time ago. Probably screwing some poor little Capuchin into giving him an interview on the greatness of America."

"I'll go see."

The rain had been falling steadily; he hardly noticed it. But once beyond the orbit of the light, slipping on the treacherous ground, it returned in all its ugliness and discomfort. The big house was scarcely fifty yards higher up. It took him five minutes to cover the distance. The water that washed his legs kept altering its level, sometimes disappearing altogether and leaving him to slide in the thick mire. He looked back over his shoulder. Harry's flashlight was popping, seeming to light up an incredibly large area. Through the heavy veil of rain the moving figures looked like something in a dream.

He was nearly there when it came. From higher up the mountain sounded another deep roar. He scrambled the last few yards to the building, to be in the shelter of its ruined wall when the flash flood came. He clung hard. The sight imprinted itself on his staring eyes.

He didn't know which he saw first. They seemed to register together, fuse into a whole. The cups, the jewelry, the statuettes, the small rolls wrapped in oilskin, were crammed high above his hand between the ruined walls. He knew it was the German commandant's stolen collection. He didn't look at it. His gaze was riveted on something else.

A short distance away Ralph Ellison was stretched, his feet pointing down the mountain. His head lay awkwardly on a small pointed rock, holding his face above the flood. His skull had been smashed in and his face was split neatly down the middle. His mouth was open and his eyes stared; his body was completely submerged. It wavered and stirred faintly, as if it still had life.

Jake Abbott thought carelessly, "Now I can marry Grace." And then he went rigid. The other thought had leaped to his head and locked there. He had killed Ralph.

The body of Ralph Ellison moved gently and disengaged itself. It floated for a moment and the shattered head turned up and smiled. The water roared. A rock came tumbling. The corpse whirled in a swift, indecent somersault and hurtled down the mountain.

Jake Abbott started to shout.

Chapter Nine

He was standing in mud, still clinging to the wall. The water had subsided. He was telling himself that the onrush must have been caused by a lake building up somewhere, a natural dam giving way. He was thinking of everything except his last sight of Ralph Ellison. He couldn't crush down his sense of guilt.

He heard the voices approaching. His fingers wouldn't loosen their hold. The men came around him, and the mayor looked up anxiously into his face. Somebody said, "Are you all right?" He tried to nod. The mayor turned his head slightly and opened his mouth to say something.

He howled. He thrust Jake aside and went on howling. The words coming from his mouth were a wild babble of art and German commandants and something about the hand of destiny. The other men crowded forward. There was a furious burst of excited talking. On the outer fringe, the big thick-set policeman stood as motionless as a statue.

Jake released his hold on the wall. He stepped forward. He said, "You'll be interested. I think that's the collection stolen during the war." It seemed very important to talk about it.

The policeman made no acknowledgement. He said coldly, "I suggest you return to town. This mountainside is dangerous." He turned aside.

The voice of Mayor Drago cut across the noise. "Captain Luca! Send someone with sacks. Quickly!"

The policeman halted in mid-stride. "I have ordered immediate evacuation, Mr. Mayor. There is peril from the viaduct. I accept no responsibility for the life of anyone who stays longer."

"But this collection, you fool!" the mayor shouted. "I should think you'd want it recovered more than anyone. Get sacks! Sacks!"

Luca gave an almost imperceptible shrug and started surefootedly for the lights. Jake Abbott ran after him. He said, "Wait a minute! There's something else."

"What?"

It was like the ringing of a bell. Jake's thoughts ran ahead. The danger signal flashed. He heard the questions, the answers he'd have to give, the whispers. Better not. Husband found dead by wife's lover. No. Let Ralph be discovered at the foot of the mountain, newspaperman lost in pursuit of duty, victim of flood, dead.

With an appalling jolt Jake's mind uncluttered. He remembered the scene with photographic clarity. The body had been clear of the building. Nowhere near any falling masonry. And yet the head was caved in. Ralph had been murdered.

"What?" the policeman repeated.

"I'll bring the sacks."

He hurried past, almost running toward the lights. The water in this part had grown deeper, almost to his knees. He didn't notice. The memory of what Leverett had said was squeezing all the breath from his lungs.

"I wish my assistant had stayed here. She disappeared."

He blundered into another figure and almost fell in the cold water. The shock restored his senses. He said foolishly, "Your father wants sacks. I found the stolen collection over there. You'd better take the sacks."

Giovanni Drago looked at him from candid blue eyes. A faint embarrassed smile illuminated the plump face. The mayor's son said in English, "Sir, you preserved for me the greatest treasure in Asceno. My father has told me how you saved his life." He put his arms around Jake, kissed him on both cheeks and held him tight for a long moment. He said, "Thank you."

"Any time." In the distance a flashlight bulb popped. Jake said, "Better take those sacks," and patted Giovanni on the shoulder. He felt detached from everything. He nodded, turned away, and waded over to where Leverett and Harry Myers were deep in conversation, up to their knees in water. It was all very unreal.

Leverett still had a pick on his shoulder. He looked like the Brooks Brothers' conception of a miner. Harry Myers was still talking about his camera. He broke off as Jake approached. He said, "I want nothing new from you, Abbott. There's pictures here to last me my life."

"I'd like to see them developed," Leverett said brightly. "There's more in this photograph business than I'd suspected."

Jake said dully, "One more. A sub-heading, Harry. Flood Collapses Wall, Revealing Stolen Art Treasures."

"What? The stuff taken by the German?"

Leverett said, "What are you talking about?"

"Over there." Jake pointed in the direction of the ruined mansion.

It was too late. A procession of men were hurrying through the water, all carrying sacks, some with one on either shoulder. The mayor waded, laughing, in the lead, up to his thighs in water. He saw Jake. "We have it all," he shouted. "Every bit. I shall see you get a reward." He reached higher ground where the water was only to his ankles and turned to urge on the others. "All right, men. Into the trucks. There's nothing more we can do here." He disappeared over a ridge.

"Except there's still somebody buried over there," Harry said. "Nine dead, three injured, another still to come. Given up by everyone except those guys."

In the declivity where the houses had collapsed, five Capuchin monks, submerged to the waist, were still pulling and digging at the broken heaps of stone. Harry said, "Let's go help."

Leverett said in the same breath, "Anyone noticed how it's still raining?" Suddenly the whole mountainside seemed deserted.

The lights were still on, but none of the few remaining men moved. A peculiar silence fell. There was only the fierce splashing of the rain. Then from far up the mountain, louder than any of the others had been, there came another roar. Harry Myers said, "Oh, God!" All but one of the men by the lights turned and ran, streaking for the ridge where the mayor had disappeared.

The remaining figure hesitated a moment, then pounded splashing toward them. It was Luca, the policeman. He was shouting, "Out! Out!" He ran right past to the edge of the declivity, yelling to the monks. "Get out of there, you fools! Immediately! Get out!"

Jake saw one of the monks shaking his head. The others continued tearing at the ruins, not looking up. Then he was running himself, Harry and Leverett on either side of him, the policeman right behind. They scrambled over the hump of the ridge.

A car was disappearing below on the distant road. Another still waited, its headlights a dim yellow. It looked far away. They fled down the incline. High off to the right, the lights shone spatteringly where the men still worked on the railway bridge. Jake felt his feet slipping. The world was rain and mud and darkness. He slid a long way. The car lights disappeared. They were standing on the edge of a wide ditch, filled with roaring water. They couldn't get across.

"Over here," the policeman shouted. Jake felt the planks under his feet where someone had flung a temporary bridge. Then they were on the other side of the ditch, scrambling up a high bank to the road. The car was there.

The rain teemed down. On the road there was no water underfoot. It was an amazing feeling. He ran to the car, feeling an almost sensual enjoyment. The policeman was opening the doors.

Luca said emotionlessly, "You're comparatively safe now, gentlemen. This road was constructed with floods in mind."

"All the same—" Leverett hurled himself into the back seat— "I'd like to get out. That protective ditch looked about full."

"Very well." The policeman got unhurriedly behind the wheel and punched the starter. The headlights flared brighter into the driving rain. The engine coughed and caught. The policeman said, "We should get a fine view from here," and they began coasting down toward the city. He pointed. He said, "Look!"

It was like a movie, the sense of participation without being part of what was happening. The water surged with a roar over the entire face

of the distant mountain, high up, curling into white crests. Harry Myers shouted something and began frantically winding down the window,
trying to get his camera outside. Jake Abbott felt Leverett next to him
break into a violent shivering. The police captain drove slowly on,
speaking casually. "The Capuchins will be dead. A fine, tragic story for
your newspaper."

"The hell with you," Jake snapped.

The policeman looked briefly over his shoulder. He was about to say
something. There was a sharp crack far off, and then a sound that grew
and strengthened until it roared continuously above the noise of rain
and seething water. Harry Myers, camera in his hands, shouted again.
Captain Luca said, "An even finer story. The bridge is going. There are
forty men up there."

They watched. It seemed to take a very long time. They could judge
only by the string of lights across the chasm. It flicked and stayed still,
then moved again. Suddenly, madly, it jiggled, as if a giant child were
shaking it in a fit of petulance. The lamps began going out one by one
from either end. The arc lights fell, burning for a short distance, like
stars. The roaring increased and there was a final great crack, the snapping of a titanic whip. All the lights dipped and curled. They swung. They
gave a jaunty little twitch and seemed to hover for a moment, and then
they were extinguished. The rumbling died slowly away. It merged again
into the sound of rain and running water.

Leverett's face was buried in his hands. He was sobbing.

Captain Luca speeded up the car. He said contemptuously, "Later, Mr.
Abbott, I will try to ascertain if any men escaped. I doubt it. But that
makes a better story."

"All right," Jake said. "You don't like newspapermen. Maybe they gave
you a bad time about the missing collection. Well, fasten your mouth.
You've nothing to complain of anymore. The collection's recovered."

"A mess." Harry Myers pulled in his camera. "A rotten, stinking mess.
Those poor bastards." He put the camera on his lap and reached into
his pocket for something. He said, "Anybody see Ralph Ellison?"

No one answered. They drove down into the town. There were no lights
in the streets.

Chapter Ten

Angelo Fuselli had a new overcoat. He had acquired it simply; he had
walked into a darkened street when all the lights went out, thumped
his elbow against a shop window, dragged the garment from a display
model, and run hard for five minutes. Mr. Turrido would have appreci-

ated and approved the maneuver. But Angelo was not happy.

The coat was too long, and it was too heavy. It had kept him warm for five minutes, and afterward the rain had soaked through, increasing the heaviness beyond measure. It now hung on his thin frame like a cloak weighted with concrete. The only consolation was that it had big pockets, large enough to hold a hand, the edge of a sleeve, and a heavy gun.

Nothing was going right. He had chased over this filthy town from end to end. He'd gone up a dangerous mountain because he'd heard the American was there. And then it turned out to be the wrong American and he had to come back and start all over again.

It was as though he could feel Mr. Turrido's displeased eyes upon him. Angelo had tried to imagine what Mr. Turrido would have done under these circumstances, but imagination failed him. And now that finally he'd run the American to earth, all he could remember was Mr. Turrido's warning that you did not kill anyone under a roof because you always left a clue. And never did you kill a person in front of witnesses.

Angelo turned again in the driving rain and peered around the frame of the window. The tall American was sitting at the bar amid a crowd of people, drinking what was certainly whisky. Americans always drank whisky. Angelo studied the quick-wristed way the drink got tossed off. It was like in the films. The man wouldn't be able to do that when he was dead. He'd be dead very soon.

He fondled the gun and decided dispassionately that he hated the American on principle. He hated all Americans. They drank whisky, drove huge cars, lived in buildings that reached to the sky, always had money, and they were tall. In the films they moved with a confidence that he would never have. And he had seen them in Rome, with their blonde women, their money, their beautiful bright clothes that he could never dare wear because other Italians would laugh at him.

His hand tightened on the gun and his hatred surged. Some day he would go to America, make a lot of money and have his revenge on the whole lot of them. He leaned against the wet wall, feeling weak. He had an overwhelming yearning to hear Mr. Turrido's voice.

Jake Abbott went swiftly from the bar and ran up the stairs. The electricity was off, the elevator not working. The only lights in the hotel were from oil lamps. He went along the corridor feeling a little better, the warmth of five brandies making him forget his soggy clothes, the pants flapping wetly about his ankles. He was still a little confused, but it was clearing. Ralph could have been near the fallen building at first and then drifted away. It didn't have to be murder.

Anyway, he'd see Grace. It would be perfectly straightforward. He'd simply tell her that Ralph was dead. He hammered on the door and waited.

Her hair was damp. It gave him a peculiar shock. He got inside the room, and she flung herself at him, she was sobbing in his arms. He held her tight. He could feel her wet clothes. It seemed all wrong that they should be doing this. He held her off at arm's length and stared down into her face.

The rain had washed off all her make-up. He thought remotely that even without it she was a beautiful woman. She looked up at him, smiling, the tears still coursing down her face. He said, "What is it?"

"You!" she said. She laughed outright. "You! Oh darling, I thought you were dead. I've been sitting here thinking you'd gone down with that rotten bridge."

He released his hold. An open pack of cigarettes lay on the table. He took one and slumped into a chair. He said, "You went up there?"

"I was down at the bar for a drink. They all kept talking about the danger to the monastery. I couldn't stand it after a while, so I got a cab."

She laughed. "He charged me a fabulous fee. Then they forced me to stay on the road and I couldn't be near you anyway. They said it was too dangerous for a woman."

"Who?"

"I don't know. Some men."

"So you didn't get up there?"

"No, but you came down, which is more important. There were only two cars left on the road when my driver lost his nerve. I got back here and they said everyone remaining had been killed. I believed them. I saw the bridge go down."

"Would you know the driver again?"

"No," she said. "He wouldn't give you back any of the money, anyway." She came toward him, smiling, the tears all gone. "Sweet, precious Jake. How it feels to see you again!" She leaned over to kiss him.

He pushed her violently aside.

She straightened up. "What's got into you?"

He didn't answer.

Her eyes narrowed. She said thoughtfully, "You bastard. Why do I live like this? I sit here sweating my soul away and then you come back and act like this."

He wanted to tell her, but he couldn't, now. The thoughts were pricking him, the words sticking in his throat like gravel. He rubbed the wet knees of his pants. The silence wrapped around them.

She said politely, "Ghastly weather, Mr. Abbott."

"Yeah."

"How is everyone keeping? Fine, I hope. Harry getting lots of good pictures?"

"He's gone to the local newspaper to develop them. Leverett went with him."

"Isn't that fascinating!" She was near tears. "And have you been to the opera yet this season, Mr. Abbott?"

He said, "Quit, Grace."

She stood up. "I know I made a psychological mistake coming here. Women should never chase men, should they, especially women with husbands. But couldn't you be at least polite? As a small reward for my eating out my heart the moment you're gone from sight?"

She gave a shaky laugh. "Shouldn't have told you that, either. Another psychological error. Puts me at your mercy, doesn't it? Well, doesn't it?"

He said, "You were up on the mountain."

"Yes," she shouted. "Thinking you'd been killed, you you bloody bastard."

She stopped. She moved forward and put a hand on his head. "Darling, I'm sorry. All those men dead. It's been terrible for you. I wasn't thinking. Forgive me. I was so worried."

"Weren't you worried about Ralph?"

"No," she said. "No, I suppose I should have been."

He tilted back his head. The hand slid over his forehead and then he was looking into her eyes. He said, "Well, he's dead too. I saw him. He's deader than a doornail. He went floating off down the mountainside."

Her eyes went a fraction wider. She stared. A smile started at her lips, then disappeared. She turned away and went back to the chair and sat down and looked at him bemusedly with her head on one side, like the faintly puzzled member of a quiz panel. She said, "Oh." Her hands came up and wiped at her face. She said, "So that's the end of it. Just like that. Poor Ralph."

A hand went to either cheek, pressing hard, framing her face. She said, "We had a hell of a life together, you know. Completely opposite types. And now it's over. Death by misadventure on a mountainside. Gone like a hero. He'll love that, wherever he is. He'll just lap it up. Good luck to him." She started to cry.

It was all so neat, so nearly conventional. He said, "Why do you say death by misadventure?"

"Wasn't it? How did it happen? What do they say it was?"

"Nobody says anything. I'm the only one who knows."

The half uttered sob died in her throat. She went rigid, eyes wide, almost cataleptic. She whispered, "Jake, you didn't—" She stopped. They both sat without moving.

He said, "No. Did you?"

"Jake."

They were in each other's arms, holding tight, saying nothing. He heard a sound out in the corridor. He thought, They're coming to tell her. It'll be great if they find us like this.

He broke away and went to the table for a second cigarette. His first was still smoldering in the ash tray. He said, "They'd have a tough time proving it, even if it was murder." Then he wished he'd kept his mouth shut. The one word went reverberating around the room.

They faced each other expressionlessly. She said, "You didn't, Jake."

"No."

"It was an accident?"

"I don't know."

"Then who?"

"I don't know."

"Who?"

He looked away.

She said slowly, "Oh. Yes, I see. Well, continue checking, Jake. Ask more questions. About my cab driver. I have a gun, but unfortunately it's still in Rome. I did wish him dead, though, didn't I? And I had a motive. How funny to be suspected by one's motive." She started to laugh hysterically. "But let's be fair. A minute ago I was suspecting you."

"Here." He held out his lighted cigarette. She took it dully and clamped it to her mouth as if she were hungry. He said, "Look, Grace." Behind him a door opened. He turned around. The girl was standing on the threshold of the adjoining room, still wearing his pajamas.

Grace said in Italian, "Go back to bed, Fausta." She crossed the room and patted the girl's shoulder, smiling mechanically. "You have nothing on your feet and you'll catch cold. Run along." The girl went back into the bedroom and closed the door. Grace said, "Oh, Jake, are we both crazy?"

"I guess so."

"Does being in love do that to everybody?"

"I don't know."

She came over and took his hand, looked into his face. "What's it all about, darling?"

"I wanted him dead, too. It makes me feel responsible."

"No," she said. "Accidents happen everywhere." She was still looking up at him. "It couldn't have been murder."

"It could have been anything," he said. "I only saw him for a few seconds. His head was beaten in. That wouldn't prove anything. But maybe there's something else, a bullet, maybe, or a knife."

"Why should there be? That's nonsense."

"We'll know when they find the body. If they do."

"You didn't tell anybody at all?"

"No. I wish I had."

She said very distinctly, "Then it's best to keep quiet."

"Why?"

Her pause wasn't uncertainty. There was a look of deliberation on her face. She said, "Because it will appear that you're making a flurry about nothing, an affair that should mean comparatively little to you. If you explain why you're so concerned and the police discover later that Ralph was murdered, you'll be the first suspect."

He had known, but to hear it mentioned scooped away the pit of his stomach. He said, "I guess so."

"But he wasn't murdered."

He released her hand. He wanted to be sick. He wondered if there was still water in his lungs. He said, "He could have been. Quite easily. I'm going to find out."

"Wait!" she said. "Jake, wait!" He was already to the door.

"I'll let you know what happens," he said, and went out along the corridor and down the stairs.

Chapter Eleven

The desk clerk, the bellboy and Giovanni Drago were all leaning on the hotel desk talking about the present moment's irksome conditions. Propped beside them was a large cardboard sign, work of the desk clerk. It proclaimed in neat ink capitals that there were no more beds, no baths, no rooms.

The dimly lit lobby was full of people. Some had fled from homes in the mountains and were seeking a safe place for the night. Some were quarreling over coveted armchairs. The desk clerk smiled happily at them. They were rich; he was not. He had never enjoyed so much power as tonight. He was making the most of his hour.

To Giovanni he said, "My dear, how infuriating for you. All these potential customers, and nowhere to take them. Flooded streets and four of the brothels evacuated. Pocketsful of lovely commission vanishing down the drain."

"Oh, shut up!" Giovanni snapped.

"Poor lad, you're not yourself tonight."

"Who could be?" the bellboy growled. "Houses falling on the mountain, people getting killed, rain coming down like there was fifty million horses up there."

"Vulgar," the desk clerk reproved.

"What are we going to do if the viaduct collapses?" the bellboy asked with gloomy relish. "Drown like rats, all of us. In mud, maybe. It's already piling up in the old part of town, two meters in places. They're trying to get people to leave, but some of them won't. Say they got nowhere else to go."

"They can come here if they have sufficient money," the desk clerk said, suddenly savage, remembering his own poverty. "But only if they have sufficient money." He switched his attention to a client approaching the desk.

"I want to contact somebody named Luigi Moretti," Jake said. "Know where I can find him?" The clerk wrinkled his nose, thinking of the disgraceful scene earlier when the same Luigi Moretti had been ejected from the hotel by five employees. He gazed loftily at the bellboy. "Friend of yours, isn't he?"

"Acquaintance." The old man leered. "Came tonight inquiring about his girl. Got a bit ugly. You know him, don't you, Giovanni?"

"Yes." The mayor's son was nervously moistening his lips. He smiled at the American. "I'm not sure where he lives, but he usually spends evenings at a wine shop near here. The owner is a friend of his. I'll take you there, if you like."

"Thanks." Jake turned to the desk clerk. "If Moretti comes back here let him in this time. Have him wait up in my room."

"Your room?" the clerk asked, surprised. The American was already crossing the lobby, Giovanni linking his arm.

The bellboy stared after them. "Now I've seen everything," he said. "Giovanni Drago offering to help somebody."

"Probably got another brothel up his sleeve," the clerk said. "Whatever it is, he's not doing it for nothing. Little Giovanni never does. One day his father will find out. That's the day I want to be there."

Jake was wishing the other man would let go of his arm. It would be less difficult to pick their way through the people. They were halfway to the entrance. The door swung open. Harry Myers came in dripping with rain, his soaked clothes making him seem thinner and taller than ever. He grinned cheerfully and held up an oilskin-wrapped package. "You should see them," he called.

The knot of nervousness in Jake's stomach eased a little. He broke away from Giovanni. "Excuse me a minute," he said, and crossed to where Harry was shaking his wet hat in a corner.

The photographer said, "Well, you make a refreshing change. That damned Leverett suddenly developed a passion for photography and he's been sitting on my neck ever since we left you. Even wanted to follow me into the dark room. Had to get the local editor to throw him out tactfully. Haven't had time to examine the shots properly yet. If you see him looking for me, tell him I'm dead."

Jake said, "Ralph is."

"What?"

"Dead."

The older man blinked at Jake in complete astonishment. He said slowly, "Ralph?" A look of real grief passed over his face. "Why, the poor bastard. How did it happen?"

"I don't know." Jake spoke very low. "He was stretched out on the mountain by that ruined house where the German lived. I seem to be the only one who saw him." He hesitated. "Listen, Harry, we've been friends a long time. Do me a favor. Don't say anything about this till later. There's an angle needs clearing up. I'm looking into it now."

Harry Myers was still off balance, blinking his eyes in bewilderment. He said, "Grace know?"

"No." Jake said the word instinctively. He wanted to protect her. The moment it was uttered he wished he had told the truth. He said, "Look, Harry, in case anything peculiar turns up, I've gone to visit a kid called Luigi Moretti."

"What is all this?"

"Luigi Moretti. Remember the name. His girl friend's up in Ralph's room."

The photographer's mouth slowly formed a round O. "And you think he might have— Now listen, kid, a story's a story, but no need to run into unnecessary trouble."

"If the guy can be dangerous, it's already over. He'd be a one-shot. See you later, Harry. Keep your mouth shut."

"Yeah." The photographer nodded slowly. "Where you say you found Ralph?"

"He got washed away."

Harry said, "You know, he'd promised me a raise. Ralph was all right."

"Yes," Jake said, and made his way back to Giovanni.

They went out into the night and it was still pelting. The mayor's son began walking quickly. Across the darkened road a figure detached from a doorway.

Angelo was not excited anymore. He was considering the prospect carefully, weighing every possibility. In this darkness he would have to get close, or he might hit the wrong one. Not that it mattered, but it might give the American another chance to run. There was a necessity to walk very softly. He rose on his toes. The other two turned a corner. They were moving too fast.

He had to stay near, or he'd be lost. He ran over the road and round the corner after them. Walking on his toes was out of the question. He was in water again. It swished across his insteps. He hated it. A long string of Sicilian curses formed in his mouth.

Giovanni was saying uneasily that the wine shop was first to the right, second to the left. His nervousness was communicative. Jake Abbott felt suddenly apprehensive. He glanced over his shoulder and could see nothing through the blackness. He put a hand on Giovanni's arm and leaned close, still urging him along.

He whispered, "I think I'm being followed by someone I don't want to see. I'll turn up the next street to the wine shop, but you keep straight ahead. Take another turning and go back to the hotel. I'll see you later."

Giovanni began to say something. The hand released his arm and the American was gone.

Giovanni splashed on. He had always prided himself on his quick wits. Tonight he needed them more than ever. Danger threatened most horribly. Up on the flooded mountain he had taken the greatest risk of his life. Discovery meant prison, or worse. Clearly, he must not be discovered. Everything now depended upon the American.

Years of touting had developed in Giovanni acute observatory powers for the more obvious emotions of his fellow men. He knew the American was frightened about something. The fact heartened him. A frightened man tended to get himself deeper into trouble. The more the American became involved, the less chance there was of suspicion falling upon Giovanni. But he was still uneasy. There was too much of an element of chance. Maybe no one would even think of blaming the American.

He thought over the matter methodically, still walking. First things first. The best plan was to increase the American's fright until he literally forced attention on himself. Where did one exert the pressure? The answer was clear. The American had just slid away up a street. At least part of his fright came from the person he thought was following him. Giovanni strained his ears. They registered nothing but falling water. On an impulse he stepped into a darkened doorway and waited.

Standing motionless, he heard the man coming. He felt a quick flash of derision for any pursuer so amateurish. The small man was splashing clumsily up the street, his long overcoat trailing in the water. He would have walked past had Giovanni not spoken. The mayor's son said, "Hey, you!"

The figure whirled. It went off balance and almost fell full length in the water. Giovanni wanted to laugh. He opened his mouth to say something genial. The gun jammed in his ribs. He sucked in a breath of pure fear. He said, "No! Wait! I can help you. I want to help you. Wait! Wait!"

The whites of Angelo's eyes glinted in the darkness. He thrust his face very close. His finger curled hard around the trigger of the gun.

The man in the wine shop said, "He was here about twenty minutes ago. Pretty drunk, I'd say. Never seen Luigi like that before. But I suppose this flood's enough to make anyone drunk."

The American said merely, "Where can I find him?"

"Up the road, first house past the Madonna. Don't suppose he'll be there. Too much water. I've lived here thirty-five years and I've never seen such—"

He was talking to himself. The door had closed.

The door of the house was slightly ajar. A crack of light escaped into the pounding rain. Jake Abbott hesitated on the step, decided not to knock, and walked straight into the tiny room. Luigi Moretti was sitting on a bed, emptying a bottle of red wine down his throat.

His eyes flicked. He continued drinking. He put the empty bottle carefully on the floor, looked up and said thickly, "Welcome. What do you want?"

It caught Jake off guard. He had expected something more truculent. He sat down on the room's only chair and said, "I just dropped in."

"For what?" Luigi fumbled under the bed and pulled out another bottle. "If you've come to talk about Fausta you can save your breath. I'm no longer interested. Want a drink?"

"No," Jake said. "You cooled off pretty quickly, didn't you?"

The guy was drunk. His eyes weren't focusing. "Had time to do some thinking," he said. "Her grandmother's a liar, but for once she speaks the truth. Fausta would have returned by now if she hadn't liked what she was doing. Not even an American can keep a girl imprisoned in a hotel room against her will. How much is he paying her?"

He took a long draw at the bottle. He said conversationally, "The grandmother fixed it because she hates me. She's greedy. She's a bad-minded old bitch. She wouldn't let me marry Fausta because I'm a bricklayer. I earn eight hundred lire a day. Seven and a half of your dollars per week."

He shut his glassy eyes for a moment. He'd been crying again. He said, "Very valuable, your dollars. More valuable than being decent or getting married or being in love. That's right, isn't it? You're an American, you can tell me."

"Hold it," Jake said. "Nothing has happened to Fausta. She's probably staying at the hotel because of the rain."

"In a man's bedroom? Undressed?"

"There's an explanation."

"Sure there is!" Luigi hurled the bottle across the room. It shattered against the wall. "I'll kill the son of a bitch," he shouted and jumped to his feet. "I'll kill anyone who's even touched her. I'm going to the hotel."

"Don't be a fool; you'll get in more trouble. The girl's all right. She's with the American's wife. Isn't that enough guarantee for you?"

"With Americans, no!" Luigi shouted. "I've seen some of them here during the summer. They're cats. If this Ellison took her to the hotel it was only for one purpose."

"He didn't take her," Jake said, getting up. "I did."

"You?" The bewilderment on Luigi's face was almost ludicrous.

"After I left you and the other man in the wine shop. Her grandmother took me to the house. She wanted to sell the girl." He was suddenly too weary to explain all of it. He said, "I saw Fausta afterwards in the street. She came back with me to the hotel."

"To your room."

"For just a few minutes." Jake went to the door. "I'm returning now."

"You're not."

"I'll send her back to you."

"After you've had the enjoyment again."

"Stop it!" Jake looked over his shoulder. "Stop the dramatics, *ragazzo*, you're making me sick. I've other things than sex on my mind."

The Italian leaped for him. Jake's feet were planted wrong. He couldn't get out of the way in time. The fist landed on his neck in a terrific rabbit punch. The room contracted. The wall rushed at him and hit him.

He rolled around, tried to straighten up. His jaw was exposed. The Italian hit him right on the point of the chin, and he felt himself going down. He fell forward, clinched his arms around the other man and held tight, trying to get his breath. The hands came to his throat and he brought up his knee. Luigi Moretti grunted with pain and sat down on the floor.

Jake Abbott stumbled against the chair. He said, "Wait a minute." He saw the glint of the blade and took a quick step forward and kicked the Italian's wrist. The knife went skidding under the bed. The boy looked almost insane with rage. He wriggled like an eel, then rolled to his feet with the neck of the shattered bottle in his hand.

He said, "Now. You did that to my girl, I do something to you." He jumped like a cat.

Jake Abbott swung up the chair and rammed hard. They both stumbled across the room and the Italian was pinned to the wall, a chair leg stabbing his wrist. The bottle fell to the floor. He writhed once and heaved and the chair came apart. They stood facing each other with broken wood in their hands. In the room it was very quiet.

Moretti jumped again. Jake side-stepped and swung the wood. It hit the Italian in the middle of the back and smashed to kindling. Jake was left holding two pieces hardly bigger than pencils. Moretti was gasping. He swung around. His lips were back, showing all his teeth. He was out of control. He said, "Now I kill you."

"Why not?" Jake panted, "you killed the other one." The boy ran at him. He put up his hands, and the wood hit him a numbing blow on the forearm. He was suddenly frightened. He clamped his arms again and the two of them stood locked together, struggling. The rain grew louder. Jake tried to pivot. The open door was swinging wider. Someone else was coming in.

The door banged hard against the wall, and Captain Luca entered with two other policemen at his heels. Jake released his hold. It was a mistake. The wood hit him on the side of the head and he fell to the ground. Moretti started kicking him in the ribs. There was a wild scuffling and the feet disappeared. Jake picked himself up, holding his head. Luigi was shouting something.

Captain Luca tried to hold him back. Luigi lashed out a foot and kicked the policeman in the shin. The other two men ran across, grabbed Moretti by the shoulders. They jerked hard and he slammed against the wall, his arms pinioned. Captain Luca lifted a huge fist. It crashed into Luigi's face and blood sprang from his nose.

The fist rose and fell like a hammer. It was very methodical and systematic. Luigi's head cracked against the wall. He started to slump. Luca didn't stop. The policemen still held the limp form upright. Jake shouted, "Enough, you bastard!"

Captain Luca drew back his hand and gave the unconscious boy a last terrific open-handed smack. He nodded his head. He said, "Let him go." The policemen released their hold and Luigi slumped in a heap to the floor. Captain Luca wiped his hands on his coat.

Jake said, "That'll make interesting reading."

"Will it?" The policeman's eyes were as passionless as ever. "A little encouragement, Mr. Abbott, and I'll do the same for you. I may yet have the opportunity."

"Yes, you fit the pattern. When you're not hitting defenseless men you make threats."

"No American conversation. Why were you fighting?"

"None of your business. Nobody called you."

"There'll be more time to question you later." Luca snapped his fingers. "All right, you men."

"*Si, signore!*" One of the policemen came smartly to attention. "You wish them both?"

"Just the one," Luca said.

"All right, Mr. Americana" The policeman looked across at Jake. "We're waiting for you."

Jake said stupidly, "Me?"

"You."

"What for?"

Luca turned from the open door. He actually smiled. He said, "You mean you have no idea, Mr. Abbott?"

"Cut the mystery," Jake snapped.

Luca shrugged and stepped from the door into the rain. The two policemen hustled Jake after him. His head was still aching from the blow. His mind raced, wondering how he could shield Grace.

There was no other explanation. They had found the body of Ralph Ellison. The panic wriggled through him. He shivered in the rain. For an instant he had an impulse to implicate Luigi Moretti. He bit his tongue. He said, "All right, quit shoving."

The four of them went swiftly down to a waiting car.

Chapter Twelve

The big room next to the mayor's office was crammed with people. There was noise and tobacco smoke and a lot of coughing. But in the light of the oil lamps and candles most of the people looked happy. They were examining the glittering collection of articles that lay upon the tables. The only unhappy ones were those who had over-insured their stolen property, collected the money, and now visualized the possibility of having to pay it back.

Three policemen stood at attention, making sure that no one did any re-stealing. The mayor bustled among the throng and took notes and names and was very important and very mayoral. He was enjoying himself. This wonderful occurrence would cancel even the bad publicity of the rain. Asceno would really be in the news. He no longer felt the least tired.

He smiled at the plump little Countess Casalbore and she smiled back. It lifted his spirits higher. He gave a little meaningful nod to his son to indicate that Giovanni get to know all these important people. One never knew what benefits might accrue in the future. Mentally he practiced: "Good evening, Countess."

"Good evening, Mr. Mayor." It sounded good.

The door opened and the American walked in. Captain Luca was behind him. The countess whispered, "Is this he?" The mayor nodded. To his astonishment the countess started a round of applause. It held fire a moment and then caught on. Everyone beamed at the American.

Jake came to a halt and looked about him in bewilderment. Behind him Captain Luca's face went stony. The mayor bustled forward with hand outstretched.

"Glad you dropped in, Mr. Abbott. The story of your lifetime, eh?" He turned to the assembly and said, "How do you like that, ladies and gentlemen? The man's best story is about the man himself. We owe it all to him."

Everyone beamed again, except those who had over-claimed the insurance. The countess murmured something about it being hardly fair to repay the American with bad aphorisms. Luca stepped forward. He said, "You mean, Mr. Mayor, that everything has now been recovered."

He got no reply. The mayor was linking Jake's arm, leading him to the tables, happily waving a hand. "See for yourself. The treasures of Asceno are restored. You came for a list, of course."

Jake said, "I don't know why I came. I was brought here by force."

The mayor blinked. "I don't understand."

Luca had followed them across the room. He said expressionlessly, "Mr. Mayor, excuse me. You said before that certain things were still missing. Did you make a mistake?"

"I never make mistakes," the mayor snapped, too loudly. A silence fell on the room. Everyone knew Captain Luca's personal stake in the affair. This was not to be missed. They watched.

The policeman said, "There are articles still unaccounted for?"

"Yes," the mayor answered irritably. He turned to Jake, trying to regain his composure. "A few things," he explained. "The bulk is here."

Luca was pulling a list from his pocket. Everyone craned with interest. The policeman said, "Two paintings by Botticelli worth more than three hundred million lire each, a quantity of small church ornaments, jewelry belonging to the Countess Casalbore worth approximately two hundred and fifty million lire—"

"Don't give me a list, dear man," the countess interrupted. "I have it engraved on my heart." She smiled warmly at Jake. "But thank you, American, for what I have recovered. I am in your debt."

"Forget it," Jake said. "It was an accident."

Luca folded the list carefully, put it back in his pocket. He said, "I'm sorry, Mr. Mayor, but it's my duty to account for everything."

Somebody coughed needlessly loud. A rustle went through the room. A small man standing at the back began whispering quickly to his wife.

The mayor had intended to say something to the captain, to indicate how pleased he was that suspicion had been lifted from the policeman's shoulders after all these years. Now he was too annoyed. Luca was ruining what had promised to be a highly successful piece of public relations. He said testily, "What do you intend to do?"

The policeman indicated Jake. He cleared his throat. He said, "This gentleman discovered the articles. Several men went immediately to the spot and were thereafter under constant supervision. When we returned and it was found that articles were still missing I had them all searched. They were carrying nothing. No man had opportunity to hide anything except on the mountain. None would have done that because they knew the flood was coming. The likelihood of recovering anything left behind was practically nothing."

"Therefore?" the mayor prompted irritably.

"The things are still missing."

"Washed away before we got there?"

"No, sir. They were lodged too high in the wall."

The countess said, "Perhaps the commandant sent them to Germany before he was killed."

Every eye in the place flicked to Luca with new interest. Her last word had caused it. Luca had killed the commandant. A whole night had elapsed before the discovery of the body. The captain's face slowly turned a deep red.

He said, "Yes, it is possible, Signora Countess. Your jewelry might have gone that way. But at the end of the war the leaders of the Allied Armies made a thorough search of Germany for all valuable paintings. The Botticellis would have been recovered."

The countess smiled. "Well, I'm not much interested in Botticellis. Although I would like my jewelry. What do you propose to do?"

Luca's face was the color of a tomato. He wet his lips. He said, "There are two people I have not yet searched."

The hush went deeper. The mayor said furiously, "What do you say? Are you implying that you suspect me or Mr. Abbott?"

"No, sir. Only official procedure will be more generally satisfied if you both consent to be searched."

The mayor looked as if he would explode. He clenched a fist, half lifted it, and became rigid with indignation.

Jake glanced about the room. He saw Giovanni and remembered that he must see him afterward. Nice to think there was going to be an afterward. Nice to think this jewelry business was all it had turned out to be. The vision of Ralph Ellison's body receded. Jake smiled. He said, "I'm willing. Though I've had plenty of time to hide anything I stole."

The mayor lowered his fist. He was seething. He said, "I am sorry you should be submitted to such indignities, Mr. Abbott. But if you can accept with good grace so can I." He faced Luca and flung his arms wide. "Search me!" Privately he thought it not a bad gesture.

In his pockets were papers, some money, a pen, a pencil, a packet of cigarettes and a great many photographs of his son Giovanni, even the one as a naked infant on a rug. The policeman laid them all on a desk. His face had changed from red to chalk white. The mayor said with great hauteur, "And would you like me to take off my shoes?"

Luca shook his head. "Would you prefer this done privately, Mr. Abbott?"

"No," Jake said, and lifted his arms. "Go ahead. Always glad to see a policeman do his duty."

Luca reached a hand into the left-hand pocket of the raincoat. It stayed there a moment. Jake felt the pressure of the groping fingers. He looked into the policeman's face. The expression did not change. Then Luca withdrew his hand and something glittered in the light.

A woman gasped. Everyone stirred. The countess said, "It's my ring. What a surprise! My marquise diamond ring."

Luca said, "I wonder how it got there."

They were all staring. Jake saw each individual face. They looked avid. He had a suffocating feeling of being trapped. He said, "Anybody's guess is as good as mine."

"Possibly better," Luca said grimly. He went swiftly, roughly through the rest of the pockets, placing everything in a little heap on the desk. He fingered through it, picking everything over. He said, "Nothing more. The ring is enough. Your explanation, please."

"I haven't one."

"Where's the remainder of the stolen property?"

"I don't know."

"I think you do."

The mayor said nervously, "Have a care, Captain Luca."

The policeman's eyes flared suddenly. His voice got a little louder. "I have had a care for many years. So have my wife and son. This seems the opportunity to be rid of it." He had started to shake. He stood very close to Jake and stared into his eyes. "Where did you hide the rest of it?"

"I didn't," Jake said.

There was a long silence. Nobody moved. The little plump countess reached out, picked the ring from the desk and slipped it on her finger. She said, "However it arrived, I'm very happy. Thank you again, American."

"You will prefer charges, of course," Luca said.

"I'll not, of course."

"It's your duty."

"Is it?" she demanded haughtily. "My dear policeman, he's an American. I knew a lot of them during the war. There were times I might have starved except for what they gave me. And I believe in reciprocity. I can, moreover, think of many ways the ring might have got into his pocket. Perhaps it fell there. He may unthinkingly have put it there during a moment of stress."

"I don't believe I did even that," Jake said.

Luca said breathlessly, "Where have you hidden the rest, Mr. Abbott?" His lips were a thin line. "Mr. Abbott, where's the rest?" He lifted a hand and could contain himself no longer. He struck out and hit the American in the face.

Jake staggered and straightened up. He started for Luca. The mayor was already between them, livid at the complete ruination of his party. That the scene should occur in his own office only added insult to injury. He shouted angrily, "You seem unusually eager to fix the blame, Captain Luca."

He was basically a fair man. He wished immediately he hadn't said that. He had once more planted the suspicion squarely on Luca's shoulders. There would be a new story. The policeman had not stolen everything. Only two priceless Botticellis and a little jewelry worth millions of lire. Fleetingly the mayor wondered what new chant the children at school would shout after the captain's son.

Luca had recovered himself. His face was a mask. He turned to the countess, speaking little above a whisper. "You will prefer charges."

She looked back at him with disdain. "I will not."

He hesitated, shook his head and glanced swiftly around at the rest of the assembly. "Then there's nothing more to be done," he said. "Excuse me." He nodded once and walked out of the room.

Nobody moved. Nobody spoke. They were reluctant to believe this was the last of what had been a remarkably interesting scene. Jake put his stuff back in his pockets. He said, "Well, I'll be going now," and smiled at the countess. "You did right," he said. "I didn't steal your jewelry."

"I know it. You look just like another American I knew in the war."

"Lucky for me," Jake said.

Somebody laughed. It broke the tension. Everyone began speaking at once, crowding back to the tables. The three policemen moved closer. The mayor began to bustle again, supervising. Jake edged over to where Giovanni was standing by the door.

"Get back to the hotel all right?"

The fine blue eyes were being especially candid. Giovanni nodded.

"There was nobody following?"

"No," Giovanni said. "I waited in a doorway. There was no one." He smiled. He still seemed nervous. "You had an uncomfortable time with the policeman, Mr. Abbott. Perhaps you would like to relax. I know a very fine place. Good wine, pretty girls, not expensive."

"No thanks. Maybe later."

"It is only five minutes away. I could take you there."

"No," Jake said.

"Or we could go in a cab. There are cabs outside."

"Sorry, I have other business." He saw that Giovanni was about to take his arm. He moved to one side. "Be seeing you," he said, and slapped the mayor's son on the shoulder and went out. Captain Luca was waiting for him in the corridor.

The policeman had regained his stolid composure. He blocked the

American's path. He said conversationally, "Unfortunate that you over-looked that ring in your pocket. Where have you hidden the rest?"

"Don't start again."

"I wish you'd tell me."

"I wish I could."

Luca said mildly, "You realize that I have a special interest. The recovery of these articles means a great deal to me. Tell me where they are, I'll pick them up and no more will be said. There'll be no charges."

"Are you as thickheaded as you act?"

"But you must at least have a theory."

"Yes," Jake said. "Yes, I do. I have it all figured out. That ring was in your hand before you searched me."

The policeman stood aside. "Very well," he said. "First I shall obtain a warrant to search your luggage. After that I shall follow wherever you go. Don't think you'll get those articles out of this town. I shall catch you."

Jake brushed past and went down the echoing corridor and out of the big swing doors. The night struck at him with a force that made him gasp. He had forgotten it was raining. He saw a cab, and sprinted for it and jumped inside. "Rialto Hotel," he snapped. The cab pulled away with a jerk. It hissed down the street with great wings of water leaping from the front wheels.

In the shadow of the doorway Angelo nursed his gun and felt bitterly angry. The fat man had promised to bring the American to him. He had not kept his word. Perhaps it was a mistake to adopt an ally. Mr. Turrido might not approve. Angelo considered this. Well, there was always one way out if matters became too involved. Shoot the ally as well. Another killing more or less made no difference at this stage.

The thought of his benefactor gave Angelo the familiar yearning. It would be wonderful if he could do something to prove his worth, a really spectacular act to make Mr. Turrido admire him. Something involving a lot of money. But he couldn't think of anything.

Suddenly he stepped from the doorway and ran splashing down the street in the direction of the hotel. He was beginning to know the town. The long coat flapped wetly around his ankles.

Chapter Thirteen

The desk clerk was still very busy, getting more arrogant every moment. He snapped something about Luigi Moretti not having appeared again and resumed being insolent to a stiff-backed old man who was insisting that he be given a room immediately. Jake Abbott turned from the desk and saw Harry Myers coming toward him across the lamp-lit lobby. The photographer looked very tired, almost like an old man.

"Some mob." Harry indicated the crowd. "It'll get worse. I've been waiting for you. A whole section's been flooded over on the east side. For the sake of the dear old Press Association we'd better get out there."

"Okay," Jake said. "I have to go upstairs first."

"Why? Oh, sure. Grace. Did you get anything new on Ralph?"

"I don't know. No. We'll have to wait till they find the body."

"They may not. There's an ocean of mud coming down. You say you haven't mentioned it to anyone?"

"No."

"Well, maybe best not," Harry said. "At least, I should think not. It might be complicated trying to explain why you didn't report immediately. Incidentally, Jake, why didn't you?"

"I don't know. Confusion, maybe. I was hanging on in a flash flood when I saw Ralph."

"So we'll go out and hang some more," Harry said grimly. "I checked the pictures. There're some real horrible beauties. I'll be sitting in the bar, dreaming how I can sell a four-page spread to *Life*."

"Five minutes." Jake hurried for the stairs.

She must have been waiting behind the door. It opened on his first knock. She'd made up her face again, was wearing a negligee, and her newly dried hair hung softly around her shoulders. He noticed how the tendrils gathered around her forehead. He was suddenly very much in love with her.

"Hello," she said nervously. "You cause me more worry!"

"Sorry about that." He crossed the room away from her, knowing that his arms would be round her if he stayed within reach. He said, "You look nice."

She smiled uncertainly, trying to gauge his mood. "Darling, you look like a drowned rat. Go change your clothes. You're dripping."

"It's wet out," he said.

Despite the room between them, they were all at once very close together. He said, "I have to get out again with Harry in a couple of minutes. I came up about Ralph."

She waited.

"That girl in there." He nodded toward the bedroom. "There's been a certain amount of misunderstanding. She has a hotheaded boy friend. I saw him up on the mountain, waving a knife and making threats. I thought maybe he'd killed Ralph, so I went to see him. He's either innocent or a very good actor."

She was looking at him intently. "Jake, you've got a bump on the side of your head."

"Courtesy of the guy in question. He may show up here. He's stewed. Handle him gently, give him the girl and send them both away with my blessings. I wish I'd never seen her."

"Then you don't think that anymore about Ralph?"

He didn't know what to answer. He said confusedly, "It was just that I felt responsible for his being here."

She shook her head. "No, darling, you can't grab it all. I've been sitting here feeling the same thing. The most dreadful part is I can't even cry about him. I've tried very hard. I should cry. But my only concern is for you. It's a mix-up. Everything gets so distasteful I don't know what to do with myself. I hate myself."

"It'll straighten out," he said. "They'll find Ralph's body, identify it, the situation will clear up and we can go back to Rome and get married."

Her faced changed. The tears brimmed out of her eyes and ran slowly over her cheeks. He said, "Stay away from me, Grace, or afterwards we'll both have that distasteful feeling. I have to go out now."

She brushed a hand across her eyes. She was smiling. She said, "I wouldn't dream of coming near you in those wet clothes. Go change them."

"The others are as wet," he said. He put a hand in his pocket. "Grace, the police found a stolen ring on me. There's a load of stuff still missing. I was suspect number one for a while. You don't have any ideas how the ring might have got in my pocket?"

"Start at the beginning, darling." She gazed at him blankly. "What are you talking about?"

"It's not important," he said, "except I've made an arch-enemy of that policeman with the mustache. He'll be along in a while to search my room. Anyone who wanted to switch the blame could easily plant more stuff in my baggage. The cop might even do it. I'd better go check."

She said, "Nobody could get in the room."

"There's a fire escape."

"Isn't that a bit extravagant?"

"So's the value of the missing stuff. Two paintings by Botticelli worth around forty thousand dollars apiece, and a lot of jewelry."

She pursed her lips in a soundless whistle. "The chance to steal them would be a fine thing. Resist all opportunities. Now go change your clothes."

He said, "I'd better not kiss you good-by."

"No," she said.

"That doesn't mean I don't love you."

She opened the door. "Get out of here, Jake Abbott, before I cry again. You have sufficient advantages already."

"I like that very well," he said, and stepped into the corridor. "You haven't said yet that you love me."

"Do I have to?" She smiled at him and suddenly put out the tip of her tongue. Then she closed the door in his face. He stood a moment, the image of her still in his mind. On the other side of the door he heard her begin to sing. He smiled to himself and walked slowly along the corridor. An oil lamp was burning dimly on a small table at the far end. He wondered if the electricity would be on again that night. He felt for his key; he had no premonition.

His door was ajar. There was a light in the room. He stood very still for what seemed a long time, then he reached out with his fingertips and gently pushed. The door swung open slowly with a faint creak. The rain hammered loud upon the window-pane.

There was no one there. An oil lamp stood on the table beside his typewriter. It was turned low, the chimney making a perfectly round reflection on the ceiling. He stepped inside. The blankets had been pulled from his bed. His eyes flicked to the cupboard containing his luggage. He couldn't tell whether it had been disturbed.

He bent over the lamp, turned up the wick, straightened and looked around. The flex of the bedside lamp trailed across the floor where the plug had been wrenched from its socket. The lamp had rolled under the bed. He saw the brass base glinting goldenly.

The limp feet, the smoke-gray trouser cuffs were protruding from the shadow of the draped bedclothes. Jake walked round to the other side of the bed. His ears began to sing. He dropped to his knees.

Leverett was lying on the floor. His eyes were open. His fingers still clutched the edges of the blankets where he had dragged them from the bed in falling. The top of his head was a broken and bloody mess. He had been dead only a few minutes.

Chapter Fourteen

He stood up quickly, went to the cupboard and examined his luggage. His fingers groped quickly through all the pockets of his other suit. He snatched up his second pair of shoes and felt in the toes. There was nothing.

The signs of struggle were clear. The carpet was scuffed, the table awry where someone had banged against the corner, the bed a churned heap. He stood in the center of the room and gazed slowly around. His eyes were aching.

The lamp had begun to smoke; the glass was blackening with soot, and he turned down the wick. Then he lifted the front plate of his typewriter and looked inside. Nothing. He didn't know where else to search. His shoes sucked as he bent down and pulled the lamp from under the bed. He felt sick and empty. The rain was drumming in a fury against the window.

The heavy brass base of the lamp was red with blood. It hadn't yet fully congealed. Two tufts of hair were gummed to the thick rim. He went back to the other side of the bed and knelt over Leverett again, endeavoring to make sense of what had happened, trying to quiet the turmoil in his brain. Everything was running together. He had a crazy composite picture; Ralph floating down the mountain, Luigi with the knife, the little girl in pajamas, Grace insisting he change his clothes, Angelo running down the street, the policeman making threats, Harry taking flash-photos of it all, the mayor offering congratulations, Giovanni looking blankly from his candid blue eyes.

He was crouched over the body. The irrelevant thought crossed his mind that Leverett had been an unusually good-looking man. He reached out and touched the dead hand. It was still warm. Then he remembered the jewelry.

He put aside the bed lamp, shuddered once and began to go quickly through Leverett's pockets. He still wasn't thinking straight, but he knew the stuff mustn't be found in this room. He had a vague idea that he'd go downstairs afterwards and report to the desk clerk.

Then the knowledge came flooding back to him with certainty that Ralph Ellison had been murdered. Leverett had been up there and had seen something; Leverett was silenced.

His mouth was dry. He slid his shaking hand into the dead man's inner pocket and touched a billfold and some papers. He was no longer thinking of anything. The sound of the smashing rain filled his ears and isolated his brain.

He had forgotten the door was open. He didn't hear the footsteps coming softly over the carpet. His fingers were right at the bottom of the pocket and he heard the almost inaudible exclamation and his heart stopped beating. All his nerves shrieked. He tried to turn around. The blow smashed into the side of his face and he fell forward and his mouth slipped sickeningly over the top of Leverett's head. He rolled, hit the floor, and continued rolling.

The foot lashed out to kick him in the head. He snatched at the ankle and pulled. The man fell hard across Leverett and the blankets slid right off the bed. The feet were still kicking. Jake clamped his arms hard around the knees and butted with his head. A hand grasped his hair and jerked, the fist hit him again in the face. He closed. For a frenzied moment the two of them were tangled in the blankets, with the dead man squashing softly beneath them. Then they fell clear and the bedclothes dragged away and Jake Abbott was at a crouch, trying to get to his feet.

The other man was quicker, more practiced. He jerked up a knee and hit the American in the chin. Jake's head snapped back. He thought his jaw was broken. Captain Luca said, "Now I have you," and Jake went crazy. His hand closed around the bed lamp and he flung it.

It hit the other man in the forehead and his eyebrow disappeared in a split of flesh. Captain Luca opened his mouth to shout. Jake lunged forward and hit the policeman square in the teeth. He felt his knuckles tear. They both fell across the bed.

Luca was dragging a gun from his holster. Jake struck hard, and the weapon went thumping somewhere on the floor. The springs creaked. They lay together and panted like two lovers. Jake was trying to get the policeman's throat. He felt the teeth sink in his hand. A blow landed in the pit of his stomach and he fell gasping from the far side of the bed and his feet landed on Leverett. The dead man gave a huge sigh.

Jake panted, "Wait a minute, you got it wrong."

The policeman was off the bed, eyes full of blood. He staggered backwards and hit a wall and he was trying to wipe his face to clear his vision. His hand went into his pocket. He said in a weak voice, "I told you I'd get you," and he started to slide down the wall. The hand came out and the whistle glinted in the lamplight. He put it to his mouth. The blast came strong and piercing. Jake ran.

The outside light had burned dim. He got to the head of the stairs and heard the others coming up and fled along to the end of the corridor and turned the lamp out. The outline of the two men hesitated at the stairhead. Jake knew they were going to come in his direction. The whistle blew again and one of them said, "This way," and they headed for his room.

He ran softly along the corridor and down the stairs. He took two at a time. He was convinced there would be other policemen in the lobby, but he had to get away from Luca because he knew that with Luca he wouldn't stand a chance.

Somebody had killed Ralph, and then Leverett. Grace had insisted he go to his room to change clothes. But Grace hadn't known of the jewelry. There had to be another explanation.

He brushed past an old man and almost knocked him down, and then he was in the lobby full of people. They were all talking as if they knew nothing of what was going on. There was still a big crowd around the desk. There were no policemen. But Giovanni Drago was waiting for him.

"Mr. Abbott!" The mayor's son came wriggling through the mob. For a frantic instant Jake wondered if he could enlist the man's aid, but he realized it was out of the question. In two minutes Giovanni would know whom the police were seeking. He would jeopardize neither his father's position nor his own to help a fugitive. Jake pushed for the door. He shook his head.

The mayor's son took no notice. There was anxiety on his plump face. He shoved through a group of people and caught Jake at the entrance.

"Mr. Abbott, I want you to go somewhere with me."

"No." Jake tried to shake loose.

The grip tightened. "It's very important," Giovanni insisted earnestly.

"No," Jake said. "Let go."

"But, Mr. Abbott—"

Jake glanced over his shoulder. Across the heads of the crowd the two policemen appeared on the other side of the lobby. Luca was behind them, holding a handkerchief to his forehead.

"Mr. Abbott," Giovanni said. One of the policemen shouted. The talking in the lobby stopped abruptly. All heads turned. Jake gave the mayor's son a ferocious push and hurtled through the big swing doors.

The rain beat hard on him. Across the road someone fired a gun and a blaze of yellow lit the deluged street. The bullet went high into the swing door and shattered the glass.

A woman screamed back in the hotel, and someone shouted. There was a great babble of voices. Jake started running, slipping in the water, and the gun fired again. The single pair of feet came splashing after him.

It was very dark. He knew the corner was near; he glanced back and saw only the one dim figure. It looked shapeless. The gun blazed a third time and Jake flung himself into the next street. The water gushed suddenly to his shins.

There was no reality anymore. The town, the rain, the gun firing were the sequence in a nightmare. But he knew he mustn't be killed until he'd spoken to Grace. He lifted his knees and ran to the other side of the road.

His clothes weighed a ton. He reached out and touched a wall and heard the other man come splashing round the corner. Somewhere off through the rain a car started up. He sank to his knees and clamped a hand tight over his mouth, and then lay down full length.

The water covered him. The thick mud oozed around his neck and into his ears. He started immediately to suffocate. He began counting and the blackness under closed eyelids turned red. He told himself that he must stay there until at least one hundred and eighty.

He was certain the man would find him. He lay waiting for the foot to kick, the bullet to enter. It would really be a relief, except that he wanted to talk to Grace, to explain something—he wasn't sure what. But if he was killed she might go back to thinking he had murdered Ralph. He didn't want that. He lay motionless and counted and started to die.

One hundred and eighty was an impossibility. At one hundred and thirty the numbers had taken actual shape. They were something like little slugs. They crawled very slowly under his closed eyelids from left to right. He had to open his mouth because his ears were humming. He pressed harder with his hands, but it was no use. His eyes flew open. Then his lips. He gulped a great draft of dirty water and beat with his hands and pushed himself to the surface. He knelt there gasping with the water flowing around his belly.

His arms flailed. His fingers scratched the wall and he pulled himself upright, leaning weakly against the brickwork. The darkness was absolute. The street seemed empty of all but flowing water. He clung to the wall and his head lolled forward. He was sick. The rain beat against the back of his hair and the mud ran in little fingers all over his face. He was shivering violently.

The car ran past on the cross street at the bottom and he heard it turn but he was still being sick and couldn't move. Then it came back, and the headlights glared full on him, and stopped at the bottom of the incline. He made a vast effort and started to run again, floundering as he went, gasping for breath. The car doors slammed and the men began shouting, but he paid no heed.

He fell and scrambled up again. The voices called for him to stop, and then a shot rang out very loud over his head. It was impossible to move another inch. He couldn't even look around. He heard them pounding up behind him, and then something hit him an enormous blow in the middle of the back. He fell down into the mud and water again, gasping with outrage. It was too much. He gave up.

He would have lain there. The groping hands grasped his shoulders and dragged him upright, pushing him against the stone wall. His vision wouldn't focus, but he knew there were only three of them. He had thought there were many more. The two policemen were holding him as they had done with Moretti. Luca was directly in front. The cut on his forehead was still open. The blood ran thinly because of the rain.

"I'll teach you to fire a gun at me, you bastard," he said. Then to one of the policemen, "Get it off him."

"But I didn't have a gun," Jake said, and his own voice shocked him. He sounded like a querulous schoolboy.

Somebody twisted his arm. "Shut up!" they said. He offered no resistance. The hands ran all over him. The voice said, "He doesn't have it, sir."

"Where did you drop it, Abbott?"

Jake waited before answering. He was trying to alter his voice. It came out just the same as before. He said, "I never had one. It was somebody else."

The hand slapped him hard across the face. Then he tried to struggle, but the policemen had him pinned. The second blow landed and his head hit the wall. The lights rocketed through his skull. He said, "Oh, you brave bastard." His voice came out normally. It pleased him. He said, "You brave and lousy bastard. Wait till I meet you on equal terms."

"You won't," Luca said. "And I haven't started yet."

He drew back an arm and grunted with the power of his punch. Jake took it full in the face. His head fell to one side. He began to lose consciousness. He was grateful for it. He knew the blows were still falling, but he didn't care. His last thought was of all the water pouring through the gutters.

They picked him up. They dragged his limp body down the street and threw him in the back of the car. The engine had stopped. They had difficulty starting it again. Captain Luca swore a long monotonous string of oaths. The other two men exchanged a nervous glance. One of them had turned a putty white, but neither spoke.

Chapter Fifteen

Jake awoke slowly, the sound of water still in his ears but farther away, only a trickle. He opened his swollen eyes, lifted both hands to his aching head, and from somewhere nearby heard an incredibly unmusical voice singing.

It ended chokingly and had a fit of coughing. Then it called in a wheezing stage whisper: "You awake yet?" Jake didn't answer. There was a moment of questioning silence and the song resumed.

Jake lifted himself. The trickling sounds were coming from all around him. He was sitting on a wall bunk in a stone cell without a window. A dim yellow light shone through the bars of the door from the corridor, reflecting faintly on rivulets of water that trickled down the walls and onto the wet stone flags of the floor.

A clatter of echoing footsteps sounded outside. A voice shouted, "Shut up!" The singer took no notice. Jake saw the shadow approaching, then his door opened and the policeman grunted, "Come on, American." He picked himself up, every muscle protesting, and went down the corridor. There were only two cells. As he passed the second the singer shouted a greeting. It was too dark to see him.

They entered a big room. A door was open, leading to the street. The cold night air blew gustily in. The rain spattered over the doorsill. The room was full of policemen, most of them moving about, agitated, waving their hands, talking loudly. A few glanced at him curiously. His escort nudged him swiftly to the far side and opened a door. They entered a small office.

Mayor Drago was waiting. So was Luca.

An expression of shock settled on the mayor's face. He opened his mouth to say something. Captain Luca smiled and said, "You appear to have hurt yourself, Abbott. Fall over in your cell?"

Jake gave him a contemptuous look and didn't answer. He turned to the mayor. "You have a cigarette? Mine got wet when the cops were beating me up in the street."

The mayor's shocked gaze switched to Luca. His voice trembled with anger. "Is this true?"

The policeman shrugged his shoulders. "I have no wish to discuss the prisoner's hallucinations. He's here on a charge of murder. Didn't you want to question him?"

"A formal charge?" Jake snapped.

"Quite. I find you bending over the victim with the murder weapon beside you. You were rifling his pockets. You resisted arrest and ran away. The conclusion is obvious."

"Mr. Abbott, is this fact?"

"A description," Jake said. "Not fact. The man was already dead in my room when I got there."

The mayor wet his lips. "Mr. Abbott, this is painful for me. Were you searching the man's pockets for the missing jewelry?"

"Yes." He saw their faces. He'd made a mistake. He said, "In case someone had planted it on him."

"But why should anyone kill a man and then put precious stones into his pockets?" Luca asked softly. "Surely it should be the other way round."

"You give an explanation," Jake said. "I'm beginning to think you could. Was anything found on Leverett?"

"No." The mayor was finally offering a cigarette. His hand shook. "You realize, Mr. Abbott, that the missing articles are of great value to the city of Asceno. If you can in any way assist in the recovery—"

"I can't. This is a mistake. It's going to be a highly publicized one. What does a man like me want with a lot of jewelry?"

Luca smiled bleakly. The mayor said, "But it's not the jewelry that perturbs us, it's the paintings."

"So?" Jake said.

The little man wet his lips again. He spoke with difficulty. "Mr. Abbott, information has reached me that you for a long time have been connected with the marketing of stolen paintings in Rome."

Jake's heart jumped. It was near enough the truth to be incriminating. "That's interesting. Is it reliable?"

There was a long silence. Luca looked from one to the other. A veil had fallen over his eyes. He said, "Mr. Mayor, from whom did you receive this information?"

Drago blinked his eyes. He started to smile, changed his mind and wiped his mouth jerkily on the back of his hand. "I got a telephone call about an hour ago. The call was anonymous. A woman's voice."

"I see," Luca said noncommittally. "Anything to comment, Abbott?"

"Nothing. Not about anything till I've been in touch with the American Embassy."

"That will take a long time," the mayor said nervously. "There are no means of communication. All the telephone wires are down. Couldn't you speak now? The water is spreading. If the paintings are hidden they might be damaged. Or lost completely. You wouldn't want that, would you?"

"I wouldn't give a damn," Jake said. "The paintings mean nothing to me. How long you intend keeping me here, Luca?"

"Years perhaps. Maybe all your life." The captain jerked his head as the door opened. "What do you want?"

"People asking for the mayor, sir." The policeman's voice was frightened. "They say the viaduct is beginning to go. Do we evacuate, sir?"

"You wait for orders," Luca snapped. "Get out!" He looked insolently at the mayor. "Better go, Mr. Drago."

"Aren't you coming?"

"You'll supervise everything perfectly, I'm sure. I'll stay behind and persuade Mr. Abbott to change his mind."

The mayor halted uneasily at the door. "I want those paintings, Captain, but no violence. You're not to touch him. Everything must be legal."

"Of course," the policeman smiled. "No need for either of us to have any fear, Mr. Mayor." He switched the smile to Jake, remaining motionless for a full minute while the mayor's footsteps retreated. Then he flung back his head and shouted, "Ianora! Take the prisoner back to his cell." He stood up. "I'll be there in five minutes."

There was a double escort this time. They marched back through the big room from which half the policemen had disappeared. Nobody bothered to look at Jake. An air of intense nervousness filled the place. There was a burst of thunder and a cold blast blew from the street through the open door, moaning a little in the corridor. The other prisoner was still singing.

The two policemen bundled Jake into his cell and stood outside the open door. In sudden unison they shouted to the other man to be quiet. He stopped. The trickling of water was suddenly very loud. Jake sat down on the bunk and waited, shivering in his wet clothes. He was frightened. He knew he wouldn't be able to stand much of it.

He heard Luca coming and something of pride prompted him to get up, to receive the other man as an equal, standing on his own feet. The captain came briskly into the cell with a rubber truncheon in his hand.

He said, "Sit down, Mr. Abbott."

"We'll talk like this."

"You are going to talk?"

"Are you?"

Luca sat down on the edge of the bunk and patted a place beside him. The truncheon dangled between his legs and swung idly. Jake didn't move. The policeman's voice was reasonable, as if he meant to argue some mild point of philosophy.

He nodded at the door. "Mr. Abbott, I'll be frank. These two policemen, like all their companions, have at times said things to each other they'd never dare to say to me. The same things have been said for years by everyone else in this city. I never hear them, but my wife, whom I love very much, gets whispers when she goes to the market. My son, who is nine years old, has heard nothing else since he began to mix with other children. You have been in this city for less than one day, but you will know already to what I am referring."

Jake said nothing.

"I need hardly tell you the rumors and whispers contain not a grain of truth. Had they been the least provable I would no longer be a policeman. But believe me, Mr. Abbott, life has been very uncomfortable these last years. For a man it is nothing. For a woman and child—"

He spread his hands, pausing a moment. "This evening the articles which for so long I have been accused of stealing were recovered; unfortunately, not all of them. All the same I had hoped the whispers would be stilled. I was wrong. The situation has been reopened, the rumors intensified. The gossips have set upon the story with renewed vigor. Tomorrow the women will carry it to the market. My son will hear it again when next he goes to school. You understand, Mr. Abbott?"

"I grieve. It's a sad story. But nothing to do with me."

"On the contrary. I think it has a lot to do with you. Mr. Abbott, you are a murderer. But even were you completely innocent and I had to choose between your suffering and the suffering of my wife and son, you would be the loser."

"Don't cover up," Jake said. "You're going to enjoy doing it."

"With you, yes." Luca put a hand to the cut on his forehead. He smiled faintly and stood up. "Won't you be seated?"

"I prefer to stand."

"But I want you to sit down."

"I'm standing," Jake said.

The end of the truncheon hit him hard in the solar plexus. He doubled over, gasping for breath. The open hand smacked his face and he fell on the bunk. The stick hit him again on the side of the kneecap. He gave an involuntary shout. The two policemen moved quickly into the cell.

One of them held his head and the other his feet. The stick came pounding down on his belly and ribs and he couldn't stop shouting. He started to faint. In the next cell the other man was singing at the top of his voice.

Luca stood back. A silence fell. The trickling water sounded like a flood. "Anything to say, Abbott?"

The breath rattled through Jake's throat. He could barely speak. "What do you expect me to say?"

"You and Leverett, the other American, stole those articles together. You quarreled over the division of them. Isn't that right?"

"It's crazy."

"Or you quarreled about the large ring we found in your pocket. Were you intending to keep it for yourself without telling your partner?"

Jake made no answer.

"Abbott, where have you hidden the pictures?"

Jake watched the water shining on the wall. The little rivulets were getting fatter.

"The pictures, Abbott. The pictures."

The grip on his ankles slackened.

"Abbott, the pictures."

"Stop it," Jake said, "you're boring me."

Luca lifted the heavy black stick onto his shoulder. The policemen tightened their hold. A peal of thunder suddenly rumbled outside. Jake felt the man at his feet give a jerk of nervousness.

"You will talk, Abbott," Luca said. "Be assured. Are you ready?" Then he swung the truncheon and Jake's intestines turned to pulp and he thought his backbone had snapped. He wanted to cry out. He had no breath. The man in the next cell was singing again. The thunder was roaring and the stick was pounding him to jelly and the footsteps were running down the corridor. A voice said, "Quick, Captain Luca! Quick!"

He heard no more. The darkness had closed over his eyes.

The rasping elderly voice said in a loud whisper, "You awake in there yet?"

The darkness swirled and took shape. Jake Abbott saw the bars of the cell door. The pain spread wide to his shoulders and converged to a sharp point of agony in the back of his skull. His stomach was full of serpents. He moved his head slightly. There was no one in the cell with him.

He desperately wanted a cigarette. He put his numbed feet gingerly to the floor, wondering if he would be sick again, and sat up. The cell whirled; the pain was very bad. He put his head in his hands and waited. The voice from the other cell whispered, "You awake?"

"Yes," he said, and was surprised he could speak. He forced himself to get up, staggered to the door and hung onto the bars. "How long they been gone?"

"Half an hour." The voice became normal inasmuch as it stopped whispering. The croaking edge remained. "They got a knife in you, friend. What you do?"

"Nothing."

"Like I always do." The man laughed. "The singing annoy you? Had to do it because I didn't want to hear. I'm sensitive. Can't stand the thought of anyone being in pain. Where'd they fix you?"

"My stomach."

"Oh, the belly treatment." The man was interested. "I got that one time in Rome. They thought I was running narcotics. Me, in narcotics. I was never lucky enough to hit a big racket in my life."

He was silent a moment. He said, "God, listen to the water. Thought it would be nice cover for a little looting tonight. Broke one store window and they grabbed me right off and brought me here. Don't like the place, do you?"

"No."

An enormous peal of thunder roared, shaking the building. Jake looked down and saw for the first time that the water was over the toes of his shoes. He peered to the back of the cell. A crack had opened in the wall. A thick film of water was seeping from the ceiling to the floor. He said, "It's wet."

"Thought it would be." The man sounded satisfied. "We're on the side of a hill, pretty high up. The water was all channeling in the other direction when they brought me in, but I guess there's too much of it now. I'll tell you one thing. If the viaduct goes there won't be time to get out and we'll all be dead. The cops too, so that'll comfort me."

Jake wished the man would stop talking. He was trying to think. Ralph Ellison and Leverett. The jewelry, the paintings. The beginning had been at the top of the mountain, by the bridge. Leverett was there. He ticked them off in his mind. And Grace, the mayor, Giovanni, Luca, Harry Myers, Luigi Moretti, maybe Angelo. And about twenty more men. Anyone could have done it. He ticked off the events of the evening. There had to be a starting point somewhere, but he couldn't find it.

Another peal of thunder tore across the sky. The man called from the next cell, "Hey, it's getting worse in here. Gives me a nice idea. What say we take a chance?"

"How?"

"Make it up as you go along," the man said, and suddenly howled. His voice rose to a shriek. "Help! Help! Come and help me! Help!"

A pair of feet came running down the corridor. Somebody asked with loud nervousness what was going on. The other man's creaking voice

shouted, "It's the American. I think he's drowning." The policeman ran
to where Jake was hanging on to the bars of the door.

He was a young man with a thin, white face. He said, "You all right?"

Jake grinned weakly. "I don't know. The water's piling up in here. I got
a bit scared. I don't feel good."

"I can understand that," the policeman said. He went to walk away,
turned back and lowered his voice. "Look, American. Don't think all Italian policemen are like that. Captain Luca's overwrought. He's got
cause."

Jake didn't answer. He slipped to his knees and sprawled full length
in the water on the floor. A key grated in the lock. The policeman ran
inside and helped him to his feet. Jake fell heavily against a shoulder.
The cop slid sideways, his feet splashing. He said, "We'd better get you
out of here," and then they were in the corridor going toward the big
room.

Jake dragged his feet, keeping his eyes closed. He heard the voices, felt
the night air blowing on him, then he was lowered to a seat. The rain
outside was splashing hard. There was a lot of confusion.

The young policeman began to argue about the condition of the cells.
A woman was talking excitedly at the same time. Somebody was trying to tell her there'd been no telephones for hours. She wouldn't listen.
The voices raged on. Jake judged where the door was and turned his face
from it in case anyone was watching. He opened his eyes. The young policeman was emerging from the corridor with a small dark man even
younger than himself. The second man was handcuffed.

He dropped on to the bench beside Jake and held up his hands. He
said, "They think I'm stronger than you." He grinned. "You did pretty
good."

Over at a table the woman talked hysterically to a group of three policemen. There were only five more present. The young one was anxiously watching the prisoners. The body from the next cell said loudly,
"Thought I was an old man, eh? Everybody does. It's drink. Liver went
first, then voice, next me."

A wind blew. Jake rolled his head wearily in the direction of the door.
The rain hung over it like a bead curtain. He could hear the water rushing down the street. The voice of the woman was getting higher and
higher, saying her husband and son were lost and the policemen must
go find them. A cannonade of thunder seemed suddenly to split the
room. The woman screamed and went on screaming and fell to the floor.

The policemen clustered round her. The other prisoner stood up. His
lips said, "Let's go," and he and Jake walked casually across the room
and out of the door and into the drenching night. With one accord they
ran.

They were sprinting side by side, the water splashing their ankles. Through the unending crash of thunder the small dark man was laughing to himself, leaping high in the air to free his feet. They ran forty yards, then everything happened at once. A thin voice commanded them to stop. A shot spat. The thunder crackled across the sky. Superimposed on it was another sound, a long continuous booming like the beating of a million loose-skinned drums. A great screaming filled the air. The little dark man stopped laughing, tensed in mid-leap, and gasped. He turned to Jake. In a scorching flash of lightning the American saw his companion was grinning. The little man pitched forward.

Jake looked back. There was nothing but darkness. He reached down and snatched the man up in his arms. He was no weight. The lightning flashed again over the whole town, flickered dim, and then blazed full force. There was a corner ahead. Jake ran for it, his burden suddenly unbearably heavy. He stumbled against the brickwork and fell. He could go no farther.

He lowered his companion, propped him against a wall. "What?" he shouted to make himself heard above the din.

The little man shook his curly head. He said distinctly, "Told you drink would get me." Then he doubled at the waist like a scissors. In the blinding glare Jake saw the spreading patch on the back of the shirt where the bullet had entered. He lifted the fallen head and put his fingers to the neck. There was no pulse. He stepped back and released his hold. The body crumpled down into the coursing water and began to drift away.

A hundred yards away a tall house crumbled and disintegrated. He held a wall for support. Near at hand an unknown man was screaming in terror and pain. The light was brighter than day. He strained his eyes. Up the hill was the other huge patch of darkness. The silhouette of a second house knelt and crashed. He knew the meaning of it and the fear choked in his throat. The landslide was pushing from the peaks, creeping over the town, crushing everything that stood in its way, an irresistible mass of slime and rubble and rocks.

He stood an instant longer. Without knowing it he shouted, "Grace!" He let go the wall and the churning water seized him and he went hurtling down the hill, trying to keep his face above water.

Chapter Sixteen

In the sky a lead-colored streak told him dawn was coming. He had walked through chaos for what seemed hours. His body was a single great ache. He felt only half conscious. He kept going. He stumbled knee-deep around a corner and on the other side of the street a group of men were working frantically without plan, scratching bare-handed at a line of fallen houses. A short fat man with a blood-covered face was loudly calling a name, standing motionless, listening, calling it again, over and over, his voice a broken counterpoint against the sound of running water.

Jake walked on. He had passed four other groups. He knew no one would bother to notice him. He reached another corner, went higher, and the water receded until it barely covered his feet. The man was still calling in the distance. He stood against a wall for a moment and shook with nerves.

He must leave the city immediately, take any possible exit and get back to Rome where accusations could be met with reason and comparative calm. He was not guilty. He'd never prove it while he remained here, isolated at the mercy of Captain Luca. The policeman was determined to get a confession. He'd illustrated his methods.

Jake couldn't take much more. He had to get somewhere to an American consul. Naples wasn't far; perhaps he could steal a car.

But first he must see Grace.

The water underfoot became a thin film. He saw the official-looking building and knew he was on the same street as the hotel. A weak light from the entrance shone farther along. He daren't risk the lobby. He went a street higher. There was no one in sight. He ran squelching along to the rear door and inside and up the service stairs. The buzz of voices from the ground floor sounded loud at first, seeming to reach up for him. He had a strong and sickening conviction he was going to be caught.

In the upper corridor the light was still extinguished. The darkness sent a faint gray through the windows. He hesitated at the top of the stairs, saw the room of his door was shut, and wondered if Leverett were still inside, if there were policemen waiting. He had an overwhelming feeling that the door would open as he passed. He forced himself to walk along the corridor, his wet shoes shrieking all the way. He reached Grace's door and almost fell against it. He tapped with his fingernails.

He knew at once he shouldn't have done it. They were waiting for him. He heard the voices. This was the first place Luca would look. He turned to run and the door flung open and Grace gave a little scream and snatched his arm. He knew then it must be all right. He pushed inside and closed the door and stood with his back to it.

She looked at him, sobs shaking her body, but she managed somehow to smile. She said, "Darling, it gets terribly monotonous. This time I knew you were dead. The man came and told us. But you're not, are you?"

"Almost," he said, and smiled and reached out and put his fingers to her cheek. He looked over her shoulder. By the open door of the bedroom was Luigi Moretti, his arm around Fausta. The girl still wore pajamas. She was deathly pale. In a corner with a glass of whisky in his hand was Harry Myers. He looked old and very tired.

He said, "Hello, Jake. You could use this."

"Yes." Jake took the drink and sank in a chair. The whisky went down his throat in a thin line and exploded like an opening fist in his stomach. He felt a little better. He said, "What do you mean Grace, dead?"

She continued staring at him as if he were an apparition. Luigi moved from the corner. He said quietly in Italian, "Mr. Abbott, I want to say how sorry—"

He was cut short by a wave of Harry's hand. The photographer took the glass and refilled it. Grace said, "Your face, Jake. What have they done to you?"

"Just one," he said. "Captain Luca."

Harry said, "He was here fifteen minutes ago. He told us you'd been killed with all the others when the police station was buried."

"Were they killed? There was a woman there." The others waited for Jake to continue. He couldn't think of anything to say. His mind wasn't working straight. He looked up again at Grace. She was beautiful. He said, "I have to get out of here."

"Of course, darling."

Luigi Moretti was looking confusedly from one to the other, not understanding the English. He cleared his throat. "I shouldn't have fought with you, Mr. Abbott. I should have trusted Fausta more. She has told me how you looked after her. I want to make amends."

"Please keep quiet a while," Grace said. She was still standing motionless. "Jake. This Captain Luca. He's made up his mind you killed Phil Leverett over some stolen property. He'll discover, you're alive and—"

"Is he coming back?"

"He may," Harry said.

"Then I get out before he fits the unbreakable frame on me. I'll try for Naples. When they find Ralph's body, there'll be two murders to hang around my neck."

Harry said, "Jake, what are you talking about? You didn't murder Ralph."

"Somebody did. I don't know. Did you?"

Grace said breathlessly, "Jake."

"All right, Grace." Harry's eyes had gone wide. His thin face was drawn and exhausted. He said, "So would I, kid, if I were in your spot. That cop's out for you. He's got the right atmosphere. This flood has made everyone a little hysterical. The finer points have gone by the board. Another life more or less won't make any difference to them or him."

The photographer hesitated a moment. He walked over and put a hand on Jake's shoulder and looked straight into his eyes. He said, "No, I didn't kill Ralph. I swear it on the head of my new wife. May she die if I did. I hope that's enough."

"Sure," Jake said. He felt ashamed. He nodded toward Luigi and the girl, continuing to speak English. He noticed for the first time that Fausta was silently crying. He said, "Were they here when Luca came?"

"No. The girl was in the bedroom. The boy hadn't arrived."

"They've heard nothing about this?"

"So far as I know."

Jake said, "Grace, when you went up the mountain the girl was left alone. Could she have followed you?"

"Yes. Why?"

"Did she have any opportunity to kill Leverett?"

"I don't know. No, I don't think so."

Luigi Moretti said, "You are speaking of Fausta. Please do not worry. I will make her forget. It is natural she should be upset, but she will recover."

"From what?" Jake said.

"I have told her that her father and grandmother were killed when the viaduct broke. For myself it is very good. The world is better without them. But women think differently. She will be unhappy a long time."

Harry said, "You don't set much price on human life."

"When it is valuable, yes."

"And who decides that?"

"Leave him alone, Harry," Jake said. "I've tried the same line of thought. I've followed every line and got nowhere. What's the point? If I had every fact in my hand I still couldn't prove a thing." He stood up. "So I'm getting out. Investigations are for the police."

Grace said, "The roads must be blocked."

"I'll walk. I don't care if I crawl." He looked across at Fausta and their eyes met briefly. She lowered her gaze. She clearly hadn't told Luigi of what had happened in Jake's room. He wondered what else she was capable of concealing. He said, "Got a gun, Harry?"

"No. I could try and get one. "

Grace said, "I'm going with you, Jake."

"Not this time."

He almost laughed. It was the same remark that had started the whole sequence of events. He realized with a shock it had been only one day before. He said gently, "It'll be too long a walk, Grace."

"Maybe not." All at once Harry looked eager. He said, "Listen, that newspaper office is on an unflooded street. The editor has a car. I know he'll lend it to me. I'll pitch him a story. You duck down in the back and we'll drive as far as we can toward Naples."

"I don't want to drag you in, Harry."

"It's nothing." The photographer grinned. "We'll head for the consulate. The guy won't be pleased to see you, but he'll at least make sure you get a fair deal. What do you think?"

Luigi Moretti lifted his head. "The rain has stopped."

They all listened. The silence was like a void. Harry Myers walked to the window and pulled aside the curtain and looked down. He said, "All the same, it's a pity to leave a story like this. There'll be pictures out there like no one has ever seen."

"You stay behind," Grace said. "I'll drive the car."

"No." Harry shook his head. "The going's too rough for a woman. Besides, I'm also getting out for personal reasons. With Jake gone that cop might decide to pick on me. I've got a wife to think of."

He picked up his raincoat from the back of a chair, shrugged into it. He said, "You'd better not wait here, Jake, in case Luca comes back. We'll take the back stairs. I'll go first and see if the coast is clear. If anyone's there I'll get them out the way. Follow in two or three minutes. Don't stick around the vicinity of the hotel. I'll check with this editor if there's a route through the flood."

"There's an official building down the front street," Jake said. "It was deserted when I passed. I'll wait in the doorway."

"Right." Harry Myers impulsively held out his hand. "If the editor's car is out of commission I'll pick us up another from somewhere. We'll get out of this, with a little luck." The photographer halted a moment and grinned. "See you soon." He squeezed the hand and nodded and went out the door. It closed softly behind him. There was silence.

"He's a good man," Grace said.

"Yeah, he's all right."

They were seeking one another's eyes. He knew why it was he'd had to see her before he left. He loved her. All at once it didn't matter that Luigi and the girl were there. It would have been the same in a crowded street. He reached his arms around her and drew her close and kissed her. He felt the hungry response. Then she buried her face in his shoulder.

He said, "You know how I feel."

She nodded wordlessly.

"I have to go now."

"Yes," she said. "I'll see you in Rome or Naples or somewhere."

"Good-by," he said.

"Good-by, darling." She hunched her shoulders. She said, "Tell me you'll be all right."

"Sure I will."

She sobbed again. The small pajama-clad girl came softly across the room and took Grace's arm and looked anxiously into her face. Suddenly the two women clasped each other. Fausta was making little soothing noises, her hand stroking the back of Grace's hair. Luigi Moretti said, "Can I help, Mr. Abbott?"

"No, but thanks. Just stay here with the lady for half an hour. Don't let anyone bother her. I'll be grateful."

"Of course. You were good with Fausta. I will look after your girl."

"That's about the size of it," Jake said. "Maybe I'll see you again." He opened the door and slipped out into the corridor.

The stillness was absolute. He could hear nothing. The ceasing of rain had left a silence so intense it seemed everything must be discovered in it. He ran swiftly down two flights of stairs to the third floor. The voices from below began drifting to him in a confused buzz. The mercury-colored light had increased through the windows and lay heavily along the corridor, seeming to increase the darkness, to fill it with waiting shadows. He started down the next flight, and his confidence increased a little. Harry would have waited had there been danger. He was more than halfway down and he heard the sound of heavy breathing. Someone turned the corner below and started to ascend.

It was too late to turn back. He had to keep going. It might be Harry. He couldn't see in the darkness. He stopped breathing. The outline was directly in his path.

He brushed against it. There was a gasp of surprise and a voice said, "Sorry, sir." The figure started to flatten against the wall. The voice said, "Can you see all right, sir?" and there was a little click. A flashlight beam shone strong down the remainder of the stairs. He daren't walk into it. He shot a glance from the corner of his eye and in the light's strong throwback saw the elderly bellboy looking down the stairs, waving the beam encouragingly.

Jake said, "Thanks." He reached out and took the flashlight and knocked off the switch. He said softly, "I'll leave it at the desk," and walked casually on down. The bellboy didn't move. His tremulous voice came from behind in the darkness. "Is that you, Mr. Abbott?" Jake didn't answer. He had reached the second floor. He turned the corner to the last flight and ran.

The rain outside had started again in a gentle drizzle. The changing color of the sky threw no light over the soaked streets. In this small section of town the houses were still intact. Jake slowed to a walk, not wanting to draw attention if anyone was watching from a window. He splashed along to the deserted cross street, wondering if all the men had been pressed into rescue work. His brief confidence was fast evaporating. He wished inconsequentially that the little man in jail had not been killed. He would have been good to go to Naples with. He was the sort of guy you always picked up in Naples.

The water underfoot was shallow, hardly covering the soles of his shoes. It was little comfort. The shoes were soaked and felt as if they were falling apart. He put his head round the corner and saw the dim light of the hotel entrance farther up the street. Nothing was coming from either direction. He crossed the road, hugged the shadows of the wall and ran hard to the deeply recessed doorway of the official building.

He waited a long time. The rain increased a little. Twice he heard cars coming, but they drove straight past. He started to shiver again, thinking bewilderedly of everything that had happened—he could make no sense of it. After a while he gave up trying. All he wanted was to get out of Asceno, to have a bath, a drink, a change of clothes, the opportunity to think things over without this pressure, this paralyzing sense of immediacy. Maybe if he could tell the story dispassionately to an unbiased listener it might clarify itself, force out issues his present state of mind was causing him to miss.

He heard another car coming and he straightened. He felt an unexpected flash of amusement that he should still be gripping the bellboy's flashlight. The tires hissed slowly along the street. He took a quick look around the edge of the doorway. The approaching car was small, Italian, the sort of thing a local editor would possess. It was traveling without headlights.

He shrank back against the wall and waited. The car pulled slowly into the curb and drew up with its engine running. Somebody wound down a window. A voice called softly, "Hey." He stepped out of the doorway.

Something was wrong. He hesitated. The street was deserted. Harry should be saying something. The car door began to open and he saw the glint of the gun. He flung the flashlight with all his strength. It bounced tinnily from the chassis of the car. Somebody started swearing in Italian. He was already running, wondering why the gun didn't fire. Then he knew.

Four policemen were coming down the street toward him, moving slowly, as if they had a lot of time. He spun around and started running the opposite way. Three more were coming from the other end of the block.

They couldn't fire while he was between them, but if he stayed there he'd be caught. And if he ran in the street they'd shoot him. He turned his head frantically, looking for an exit. Captain Luca was leaning nonchalantly against the little car, dangling a gun in his hand.

A great wave of hatred went through Jake. Then he was weary. He walked slowly to the wall and leaned against it. He put up his hands. He said, "All right, Luca, you win. Start the beating, you bastard. You got more men to hold me this time." Momentarily he felt like crying.

The other policemen were coming running. Luca sauntered over casually from the car. In the growing gray light his teeth gleamed in a smile. He said, "Mr. Abbott, you have the nine lives of a cat." He pushed the gun lightly against Jake's stomach. "And I want every one of them."

"That shouldn't present much difficulty."

Another policeman began patting his hands all over Jake's body, searching for weapons. Luca said, "But I prefer you alive for a while. The confession. They'd never really have believed me without your signed statement. We go now to make it."

He waved the gun toward the car. The other policemen were crowding round, some of them wet to the waist, their clothes plastered with mud and grit. Luca said, "All right, men, back to your more important duties. See the gangs keep working. Watch out for looters. I'll be along presently."

He opened the rear door of the car. Another cop was sitting inside with a gun in his lap. He reached out and pulled Jake to the seat. Luca crushed in behind them. Jake was wedged between the two. The door slammed. The car started.

Jake said, "The editor didn't mind lending you this?"

Luca was still smiling. "What editor?"

"How did you know I was in that doorway?"

"I have second sight. It is similar to those anonymous phone calls the mayor receives from women."

Jake said, "I guess you'll pick another truncheon this time. It wouldn't be artistic to use the same one twice."

"Admirable American spirit." Luca patted him on the knee. "Unfortunately we have no cell, because the police station is buried under several hundred tons of rock." He paused and chuckled. "But there might be another truncheon. I wonder if the mayor has an old one in his desk."

Jake saw headlights. He looked from the window. Harry Myers drove past in a small gray car.

Chapter Seventeen

Mayor Drago burst into his own office and went white with fury. He'd been through a grueling night. The sights in the streets demanded a strong reaction and he had either to be sick or angry. He chose the latter.

When the policeman arrived for him he'd been supervising rescue work on the collapsed orphanage. There were fourteen children still in the ruins, and the mayor was fond of children. He had seized a pick to join the rescue work, but the policeman had insisted he come at once. Captain Luca was waiting. A matter of great importance. He had driven here and entered and opened the door of his own office only to find the unfortunate American sitting handcuffed in a corner while Captain Luca lounged behind the mayoral desk as if he himself had been elected.

The mayor bristled. "You sent for me, Captain Luca?"

"Yes, sir." The policeman straightened, a smile lingering on his face. "As you see, I have recaptured Abbott. He was not after all dead. In pursuance of my investigation, I thought—"

"You thought?" The mayor stood with his back to the door. "You had the audacity to send for me at a time like this? Get out of my chair, Captain. Explain yourself. Your reasons had better be good."

"It's very simple," the American said. "He wants permission to beat me up again."

"Shut your mouth, Abbott!" The smile had disappeared. Luca stood up with a dull flush creeping into his face. "I had to bring him here, Mr. Mayor. The police station is finished."

"I'm aware of that. You can leave him here. Get out and do some work like every other able-bodied man in the city. Lock him in an office."

"He would escape again."

Mayor Drago's mouth became a thin line. "Captain Luca, you still haven't explained why you brought me here."

"You haven't given me time," Luca snapped.

"I have no time. I know your interest in the case, but this is not the place nor am I the person to assist you in prosecuting your little personal feuds. At present there are matters of more importance."

"Not to me." The policeman's voice became flat and toneless. He was fighting to keep his temper. He said, "It's unfortunate you've never liked me, Mr. Mayor. I wanted to clear the case immediately. I hoped you might help. I should have realized you had other things to do, but in my anxiety I overlooked the present emergency. Accept my apologies. Perhaps we can have a discussion later. The question, as you say, is not important. I merely wanted an explanation of how you received an anonymous phone call from a woman when the phones have been out of order all night."

The mayor remained leaning against the door. He went very pale. He said, "Captain Luca, it is true I don't like you. I shall take great pleasure in reporting your present conduct to the proper authorities. The whole of the Via Frascati has been washed away. The old part of the city has disappeared under a layer of mud. Yet you stand here prattling away and trying to shift the blame for a theft that everyone says you committed yourself. Captain Luca, I begin to believe them." He wheeled around and went out, slamming the door behind him.

Jake said, "Luca, did you kill Leverett too?"

The policeman was still standing at the desk, head lowered, hands hanging limp. All at once he laughed. It made him seem almost human. He said, "I hear many complaints of the police persecuting a man. Did you ever hear of men persecuting a policeman?"

"Once in a while. Only they didn't use rubber truncheons on him."

"Yes," Luca said. "You've made a personal affair of it. You'd like to do the same to me."

"I will eventually. You can't imagine the pleasure I'll get."

"Exactly. No one ever understands the point of view. The method is only to save time when we know a man is guilty."

"Like me."

"Like you."

Jake said, "Shame you can't start again, but there's no one to hold me down. I'll make a deal. You get a truncheon and I'll use my bare hands, with handcuffs. Or are the odds too great for you?"

"Get up. We're going out."

"You're a brave bastard," Jake sneered.

The policeman came across the room and dragged him to his feet. The moment of near-humanity was past. Luca said, "You're the only man can solve my difficulties. But if I stay here and work on you I'll be reported by Drago. The difficulties will increase. I've had enough ironies in my life. I'm going out on the job and you're going with me. You'll not be out of my sight. We'll get to the rubber work later."

Jake said, "But I don't want to go." He saw the cop's fist tighten. His stomach contracted. He said, "All right. But one day we'll meet on equal terms. Luca, you'll be awful sorry."

The policeman had the door opened. He clamped a hand on the back of the American's neck and hurled him outside. He said, "Get moving."

They went down the passage and out into the increasing grayness of the morning.

Jake wiped his forehead on the back of his sleeve. An open jeep, fitted with a siren, wound its slow way up the cluttered street. Luca was directing operations from a mound of rubble twenty yards away. Every so often he'd blow a whistle and shout and wave his arms. Jake stopped digging.

He couldn't use the shovel properly because the handcuffs were still around his wrists. He looked back over his shoulder. Luca's eyes were fixed unwaveringly on him. A pistol butt gleamed dully from the loosened holster around the policeman's hips. There wasn't much hope.

A few yards away a man in a beret said, "Here's some more." Jake dropped the shovel and went over, stooping down, helping the man lift the cement block. The woman was underneath, and then the two children. They made twenty-one dead in this single row. They must have been in the upper stories, to be so near the surface. He clawed at the stones, forgetting his own troubles.

He tried to help strap the bodies onto stretchers, lift them to the jeep. His handcuffs impeded him. The man with the beret nodded with understanding, the rest watched curiously. Jake picked his way over the broken brickwork to Luca. He held out his wrists. "Here, take these off."

"You want to make the confession?"

"No."

"Then get back to work." Luca looked at him bleakly. "Don't try any tricks. I have a good wide range to take aim at you." The policeman turned away and blew his whistle again and shouted another order.

The open jeep bumped slowly away over the rubble, its siren wailing. The stretchers were tilted at an angle through lack of space. The corpses were head downward, necks limp, feet in the air. The ghastly freedom with which their necks rolled was more dead than anything Jake had ever seen. He watched the vehicle disappear around the corner. He calculated the distance—about sixty comparatively free yards. He wondered if he could make it. He looked back to Luca again, and a few yards beyond Harry Myers was approaching. The photographer lifted a hand and waved. Jake waited. A shaft of hope went through him. He daren't allow it.

Luca saw the other man and said something very rapidly. Jake couldn't make out what it was. Harry answered clearly, "Look, copper, I'm a member of the press. Unless I actively interfere you can't stop me going anywhere." He flipped his fingers at the policeman and came ahead to Jake. The man in the beret moved a little farther away. Jake liked him for that. He said, "Hello, Harry."

The photographer stumbled the last few feet. He didn't have his equipment with him. His face was unbelievably haggard. He came very close, lowering his voice to a murmur. "What happened, kid? They were dragging you away when I got there."

Jake put a foot on the edge of his shovel. "I got turned in."

"How do you mean?"

"I was standing back in the doorway. They couldn't have seen me from the street, but they knew exactly where to come. They drove right up and stopped. They had the place cordoned. Somebody had been chattering."

Harry looked completely blank for an instant. He said, "Up in Grace's room. The Italian fellow."

"So far as I know he speaks only his own language. The same with the girl. We made all the arrangements in English."

Harry said, "But nobody else knew except me and Grace." He stopped abruptly. His eyes narrowed. He said, "It must have been the Italian."

"Yeah," Jake said. "It must have been." He nodded at his wrists. "Anyway, it makes no difference now. I'm stuck good. Luca's over there and he's not moving. Even if I got out from under him I couldn't leave town wearing handcuffs. I'd be spotted in five seconds."

"Get on with your work!" Luca shouted. Jake bent to the shovel. Harry said softly, "I have the car, kid. There's still a road going part way towards Naples. We're going to get you out."

"How?"

Luca must have crept up behind them. He said in very bad English, "You enjoy your talk?"

They both jumped. Harry said, "We were." He eyed the policeman from head to foot. "I ought to get a picture of you, Luca. I've a feeling there'll be a big story attached to you pretty soon."

"I have a feeling too," Luca snapped. "You'll soon be arrested. I warned you against interfering with the prisoner. Now get out. I give you two minutes. I have another pair of handcuffs."

"Better go," Jake said. "He can do it."

"Sure." Harry turned his head slightly and gave a tiny wink. He said distinctly, "I'll be at my hotel if you want to contact me, Luca. Bring all your troubles to Uncle Harry. He can fix anything. He's going to." He gave a last grin and picked his way off over the rubble.

"Well?" Luca said.

"I'm working."

"And the confession?"

"You can go to hell any time," Jake said, and started digging again. Another jeep came wailing up the street. Somebody called Luca's name. He stamped away.

Time passed. The sky seemed to get no brighter. The dull leaden light was giving to everything the appearance of a badly reproduced etching. The awkward position in which he was forced to hold his hands was making Jake's back ache. He kept working. All the while he used physical energy his mind couldn't concentrate too clearly on Grace. He didn't want to think of her. He daren't. He loved her too much to suspect her. But there was no other train of thought, once he got started.

The man in the beret had just given him a drink of wine. Jake was turning around, wiping his mouth, and Giovanni Drago said, "Hello, Mr. Abbott. I came to see if there was anything I could do for you." He spoke softly in English.

Jake glanced over his shoulder. The cop was watching closely. He said, "Look out for Luca."

Giovanni smiled, frank blue eyes gleaming with amusement. "The captain will say nothing, Mr. Abbott. He is afraid of my father. My father could lose him his job."

"Try and persuade him."

"Yes." Giovanni nodded. "I have heard rumors of what you suffered. You know, Mr. Abbott, I think Captain Luca is determined to blame you for something he did himself. He'll treat you very badly if he gets you alone again."

"I know it."

"That made me wonder if you would like to escape."

A jeep was approaching from somewhere. Its siren sounded thin and far away. Jake looked down into the soft chubby face. "I don't understand."

"To escape," Giovanni said. "I come as a friend."

"Harry send you?"

"Harry?" Giovanni blinked. "Harry Myers, the photographer? Yes, he did."

"And why did you come?"

The smile faded from the mayor's son's plump face. His fine eyes became serious. He said simply, "You saved my father's life. I understand in America it is very different, but here a father and son are very close. I am in your debt. To assist your escape is small repayment."

He paused, eyes searching Jake's face. "There is a car. You could run away to Rome. Captain Luca will never catch you."

"Not till I run ten yards. Then he'll shoot me."

"But no." Giovanni's gaze flickered from side to side, coming into focus again. "It is very simple. That corner over there. There is mud in the next street, so be careful. Halfway along you will find an alley to the left. It ends at the front of a house which has been emptied. I unlocked the door a few minutes ago. You will run down the alley, through the door, close it behind you, and then make your exit through the only other door on the ground floor. You will find yourself in a street full of rocks. On the opposite side is a baker's shop with the windows smashed. No one will see because the district is entirely evacuated. In a while I shall come and collect you, lead you to the car." He nodded gravely. "Please repeat those instructions."

"I have them," Jake said. "You've gone to a lot of trouble and I still don't understand why you did it. Anyway, thanks for the effort. But there's one important point you overlooked. How do I get from here to the corner?"

The jeep came slowly up the street. Giovanni opened his mouth to say something. Captain Luca shouted politely, "Mr. Drago. I wish to speak to you for a moment."

The frank blue eyes flickered. "A few minutes more."

"I'd like to speak to you now."

Giovanni hesitated a moment, still watching the jeep, timing himself. He shouted, "Very well, if you insist, Captain," and started to walk away. Jake watched him go.

It was beautifully done. The jeep was traveling at no more than ten miles an hour. Giovanni judged its direction, fixed his eyes firmly on Luca. The policeman was still watching Jake. He had no way of knowing whether it was accident or not.

The jeep driver gave a sudden shout and jammed on his brakes. Giovanni flung up a hand. The flat of his palm hit the nearside fender. In the single movement he pushed backwards, fell flat on the ground and started to scream.

Luca leapt from the mound. He was swearing. The driver scrambled over the side of his vehicle. Everyone was gazing in one direction. Some of the workmen ran toward the jeep.

Giovanni screamed, "Captain Luca, you did it intentionally. I shall tell my father. You did it intentionally." He let out a great moan. The policeman fell swearing to his knees beside him.

Jake dropped the shovel, hugged his handcuffed hands to his chest and streaked for the corner.

It was like ninety miles. Giovanni still howled accusations. Jake was nearly there. Another voice cut across the racket. "Captain Luca! He's running away!"

The shot rang out and Jake lurched around the corner and slithered through the sucking mud to get across the road to the mouth of the alley. The walls closed about him. He saw the door far ahead and pelted toward it, filled with a sudden conviction that it would be locked, that this was all an elaborate joke of Giovanni's. He expected the gun to fire again. They couldn't miss him in this alley. His feet dragged and he had a pain in his side.

He hit the door with a force that slammed it right back against the wall. His manacled hands snatched clumsily and he had a last glimpse of the empty alley. Then the door was closed. He was leaning against it, sliding a bolt. He stood there panting. The exhaustion was so great he wanted to fall down. He said, "Grace," and began to weep.

It lasted only a few seconds. He went quietly through the empty, soaked house, found the other door and peeped cautiously into the rock-smashed street.

Chapter Eighteen

The baker's shop had an oven somewhere at the back. The smell of yeast persisted amid the reek of mud and wet dust and ruination. Jake eased to the broken window and looked out again. His vision was restricted. Both ends of the street were completely blocked with rocks and rubble, the sound of trickling water coming from beneath the pile. Every so often a boulder changed its level and fell grindingly as a spasm of pressure was exerted from high in the mountain peaks. To Jake's tired eyes the whole street seemed to move.

He went back and sat behind the counter. A long time had passed. He wondered if he had done wrong to bolt the door of the house in the alley. There seemed no other way of entering the street. Perhaps Giovanni was unable to get here. He'd give him a few more minutes, and then strike out on his own. He'd not get far wearing handcuffs. He started to grind the connecting chain again on the rock clamped between his knees. It had no effect but to hurt his wrist.

Far off the jeeps were whining. He experienced a peculiar twinge of conscience that he should be there helping. And there was a story to be written. He visualized the by-line and smiled grimly. Personal story: Jake Abbott: composed in a prison cell. At another time and place it might be funny.

Nevertheless the sense of pressing urgency had left him. He felt already half liberated; his mind was moving more freely. He began again to reconstruct the night's happenings, taking them step by step. Ralph murdered on the mountain. Why? Exclude Grace—he refused to entertain that anymore—there had to be another motive. The alternative was clear. Theft.

Ralph was near the missing articles. Conjecture that he saw someone stealing them. He was immediately killed for it. The weapon appeared to be a rock, and that was feasible; it would be the nearest thing at hand. But the damage to Ralph's head may have been sustained after death. There could be a knife or bullet in him. For the moment that was relatively unimportant. The next step was identity. Who had done it?

There had been many men on the mountain. He could deal only with those he knew. They made a surprisingly short list: Leverett, Myers, Giovanni, the mayor, Captain Luca and Luigi Moretti. Maybe Angelo. He'd forgotten Angelo. He ran through them.

Not Leverett. He had been seen or stumbled on something incriminating to the murderer and promptly got killed himself. Keep the list in order. Harry? No. Back at the hotel he had sworn on the head of his wife he didn't kill Ralph. It was more than enough. And if he were guilty he would not have tried so hard to assist Jake's escape.

The same mitigation now applied to the mayor's son. Harry obviously trusted him enough to enlist his aid. Jake had a suspicion Giovanni could be bought, but he dismissed it. There wasn't enough money anywhere to persuade one man to help another on whom he was trying to pin a crime committed by himself. Giovanni might be greedy, but there was no possible financial incentive to make him take the present big risks. He must have meant all that he said about gratitude.

So who was left to qualify? Angelo, the mayor, Luca and Luigi. But Angelo must be ruled out. The murderer was also the thief. Someone had slipped the countess's ring into Jake's pocket, and Angelo had not been near enough. That left only three.

They'd all had ample opportunity to plant the ring. The mayor on the mountain or in his office; Luigi while they were fighting in the room. Captain Luca—most chance of all: on the mountain, in the car, at the mayor's office, in Luigi's room, in the street. Significantly, he had arrested only Jake after the fight, leaving Luigi on the floor. Maybe because he knew the ring was already in Jake's pocket.

Jake leaned his head back against the counter. He hated the policeman. He wanted him to be guilty. But there was one exonerating fact that stood out a mile. Luca had known where to come with the car when Jake was hiding in the doorway. He didn't have second sight. He must have been told. Whoever carried the information didn't want Jake to escape. The obvious indication was that it had been the guilty party.

There were only two remaining. The mayor and Luigi Moretti. And the mayor had known nothing. Only Luigi was present when the escape arrangements were made. The deduction was clear. Moretti spoke English. He had understood everything. He had left the hotel room directly after Jake, and had run to tell Luca.

Jake took it slowly. The Italian had already been seeking Ralph Ellison on the mountain. Maybe he'd even killed him first and discovered the missing collection afterwards. The sequence wasn't important. There were good firm motives for both the theft and the second murder. Luigi wanted to marry Fausta. He was a bricklayer earning seven and a half dollars a week. The jewelry and paintings must have represented the answer to everything he wanted. It looked airtight. Luigi Moretti.

But one question remained unanswered. If Leverett had seen or known something why did he keep quiet about it until he was murdered himself?

Jake went suddenly rigid—footsteps had shuffled. On the other side of the counter someone had entered the shop. Glass crunched. A brick was kicked. Someone swore very softly. Jake remained motionless and a voice whispered, "Mr. Abbott." Giovanni came guardedly round the counter.

He saw the American and sank to the floor. He was smiling. He whispered, "What a big confusion back there. My father heard I was hurt and came running and had a big quarrel with Captain Luca. The captain was swearing about your escape. He wanted ten policemen to hunt for you. But my father said no, because there was more important work for them to do and Luca had already taken them once before. The quarrel got bigger. Everyone was shouting. Captain Luca said he would search himself, and my father ordered him to stay where he was and supervise the workmen. Captain Luca told my father to go to hell. I thought they would fight."

"What happened?"

"Captain Luca hit the driver of the jeep and walked away. He really is looking for you, Mr. Abbott. We must be very careful. He has a gun."

Jake said, "Did you see Harry again?"

Giovanni nodded emphatically. "Yes," he said. "Yes, I did. Everything is arranged. I take you to an empty house near the main street and you wait there while I fetch Mr. Myers with the car. It is very simple. There is still a clear road leading out of town. If the mountains are not completely blocked you will be in Naples for lunch. I am happy for you."

Jake said, "Harry paying you for this?" He saw the look of injury come into the blue eyes. He said, "Sorry, Giovanni. You're taking so many risks. You deserve something."

"I shall get something," Giovanni answered, smiling. "I shall have the satisfaction of knowing I discharged my debt to you. We go now." He stood up cautiously.

"Any way I can get rid of these handcuffs?"

"Not unless you ask Captain Luca for the key." Giovanni patted him happily on the shoulder and smiled again. For an inexplicable instant Jake felt uneasy. They stepped warily into the street.

The light was increasing slightly. Far to the east a wisp of pure blue shone through a rift in the heavy overcast. The wind had dropped. In the oppressive silence the sirens of the jeeps, the distant voices of men echoed, as if they worked in a huge and far-off canyon. There was an air of the fantastic over everything. Only the sound of running water remained real.

They skirted the mud, going up alleys and through the broken ruins of houses. The flood had followed no apparent pattern, but the whole area was deserted. One street was filled with rushing water, the next was bone dry. The landslide of rocks and mud was everywhere, still creeping forward. They picked their way down a completely ruined street, and Jake wondered how many people lay buried beneath the piles of bricks. His conscience was gnawing. He whispered, "Why is no one working here?"

Giovanni turned a white face. All at once he was much more nervous. "Impossible to bring in jeeps and equipment. Everything blocked."

"But aren't we near the main road yet?"

They were almost to a corner. Giovanni shrugged and started to say something, but his jaw closed with a snap. His eyes went big. He waved a frantically quieting hand, but Jake had already heard. The footsteps were approaching up the next street. Someone was tramping softly on broken glass.

Giovanni turned quickly from side to side, hunting an exit. He whispered, "Hide," and pointed vaguely across the rock-strewn road. He started to run. Jake turned and took one step and stopped.

He had come a long way. He was weak. He was tired of running. They must be near the main road by now and there was a possibility this was Harry looking for them. He held his manacled hands to his chest, edged to the corner and peered round it. The man was twenty yards down the street, advancing with a gun in his hand. He was taking his time. He was Captain Luca.

Jake backed away and stumbled over a large piece of wood. He looked around. Giovanni had disappeared. He could see no place to hide. He hovered irresolutely on his toes, and then the last thing he wanted to do was hide. He had promised himself this. His chance had come. He bent down and picked up the piece of wood. It was very heavy.

The gambit would be lost if Luca moved to the other side of the street. The risk must be taken. He clamped both hands tight on the wood and swung it over his head and eased back to the corner. The footsteps were coming in measured treads. He waited. A sudden fierce pleasure filled him.

He didn't much care then if he won or lost, so long as he made the effort. He'd been forced all night into the passive role of victim, unable to make any positive act of resistance. His opportunity had arrived. He owed it to his own spirit to make the most of it. For no reason at all he thought of the little prisoner now dead, being beaten up in Rome. His grip tightened. He tried to wet his dry mouth. An extra hard wallop for the sake of the little man.

The footsteps approached slowly, now spasmodically. Luca was looking into all the buildings as he advanced, staying on one side of the road. A rock slipped. The glass crunched underfoot. Jake's arms began to ache. He had stopped breathing.

It was ridiculously simple. The gun came first, and after it the arm.

No more. Luca had halted. He was looking back down the street. Jake took a propulsive step forward and swung with all his force. The wood smacked the forearm just below the elbow. Luca gave a tremendous howl of pain and the gun dropped. Jake stepped round the corner.

He kicked the gun. It went clattering off among the rocks. He brought up the wood. It hit scrapingly on Luca's chin and the policeman's lips split. Jake saw the terror in the man's eyes. He reveled in it. Briefly he had no room for a second swing. He jabbed the stake hard into the policeman's stomach and Luca gave a great gasp and started to fall, clawing at nothing. Jake stepped back. Luca tried to yell, but he didn't have a chance. The wood whistled down and hit him on the side of the neck and he went full length on his back. Jake stood over him.

He did it scientifically, exactly as Luca had. He started at the policeman's chest and flogged methodically all the way down to the ankles. He felt lightheaded, detached from what he was doing. He didn't realize that Luca had lost consciousness. He stopped only when he was gasping for breath and his arms would yield no more. He tossed the wood aside, bent down and propped Luca's limp body in a sitting position against the wall.

The key was in the right-hand trouser pocket. He twisted his wrists, released the handcuffs, clamped them on Luca and tossed the key far down the street. Then he looked for the gun. It was nowhere. He walked to the rocks and started to search. Giovanni looked around the corner. He jerked his head.

"Come on!" the mayor's son hissed. "Mr. Myers will be waiting."

"Yes," Jake said dully. He took a last glance at the policeman. Giovanni was already going swiftly down the other street. Jake went after him. They broke into a trot, turning a first corner and then a second. The morning was suddenly a lot brighter.

"Not far," Giovanni said, and all at once he giggled. "I saw what you did to Captain Luca. It made me very happy. I don't like Captain Luca, do you?"

Jake felt a strong revulsion. There was something sickening in the way the man laughed. He said shortly, "Thanks for the help you didn't give."

Giovanni's eyes went wide and honest. "But you understand I couldn't let him see me. I can't take too many risks. I am doing a great deal for you now." He came to an abrupt stop, standing motionless. He was still smiling.

"What is it?" Jake said.

"You're not angry at me?"

"No. When do we get to this place?"

"What?" The smile became radiant. "We are here now." Giovanni pointed to the house. It had one shattered window. Its door was broken. "We are here now," he repeated, a little louder. "Go inside. I will show you where to wait."

Jake automatically stepped aside to let the other man pass. Giovanni moved forward impulsively and put an arm around the American's shoulders. It was uncomfortable. They were squeezing through the door together. Giovanni was exerting too much pressure. He was pushing.

The alarm signals suddenly tensed every fiber of Jake's body. He shoved Giovanni from him. He tried to get out. He was too late.

The shadow moved from behind the door. The big gun jammed hard into his chest. He looked down frozenly into the little cruel white face of Angelo. Giovanni giggled again.

He said, "Mr. Abbott, we want those two paintings."

Chapter Nineteen

A flow of happiness filled Angelo's breast. The discomforts and fears of the night were gone—his mistakes were rectified, his goal had been reached and surpassed, his success promised to be overwhelming. He grinned hungrily at the American and quick pictures of the exultant homecoming were flitting through his mind.

Mr. Turrido was going to be angry at first when he heard of the temporary ally. He would shout and talk of bad tactics and say many harsh words. But Angelo would endure them patiently, certain in the strength of his position. And when Mr. Turrido was quite finished he would give his triumphant explanation, telling how the night had reached its lowest ebb, the situation become most difficult, and then this same fat ally had presented the golden opportunity for that long-dreamed-of spectacular coup. It was a delightful contemplation.

Angelo had been furious when Giovanni had failed to bring the American to him. He thought then that the mayor's son had promised to help only to save his own skin. But finally Giovanni reappeared outside the hotel, full of suspicions and very excited. Angelo listened and did not believe until the fat man mentioned paintings. Then he knew.

It was his turn to become excited. Without mentioning names, he told how the American had been mixed up in the sale of counterfeit pictures in Rome. They had convinced each other. Abbott was the only logical person to have stolen the Botticellis. Giovanni spoke of their value and Angelo's head spun like a top. What a gift for Mr. Turrido!

Giovanni said, "Where are the paintings, Mr. Abbott?"

The American looked white and very ill. He said slowly, "You fat, dirty little rat," and made a sudden motion as if to attack. Angelo jammed harder with the gun. It would have been satisfying to pull the trigger right then, but the result, without paintings, would now be only half a triumph. He edged the American away from the shattered window and back to the wall. He said, "The paintings. I want them."

"So do I," the American said.

"No need to be elusive, Mr. Abbott." Giovanni's eyes glinted. "Remember that I was on the mountain also, watching very carefully all the time. Only two other people went near the collection before you discovered it—Mr. Ellison and Mr. Leverett. When I heard the Botticellis were missing, I knew it must be either them or you. But then you killed Mr. Leverett in your room. The motive was obvious. It cut out Mr. Ellison and left only you. Where are they?"

Jake looked fixedly into the honest blue eyes. The first ray of light penetrated. He said, "Why were you watching so carefully?"

Giovanni's gaze flickered. For no apparent reason he stepped forward suddenly and kicked Jake viciously in the shin. "I am asking the questions. We wait for the answers." He smiled again. "If you tell us where the paintings are we'll let you go."

"What paintings?"

"Inside his coat," Angelo said.

"No. I had my arm round him. There's nothing. The police would have found out if he were carrying them. Where are they, Abbott?"

Jake stood tensely against the wall, his mind clicking like a comptometer. He had to play for time while he figured an angle. He said, "Harry didn't send you."

Giovanni laughed gleefully. "That was your suggestion, Mr. Abbott. Don't blame me that I seized it. I would have become tired about being grateful over my father."

"I should have known," Jake said. "Harry and I fixed Naples. You started talking Rome again. I was a fool."

"Not if you give us the paintings."

"I don't have them."

Angelo nudged with the gun. He was growing nervous again, tired of all this talking. He said childishly, as if reciting a lesson: "When I shoot a man in the stomach he takes a long time to die."

"I know," Jake said. He saw one chance now. Giovanni was the almost pathological type who had to outsmart everyone. Probably he was even trying to outsmart Angelo. Jake composed his expression, looked interestedly at the Sicilian. "What is it exactly you're after?"

The boy's finger tightened angrily on the trigger. The American was making fun of him. He said, "I want two paintings by a man named Botticelli."

"Why? They'd be worth nothing."

Giovanni laughed abruptly. "Listen to it," he sneered. "The man lived five hundred years ago. His paintings are worth millions."

Jake made his great effort. He smiled. He said, "Angelo. Check with Mr. Turrido. Signor Botticelli lives on the Via Lima in Rome. He has supplied us with most of our forgeries."

"What?" Giovanni gasped, started to laugh again and changed his mind. He reached out and slapped Jake hard across the mouth. "What are you trying to arrange?"

"I'm not talking to you." Jake forced himself to remain calm. "Angelo, there are no paintings by Botticelli. This is a trick of Giovanni's. He's already used me, now he's trying to do the same with you."

The mayor's son made another lunge. Angelo caught him off balance and hurled him with surprising strength against the wall next to Jake. The gun waved; he covered both of them. The confusion swirled in his mind. The anger and fear churned in his stomach. Someone was making a fool of him. The imagined idyll with Turrido was receding dangerously. He nodded at the American. "All right, what is this? Speak!"

Jake said slowly, "Nothing has been stolen except some jewelry, very valuable jewelry. Giovanni and I stole it together. This present maneuver seems to be an attempt to cheat me out of my share."

"You liar!" Giovanni gulped his lips incredulously for a few moments, like a sick goldfish. He looked frantically at Angelo. "You mustn't believe him. I don't know anything about any jewelry."

He had gone gray in the face. Angelo studied them both. The American was calm, steady-eyed, not frightened. Mr. Turrido had said Abbott was an honest man. He had used him for that reason. Honest men were more easily gulled. The fear was fluttering all over Angelo's stomach. He had to believe one of them. He said, "I'm waiting, American."

"A moment." Jake grimaced another smile, turned his head to Giovanni and spoke in English. "This guy was going to kill me anyway. You'll keep me company by the time I'm finished."

"What are you saying?" Angelo rapped.

Giovanni's blue eyes were no longer frank or honest. They bugged. "No," he said. "He's going to make you kill me. Don't let him. I don't know what he's talking about."

"Jewelry," Jake said calmly. "Angelo, why should I want you to kill him? I'm trying to persuade him to split the stuff three ways, but he wriggles too much. A moment more."

He turned back to Giovanni, lapsing again into English. "I've got it clear," he said. "You were looking all the time in the direction of the commandant's house because you'd already been there and stolen the jewelry. But why only that? Didn't you know the value of the paintings?"

Giovanni wet his lips and took a deep breath. He said, "Look, Abbott. You and I can get out of this if we work it right."

"Thanks, no. You got me into it, up on the mountain when you thanked me for saving your father's life and slipped the ring into my pocket. A smart move. You knew there'd be uproar when the police discovered some of the stuff was missing, so you had to frame someone else. You elected me. I was a natural. I was the man who'd found the stuff."

Giovanni's eyes flickered almost imperceptibly to Angelo. "All he wants is one of the paintings. We can pass anything off on him. He's just a kid. What do you say?"

"Hand him the jewelry."

"But I don't have it."

"And I don't have the paintings."

Angelo snapped, "You've talked long enough. Speak in Italian."

Jake smiled thinly. "The language won't make much difference. I'm trying to persuade him to give you the jewelry, but he's too greedy. Wants it all for himself. He's going to claim he doesn't have it."

"I haven't," Giovanni insisted desperately.

"Call his bluff. He wouldn't have risked hiding it anywhere with these floods on."

Angelo stepped back a pace. The big gun was sagging. His wrist still hurt from the stamping he'd received in Rome. He said, "Fat one, turn out your pockets."

Giovanni's eyelids flittered like the wings of a moth. He creased his fat face in a quavering smile. With a sudden boyish sincerity, completely unconvincing, he said, "Such a liar, this American. He's just trying to confuse us about the paintings."

"Turn them out."

All at once Angelo had an overwhelming desire to cry. The night had been exhausting. He had endured such discomforts and uncertainties of mind as he had never before thought possible. He had been without Mr. Turrido, completely on his own, forced to make decisions of which he did not know the value, that had left him feeling wrong and inadequate and feeble.

"Your pockets," he shouted.

Jake heard the mayor's son start a high-voiced protest. He shot a quick glance at the shattered window. He looked back to Angelo and smiled and said, "Don't get nervous, son, I'm here to help. There's one sure way." Then he hooked the tips of his fingers into Giovanni's pocket and jerked hard. The cloth ripped clear away. The mayor's son squealed high with despair. The jewelry fell in a tinkling cascade and lay gleaming on the sodden floor.

There were rings, little brooches, a necklet, other things Angelo could not identify. He didn't mind. His heart was lifting. Paintings were all very well. But jewelry was something you could hold, could trickle piece by piece into Mr. Turrido's waiting hand. He looked at the fat man's quivering, sweating face and smiled. He said, "Pick it up."

"Sure." It was the American who stooped, gathering everything into a cupped palm. He straightened, hesitated, looked at the collection and with a tiny grin handed it to Angelo. He said, "Diamonds, emeralds, rubies. Nice words. Nice price they bring. That fistful is worth a small fortune."

Angelo tilted the jewelry into the huge pocket of his long overcoat, glorying in the tinny sounds it made. He gripped the gun tighter, raised it a little and aimed directly at the trembling fat man. The American said, "And there's more."

"No." Giovanni shook his head violently. "It was a joke. I didn't intend keeping it from you."

"More," the American said.

Angelo grinned wolfishly. A sackful to take back to Mr. Turrido. "Where?" he asked.

The American remained motionless. "Probably in the pocket on the other side."

"Get it."

"There's nothing," Giovanni whispered.

"Get it."

The American moved slowly. He gave no warning. He eased Giovanni from the wall and reached an arm round behind him. Then abruptly he shoved.

There wasn't even time to shoot. Giovanni fell forward and clamped his arms around Angelo for support. Angelo's hurt wrist was bent. He saw the American run across the room and leap through the broken window. Everything was happening too quickly. He couldn't get the gun free. Giovanni said, "No!" just once and broke away and tried to run. Angelo aimed at the small of the fat man's back and pulled the trigger.

The big gun jumped. The roar was deafening. Giovanni pitched to the floor and started to scream, long and high without stopping. Angelo felt that his wrist was broken. He ran for the door and stumbled. His shoe caught on the bottom hem of his long coat and he almost fell full length. He clutched at the door frame, pulling himself upright. He catapulted into the strewn street.

It was a terrible moment. It was as if his head were suddenly caught in a clamp. Giovanni was screaming; that was nothing. But inside Angelo's skull the voice of Mr. Turrido began shouting imprecations, calling him a fool, a bungler, telling him to get out and never return. A choked sob burst from Angelo's throat. He saw the American twenty-five yards away, scrambling across a pile of rocks. There was somebody else, too, running down from the other end of the street, but he couldn't be bothered with that one. Mr. Turrido had sent him for the American. Angelo must obey. He lifted the gun and couldn't aim properly because his wrist hurt and he was running. He tried to steel his arm. He pulled the trigger.

It was useless. The heavy weapon leaped sideways. His whole arm, clear to the shoulder, jumped to the right. He saw the bullet pluck a plume of dust from high in the wall on the other side of the street. He gave another sob and fired again. He missed. The fat man screamed on and on. Mr. Turrido shouted from somewhere. The other person was running down the street from behind.

Angelo knew all these things with a preternatural sharpening of the senses. He was conscious of everything—the whole town, the entire world. But he was alone in it. It was as if the street had grown immensely wider, turned into a Sahara of mud and rocks. The only realities in all the desert were the shouting voice of his employer and the figure of the American, still scrambling ahead over the rocks.

He had to remain calm. What would Mr. Turrido do in this position? Mr. Turrido would be cool, unflurried, judicious. Angelo came to a sudden halt. He forced down his panic and took a deep breath. He even smiled slightly. Then he raised the gun very slowly, steadied his forearm with his left hand, closed one eye and sighted along the barrel.

It was going to be utterly simple, something like a sport. The fleeing figure of Abbott grew very large. He reached the top of a mound of rocks, hesitated a split second and stood silhouetted against the gray sky. Angelo squeezed the trigger.

It wasn't only his arm that jumped. His whole body went. The blow hit him with appalling force between the shoulder blades and he fell full length to the ground, lying there a second, stunned. The voice of Mr. Turrido shrieked at him. He scratched to his knees and tried to fling himself upright. It was the long coat again. He was standing on the skirt. His wrist hurt. His knees were bent and his balance uncertain. He jerked his shoulders. The gun went off.

Angelo's little white face disappeared into a jammy mask. He crouched for a crawling moment on the ground and his hands twitched forward and he lay down. His last living image was a memory. He saw Mr. Turrido with his trousers down and his shirt up and the bright pink corset exposed. The picture was very vivid, horrifyingly amusing. No man like that was worth dying for. Angelo started to protest.

A breath whistled from where his mouth used to be. He died.

Chapter Twenty

The gun had stopped firing. The voice called again. "Mr. Abbott!" Jake flung a look back over his shoulder. There was no Angelo any more. Luigi Moretti was standing perfectly still, both arms above his head, beckoning. A crumpled heap lay unmoving at his feet.

It was no cause for turning back. Moretti was the thief, the murderer. It had all been deduced back in the baker's shop. Jake heard Giovanni screaming. His mind clicked—that was one count at least on which he'd been mistaken about Luigi. Maybe everything else was wrong. He came to a halt, looked back again. "Signor Abbott," the Italian shouted. "Your girl sent me." It was enough.

He went slowly back down the street, staying near the doorways, waiting for tricks. Luigi beckoned once more, then ran and looked through the broken window at Giovanni. "Shut up!" he said, and disappeared into the house. Jake saw the big gun lying beside Angelo. He ran forward and picked it up.

Suddenly Giovanni stopped his noise. The silence flowed almost palpably down the street. Far away the jeeps whined, raising echoes; the unconcerned voices of men rang distantly. Jake clutched Angelo's thin shoulder, lifted him up, knowing by the limpness that the boy was dead even before he saw his face. He lowered the body gently, fought the gagging sensation in his throat, continued on down the street to enter the shattered doorway of the house.

Giovanni was propped in a corner. Luigi stooped beside him, a hand clamped over the straining mouth, stifling the shouts in the fat man's soft throat. "Shut up!" Luigi said again, and grinned at Jake. "I have to stop his row or everyone in town will be here."

Jake slipped the gun in his pocket. He said, "I'm pleased to see you. What happened?"

Luigi squeezed the hand tighter, rattled Giovanni's head. "Your girl heard you'd escaped again. She sent me to look for you. The screaming started when I was in the next street. I came through one of the broken buildings, and that kid out there was chasing you with a gun. I threw a big brick at his back. He fell over and shot himself. Probably deserved it."

"Yeah. Thanks."

"Who was he?"

Jake didn't answer. In the troubled cross currents of his mind he could think clearly of nothing. He only knew he must stay on guard with everyone. He looked down at Giovanni. The mayor's son had stopped moaning and was watching them both with eyes that seemed swollen with fright. Jake said coldly, "All right, let him go. Where's my girl now?"

"Back at the hotel." Luigi kept his hand a few inches from Giovanni's mouth in case the shouting started again. She has a car. She told me why you have to escape, and I want to help. If you wait here I'll fetch her. The main thoroughfare is only two blocks away."

Giovanni made a whining noise. His head fell to one side. He said, "I'm dying."

"Good. No one will miss you." Luigi grinned, raising his eyebrows at Jake. "What did he do?"

"Stole the jewelry I was accused of taking."

"I'm not surprised. He's always been a thief. Everyone in town knows that except his father."

"He's played a tricky game. He may also be a murderer."

"You mean the American?"

"No." Giovanni moaned faintly. "I intended to give everything back. Take me to a hospital. I'm dying." His eyes started to glaze. He opened his mouth very wide. Suddenly he slumped in a dead faint. They saw the blood on his back where the bullet had entered.

Luigi stretched him on the wet floor. "You really think he is dying?"

"Either way, we can't leave him here. You'd better get somebody."

"Let him lie. Anyone else will report you to the police."

Jake looked down into the Italian's vehement face. His doubts disappeared. He couldn't fathom it, but the guy really wanted him to escape. He said, "I'll go. You'd better not become involved."

Luigi leaped to his feet. "I'll think of something. Stay here." Jake started to protest. The Italian was already through the door. A brick was kicked as he hurried off down the street. The silence closed in again.

Jake leaned against the wall and studied Giovanni. The torn pocket was flapped open. Two or three small pieces of jewelry still lay at the bottom, near the seam. Blind luck to have ripped the right pocket first time off. Giovanni was a thief. Was he also a murderer? The answer could be left to others. Maybe with this much to go on even Luca would relax his personal pace a little.

Jake considered how much actually there was. His spirits flagged. Giovanni had stolen the jewelry; even that might be hard to prove with the only other witness dead. And the paintings: the plump man's sole apparent motive for helping the escape was to get his own hands on the Botticellis. In that case, where were the pictures now? How many thieves were there?

He bent over the mayor's son and felt his pulse. It was beating strongly. He looked at the wound and the bullet seemed to have entered diagonally and lodged in the flesh behind the collarbone. There was no longer any blood. Giovanni wasn't dying, or anywhere near it. He propped the unconscious man against the wall and gently slapped his face a few times. Giovanni moaned, stirred. He didn't open his eyes. He sagged again.

Jake went to the door and looked into the street. He saw the body of Angelo, and his hand went instinctively to the big gun in his pocket. With the sort of luck that had been dogging him all night he wouldn't be surprised if they tried to pin even this death on him. He wondered briefly if he should wipe the gun and put it back beside the body.

His hand relaxed. He remembered that Luigi Moretti had witnessed what had happened. Unexpectedly he felt a wave of pity for the screwed-up little shape in the big overcoat. He thought of Mr. Turrido sitting in the Rome apartment, perfumed, smoking cigars, drinking brandy. Something had to be done about Mr. Turrido. More immediately something had to be done about himself.

He saw the figure turn the corner and tried to dodge back in the doorway. He was too late. He had been seen. Mayor Drago halted a moment, then came on cautiously, looking faintly comic as he picked his way over the mud and rubble. Jake's hand tightened again on the butt of the gun. He advanced toward the mayor, knowing he'd not be able to shoot if the occasion arose but thinking he might use the weapon as a bluff if Drago got troublesome.

The little man's face was agitated. He said breathlessly, "Hello, Mr. Abbott." Then he looked beyond and saw the body of Angelo. A peculiar little whimper broke from his throat. He said, "Giovanni!" and started to run forward.

Jake grabbed him by the shoulders. "No, it's somebody else. Better not look. He's an unpleasant sight."

Some of the tension went out of the mayor's body. He gazed wide-eyed into Jake's face. "A young man approached me just now. He told me you were here and I'd better come immediately because Giovanni was in trouble. He advised me not to tell anyone if I wanted my son to be safe. What did he mean? Was it a joke?"

Jake held on, trying to think, to organize a pattern with which he could help himself. He said, "It's complicated. I'm afraid it may prove painful for you."

"Tell me at once."

"That boy there." Jake nodded toward the body. "He was a gunman from Rome. Giovanni met up with him and entered into some sort of deal. I think they were trying to steal the Botticelli paintings between them. Your son had already stolen the missing jewelry."

The mayor remained staring for five long seconds, the incredulity gradually spreading across his face. A high pitched laugh came from his throat. He stepped back a pace. He said, "You ridiculous liar. Who do you think will believe that?"

"I don't know," Jake said soberly. "Probably no one. I'm just giving you the truth." He withdrew the gun from his pocket. "The boy shot himself accidentally with this. I have a witness. Beforehand he and Giovanni had quarreled over the jewelry. For that I don't have a witness."

The mayor was looking at the gun. Suddenly he lifted his chin. In an odd way he contrived to appear proud and fearless. He said, "Of course you have no witness. In all the world there is nobody can testify that my son is dishonest. He is a good boy, the best a father ever had." The mayor paused, his chin going even higher. "It grieves me deeply to hear you say these things, Mr. Abbott. You are the man who saved my life. Until now I have wished you well. But no longer. I must go at once and tell the police where to find you." He started to walk away.

Jake said dryly, "And during the quarrel Giovanni got shot."

The mayor froze. He turned slowly and came back, his face drained of all color.

"A flesh wound," Jake said. "Nothing serious." He pointed up the street to the shattered door. "In there."

The mayor gave a sob, raised both hands above his head and ran past. Jake followed slowly, trying to figure a way he could clear himself. One thing at a time. The jewelry first. He replaced the gun in his pocket and entered the door.

The mayor was weeping, holding Giovanni's head tight to his breast, rocking to and fro, whispering, "My son, my son," as if the fat man was a small child that needed soothing. Giovanni began stirring into consciousness. It would be fatal if he regained his senses immediately. Jake edged the mayor aside. He said authoritatively, "Here, let me look at him."

"Is he dying?"

"He'll be all right." Jake stopped down, seized the fat man around the lower chest and hauled him upright. Giovanni's feet shuffled, seeking purchase on the ground. His eyelids fluttered. The torn pocket rolled right open and the remaining jewelry fell on the floor.

Jake saw the mayor look at it. He said, "He may have stuff in another pocket. There's more on the dead boy out there."

"You distributed it well. I shall fetch a doctor. Also the police."

"One moment." Jake leaned close to the unconscious man's ear. He whispered fiercely, "Angelo's coming back! Quick! We have to get out."

Giovanni moaned again and his whole body twitched convulsively. The mayor made a move to intercept. Jake heaved with a shoulder and the little man went stumbling backwards across the room. Jake shouted, "Wake up, Giovanni! We have to give him the rest of the stuff you stole.

He'll kill us."

Giovanni gave another great twitch. His eyelids flicked open. The blue eyes were glassy with panic. He gasped, "Where is he?"

"The other jewelry you stole."

"There isn't any more." Giovanni flung his arms around Jake, seeking protection. He sobbed, "I didn't have time to get any. Someone was calling me from over by the lights. I was afraid."

"And the church ornaments?"

"I dropped them on the mountain. They were too big. Maybe I could tell him to look for them."

"It wouldn't be any use."

"But I don't want to—" Giovanni began. Then over Jake's shoulder he saw his father. He straightened up, pushed himself away from the American, tried to smile. He took a deep breath. In complete anti-climax he said weakly, "Hello, Papa."

The little man was advancing, nearly tottering, his face an incredulous mask. His voice came almost inaudibly. "You did steal the jewelry."

"Well—no, Papa."

"A liar also. You stole it, didn't you?"

"Yes, Papa," Giovanni said frantically, "but it was only a joke." "Thief!" The little man took two measured steps, drew back his hand and hit his son full in the face. "You thief!"

"No." Giovanni put up his hands for protection. Suddenly he wailed, "Papa, the other man shot me. I'm hurt."

"You should be dead," the mayor said icily. He struck again. A frenzy seemed to seize him. His fists flailed. He shouted, "I should have done this years ago," and then he was beating his son about the face and head and Giovanni was cringing against the wall, sobbing, his voice getting higher.

There wasn't time to waste. Jake pinioned the mayor's arms and pulled him away. The mayor struggled for only a second. He made a great effort and drew his composure around him again, like a visible cloak. "Mr. Abbott," he said. "You were going to give me an explanation."

"It's not much. Giovanni stole the stuff and planted the ring they found in my pocket. He wanted to shift the blame."

"He went to greater lengths to implicate you," the mayor said. "I trusted him. It was he who told me he'd received a phone call from an anonymous woman." He looked emotionlessly at his cowering son. "You received nothing, did you?"

"It was Angelo told me."

"Where are the missing paintings?"

"Papa, I don't have them."

"Does he, Mr. Abbott?"

"I don't know. I think not. He was trying to get them from me."

"You know where they are?"

"I've never even seen them."

The mayor nodded. He was showing a completely different personality. "I believe you. You were a good man when you saved my life. I think you are still." He turned again to his son, lips a thin line. "One more question, thief. Did you kill the American at the hotel?"

"No, Papa," Giovanni whispered.

Jake said, "Did you kill anybody?"

"No. Why should I?"

The mayor looked up into Jake's eyes. The protective composure fell from him. All at once he was a helpless old man. He said pathetically, "Mr. Abbott, I understand nothing. What has happened?"

"I wish I could tell you for my own benefit," Jake said. "Apparently there were two thieves last night. Giovanni went first and took the jewelry. Somebody went later and got the paintings."

"Ellison, then Leverett, then you," Giovanni said. "Nobody else went near. Papa, at least I didn't steal anything as valuable as that."

"Shut up, thief! Neither did Mr. Abbott."

"No," Jake said. The breath was caught at his throat. A hundred scattered pieces were drawing together in his mind. Ellison first, then Leverett. Ellison and Leverett both dead. He'd made a huge error in deduction back at the baker's shop. Leverett, as Ralph had said, was another guy on the make for a swift buck. He'd kept quiet about the first murder for one starkly obvious reason.

Jake fought to keep the composure in his face. "Thanks for the confidence, Mr. Drago. Pity Luca doesn't feel the same way."

"I shouldn't have left you alone with him." The mayor lowered his gaze. "It won't occur again."

"I know. I'm getting out."

"How?"

The footsteps hurried like an answer down the street outside. Giovanni opened his mouth to shout, and shut it again. Jake had whipped the gun from his pocket. The mayor looked scared for a moment, and then nodded in resigned approval as Jake covered the door. Luigi Moretti walked in.

He said brightly, "All arranged. We give them two minutes. We'll have to be careful, though, because Captain Luca's on the prowl again. He looks a mess. That makes me really happy."

"Who has the car?"

"Mr. Myers and your girl."

He was trying to make it fit a pattern. "Who's driving?"

"Your girl." Luigi turned to Drago, his face splitting in a grin. "Hello,

Mr. Mayor. See you finally caught up with your fine boy."

The mayor colored. "He's a thief."

"That's right. We've all known it for years. The bets were on how soon you'd find out."

"That's impossible," the mayor said dully. "Why was I elected?"

"Because your reputation's good. They'll pick you again."

Jake said, "We'd better go." He held out his hand. "Thanks for helping me over a bad patch. I'm sorry it's costing you so much."

"I'll try to do more," the mayor said. "Why don't you stay?"

"There's still the murder hanging over my head, and the pictures. I must get away from Luca before he complicates things too much. It's important I remain free for the next hour or so."

They all looked at him, detecting the tone in his voice. The mayor said, "You know something?"

"I guess something. There's no sure way of proving it. But at least I can try if that cop isn't on my neck."

"It can be managed." The mayor was an old man again. "I'm taking Giovanni to Luca immediately. We should occupy him for some while."

"Thanks," Jake said. Giovanni remained mute.

Luigi said, "I'll come later and explain about the dead man out there."

"Which man?" Giovanni raised his head.

"The boy in the long coat. He shot himself."

Giovanni's plump face quivered. He looked unbelievingly at Jake. He said, "You son of a filthy whore, you tricked me." A stream of abuse began pouring from his mouth. His father hit him again.

The curses stopped. The mayor said, "Better go, Mr. Abbott." He was near tears.

"Sure." Jake reached out and touched the old man on the shoulder. "Thanks again. Come on, Luigi."

"We're off," Moretti said, and waved a cheerful hand. They went together into the street. They started to run.

A big patch of blue was widening in the sky. The air was still filled with the sound of running water, and Jake heard the jeeps again, far off. His mind was briefly a kaleidoscope of unintegrating thoughts—Luca, the number of people killed, the story he should have written, Grace. He mustn't think of her now. He shook his head. He must concentrate on Leverett's attack of modesty on the mountainside. It was the single connecting thread.

All at once he didn't know whether he could run away or not. He wouldn't know until he saw the car.

Luigi was ahead. He looked around the corner, then turned and waved. A jeep swished swiftly past on the lower street, raising a thin spray of water. Jake guessed it was the main thoroughfare. He moved up behind Moretti and looked over his head. The small gray car was sitting a little way down the road, its engine running. Harry was in the back, Grace behind the wheel. Jake knew then that he could run away if he was quick. He stepped into the open.

He didn't say good-by to Luigi. He hoped he'd be seeing him again. He pushed him out of the way, caught a glimpse of the Italian's surprised face, and then he was pounding for the car. The rear door opened. He saw Grace's tense face, the beginning of Harry's encouraging grin. The photographer said, "In here! Quick!"

Jake was already pushing in the front. Grace said, "Darling," like a sob. He shoved her from behind the wheel, seized it in his own hands, then the car leaped down the road and he was in control.

The rear door swung hard and slammed shut. Harry said urgently, "Wait, kid!"

Jake took no notice. He was suddenly glad of the gun in his pocket.

Chapter Twenty-one

A jeep flashed past. Behind it was a small open truck loaded with standing soldiers, digging implements on their shoulders. Grace turned a strained face. "Darling, someone will see you."

He didn't answer for a while. Then he said, "No, they're all too preoccupied. And they don't expect me to be in a car."

"But, darling—"

He swung the wheel and steered swiftly round a pile of brick. The tires screeched. Harry Myers held hard on the front seats and leaned forward. "Kid, you're lousing it up. Stop and let me out."

"Why?"

"We've got it all arranged, Jake," Grace said desperately.

"That's right." Harry nodded. "If somebody finds the two of us gone they'll get suspicious. The owner of this car is due to call at the hotel in ten minutes."

Grace said, "No one saw us leave except the bellboy. Harry gave him some money. Don't ruin it, Jake. We can make a clear getaway. Lie down in the back of the car. I'll drive as far as Naples. Harry can return and cover our tracks."

"How?"

"I'll wait a while then tell everyone I saw you running in the other direction."

"We'll do better this way."

Harry said nervously, "But, Jake, I can't go with you. I've left all the photographs back there. Every wire service in the country will have a man in town by this morning. I'll lose my scoop."

"What did you tell the bellboy?"

"How do you mean?"

"What did you tell him?"

"That when the local editor arrives for his car he's to say I'll be back in a few minutes. Jake, if I don't return, the search will start immediately."

Another jeep flicked by. Jake steered with one hand and eased the gun into a more accessible position in his pocket. His mind was calm now. He was getting corroboration. But he could still demonstrate nothing until he had at least one article of solid proof in his hands. His only hope was to keep driving and pray for something to turn up.

The road was widely scattered with bricks from a line of fallen buildings. He bumped over them without slackening speed. The mountains loomed ahead, the large patch of blue spread widely behind them. A few peaks were touched with yellow.

Grace stared at him, her face gone taut. "Jake, are you all right?"

"I feel better than I have for a long time."

"Why don't you let Harry out?"

"It wouldn't be wise in the middle of town."

"We're nearly to the outskirts."

He didn't answer. The list was unrolling. He took everyone in turn, ignoring the tricking paths of deviousness, double checking the conclusion in his mind. Start with Angelo, sent to kill a man, finding death himself. No conceivable reason why he should have tried to kill anyone except the one man, Jake. Strike off Angelo.

Then—Ralph Ellison, number one victim, innocent. Leverett, not wanting his photograph taken, number two victim, much less innocent. The rest conceivably had involved motives. Ignore that aspect. Take them on face value; judge from their behavior.

The mayor and Giovanni. They'd just taken care of themselves, been cleared of the main issue. Fausta was nothing; it was doubtful she even knew what had been going on. The boy friend—

Jake said, "Grace did you send Luigi Moretti looking for me?"

She nodded. "He's a good boy, Jake. It was because you looked after the girl. He wanted to do something for you."

"When did he leave the hotel?"

"After we heard you'd escaped the second time." She looked from the car window. "Jake, we're out of town. Let Harry out. We'll soon be in the mountains."

"Wait a minute."

"Not too far," Harry said. "Remember my rheumatism."

"I'm remembering everything."

Grace turned her head sharply to him. The car engine began to roar as the road sloped up toward the first mountain. They skidded over an area of deep mud. A spread of sunshine began creeping down the highest peak.

So strike off Luigi. He couldn't have betrayed Jake to Luca because he was still in the hotel when the car drove up to the doorway. Strike off Luca. He was absolved by the simple fact that there had been a betrayer. Jake checked his list again. It had shrunk. Only two people left. He knew which one it was. He had to prove it. He had to provoke something.

He said grimly, "It's been a long, hard night."

Grace put a hand on his knee. "Darling, it's over."

"That's right." The photographer grunted cheerfully, leaning forward again on the back of the seats. "It'll turn out fine, kid. A couple hours more and you'll be telling the story in the Naples consulate. I'll handle things at this end, discover what I can and try to knock some sense into that dumb cop." He laughed. "That's if you let me out."

Grace turned around to say something. Jake felt her stiffen. She said, "Oh."

They were climbing sharply now, hurtling along a wide highway. A thin film of water was still coming from the peaks, washing the paving clear of mud. The tires of the car made a curious humming sound. Harry said, "What, Grace?"

She was staring past his shoulder. "There's a car coming after us."

Harry took a look. He said, "It's the police."

It was the clincher, the last touch of certainty. There was still no way to prove it. Jake shot a glance through the rear window. The city lay below, partly obscured by the gray overcast. The sloping highway behind was clear. The pursuing car, traveling at high speed, looked like a small, venomous insect. Jake stood hard on the accelerator.

"They won't catch you." Harry put a hand on Jake's shoulder. "Let me out. I'll delay them."

"Nobody gets out."

"Don't be foolish." The hand tightened. "It's your only chance. I'll pitch a story, make them turn around."

Jake said, "Who told them to follow us?"

There was a silence. He wondered if it was imagination that made him feel the sense of guilt pulsate through the car. Grace said shakily, "Somebody must have seen you. One of the soldiers in the truck."

"I doubt there's a soldier in Italy knows what I look like."

"Well, somebody." Suddenly she beat on his knee. "Jake, for God's sake let Harry get out and stop them."

He shook his head determinedly. The tires whined a high angry song.

The black base of the rock-face loomed ahead. The road was entering a pass. He leaned forward, trying to urge more speed with his body. Harry's hand clutched hard at his shoulder. Grace was still beating helplessly at his leg.

He swung the wheel.

The mountains closed in on either side of them. He saw the fall of rocks ahead. He jammed on the brakes, but they were traveling too fast. There was a great squealing. The car skidded for ten yards. They hit.

The rocks weren't big or high, but they were enough. The two front tires burst with a noise like a cannon. The car gave an enormous jolt. Jake flung an arm to protect Grace, his own head hit the windshield, and the wheel jammed hard in his stomach. He sat gasping for breath, half stunned, hearing Harry scramble out of the back.

The door opened beside him. The photographer's hand reached in, dragging him out. Harry's voice said, "Jake, run! Run!"

He was already halfway from the car. He shook off the hand and said, "You all right, Grace?" His vision cleared. He saw that she was. He scrambled to the ground, stood up shakily as she was getting out at the other side. Harry said, "Jake, they'll catch you. Run!" He reached out and gave a propulsive push.

Jake's knees gave way momentarily. He clutched at the photographer for support. His arms went right around Harry's chest. He knew then he'd got what he wanted. He pulled himself upright. He said slowly, "So that's it."

They looked deep into each other's eyes, like a pair of adolescent lovers. Harry said once more, "Run!" His voice was without conviction.

Jake said, "But they'll kill me if I run," and Grace put her hand on the hood and came slowly round from the other side of the car. For a moment they were a motionless tableau. The silence of the mountains fell on them, broken only by the faint sound of the approaching car, the faint trickling of water.

Grace put a hand to her forehead. Her voice was exhausted. "It's no use, Jake. They have you."

"Not me." He released his hold on Harry, stepped backwards and pulled the gun from his pocket. He said, "It's over."

"You gone crazy?" Harry asked.

He wondered if he had. He wanted to laugh wildly. He said, "We'll wait for the cops. They can check. Try to dump evidence and I'll shoot you in the legs."

Harry looked unblinkingly at the gun. "You wouldn't."

"Try."

Grace said, "Jake. Not him."

He nodded.

She looked at the photographer in complete disbelief. "Harry, you swore you didn't kill Ralph."

"He didn't," Jake said. "Leverett did."

The car was getting nearer. Harry said, "Kid, I'm going to walk away now over these rocks. I'll dump the stuff I'm carrying and you'll never prove a thing." He turned around and took three steps. Jake shot him in the foot.

The sound boomed among the mountains. A little way off, the car ground to a stop and the silence was complete. Harry Myers pulled himself upright, looking down at the blood that poured from the heel of his shoe. His teeth were clenched. He said, "That hurts like hell. I didn't think you would."

"Next I'll shoot you in the knee."

"I'm not moving."

They stood waiting. The silence was ear-aching. The gun was heavy. There was no sound of the police. Harry's face had gone paste white. The beads of sweat stood out on his, forehead. Suddenly he shrugged. He said, "So that's it. I don't suppose it'll help that Leverett attacked first. He wanted the photographs."

"It was the flashlight," Jake said. "When I was over by the missing collection it seemed to light up the whole area."

"He must have been nuts. No camera could have taken a picture at that range in the rain we were having."

"Leverett didn't know anything about photography."

"Only art," Harry said. "Recognized a Botticelli the moment he set eyes on it. Funny thing he didn't mention the missing jewelry. It wasn't in his pockets."

A faint smile hovered around Harry's mouth. He turned his head. "Cops are taking a long time. They probably heard that shot. They'll give it to you on sight when they see you holding the gun."

They stood waiting in a frozen group, staring at each other. Grace said faintly, "Jake, I don't understand."

He saw her look compassionately at Harry. He liked her for that. He said, "It's difficult till you know that everything came in pairs. Two thieves, two murders. Giovanni Drago went first and helped himself to the jewelry. He saw Ralph go afterwards, probably looking for copy, then Leverett. I guess Ralph surprised Leverett taking the pictures."

"He did," Harry said laconically. "Leverett lashed out with a rock, then ran. It accounted for his modesty afterwards. He wasn't sure I'd got a long-distance picture, but he didn't want me taking any more, in case I made comparisons. He was nervous. He wanted to check. He developed an interest in photography, followed me everywhere and tried to get a look at the shots. He ran me to earth in your room when I was waiting to show you what I'd got. There wasn't a thing that could have incriminated him."

Grace said in a frightened voice, "Jake, they're coming. Put away the gun."

He hesitated, slipped it into his pocket and looked levelly at the photographer. "Sorry you did it, Harry."

Harry shrugged again. "Me too. I had no intention. He kept asking all the time in which direction I'd taken the shots. I didn't get suspicious till you told me about Ralph and where you'd found him, and then in the room when Leverett tried to snatch the photographs from me. He started babbling. It all came out in a rush. I said I had to go to the police. He tried to bribe me with one of the pictures. I was nearly to the door. He jumped me. I hit him with the lamp in self-defense."

"You could still have gone to the police."

"Not after having met your friend Luca. I didn't want to be involved." Harry laughed mirthlessly. "So I succumbed to the temptation. Eighty thousand bucks' worth of Botticelli. He had them with him. Enough for me to take Lucia back to the States, set up in private business and buy her a few things."

Grace said softly, "Poor Lucia."

"I forgot you'd met her." Harry looked at them curiously. A spasm went across his face. He said irrelevantly, "I'll get prison for life. There's no death penalty in this country. I doubt she'll divorce me, not for a long time anyway. Yeah, poor Lucia." He paused, looking down again at his bleeding foot. "You know, this doesn't hurt so much after all."

"Here they come," Grace said.

The five policemen emerged into the pass, one at a time, coming cautiously, all holding guns. Jake thought inconsequentially that they were being brave. He turned to face them, saw Captain Luca and put his hands high as a sign of good faith. He shouted, "All right! Nothing to worry about!"

The hand dived into his pocket. He felt the gun jerked out. He waited for the bullet and an overwhelming sense of his own stupidity surged through him. He heard the shuffling behind him and turned around, still keeping his hands high, and Harry Myers was scrambling over the low barrier of rocks, his bleeding foot leaving a trail, Angelo's gun clutched in his right hand. The policemen were running.

Jake reached out. Grace pulled him back, clinging to him. Harry disappeared over the ridge of the rock, the feet pounded, and then Luca's voice said, "Don't move, Abbott." The policemen were all around him, five guns at the ready. Luca's face bore marks of the beating. Jake noticed it without pleasure.

He said, "Who brought the news? The bellboy?"

The policeman nodded, a puzzled expression in his puffed eyes. He started to say something.

Jake said, "Mr. Myers couldn't get there this time. He got dragged along on the trip. Hurry and you'll catch him with the Botticellis still on him."

"What?" Luca jerked so hard with surprise it was almost comical.

"They're tied around his chest, under his shirt. He killed Leverett."

Jake was suddenly so tired that he wanted to sit down. His arms dropped to his sides. Vaguely he was aware that the police were moving again. He went over and put his arms around Grace. They stood holding tight, saying nothing. He felt her trembling.

He raised his head. The policemen had halted in a momentary line on top of the ridge. They looked for an instant like a posed picture. Then from near at hand, much nearer than Jake had expected, Harry fired a shot.

The five guns answered simultaneously. A young, pale-faced policeman kept pulling the trigger long after the others were done, pumping slowly and automatically as if he were at target school. The five men disappeared with a rush on the far side of the rocks. The noise still boomed, reverberating among the peaks.

Jake led Grace to the wrecked car. They sat side by side on the running board. He realized at the back of his mind that the sun had come out. He was appallingly tired and sick. He put an arm round Grace's shoulder.

It seemed hours before the footsteps came back. His head was lowered. The shoes approached and Luca's voice said, "He's dead. They were under his shirt."

Jake lifted his gaze. The paintings were unrolled in the policeman's hand—the heads of two young women with ugly curved eyelids, chinless and pouting, enough alike to be sisters. The fresh blood smeared darkly over the bright unfading colors of the paint. Both pictures were punctured where the bullets had penetrated.

Luca said, "They don't look like all that money to me, but people must be right. I suppose an expert can fix these holes."

Jake stood up. "There're explanations to make."

"He didn't die right away. He told us."

"What?"

"He killed Leverett over these things. Didn't you know?"

"Yes."

There was a silence. "I saw the mayor for a moment. I owe you an apology."

"Don't bother."

"Yes, I'd feel the same." Luca put out a hand and took Jake's arm.

"Come over here a minute." They withdrew a few paces.

"What now?"

Luca whispered, "How did the lady happen to be with you?"

"She was in the car. She didn't know what was going on."

"It's not important." Luca's voice dropped even lower. "Only I have bad news for her. Her husband has been found. He got killed in the flood."

Jake fought down a wild impulse to shout with laughter. He said, "What exactly did Harry tell you?"

Luca looked surprised. "Leverett had the paintings. He killed Leverett and stole them for himself. Why?"

"Like you say, it's not important. Not for the moment, anyway." Jake turned back to Grace. The four policemen were stumbling over the rocks, carrying Harry between them.

Luca said, "I'll give you and the lady a lift back to town."

"Thanks, we'll walk."

The policeman became suddenly nervous. "Don't you have a story to write."

"Half a story." Jake shook his head. "Just half. There's no rush."

He went and sat down again beside Grace. She offered him a cigarette, not speaking. The policemen went down the road, Luca bringing up the rear. He glanced back twice. He seemed frightened.

After a while they heard the car start. They remained sitting, smoking the cigarettes. The sun began to shine strongly. Jake said, "About living in Paris. You think you'll like it?"

She waited before answering, as if pondering the question. Finally she said, "I believe so. Yes, I'm certain. I shall be even more certain as time goes by."

"You're not getting much."

"It's what I want," she said.

"I'd hoped that." He stood up, helping her to her feet. They looked at each other for a long moment, and there was the beginning of happiness in her eyes. He said, "I guess we'd better get back to town."

"Yes," she said. "Jake, you'll have to get a shave."

He said, "There's a razor at the hotel. I'll do it as soon as I get there."

They started back down the mountain.

THE END

DOUGLAS SANDERSON BIBLIOGRAPHY
(1920-2002)

Dark Passions Subdue (US, 1952)

Final Run (UK, 1956) aka *Flee from Terror* (US, 1957) and *Un bouquet de chardons* (Fr, 1957) both as by Martin Brett

Night of the Horns (UK, 1958) aka *Murder Comes Calling* (US, 1958) as by Malcolm Douglas

Cry Wolfram (UK, 1959) aka *Mark it for Murder* (US, 1959) and *La semaine de bonté* (Fr, 1958) as by Martin Brett

Catch a Fallen Starlet (US, 1960) aka *The Stubborn Unlaid* and *Cinémaléfices* (Fr, 1960) as by Martin Brett

Lam to Slaughter (UK, 1964) aka *As-tu vu Carcassone?* (Fr, 1963) as by Martin Brett

Black Reprieve (UK, 1965) aka *White Man Dead* and *Couper cabèche* (Fr, 1964) as by Martin Brett

No Charge for Framing (UK, 1969)

A Dead Bullfighter (UK, 1975)

As Martin Brett

Exit in Green (US, 1953) re-written as *Murder Came Tumbling* (UK, 1959)

Hot Freeze (US, 1953) aka *Mon cadaver au Canada* (Fr, 1955) and *Heisser Schnee* (Germany, 1975) as by Malcolm Douglas

Darker Traffic (US, 1954) aka *Blondes are My Trouble* (US, 1955) and *Salmigonzesses* (Fr, 1956)

Flee from Terror (US, 1957) aka *Final Run* (UK, 1956) and *Un bouquet de chardons* (Fr, 1957).

The Shreds published as *Sables-d'or-les-pains!* (Fr, 1958)

The Dead Connection published as *La came á papa* (Fr, 1961)

A Dum-Dum for the President (UK, 1961) aka *Estocade au Canada* (Fr, 1961)

Shout for a Killer published as *Chabanais chez les pachas* (Fr, 1963)

Score for Two Dead published as *Le moîne connait la musique* (Fr, 1964)

As Malcolm Douglas

Prey by Night (US, 1955) aka *A boulets Rouges* (Fr, 1956) as by Martin Brett

Rain of Terror (US, 1955) aka *And All Flesh Died* and *Le Fête a la grenouille* (Fr, 1956) as by Martin Brett; and *Alptraum auf Italienisch* (Germany, 1975) as by Malcolm Douglas

The Deadly Dames (US, 1956) aka *Du Rebecca chez les femmes* (Fr, 1956) as by Martin Brett

Pure Sweet Hell (US, 1957) aka *Zum Sterben hat jeder mal Zeit* (Germany, 1975)

Murder Comes Calling (US, 1958) aka *Night of the Horns* (UK, 1958) as by Douglas Sanderson; and *Ruh in Frieden, lieber Schatz* (Germany, 1974) as by Malcolm Douglas

And for more twisted tales of obsession, we offer...

Douglas Sanderson

"There is more going on than you can believe, with backstabbing and double crosses galore."—Bruce Grossman, *Bookgasm*

www.ingramcontent.com/pod-product-compliance
Lightning Source LLC
Chambersburg PA
CBHW071745190726
48292CB00003B/868